THE
LONG
SHADOW

ALSO BY LIZA MARKLUND

THE LONG SHADOW

A NOVEL

LIZA MARKLUND

EMILY BESTLER BOOKS
—
WASHINGTON SQUARE PRESS

NEW YORK LONDON TORONTO SYDNEY NEW DELHI

W

WASHINGTON SQUARE PRESS
A Division of Simon & Schuster, Inc.
1230 Avenue of the Americas
New York, NY 10020

EMILY
BESTLER
BOOKS

Copyright © 2008 by Liza Marklund

English language translation © 2014 by Neil Smith

Originally published in Swedish as *En plats i solen*. Published by agreement with Salomonsson Agency.

First Emily Bestler Books/Washington Square Press trade paperback edition April 2014

EMILY BESTLER BOOKS/ WASHINGTON SQUARE PRESS and colophons are trademarks of Simon & Schuster, Inc.

For information about special discounts for bulk purchases, please contact Simon & Schuster Special Sales at 1-866-506-1949 or business@simonandschuster.com.

The Simon & Schuster Speakers Bureau can bring authors to your live event. For more information or to book an event, contact the Simon & Schuster Speakers Bureau at 1-866-248-3049 or visit our website at www.simonspeakers.com.

Cover design by Anna Dorfman
Cover photograph by Gremlin/Vetta/Getty Images

Manufactured in the United States of America

10 9 8 7 6 5 4 3 2 1

Library of Congress Cataloging-in-Publication has been applied for.

ISBN 978-1-4516-0703-1
ISBN 978-1-4516-0707-9 (ebook)

THE
LONG
SHADOW

PART 1

After New Year

The night was pitch-black. She could just make out the orange trees lining the road as black shadows on the edge of her vision. Three cats' heads stuck up out of a rubbish bin, the headlights catching their eyes.

The rain had stopped, but the tarmac was still wet and shiny, reflecting the light from the streetlamps. She had the car window wound down and was listening to the wet hiss of the tires on the road surface, the crickets chirping, the wind rustling the trees. The air coming through the window was chill with damp.

It was as peaceful as could be.

She braked and stopped uncertainly at a crossroad. Was this where she was supposed to turn left, or was that the next one? She was clutching the steering wheel in a cramped ten-and-two grip. All this random building work; they didn't have any planning regulations, no town planning, and therefore no maps. Not even Google Earth had been able to help with these new districts.

Well, this must be it. She recognized the golden knobs at the top of the gate to her right. Everything looked so different in the dark.

She put the indicator on so that the truck behind her could see which way she was heading.

The two vehicles were driving with dipped headlights; anything else would have been impossible on such terrible roads. And a car with no lights would arouse more suspicion than one with headlights on. She swerved to avoid a large pothole in the middle of the road, then checked in the rearview mirror that the driver following her did the same.

Then the car's headlights swept across the gateway at the edge of the neighborhood, an overblown affair in black wrought iron with a pair of concrete lions on either side of the gates. She felt her shoulders relax in relief. She quickly tapped the code on the pillar below one of the lions, and the gates shuddered and then slid open. She peered up at the night sky.

The clouds had rolled in from Africa during the afternoon and settled like a thick blanket over the whole coast. Somewhere behind them was a full moon. She noted that the wind was picking up and hoped they'd be finished before the cloud cover started to break.

The roads inside the gates were, in marked contrast to those outside, smooth, with perfectly edged pavements and hedges that were absolutely straight. She passed three turnings before she swung off to the right and carried on down a slight hill.

The villa was off to the left, with its terraces and pool facing south.

She drove some ten meters past the house, parked by the pavement in front of a vacant plot, and waited patiently as the truck driver pulled up behind her.

Then she took her briefcase, locked the car, went over to the truck, and clambered up into the cab.

The men looked focused, slightly sweaty.

She pulled on a pair of latex gloves, then took out the syringes for the injections and attached the first needle.

"Lean forward," she said to one of them.

The man groaned quietly and obeyed; there was hardly room for his fat stomach under the dashboard.

She didn't bother cleaning the area on his buttock, just stabbed the needle quickly almost the whole way into the muscle and injected the liquid.

"There you go," she said as she pulled it out. "Start getting the stuff out."

She moved so the fat man could get out. Then she sat next to the driver.

"And this is better than gas masks?" the driver asked, staring in some trepidation at the needle in her hand.

He spoke relatively good Spanish, but of course Romanian was also a Romance language.

"I'm going to be having one as well," she said.

He unbuckled his belt, put his hands on the wheel, and leaned forward so that she could get at his backside.

"It stings," he said.

"Don't be such a baby," she replied.

Then she pulled up her skirt and stuck the last syringe into her own thigh.

"And you only want the safe?" the man asked as he opened the door and got out of the cab.

She smiled, leaned down over the briefcase, and put two one-liter bottles of San Miguel into the little cubbyhole between the driver's and the passenger's seats.

"Only the safe," she said. "The rest is yours. Help yourselves."

The driver looked at the bottles of beer and laughed.

The fat man had already got his tools and the tubes out, and had put them all down beside the entrance.

"And you can guarantee that this is going to knock them out?" he wondered, looking at the canisters with a degree of suspicion. They didn't look like they usually did.

He looked up at the house as the full moon peeped out between a gap in the clouds. They needed to get going.

She concentrated and tapped in the code. The panel on the alarm turned green, and the lock on the gate opened with a click.

"Oh yes," she said. "It's guaranteed to knock them out."

TT News Agency, 09:13.

URGENT

ATTORNEY GENERAL DEMANDS JUDICIAL REVIEW OF TRIPLE MURDER CASE

STOCKHOLM (TT) On Monday, Attorney General Lilian Bergqvist will submit a request for the judicial review of the case against the so-called Ax-Murderer, financier Filip Andersson, TT has learned.

Filip Andersson was sentenced to life imprisonment for three brutal murders on Södermalm in Stockholm. He has always maintained his innocence.

"In December last year, once the real murderer was killed, Filip Andersson was finally able to tell the truth," says his lawyer, Sven-Göran Olin. "Filip's sister, Yvonne Nordin, carried out the murders."

Almost four years ago Filip Andersson was found guilty in both the City Court and Court of Appeal, and received the maximum sentence available for three counts of murder, blackmail, extortion, and desecration of a grave. All three victims, two men and a woman, were mutilated during the attack.

The evidence against Filip Andersson was regarded as weak even during the previous trials. He was convicted on the strength of a DNA trace from one of the victims found on his trouser leg, a fingerprint on a door handle, and an unpaid debt.

The attorney general's submission to the Court of Appeal will summarize the evidence the prosecutors are planning to present.

(cont.)

© TT News Agency and the author of the article.

THE PRINCESS IN THE CASTLE AMONG THE CLOUDS

The light was utterly white. It drifted through all the rooms like little streams, around chandeliers and drapes and stags' heads; she could hear it whispering and giggling up by the beams in the ceiling.

It was so easy to breathe.

In fact the air was so clear and pure that sometimes she became a little feather, a silent little pale-blue feather that swirled around in the white light on sunbeams and tapestries of hunting scenes.

I said she was silent, didn't I?

Oh, she was silent, so silent, because the Führer mustn't be disturbed.

Everybody spoke quietly and respectfully in the castle up among the clouds, and thick rugs on all the floors and stone staircases took care of their whispers and hid them away in a safe place.

Her favorite place was *die Halle,* the room which was as big as an ocean, with windows looking out onto the clouds and the snowcapped mountain below.

Sometimes she danced in *die Halle,* silently of course, and lightly on her bare toes, with the sculptures and paintings and all the dolls as her appreciative audience. Her dress, all that thin fabric, fluttered around her with a life of its own, and she jumped and twirled until her head was spinning. Yes, she was a princess, the Princess in the castle among the clouds, and she danced for the horses and the dead deer and all the beautiful wooden carvings on the ceiling. Nanna always tried to stop her, of course, but she ignored her. Nanna was just a grubby *Landwirtmädchen*, who had no right to tell her what to do, because she was the *Princess in the castle among the clouds*.

Once she danced right into the Führer.

Nanna, the stupid cow, had run off crying because she had bitten her on the arm, and she had been able to dance for ages all on her own in *die Halle*, but the Führer wasn't angry with her, not angry at all.

He just caught her in his long arms, leaned over, and put his hands on her shoulders. He had blue eyes, red-rimmed, but the Princess wasn't looking at his eyes. Instead she was staring in delight at the hairs sticking out of his nose.

She knew she had misbehaved.

Now Mother would be cross!

It was Nanna's fault!

"You're a proper little Aryan, aren't you," the Führer said, then touched one of her blond ringlets, and she felt the force flowing out of him, just like Father had explained to Mother, and she said:

"Am I blessed now?"

He let go of her and walked off toward the residential quarters, and Blondi trotted after him with her tail wagging, and that was the last time she saw him.

She wasn't always in the castle among the clouds, obviously.

When they were in Obersalzberg, she and Father and Mother lived down in the Hotel Zum Türken, along with the other officers' families. Mother called it the Turk: "*Why do we get shoved away in the Turk while the Goebbelses get to stay up at Berghof?*"

Mother often spoke of the apartment, the one on Friedrichstrasse which had been bombed to ruins by *die verdammten Verbündeten,* the damned Allies.

"It was lucky for us that one of us is still thinking rationally," she would say, looking sharply at Father, because Father hadn't wanted to evacuate. He thought it was a betrayal of the Führer, a sign of loss of *faith,* but Mother had insisted and had emptied the whole apartment and arranged for all their belongings to be taken by train to the house in Adlerhorst.

As the Russians got closer, Mother ordered a car from the Party and sent the Princess and Nanna and three trunks with all her beautiful dolls and dresses to Harvestehuder Weg.

The Princess didn't want to go. She wanted to stay in Adlerhorst; she wanted to go to the castle.

But Mother put a label round her neck and was very abrupt, and her face was red, and she gave her an awkward farewell kiss that the Princess wiped away at once. The car door slammed shut.

They never made it to Harvestehuder Weg.

They were stopped outside a town that she didn't know the name of, and the soldiers took her things and dragged Nanna off with them into the woods, and they shot the chauffeur in the head, getting muck and goo on the Princess's coat.

All she had left when she got to Gudagården was her coat and dress, and her doll Anna.

Because on the label tied round her neck was Onkel Gunnar and Tante Helga's address, Gudagården in Södermanland, Schweden, that was where the Princess was sent when there was no one left who could look after her.

I don't remember anything myself, but I've been told.

How Onkel Gunnar put the rich kid's clothes and the doll in a pile in the courtyard, poured paraffin over them, and lit a fire that would echo through the decades.

"The sinner must burn in hell," he was supposed to have said, and that might well be true.

MONDAY, JANUARY 3

Annika Bengtzon poked her head through the editor in chief's half-open door and knocked on the wooden frame. Anders Schyman was standing with his back to her, sorting through piles of paper spread out across his desk and all over the floor. He turned round, saw the expectant look on her face, and gestured toward a chair.

"Close the door and sit down," he said, going round the desk and sinking onto his own chair. It creaked ominously.

She closed the door behind her and glanced suspiciously at the pile of paper by her feet, noting something that looked like a plan of the newsroom.

"Don't say we're going to rearrange everything all over again," she said as she sat down.

"I've got a question for you," Schyman said. "How do you see your future here on the paper?"

Annika looked up quickly and met the editor in chief's gaze.

"How do you mean?"

"I'll get straight to the point. Do you want to be lead editor?"

Her throat tightened, she opened her mouth but closed it again, then looked down at her hands on her lap.

"You'd be in charge of all news coverage throughout the day. Five days on, five days off. Coordinate sport and entertainment with the editorials, opinion pieces, and news. Make the final decision about what to put on the front page. You'd have to sort out the setup of the various departments with their respective bosses. No web stuff or any of that crap. You'd sit in on management meetings and would be able to influence budgetary decisions and marketing strategies. I want you to start as soon as possible."

She cleared her throat, but the words kept catching.

Lead editor was big, a huge responsibility. She'd be the second most powerful person on the paper, just below the editor in chief, and head of all the subsidiary departments. She'd be in charge of the news editors and entertainment editors and the head of sport and all the other little potentates who considered themselves so important.

"I have to restructure things," Schyman said in a low voice when she didn't respond. "I need to be able to rely on the people who are directly answerable to me."

She was still looking down at her hands. His voice was going over her head, bouncing off the wall, and hitting her on the back of the neck.

"Are you interested?"

"No," Annika said.

"I'll double your salary."

She looked up.

"I've tried having money," she said. "It's nowhere near as much fun as people say."

The editor in chief got up and went over to the window.

"This time last year we were under threat of closure," he said. "Did you know that?"

He glanced over his shoulder to see her reaction. She didn't let him have anything, just played with her grandmother's emerald ring on the forefinger of her left hand.

"We managed to turn the ship round," Schyman said, facing the newsroom that stretched out in front of him on the other side of the glass. "I think it's going to work, but I don't know how long I'll be staying."

He turned round and looked at her. She moved her head and let her gaze slip past him, out toward the newsroom.

"I don't want your job," she said.

"I'm not offering you my job. I'm offering you the position of lead editor."

"What about Berit? She could do it."

"What makes you think she'd want it?"

"Jansson, then? Or Spike?"

He sat down on the desk with a sigh.

"There's no shortage of volunteers. But I need someone with decent judgment."

She laughed in spite of herself.

"And you're asking me? That says a lot about the level of competence in this newsroom."

"The alternative is for you to accept a normal rota. Sitting at the desk, making calls, doing whatever the news editor tells you."

She suddenly realized how uncomfortable the chair was and shuffled to stop herself getting a bad back.

"Doesn't this need to have union approval?" she asked.

"The union's no problem, believe me," he said.

"Putting me on a rota would be crazy," she said. "You know I manage to get far better stories if I'm allowed to look after myself."

He leaned toward her, and she stared at his knees.

"Annika," he said, "the cutbacks we negotiated last autumn have all gone through. We no longer have the resources to support any reporters on special conditions. You'll report to Patrik as your immediate superior."

She looked up at him.

"You're joking."

He folded his arms.

"We arranged it between Christmas and New Year's. As lead

editor you'd be his boss. You could steer him, make sure he stays on the right track. If you start working as a reporter on a rota, you'll have to do whatever he tells you."

"But I was the one who gave him a job," Annika said. "I can't have him as my boss. And if you're after someone with judgment, then Patrik's pretty much the last person . . ."

"We need good judgment further up the organization. At the level of head of news I need someone with Patrik's enthusiasm, someone who finds everything interesting."

Annika stretched her neck and looked over toward the decimated crime desk, where Patrik was sitting with his nose pressed up against his screen, typing something with his elbows in the air. She remembered how he had managed to get the only comment from the prime minister the day the minister for business resigned: He'd run after his cortège all through central Stockholm and had finally been rewarded with the words "Are you crazy, you stupid bastard?" When he got back to the newsroom he described the whole event as a triumph.

"Well," she said, "if you're after passion, then you should certainly promote Patrik."

"You'll be on the day shift, Monday to Friday," Schyman said, standing up. "No overtime and no antisocial hours payments. Because we've been shutting down our local news teams around the country, you could be sent anywhere at a moment's notice, even abroad. You'll have to take over the series of articles about the Costa Cocaine that Patrik was planning, for instance. You can go and sit down at the news desk, and Patrik will be over to give you your papers."

"What, that bit of fluff?" she said. "Wasn't that just an excuse for Patrik to fly down and go swimming?"

"You're wrong about that. The Costa Cocaine is an exclusive series of articles; the initiative came from the editorial management of the paper. We've set up a collaboration with the Police

Authority and the Justice Department to have access to privileged information. So we're going to go through with it."

"What's going to happen to the day-shift desk?" she asked, looking over at her workplace with her computer, jacket, bag, and an array of notes.

"That's going to be the features department," Schyman said, gesturing toward the plan on the floor. "The crime desk is turning into the op-ed section."

She got up and left the editor in chief's glass box of an office without looking back.

She really couldn't care less which chair she sat in or which articles she had to write. He husband had left her and had taken half her time with the children with him, her house had burned down, and the insurance money couldn't be released. She was living in a three-room flat in a building owned by the police association, arranged by her contact in the forces, Detective Inspector Q, under highly dubious circumstances, knowing someone could show up any day and take it from her.

She gathered together her things and, balancing everything in her arms, made her way over to one of the cramped spaces around the main news desk. She hardly had space for the computer on the desk in front of her, so she dropped her jacket, bag, and all her notes on the floor beside her chair. She sat down, raised the seat, checked that the computer was connected, and sent an email to Inspector Q: "I've moved into the flat, but I still haven't seen anything that looks like a contract. And FYI I'm thinking about digging into the extradition of the kitty-cat. /a"

That would give him something to think about.

Then she reached for one of the telephones and dialed the number of the Justice Department. She asked to be put through to the justice minister's press secretary, a woman who sounded very stressed when she answered, with the wind whistling in her mobile phone.

Annika introduced herself and said where she worked.

"I'd like a comment from the minister about the extradition of an American contract killer who goes by the name of the Kitten," she said.

"A what?" the press secretary said.

"I know she was handed back to the US in exchange for us getting the cop killer Victor Gabrielsson home from prison in New Jersey. I want to know why, and how it came about."

"The minister never gives statements on matters concerning national security," the press secretary said, trying to sound robotic and uninterested.

"Who said anything about national security?" Annika said. "I just want to know what you did with the Kitten."

"Can I get back to you?"

Annika gave the woman her mobile number and direct line, as if there was actually any chance of her calling back. Yeah, right! She hung up, then dialed Berit Hamrin's mobile number. Her colleague answered at once.

"Have you been demoted as well?" Annika asked.

"With Patrik as boss," Berit confirmed.

There was the sound of traffic in the background.

"Where are you now?"

"I've just pulled out onto the E18."

Annika could see Patrik sweeping toward the news desk with a bundle of notes in his right hand, and moved the receiver closer to her mouth.

"Here comes the boss," she said quietly. "This is going to be interesting."

She hung up just as Patrik sat down on her desk. She quickly moved the computer aside.

"Okay, now things are really going to start moving," the newly appointed head of news said, leafing through his notes. "We've got a fire in a flat out in Hallunda, people gassed to death on the

Spanish coast, and a bus crash in Denmark. Start with the bus and check if there were any Swedes on board. Who knows, if things are really bad it could be a load of Swedish schoolkids on their way home from Tivoli."

"Lilian Bergqvist is asking for a review of Filip Andersson's case," she said, switching the computer on next to Patrik's thigh.

"Old news," Patrik said. "We all knew she was going to do that as soon as we revealed that his sister was the real killer. Berit can write a little note about it."

When *I* revealed who the real killer was, she thought, but said nothing.

"The gassing in Spain sounds pretty grim," he went on, handing over the notes. "Looks like an entire family is dead, including the dog. See if you can make anything out of it, ideally a picture of them all, and with the name and age of the dog. People are always interested in Spain: It must still be the biggest tourist destination for Swedes."

"Haven't we got a stringer down there?" Annika asked, remembering a picture byline of a suntanned man with a clenched smile.

"He's back home in Tärnaby for Christmas. The fire in Hallunda feels a bit thin, but maybe they had to evacuate and poor old Hedvig couldn't get down in her wheelchair, or something else that would look good in the mix."

"Okay," Annika said, thinking that he'd already learned the vocabulary.

Good in the mix. Bloody hell.

"There's a couple of other things I was going to check out," she said, making an effort to sound calm and composed. "I got a tip-off that the government was involved in a peculiar extradition case, and I've got a meeting at two o'clock with a woman which might lead to an interview about . . ."

But Patrik had already got up and was on his way over to the features department.

Annika stared at him as he went, but made up her mind not to get upset. If he chose not to listen to his . . . subordinates, then that was his problem.

She leaned back in the chair and looked around the newsroom. She was pretty much the only person there.

She'd been called in by Schyman at eight o'clock in the morning and had assumed that it would be another attempt to persuade her to accept one of the senior editorial positions. There were usually a few years in between the offers, but this time it was different. He'd tried to push her into accepting the positions of head of news and head of supplements before, and she had even accepted the post as head of crime for a short while, but never before had he offered her the position of lead editor.

She let out a sigh. The way he had described it, five days on, five days off, she would still have been sharing the job with someone, probably Sjölander. She wouldn't just have been held responsible for all the idiotic things that would inevitably have arisen during the course of putting together the news section, but would also have had to sit through interminable meetings about budgets and marketing plans and long-term staffing issues.

Sooner fires in blocks of flats out in Hallunda, she thought, as she called the direct number of the section head of the emergency services control room.

Smoking in bed, the section head told her, one dead, someone who'd taken early retirement. Fire extinguished. Limited smoke damage. No evacuation.

"And who was the person who died?" Annika asked.

He leafed through his papers.

"The flat belonged to a . . . I've got it here somewhere . . . something Jonsson . . . well, no one famous, anyway."

No one famous = no story.

They hung up.

The bus crash did turn out to involve a group of kids, not from a school but a hockey team on their way to a tournament in Aalborg. The accident had occurred when the bus slid slowly off an icy country road in Jutland, and ended up on its side in a ditch. The children had had to clamber out through the driver's window.

Annika emailed the details to the picture desk and asked them to keep an eye out in case any pictures of terrified children appeared. The story wasn't worth anything except as a caption to a photograph.

The gassings in Spain were trickier to get to grips with.

Patrik's note had been a printout of a telegram from the main news agency, consisting of three lines stating that a family with two children and a dog had been found dead after being gassed in connection with a break-in.

She started by going onto the website of the only Spanish newspaper she knew the name of, *El País*. She got caught by the main headline: *"España es el país europeo con más atropellos mortales de peatónes."*

She squinted at the screen—she really ought to be able to understand this. Two years of Spanish in high school wasn't much, but online newspaper language was hardly splitting the atom. Spain was the European country with the highest mortality rate for pedestrians, she imagined that it meant. Six hundred eighty last year.

She closed the article and went on looking. It ought to be something like *Familia muerta Costa del Sol*.

Nada, ninguno, vacío.

But of course *El País* was a national paper, presumably based in Madrid. Maybe they didn't bother with things that happened down near the edge of Africa.

But surely a whole family dying ought to warrant a mention, at least in the online edition?

She went and got a plastic cup of coffee from the machine, sat back down with it, and thought. Gassed in connection with a break-in? She'd never heard of that before. Was that even a real phenomenon?

She typed "gassed in connection with a break-in" into Google and got one single hit.

Had something gone wrong with the translation? Had the news agency got it wrong?

She blew cautiously on the coffee and took a careful sip. It shouldn't be possible, but it actually tasted even worse than yesterday.

She went back to Google and tried "gas" and "break-in," and this time the results were better.

"Driver knocked out with gas during break-in," was fourth on the list. The article was from Radio Sweden and had been published on December 14, 2004. Several pallets of flat computer screens had been stolen from a lorry at the Shell garage at Västra Jära on highway 40, just west of Jönköping. Neither the driver nor his dog, who had been asleep in the cab at the time, had noticed the robbery. When he woke up, the driver had a headache and felt badly sick. The police suspected that he had been knocked out by some sort of gas. They had taken blood samples to see if they could find any trace in his blood.

Here we go, she thought and scrolled down the screen.

"Thieves drugged dog with gas—rapid rise in burglaries in Stockholm," she read. The article was from *Metro*, and was only a week or so old.

She went into the paper's own archive and carried on looking.

"Thieves used gas on tourists—Four people knocked out in camper van—Heavy doses of hexane gas can cause serious injury," and "Action-film director robbed with gas—*The whole thing was terrible.*"

The article was about a Swedish director whose home on the Spanish coast had been broken into. He and his girlfriend had woken up the next morning to find all the doors wide open and the whole flat empty.

"So, we're back to being foot soldiers again," Berit said, putting her handbag down on the other side of the news desk.

"Happy New everything," Annika said.

"How are you?" Berit asked, hanging her coat on the back of her chair.

Annika's hands hovered above the keyboard.

"Pretty good, thanks. This year has to be better than the last one, because anything else just isn't possible . . ."

Berit put her laptop on the desk and looked around the newsroom.

"Is it just you and me left?" she asked. "Has everyone else been rationalized out of existence?"

Annika looked round.

Patrik was talking animatedly into his mobile over by the sports desk. There were a few people from the online edition over in what had once been the entertainment section but now produced copy for cyberspace, and one of the editors of the Sunday supplement was hanging around the picture desk. Tore, the caretaker who gave unhappiness a face, was laboriously fixing that day's flysheets to the notice board.

"Newspaper wars are just like any other," Annika said. "The ground troops get cut, and everything gets spent on technology and smart bombs. When did Schyman talk to you?"

Berit pointed at Annika's coffee.

"On Friday. Is that drinkable?"

"Negative. He called me this morning. Did he want you to join the management team?"

"Head of news," Berit replied. "I said thanks but no, thanks."

Annika looked down at her computer screen. Schyman had offered her a more senior position.

"So now I'm looking into a fatal gassing in Spain," she said. "A whole family was killed in a break-in on the Costa del Sol."

Berit switched her computer on and went over to the coffee machine.

"Give Rickard Marmén a call," she said over her shoulder. "I don't know his number, but if there's anything going on in Spain that's worth knowing, Rickard will know about it."

Annika picked up the phone and dialed directory inquiries.

Engaged.

Instead she went back into Google, thought for a moment, and then typed *"buscar numero telefono españa."* Was that the right spelling? Search telephone number Spain?

The first result was for something called *Pàginas Blancas,* White Pages.

Bingo!

A search form appeared on the screen and she narrowed the search to Málaga and typed in the name Rickard Marmén, then pressed *"encontrar."*

Who'd have thought it?!

He lived on the Avenida Ricardo Soriano in Marbella, and both his landline and mobile numbers were listed.

Berit sat down with a cup of steaming coffee.

"So who's this Rickard, then?" Annika said, with the receiver in her hand.

"An old friend of my brother-in-law's. He's lived down there for twenty years now, and has tried his hand at pretty much everything you can think of, and failed at all of it. He's rented out sunbeds and bred stud horses and run a guesthouse, and once he had a share in a company selling log cabins."

"On the Costa del Sol?" Annika said dubiously.

"I said he always fails."

"What's the dialing code for Spain?"

"Thirty-four," Berit said, pulling as face as she tasted the coffee.

Annika tried the landline first. After five rings an electronic voice said something unintelligible in Spanish and she hung up. She tried the mobile number, and two seconds later a male voice said loudly: "*Sí dígame!*"

"Rickard Marmén?"

"*Hablando!*"

"Er, my name's Annika Bengtzon, I'm calling from the *Evening Post* in Stockholm. Is that Rickard Marmén . . . you do speak Swedish, don't you?"

"Course I do. What can I do for you?"

He had a strong Gothenburg accent.

"I'm calling because I've been told you know about everything that happens on the Costa del Sol," she said, glancing at Berit. "I was wondering if you knew anything about gas being used in a break-in somewhere down there?"

"Gas? In *a* break-in? Listen, love, we don't have any other sort of break-in here these days. Every break-in uses gas. Gas detectors are more common than fire-alarms in the villas of Nueva Andalucía. Anything else you want to know?"

There was a lot of noise in the background; it sounded like he was standing next to a motorway.

"Er, okay," Annika said. "So, what exactly is a break-in involving gas?"

"The thieves pump some sort of knockout gas in through the windows or air-conditioning; then while the occupants are asleep the thieves can go through the whole house. They usually take their time, have some food in the kitchen, open a bottle of wine."

"And this is the most common type of break-in, you say?" Annika asked.

"It's an epidemic. It started five, six years ago, although gas was sometimes used before that as well."

"Why is it so common down there in particular?"

"There's a lot of money down here, darling. Thick bundles of cash under mattresses all round Puerto Banús. And there's a significant criminal element here, of course, and plenty of poor bastards who'll do anything for a bit of cash. They caught a gang of Romanians last autumn. They'd cleaned out over a hundred villas right along the coast, from Gibraltar up to Nerja . . ."

"The news agency has just sent out information about a whole family being killed by gas in a break-in," Annika said. "You don't happen to know anything about that?"

"When? Last night? Where?"

"Don't know," Annika said. "Just that everyone died, including two kids and a dog."

Rickard Marmén didn't answer. If it hadn't been for the sound of traffic in the background she would have thought the line had been cut off.

"Does he know anything?" Berit asked.

Annika shook her head.

"Killed by gas in a break-in, you say?" he said, and the sound of traffic behind him changed. "Can I call you back?"

Annika gave him her direct line and mobile number.

"What do you make of this?" she said once she'd hung up.

Berit took a bite of an apple. She seemed to have given up on the coffee.

"What, crime on the Costa del Sol or this latest reorganization?"

"The reorganization."

Berit put on her reading glasses and leaned over toward the computer screen.

"You just have to make the best of things," she said. "If someone else is responsible for what I do, that gives me more time for the things I really want to do."

"Such as? Your own articles? Gardening? Deep-sea diving?"

"I write songs," Berit said, and she concentrated on the screen.

Annika stared at her colleague.

"Songs? What sort of songs? Pop songs?"

"Sometimes. Once we sent in an entry to the Eurovision Song Contest."

Berit was still staring at the screen. Annika realized that her jaw had dropped.

"You're kidding. You made it to the *greenroom*? What was it like?"

Berit looked up.

"The song didn't make it into the one thousand two hundred best songs. The last I heard, it had been picked up by a local group in Kramfors who play it at gigs around southeast Ångermanland. Have you read Lilian Bergqvist's report to the Court of Appeal?"

"No, I haven't had time. What's it called?"

"Application for judicial review in the case . . ."

"The song."

Berit took her glasses off.

"'Absolutely me,'" she said. "One of the lines is the groundbreakingly innovative 'to be or not to be.' I've spent thirty-two years working on this paper, and if I'm lucky it'll stay afloat for another ten. By then I'll be sixty-five, and ready to retire. I like finding things out, writing articles, but I don't really care who gives me the jobs or which desk I sit at."

She looked at Annika intently.

"Does that make me sound bitter and resigned?"

Annika took a deep breath.

"Not at all," she said. "I feel exactly the same. Not that I can retire anytime soon, but we've changed direction so many times that I don't even feel travel sick anymore. 'To be or not to be.' What about the rest?"

"'No more crying, no self-denying,'" Berit said, putting her glasses back on and turning to the computer again. "What do you make of Filip Andersson's chances of getting a pardon?"

"The fact that it's the attorney general herself requesting the judicial review adds weight to the argument," Annika said.

She went onto the attorney general's website and clicked through to the request.

"You met him in Kumla Prison a few months ago, didn't you?" Berit said. "Do you think he's innocent?"

Annika glanced through the attorney general's report. Reading about these murders always unsettled her. She had been in the patrol car that had been first on the scene that evening, and had wandered blithely in among the victims.

Then she had come across Filip Andersson's name several times when she was digging into the case of the murdered celebrity police officer David Lindholm last autumn. Filip had been a reasonably successful financier who was more famous for his appearances in gossip magazines than for any mentions in *Dagens Industri* before he became known throughout Sweden as "the Södermalm Ax-Murderer." He had been good friends with David Lindholm.

"Those people were killed by Filip's lunatic sister," Annika said. She shut the website.

"How well do you know Rickard Marmén?"

"I wouldn't exactly say I know him well," Berit said. "My brother-in-law, Harald—Thord goes fishing with him sometimes—he's had a flat in Fuengirola since the late seventies. When the children were small we used to borrow it for a week every summer. Rickard's the sort of person you bump into sooner or later if you spend any time down there. I'm not so certain that Filip Andersson is innocent."

"He's a fairly unpleasant character," Annika said, typing the words *Swedes Spain Costa del Sol* into Google. She clicked a link and found herself at www.costadelsol.nu. As the site loaded Annika leaned forward to look.

She read that the Costa del Sol had a Swedish-language commercial radio station, broadcasting twenty-four hours a day. There was a monthly Swedish magazine and a Swedish newspaper, Swedish estate agents and Swedish golf courses, Swedish restaurants and Swedish grocery stores, Swedish dentists, vets, banks, construction firms, and television engineers. She found a few comments that suggested that everything was better in the olden days, and a diary that informed her, among other things, that the Swedish Church was planning to celebrate "cinnamon-bun day." Even the mayor of Marbella turned out to be a Swede, or rather married to a Swede. Her name was Angela Muñoz, but she was evidently known as Titti.

"Bloody hell," she said. "Marbella looks as Swedish as a rainy Midsummer Eve."

"But with rather better chances of sun," Berit said.

"How many Swedes live there?"

"About forty thousand," Berit said.

Annika raised her eyebrows.

"That's more than Katrineholm," she said.

"And that's just the permanent residents," Berit said. "There are plenty more who only live there for part of the year."

"And a whole family has been murdered," Annika said, "in the midst of this Swedish idyll."

"Good angle," Berit said, picking up the phone to call the attorney general's office.

Annika clicked and read the contents of "Latest news from Spain."

The Spanish police had seized a large shipment of narcotics in La Campana, 700 kilos of cocaine hidden in a container load of fruit. Three leaders of the controversial Basque party ANV had been arrested. There were fears of drought again this year, and a whale had beached outside San Pedro.

She clicked to close Google and went into the paper's own archive.

Loads of Swedish celebrities seemed to have houses or apartments down there, actors and artists and sports stars and businessmen.

She picked up the phone and dialed international inquiries, and had better luck this time. She asked for the numbers of the La Garrapata restaurant, the *Swedish Magazine,* the *South Coast* newspaper, and the WASA estate agency, all of them in the district of Málaga.

Then she started ringing round.

None of the Swedes who answered on their crackly Spanish telephones knew anything about anyone being gassed to death in connection with a robbery, but they all had juicy stories about other break-ins, the history and development of the area, the weather and the people and the traffic.

Annika found out that there were more than a million people living in the province, half a million in Málaga, and a couple of hundred thousand in Marbella. The average temperature was seventeen degrees in the winter and twenty-seven in summer, and there were three hundred and twenty days of sunshine. Marbella had been founded by the Romans in 1600 BCE, when it was known as Salduba. In 711, the city had been conquered by the Arabs, who renamed it Marbi-la. The oldest part of the city was built on Roman remains.

"We were still running round in animal skins when people down there had running water and air-conditioning," Annika said in surprise when she hung up.

"Do you want to go and get some lunch?" Berit asked.

They logged off their computers so no one could send fake emails from their accounts while they ate.

Annika was digging out a lunch coupon from the bottom of her bag when the phone on her desk rang. The number on the little screen was eleven digits long, and started with three-four.

"Annika Bengtzon? Rickard Marmén here. Okay, I've looked into that break-in. It seems to be true."

He must have moved from the motorway, because now there was nothing but silence in the background.

"I see," Annika said, starting to lose hope in finding a lunch coupon.

"Did you have any information about the family?"

"The victims?"

She found a crumpled coupon in the side-pocket.

"Did you know it was Sebastian Söderström's family?"

She was about to say "Who?" then gasped instead.

"The ice hockey player?" she asked, letting the lunch coupon fall to the desk.

"Well, it must be ten years since he last played in the NHL. He's been living down here for a while, runs a tennis club. As far as I've been able to find out, his whole family was wiped out, including his mother-in-law."

"Sebastian Söderström is dead?" Annika said in a loud voice, waving her arm at Berit to stop her heading off to the canteen. "So the family that died was Swedish?"

"He had a wife and two fairly young kids."

"What did you say about Sebastian Söderström?" Patrik asked, suddenly materializing beside her.

Annika turned her back on him and stuck a finger in her free ear.

"How reliable is this information?" she asked.

"Hundred percent," he said.

"Who can confirm it?"

"No idea, darling. But now you know."

He hung up without waiting for a reply.

"What was all that about?" Patrik asked.

Berit came back to the desk and put her bag down again.

"Check out Sebastian Söderström on paginasblancas.es," Annika said, and Berit logged back in, typed in the details, and read: "Las Estrellas de Marbella, Nueva Andalucía."

The number had nine digits, and began with 952.

"What's going on?" Patrik asked, holding his hands up to show his frustration.

"Just need to check something," Annika said, dialing the number of the villa in Las Estrellas de Marbella. After five rings an electronic female voice said, "*Ha llamado a nueve cinco dos . . .*" She hung up and dialed the press office of the Foreign Ministry.

"Don't get your hopes up," Berit said, who could see what number she was dialing. "They're usually always last to know."

After the Asian tsunami the Foreign Ministry had got its act together and had been almost helpful for a while, but now they were back in the same old arrogant attitude as before the disaster.

"My name's Annika Bengtzon, I'm calling from the *Evening Post,*" she said when the call was finally answered. "I'd like confirmation that the family that was gassed to death in a break-in in Las Estrellas de Marbella in the south of Spain last night were Swedish citizens."

"We haven't received any information to that effect," the woman at the Foreign Ministry said abruptly.

"Perhaps you'd like to check?" Annika said in a silky voice, and hung up.

"My Spanish is too bad for the Spanish police," Berit said.

"Mine too," Annika said.

"Interpol," Berit said.

"Europol," Annika said. "They're more active."

"WHAT?!" Patrik shouted.

Annika jumped and looked in surprise at her colleague or, rather, the head of news.

"I have a source who says that the family that was gassed on the Costa del Sol is Sebastian Söderström and his wife, children, and mother-in-law."

Patrik turned on his heel, put both hands to his mouth, and yelled, "*Sport!*"

Annika took three long strides and put her hand on his shoulder.

"Calm down," she said as he spun round and was standing face-to-face with her again. "I need to get confirmation. You can't get the lads in sport to start writing his obituary until we know that this is true."

"They need to start making calls," Patrik said.

"And say what? That we *think* he's dead? And even if it's true, we don't know that his family has been informed."

"You said they all died."

Annika groaned.

"Maybe he's got parents, brothers, and sisters."

She took another step forward, stopping right in front of him. She only came up to his Adam's apple.

"A bit of advice, head of news. Try to curb your enthusiasm. You'll end up flying off into the ditch if you carry on like this."

Patrik went pale.

"Just because you didn't get promoted," he said, and headed off toward the sports desk.

"We'll have to try to get confirmation," Berit said, picking up the phone.

After several phone calls the Spanish police had confirmed that five people had been killed the previous night just outside Marbella in what looked like a gas attack in connection with a burglary. There would be no comment on the identity and nationality of the victims until tomorrow lunchtime at the earliest.

They took a break and hurried down to the canteen.

"Sport isn't exactly my strong subject," Berit said once they were sitting down at one of the window tables with two portions of beef stew.

Annika took a bite of a piece of crispbread and looked out at the grayness beyond the window.

"He played professionally in the NHL for several seasons," she said, "first with the Anaheim Ducks, then Colorado Avalanche. He played defense. In the early nineties he was selected to play for the Three Crowns national team several years running. I think he was in the team that won gold in the World Championships in Finland in '91, and Czechoslovakia in '92 . . ."

Berit put her fork down.

"How do you know all this?"

Annika took a sip of mineral water and gulped hard.

"He was Sven's idol," she said, and Berit let the matter drop.

"There's something about fading sports stars," she said, joining Annika in looking out of the window. "They're like black holes, they seem to attract misery."

Large raindrops were hitting the glass.

"Imagine hitting the top when you're twenty-four," Annika said. "You'd spend the rest of your life as a *has-been.*"

They skipped coffee and went back up to the newsroom.

Patrik was practically jumping up and down beside Annika's chair.

"I've got something for you," he said. "As of this afternoon Kicki Pop is going to be presenting the radio program that goes out before P1's in-depth news program. I want you to call Erik Ponti at Radio News and find out what he thinks about that."

Annika stared at the . . . head of news, and waited for the laugh that would tell her it was a joke.

It didn't come.

"Are you kidding?" she said. "I'm busy with the murders in

Marbella, that's a huge story. There are loads of Swedes down there who . . ."

"Berit can deal with that. I want you to do this now."

She couldn't believe her ears.

"You're telling me to call Erik Ponti and try to get him to bad-mouth a female colleague? And one who just happens to be young and blond?"

"He's famous for saying that bimbos are the lowest of the low."

Annika sat down on her chair, her back ramrod straight.

"Ponti may be pompous and self-important," she said, "but he's not stupid. He criticized a blond female colleague once before, when he had every reason to. But considering the amount of shit that got him, do you really think he'd do it again?"

Patrik leaned over her.

"Make the call," he said.

Annika leaned over, picked up the phone, and dialed radio news.

Erik Ponti didn't feel like making any unpleasant comments, not about Kicki Pop personally, and not about her program.

"What a surprise," Annika said, pulling her jacket on and heading toward the caretaker's desk.

"Where are you going?" Patrik called after her.

"I've got a meeting at two o'clock," she said over her shoulder.

"Who with?"

She turned round and looked at him.

"There's such a thing as confidentiality of sources," she said. "Ever heard of it?"

"Not where your superiors are concerned," he said, and Annika could see that his earlobes were dark red.

"Not where the legally responsible publisher is concerned," she corrected.

Then she went over to the caretaker's desk and booked out a car from Tore.

*   *   *

The rain was getting worse; she had to have the windscreen wipers on the whole time. It was only half past one, but darkness was edging closer, creeping up on frozen pedestrians and filthy streetlamps and lorries with flickering headlights.

She was heading west, toward Enköping, past Rissne, Rinkeby, and Tensta. She passed blocks of flats, row houses, empty schools, and an abandoned football pitch. The traffic on the motorway ground to a complete halt outside the railway station in Barkarby, and Annika leaned forward and peered through the windscreen of the car in front to see if there had been an accident she could phone to tell the paper about. It didn't look like it. Maybe a pedestrian had been knocked down. Or someone had jumped in front of a train. That was fairly common.

Soon the traffic started moving again, heavy and slow. The residential buildings thinned out, and pine forest and industrial units took over. The road surface was terrible. Brownish gray sludge was being thrown up at the windscreen by the car in front, and she had to put the windscreen wipers on maximum. She switched the radio on, but it was in the middle of a block of adverts, and she turned it off again.

The scenery outside became increasingly monotonous. The industrial units vanished, leaving just the pine trees. Their branches reached out toward the car, the same dirty Volvo she had driven out to Garphyttan with on the December day when she had found Alexander.

At Brunna she turned right, toward Roligheten. All of a sudden the rain stopped, and everything went quiet. Annika had a terrible sense of direction, something she compensated for by scrutinizing maps and writing detailed directions for herself. Left at Lerberga, then left again after 800 meters, past Fornsta. Through an army training area, then right.

She was heading for Lejongården, a sheltered home for families, situated by the water of Lejondalssjön, where Julia Lindholm had been staying with her son since he was found.

Annika had promised to visit them, but had kept putting it off. She didn't know what to expect. They had only met twice before, both times under extremely difficult circumstances.

The first time they met, they had stumbled upon the gruesome murder scene on Sankt Paulsgatan on Södermalm. Annika had been shadowing Julia and her colleague Nina Hoffman on their shift in patrol car 1617 that evening. The call hadn't sounded terribly serious, a domestic dispute, so Annika had been allowed to go up with them as long as she agreed to stay in the background. She had been quickly ushered away by Nina as soon as they found the bodies.

The second time they met, Julia was under arrest on suspicion of murdering her husband, police officer David Lindholm, and her son, Alexander. She had been sentenced to life imprisonment by the City Court. No one seemed to care about the fact that she had always maintained her innocence and claimed that another woman she had never seen before had shot her husband and abducted her son.

Annika had only met the son, Alexander, once, on the night she found him at Yvonne Nordin's cottage outside Garphyttan. The boy had been missing for seven months when Annika rescued him.

The headlights lit up a rough-hewn red wooden façade, the sort of red that reflected slightly and gave away the fact that it wasn't proper, old-fashioned paint, but a modern oil-based version. Annika realized that this was the place she was looking for. She pulled up in front of the house, put the hand brake on, switched off the headlights, but remained seated in the darkness with the engine idling.

Lejongården was a dark, squat single-story building located on the shore of Lejondalssjön. It looked like a day center, or perhaps a small old people's home. A small playground was visible in the light from the porch. The water lay still and gray in the background.

"I really do want to thank you," Julia had said on the phone, and her words had embarrassed Annika.

She adjusted her hair, switched the engine off, and stepped out onto the gravel drive.

At the porch she stopped and looked out across the lake. A few naked birch trees shivered hesitantly along the shore, their branches as gray as the water. There was a wooded island a hundred meters or so out in the lake. In the distance she could just make out the faint rumble of the motorway.

The door opened, and a woman in a Norwegian-patterned cardigan and sheepskin slippers leaned out into the porch.

"Annika Bengtzon? Hello, I'm Henrietta."

They shook hands. Henrietta? Should she know who this woman was?

"Julia and Alexander are expecting you."

She stepped inside the rehabilitation home. There was a vague smell of damp and the seventies. Pale linoleum floors, pink glass-fiber wallpaper, plastic baseboards. Straight ahead, behind a half-closed door, was something that looked like a meeting room. She could make out some brown plastic chairs around a veneered table, and heard someone laughing.

"I'd like you to concentrate on acting perfectly normally," Henrietta said, and Annika instantly felt herself clench.

"This way . . ."

Henrietta turned off to the left and led her down a narrow corridor with a row of doors to the right and windows facing the car park on the left.

"This reminds me of the only time I ever went InterRailing," Annika said, hoping she sounded normal.

Henrietta pretended not to hear her. She stopped at one of the doors halfway along and knocked.

There were no locks or room numbers, Annika noted. She had read on the home's website that they tried to maintain "a cozy atmosphere to make people feel cared for and safe."

The door opened. A triangle of yellow light stretched out across the floor of the corridor.

Henrietta took a step back.

"Alexander's baked a cake," she said, ushering Annika in. "Just let me know if you'd like me to take him out to play for a bit."

She addressed this last remark inside the room.

Annika stopped in the doorway.

The room was much bigger than she had expected. It was rectangular, with a big picture window at the far end and a door leading out to a terrace. A double bed and a small child's bed stood next to each other just inside the door, and farther in there was a sofa, a television, and a table with four chairs.

Julia Lindholm was sitting at the table, in a sweater whose sleeves were too long, her hair in a ponytail. Her son had his back to the door; his arms were moving as though he were drawing frantically.

Julia got up and ran over to her, and hugged her hard.

"I'm so glad you could come," she said, holding Annika tight.

Annika, who had been holding her hand out, felt stupid and hugged her back rather feebly. The door closed behind her.

"Yes, absolutely," she said. "Of course, I wanted to visit."

"Not many people have been allowed to visit yet," Julia said, finally letting go and walking over to the sofa. "My parents were here for Christmas, and Nina's visited us a few times, but I've said no to David's silly mother, I don't want her here. Have you ever met her?"

"David's mother? No."

Annika let her bag and padded coat fall to the floor beside the sofa. She looked over at the boy, could see his fragile profile behind his hair. He was drawing with thick crayons, firmly and intently, without looking up. She moved gently closer, sank down beside him, and tried to catch his gaze.

"Hello, Alexander," she said. "My name's Annika. What are you drawing?"

The boy clenched his jaw and went on drawing with even greater concentration. The lines were thick and black.

"His grandmother's so confused," Julia said, "and it would just get worse if we met at such a strange place as this. We'll wait and see Grandma once we get back home, won't we, darling?"

The boy didn't react. The sheet of paper was covered by pitch-black stripes. Annika sat down next to Julia Lindholm.

"He's not talking much yet," Julia said quietly. "They say it's nothing serious, it's just going to take time."

"Does he say anything at all?" Annika asked.

Julia's smile vanished. She shook her head.

He spoke to me, Annika thought. That night. He said several things. *Are there any more sweets? She's horrid. She's really horrid. I like the green ones.*

Julia went over to the window and stopped with her back to the room; Annika could see from her reflection that she was biting a fingernail. Then she suddenly rushed for a phone on the wall next to the terrace door.

"Henrietta, can you look after Alexander for a bit? Now, right away. Thanks ever so much."

The silence when Julia hung up was electric. Annika's mouth felt dry, and her fingers started to itch. She squeezed her hands in her lap and looked down at her grandmother's emerald ring. A long minute passed before the carer, or whatever she was, came into the room, took Alexander by the hand, and said:

"Shall we go and watch a film, you and me? *Finding Nemo*?"

She turned to Annika.

"It's about a little boy fish who gets lost from his dad, but then he finds his way home again."

"Yes," Annika said, "I know."

The silence lingered once they were left alone.

"Well, as you know, I work for the *Evening Post*," Annika said, to break the silence. "So I'd like to ask you if you want me to write about you in the paper. About you and Alexander. About how things are for you here."

Julia bit her thumbnail.

"Not yet," she said. "Later, maybe. Yes, later. I want to explain, but right now my head's in too much of a mess."

Annika waited quietly. She hadn't been expecting Julia to want to talk about what had happened since her release, at least not this afternoon, but she had been hoping that she might want to at some point. For the media, crime stories always ended when the case was solved and the perpetrator convicted. The consequences of crime, the victim's long and difficult path back to a relatively normal life, was something that very few people wrote about.

"I'm so angry," Julia said, quietly, almost with surprise. "I'm absolutely furious with the whole world."

Slowly she walked over to the table and sat down on Alexander's chair. She was so slight that she almost vanished inside the big sweater.

"And they tell me that's normal as well. Everything's so fucking normal here!"

She threw out her arms in frustration.

"Have you been here ever since you were released?" Annika asked.

Julia nodded.

"It was the middle of the night. They took me down to the duty court and held the custody hearing at half past one in the morning, then they drove me out here. Alexander was already here."

She looked out through the window. It was dark outside now.

"I wasn't well in prison," she said. "I wasn't well here either to start with. Alexander didn't want anything to do with me. He just turned away and wanted to be with Henrietta."

"And that's perfectly normal as well?" Annika said, and Julia actually laughed.

"You've got it," she said. "But they're very professional here. Nina says so, she's checked them out. This is the Rolls-Royce of family rehabilitation centers, according to Nina, but it's only reasonable that society should have to compensate us a bit for the injustice we suffered . . ."

Annika could hear Nina Hoffman's voice behind Julia's words. Julia's best friend, the police officer that she had shared her training and patrol car with, had been one of Annika's sources in her investigation into David Lindholm. Annika could see Nina before her, her tight ponytail, firm gaze, determined expression.

Julia stood up again.

"Do you want coffee, by the way? There's some in the flask. And Alexander didn't make the cake; Henrietta did while Alexander sat beside her scribbling bird's nests."

She picked up the picture on top of the pile and held it up to Annika. A chaos of heavy black lines covered almost every square millimeter of the large sheet.

"That's normal too," she said, putting the picture down again.

"Maybe a bit of coffee," Annika said. "The stuff we have in the newsroom is undrinkable. We reckon someone poured cats' pee in the water tank."

Julia gestured toward the flask but made no effort to stand up.

"We're going to be here for at least three months," she said. "It's for Alexander's sake, they say. He's the one being taken care of. Right now we're an emergency case, still under investigation."

Anger made her voice crack on the last word.

"It takes the doctors eight weeks to evaluate how disturbed we are. Then we get treatment anything between two and six months. Then we get to live on our own, but fairly close to the home. The emphasis at this place is on relationships between parents and children. I'll be getting support and advice on my parenting. Afterward I can carry on getting follow-up support at home . . ."

She hid her head in her hands and started to cry.

Annika, who had been pouring a cup of coffee from the flask, screwed the lid on, and put it back on the table as gently as she could.

"It's only natural for you to be angry," she said. "Alexander too. I'm not particularly fond of shrinks, but I daresay they're right. It's probably absolutely normal for the two of you to be utterly furious."

Julia took a napkin from the pile beside the cake and blew her nose.

"They say that six months is like a lifetime for a small child. Alex spent seven months up in the woods with that madwoman, so of course he's angry. He probably didn't get any answer to his questions about where David and I were, so as far as he was concerned, we might as well have been dead. And the doctors say that he was aware that his life was in danger. He had a lot of bruises and cuts on his body, so she evidently didn't hold back on hitting him."

"How is he now?"

"He'll come to me, but he doesn't want to look at me. He sleeps badly at night, keeps waking up and crying. We've had to start putting him in nappies overnight again, even though he'd been dry for almost two years."

"So how do you spend your days?" Annika asked, sipping the coffee. It tasted incredibly good.

"I have individual counseling sessions, and soon I'll be able to join in with group therapy and talk to some other mothers; that's supposed to be very helpful. Alexander just plays. He messes about in the sandpit and draws and plays with balls. When we're discharged from here, the childhood psychiatry unit will take over his case."

She let out a laugh, suddenly nervous.

"Oh, listen to me, going on," she said. "I really just wanted to thank you, for everything you've done for us. I mean, you were the one who . . ."

Annika was clutching her cup hard.

"That's okay," she said. "I'm just glad I could be useful."

Silence descended again.

"So," Julia said, "did you have a good Christmas?"

Annika put her cup down on the saucer.

Should she tell the truth? That she and the children had spent Christmas Eve surrounded by boxes in Gamla Stan, eating ready-sliced ham from the Co-op and watching Donald Duck on the laptop? That she had handed her children over to their father for New Year and Twelfth Night, and that they were much happier there?

"Oh yes," she said. "I've just got a lot on at work, that's all. Today I've been working on a really gruesome murder down on the Costa del Sol in Spain."

Julia stood up and turned her back on Annika.

"The Costa del Sol's a terrible place," she said. "Estepona's absolutely awful."

Annika looked down at her hands; her choice of subject for small talk really was dreadful. After all, she knew that Julia had had a terrible time down there with her husband, David.

"Sorry," Annika said, "I didn't mean to . . ."

"We spent six months there," Julia said, "and David was off traveling almost the whole time. I was pregnant and didn't have a car, and it was several kilometers to the nearest shop, and I had to drag those bags of groceries home in thirty-degree heat . . ."

"It must have been awful," Annika said.

Julia shrugged.

"He was working deep undercover; sometimes he could be gone for weeks at a time without getting in touch. That went on for several years, for the duration of that bloody operation. Years!"

She spun round.

"And I never did find out what it was all about. Drugs or money laundering or some crap like that, I've no idea, I never found out . . ."

She leaned toward Annika.

"And do you know what the worst thing is? That I was so terrified that he was going to get hurt. That something would happen, something dangerous. And what happens?"

She laughed out loud.

"He fucks a crazy bitch once too often and she shoots his head and his cock off, and they lock me up, and Alexander . . ."

She was leaning close now, staring into Annika's eyes.

"They say Alexander's going to carry the scars of this for the rest of his life. And no one believed me."

She slammed her hand down on the table so hard that the porcelain jumped.

"*No one believed me!*"

Suddenly Annika realized that visiting time was over.

She pushed the coffee cup aside and stood up.

Julia slumped down on her chair and stared vacantly ahead of her.

"Who'd have thought it would be Yvonne Nordin, of all people?" she said.

Annika stiffened.

"What? Did you know her?"

Julia shook her head.

"No, I never actually met her, or Filip Andersson."

Annika went over to pick up her coat.

"Speaking of Filip Andersson," she said, "the attorney general has applied to have his case reviewed."

Julia looked up.

"Nina will be pleased," she said in a toneless voice.

Annika stopped, coat in hand.

"Nina Hoffman? Why would she be pleased about that?"

Julia scratched the back of her left hand hard.

"Of course she'll be pleased. Filip's her brother, after all."

Annika tore her mobile out before she had even opened the car door, then sat in the driver's seat and dialed Nina Hoffman's number from memory.

Why the hell hadn't she mentioned that she was the sister of both Filip Andersson and Yvonne Nordin?

The line buzzed and crackled, and it took ages for the call to go through. Annika stared out at the dark windows of the rehabilitation home as the phone rang.

How many times had she and Nina discussed the Södermalm murders? And whether Filip Andersson was innocent or guilty? And Filip's contacts with the underworld, and with David Lindholm? After she went to visit Andersson in prison last autumn she had even gone straight round to see Nina and tell her about the visit . . .

There was now an engaged tone on the line, as if the call had been rejected.

Throughout all their conversations Nina had had a hidden agenda. Maybe she had been lying the whole time, maybe she had only talked to Annika to find out what she knew, and try to direct what she was going to write?

Annika dialed the number again as she watched the lights go on in the corridor inside the building. Henrietta was walking along with Alexander; he was so small that Annika could only see the curls on the top of his head bouncing as he walked.

There was a click on the line, and Telia's message service clicked in.

Annika hurriedly ended the call, as if she'd been caught doing something she shouldn't.

She'd trusted Nina, but Nina hadn't been honest with her.

Annika had asked her to dig out Yvonne's passport picture, and Nina hadn't said a thing about the fact that they were sisters.

Annika dialed the mobile a third time. Voicemail again. She cleared her throat.

"Er, hello, this is Annika Bengtzon," she said. "Happy New Year. Listen, can you call me when you get this? Okay? Bye for now."

She called reception at Police Headquarters and asked to be put through to the duty desk of the station on Torkel Knutssons-gatan. The man who answered gave his name as Sisulu.

"Nina Hoffman's on leave," he said. "She'll be back on duty on Sunday."

Annika thanked him and put the mobile down on the passenger seat, started the car, and pulled out onto the road, heading quickly back toward the office.

When she reached Kallhäll she realized that she had no good reason to hurry anywhere.

She didn't want to get back to Patrik and his little notes, and she was in no rush to get back to the as-yet-unfurnished flat on Agnegatan.

When the mobile rang on the seat beside her and she saw her ex-husband's number on the screen, she felt strangely elated.

"Hello, this is Thomas."

She took a deep breath, not remotely pleased at the way her chest was fluttering.

"Hi," she said, her voice sounding slightly too bright.

"What are you doing? Are you driving?"

She laughed, feeling the warmth spread.

"I've just been out on a job, I'm on my way back. No problem."

"Listen, we're planning Easter here, and we were wondering how you're fixed that week?"

The happiness was wrenched from her body with a force that felt quite physical.

"Have you started using the royal *we*?" she asked, trying to sound lighthearted. It didn't work at all.

"Easter's late this year, Maundy Thursday's the twenty-first of April, and it's the following week that's a bit tight. I'm away at a conference, but that's my week, so I was wondering if we could maybe swap . . ."

"I can't answer that," Annika said. "I got a new job at the paper today, and it's going to mean a few changes."

He fell silent.

"Don't you think you should have discussed that with me first?" he said curtly.

Raw anger flared up instantly. She clenched her teeth and swallowed.

"It won't affect my weeks with the children, so I couldn't see any reason to do that."

"Okay," he said crossly. "Sophia wants to talk to you."

He passed the phone to his new partner without saying good-bye.

"Hi, Annika, this is Sophia."

"Hello," Annika said.

"Well, we've been having a discussion in my network, I mean, my private network, my girlfriends, and we've got a little invitation for you."

Annika took a deep breath and forced herself to stay calm and reasonable.

"You work with the written word and all that, so we wondered if you'd like to be part of our reading group?"

Reading group? Jesus fucking Christ.

"Erm," Annika said, braking at the traffic lights at the Rissne junction.

"This week we're reading a wonderful book by Marie Hermanson, *The Mushroom King's Son*, have you read it? It's about working out what really matters, finding your place in the world. The son grows up in the forest, but he really belongs on the coast. It's a really beautiful story. Do you like Marie Hermanson?"

Annika had read *The Clam Beach*, and had started a book about a man who lived under some stairs, but she hadn't finished that one.

"I don't know," she said. "Things are a bit tricky right now, I just started a new job at the paper today, so everything will be a bit up in the air for a while . . ."

"A new job?" Sophia said. "But how's that going to affect our weeks with the children?"

There, right there, was the limit for how much crap Annika felt she had to put up with.

"Listen," she said, "there's a slim chance that I might discuss a serious change in my work with the father of my children, but I will never, ever discuss my career with you. Have I made myself clear enough?"

Sophia Fucking Bitch Grenborg sounded rather put out.

"Why are you so aggressive? I only want what's best for your children."

Annika let out a shrill, evil laugh.

"You're such a fucking hypocrite," she said, far too loudly. "If you wanted what's best for my children, you wouldn't have torn our family apart, you fucking . . ."

She had been on the point of saying "bitch in heat," but felt that the term wasn't quite adequate.

"I haven't got time for you and your book group," she said instead. "There isn't a chance in hell that I will ever be friends with you, so just drop it, okay?"

She clicked to end the call without waiting for an answer.

For the first time she didn't feel remotely ashamed of shredding Sophia's absurdly expensive bra at a petrol station outside Kungsör.

And the fact that she had sent a tip-off to the paper from a fake email address that made sure Thomas's investigation at the Ministry of Justice got closed down suddenly felt a bit better as well. He didn't seem to be suffering, exactly. Thomas had instantly been given a new appointment, organizing new legislation in the area of international financial crime, and he certainly hadn't seen fit to discuss that with her.

Considering that it was rush hour, the traffic was surprisingly light, but then it was a short week after a public holiday, and a lot of people had taken the chance to get a full week off for fewer days of their holiday, like Nina Hoffman.

She got back to the paper just in time to pack up her laptop and go home.

"Oy!" Patrik yelled the moment he caught sight of her. "You're flying to Málaga first thing tomorrow morning."

Annika, who had started gathering together her things, dropped everything on the desk.

"What are you talking about?" she said.

"You're booked on a flight that leaves at 0630," Patrik said.

Annika threw out her arms.

"For fuck's sake," she said, "I can't go anywhere. I've just moved, I haven't even had time to unpack . . ."

"You can't have that many things, can you?" Patrik said. "I mean, your house burned down, didn't it? Clobbe from sport is on holiday in Marbella. He's not going to win any prizes, but he can do the main piece for tomorrow. You can have a handover meeting with him when you get there. Then you need to concentrate on getting confirmation of the victim's identity, and if it *is* Sebastian Söderström, you'll probably be there the rest of the week."

Annika stared down into her bag. Erik Ponti's arrogant lies about how much he valued Kicki Pop and had nothing whatsoever against P1 being invaded by noisy talk shows were still ringing in her ears.

But of course she was working to a rota now.

"The tickets, then," Annika said, "where are they? Or have I just got a booking number. Where I going to be staying? Do you want me to hire a car? Have we got an interpreter? Have we established contact with the local police? And who's going to be taking the pictures?"

Patrik stared at her with a vacant look in his eyes, then he puffed out his chest.

"You can sort all that out once you're there," he said. "There must be freelance photographers in Spain. And take the chance to do a bit of research on the Costa Cocaine as well; you're going to be taking over the series of articles about drugs and money laundering, the ones I'd have written if I hadn't been promoted . . ."

Then he turned on his heel and hurried off to the entertainment desk.

Annika turned to Berit.

"Unbelievable!" she said. "He thinks the job of head of news means running around and giving people advice about things that are bloody obvious."

"The booking number of your flight to Málaga's in your email," Berit said without looking up. "There are a couple of Scandinavian police officers stationed in Andalucía. You've got their names and numbers in another email. Start by calling them; they're bound to know a local interpreter. Take your own pictures; that's easiest. I managed to book out a completely automatic camera; you just point and click. Call as soon as you know anything."

She pointed at a little camera case on the desk beside Annika and looked up over the frame of her glasses.

"Fly carefully," she said, "and good luck."

Annika groaned.

"Why didn't you take the job, Berit?"

There was an echo as she closed the door of the flat. She stopped in the hall for a minute or so, the way she usually did, listening to the sounds from the street and feeling the draft trying to get into the stairwell.

This flat was much darker than any she had ever lived in before. It was higher off the ground, on the fourth floor. Large tree-tops swallowed the light from the streetlamps down in Agnegatan. Outside her bedroom window she had nothing but a starless sky.

From the hall she looked through the living room into the darkness that would be Ellen's room. The kitchen was immediately to the left, a modern, minimalist affair that she had taken an instinctive dislike to.

She turned on the lights, took off her padded jacket, and let it fall in a heap on the floor. She went quickly past the kitchen, not wanting to see the boxes of belongings.

She went into her room, curled up on the bed, and leaned back against the headboard.

There wasn't much wrong with the flat itself. It was actually quite nice. It only had three rooms apart from the kitchen and bathroom, but it was fairly roomy, 104 square meters, with a large hall that could be used as a living room, which meant that she and the children could each have their own bedroom.

The keys had been delivered by courier to her temporary home in Gamla Stan the day before New Year's Eve. She had spent New Year's Eve itself hiring a car and moving the few possessions she had managed to acquire since the fire.

She looked up at the smooth ceiling. There must have been

some heavy plaster detail up there at some point, but the building had been renovated at the end of the 1930s and all the unnecessary ornamentation had been stripped out.

She had found out that the building, known as No. 1 Walnut Block for bureaucratic purposes, was a cooperative apartment block, where each occupant owned a share of the building. This particular flat was owned by the National Property Board.

She had no idea what Q had done to get hold of it, and she had no idea how long she would be able to live there.

She lit one of the bedside lamps and plumped up the pillows behind her back, turned her head a little to the right, and looked up at the sky.

She could see the bedroom in the villa out on Vinterviksvägen before her, how abandoned and alone she had felt there. She closed her eyes and remembered the fire, the smoke, the panic.

Thomas hadn't been at home. That same evening he had left his family and gone off to Sophia Grenborg, and Annika had to save herself and the children as best she could. She had lowered Kalle and Ellen out of the bedroom window on the first floor using sheets, then she had jumped out and landed on the table on the terrace.

And then she was suspected of arson.

After several months of forensic investigation, they had found a fingerprint on a Molotov cocktail in the remains of the house that could be linked to the real culprit: an American contract killer known as the Kitten.

Which made little difference to Annika.

The Kitten would never be held responsible for the fire.

Instead of arresting her, Inspector Q had used her to negotiate a prisoner exchange with the American authorities: The FBI got the Kitten, and the American justice system sent home a Swedish citizen from a prison in New Jersey.

"You sold out my home, *my children's home,* just to get a bit of credit with the CIA and bring home a cop killer," she had said to Inspector Q.

That was when he had joked about organizing a new home for her, and now here she was, in number 28, Agnegatan, in the same block as the flat she had lived in when she first arrived as a summer temp on the *Evening Post* ten years before. She had no windows facing that direction, otherwise she could probably have looked into the little house in the courtyard where she had spent that hot summer when everything began, before the children, before Thomas, when Sven was still alive . . .

The phone started to ring somewhere in the flat, not her mobile but the landline. She flew up, unable to remember where she had plugged it in.

After the fourth ring she found it on the floor of Kalle's room.

"Annika Bengtzon? This is Jimmy Halenius."

The undersecretary of state at the Ministry of Justice, the minister's right-hand man.

Thomas's boss.

She cleared her throat audibly.

"Thomas has moved out," she said. "I told you."

"I want to talk to you, not him."

She moved the receiver to her other ear.

"Oh," she said, "really?"

"I heard from Britta that you wanted a comment about the extradition of an American citizen toward the end of last year. As you know, the minister isn't in a position to comment on individual cases, but if you like I could outline some of the issues involved in a more informal way?"

"Britta?" she said.

"I'll be at Järnet on Österlånggatan from seven pm. Come if you're interested."

"On the record?" she asked.

"Absolutely not," he said. "But I'll pay for dinner."

"I don't eat dinner with politicians," she said.

"As you like. Well, thanks, and good-bye," he said and hung up.

She put the receiver back and lowered the phone to the floor. There were no lights in Kalle's room yet, she was standing in the dark by the window, looking down on the naked treetops a couple of floors below.

Really, she ought to unpack.

She looked at the time.

Mind you, she didn't have to do that this evening. She had never expected to hear back from anyone in the department. Shouldn't she go and hear what they had to say? Besides, she'd met Halenius before when Thomas had some colleagues round for dinner.

She looked round at the boxes.

It's a tough decision, she thought. Dinner at a fancy restaurant with a highly placed source, or spending the evening with Kalle's Brio train set?

Järnet turned out to be one of the restaurants in Gamla Stan that Annika had walked past so many times and peered into, as if the people inside lived in a different, much more beautiful world than her own. It always looked so cozy, with candles and gleaming cutlery, glasses full of wine, and tables resounding with laughter. Outside in the street as she passed there was always a bitterly cold wind blowing.

A simple little sign with the name of the restaurant in joined-up writing was swinging and creaking above the entrance. She pushed open one of the gray-green double doors and found herself in a lobby. At once a waiter appeared out of nowhere; he looked very friendly. He took her padded jacket without giving her a numbered ticket or asking for fifteen kronor as a wardrobe fee.

It was ten past seven. She had chosen the time carefully, didn't want to seem too keen, but didn't want to leave him waiting on his own for too long either.

The dining room itself was small, only ten or so tables.

Jimmy Halenius was sitting in one of the farthest corners, immersed in one of the evening papers with a glass of beer in front of him.

Not the *Evening Post,* she noted, but the main competitor.

"Hello," she said. "You're reading the wrong paper."

He looked up. His brown hair was sticking up in all directions, as if he'd got into the habit of rubbing it in frustration.

He got up and held out his right hand.

"Hi," he said. "Have a seat. I've already read the right paper. Memorized it, in fact. Do you want something to drink?"

"Mineral water," she said, hooking her bag over the back of the chair.

"Throw caution to the wind and have a Coke. My treat."

She sat down.

"Not the benevolent state, then?"

He folded his arms and raised his shoulders slightly with a smile.

"Unlike your expense account, my expenses are in the public domain," he said. "I think we'll keep this in the family."

Annika unfolded her napkin, glancing surreptitiously at the undersecretary of state, his demeanor, and the way he was dressed.

He didn't exactly exude power. Self-confidence, certainly, but nothing formal. He was wearing a blue-striped shirt under a fairly crumpled jacket. No tie. Jeans.

"So am I to understand that the Kitten's extradition is something else that we're going to keep in the family?" she said, looking him right in the eyes. "Why are you being so secretive about it?"

Jimmy folded the paper and put it away in a shabby briefcase.

"I need to know that this will stay between the two of us," he said.

Annika didn't answer.

"I can tell you some of what you want to know," he went on, "but you can't publish it."

"Why should I listen to you if I can't write about it?" she asked.

He smiled and shrugged.

"The food here is good," he said.

She looked at her watch.

He leaned back in his chair.

"The Kitten was responsible for the murders at the Nobel banquet just over a year ago," Annika said.

"Correct," Jimmy said.

"And she murdered that young scientist out at the Karolinska Institute."

"In all probability."

"And she burned down my house by throwing firebombs into the children's bedrooms."

"We're assuming that's what happened."

Annika rubbed her forehead.

"This is completely incomprehensible to me," she said. "How can you refrain from prosecuting one of the most ruthless criminals ever to have been caught by the Swedish police?"

"Obviously this is about what we got in exchange," the under-secretary of state said.

"And that's what you were thinking of telling me?"

He laughed.

"What would you like to eat?" he said. "The menu's actually comprehensible, for the most part."

Annika picked up the menu.

"This can't just be about some shabby little cop killer in New Jersey," she said.

She could identify a lot of the dishes on offer, fried herring with dill butter and puréed potatoes, for instance. But things like the "gremolata emulsion with potato confit" were rather more difficult.

Jimmy Halenius chose the carpaccio of venison with black chanterelle mushrooms and Västerbotten cheese as a starter, and grilled steak with shallot purée, roasted Hamburg parsley, and Västerbotten croquettes as his main.

She ordered vendace caviar and shredded reindeer meat stew.

"Looks like you're very fond of Västerbotten cheese," she commented as the waiter glided off to fetch their wine, a South African Shiraz.

"Well, you're sticking to Norrbotten," he said. "Reindeer and vendace."

"Even though I'm from Södermanland," she said, raising her glass of water.

"I know," he said.

She opened her mouth to ask how he knew, then she remembered their last meeting out at the villa in Djursholm.

"You used to have an old Volvo, didn't you?" he had asked back then. "A 144, dark blue, lots of rust?"

Annika could still feel how the blood had coursed through her body, turning her face dark red.

She put the mineral water down.

"How did you know I'd sold Sven's car?" she asked.

"It was my cousin who bought it," he said, drinking his beer.

She stared at the undersecretary of state.

"Roland Larsson?" she said. "He's your cousin?"

"Of course. We were best friends growing up."

"He was in my class in the Works School in Hälleforsnäs!" she said.

Jimmy Halenius laughed.

"And he had a huge crush on you all those years."

Annika started to laugh as well.

"God, he did, didn't he?" she said. "I almost felt sorry for him."

"We used to lie in the hayloft at Grandma's on summer evenings, down in Vingåker, and Roland would spend hours talking about you. He had an old photograph he'd cut out of the paper, of you and a few other people, but he'd folded it so only you showed. He kept it in his wallet the whole time."

The waiter came over with their starters and poured wine in their glasses. They ate, silent and hungry.

Annika pushed her empty plate away and looked intently at the man opposite her.

"How old are you really?" she asked.

"Two years older than Roland," he said.

"Who was one year older than me, because he had to repeat a year."

"Education wasn't exactly a priority in the Halenius family. I was the first one to make it to university."

"Are you from Södermanland as well?"

He took a sip of wine and shook his head.

"Östergötland, Norrköping. I grew up on the third floor of a block of flats on Himmelstalundsvägen."

"So are you Social Democrat royalty, then? You know, mum a local councillor, dad a union boss?"

"God, no," he said. "Dad was a communist. I was in the Red Youth to start with, but the Social Democrat youth movement had better parties. And much prettier girls. I got Roland to join as well. He's still on the town council for the Social Democrats down in Flen."

She could see Roland Larsson in front of her, his slightly squat frame and long arms. He and Jimmy Halenius were actually fairly similar. She didn't know he had gone into local politics.

"What else is Roland up to these days?"

"He usually works in the ice-cream factory each summer, but he's signing on at the moment."

"Does he still live in Hälleforsnäs?"

"No, last autumn he took the leap and moved all the way to Mellösa. He moved in with a divorcée with three kids who lives just behind the local shop, you know, the one on the road out to Harpsund . . ."

"Not Sylvia Hagtorn?"

"Yes, that was her name! Do you know her?"

"She was in the class above us. Three kids? I wonder who with?"

The waiter removed their plates and brought the main course. He refilled Jimmy Halenius's glass.

"Are you married?" Annika asked, glancing at the ring finger of his left hand.

"Divorced," he said as he attacked his steak.

"Children?" she asked, picking at the reindeer stew.

"Two," he said, looking up. "Twins. One of each. They're six now."

"And you have them every other week?"

"Since they were eighteen months."

"How do you think it works?"

He drank some wine.

"Oh, you know," he said. "How do you think it works?"

He looked up at her and went on chewing.

She swirled her wine round in the glass. She didn't usually like red wine, and this was particularly dense and heavy.

"I hate being divorced," she said, meeting his gaze. "I miss my children so much I feel like dying when they're not with me. And I . . . well, I have a few problems with Thomas's new . . . partner."

She had been on the point of saying, "I hate Thomas's new fuck."

"Really, why?"

He sounded almost amused.

"She's a walking cliché. I don't understand what Thomas sees in her."

"So you don't think she tore your family apart?"

Annika gripped her cutlery hard.

"Well, of course she did. If it hadn't been for her, I'd have my children with me all the time."

Jimmy Halenius looked down at his plate.

"Do you really believe that?" he said without looking up. "Didn't you and Thomas do a pretty good job of tearing your family apart without anyone else's help?"

She was so taken aback by his question that she dropped her fork.

"What the hell would you know about that?" she said, and she could hear that her voice sounded strange.

He looked up and let out a short laugh.

"Oh," he said, "I don't know anything about the two of you. I just know what mistakes I made. I was awful to live with. I didn't communicate. I could start a world war about the tiniest things, but when it came to the really big issues I never made any demands. I just expected her to know what I wanted. And now I've started five sentences with the word 'I.' I'm fairly self-absorbed as well, did I mention that?"

She stared at him, then burst out laughing.

"That could have been me you were describing," she said, astonished. "I was a terrible person to be married to."

And the moment she said the words, she knew they were true.

"I never even told him that I knew he'd been unfaithful. I just took my revenge, over several months, without explaining why. He didn't realize a thing, obviously."

The waiter asked if they'd like anything else, and Jimmy Halenius looked at his watch.

"Shall we move on somewhere else and have a few drinks?" he asked.

Suddenly Annika remembered the flight to Málaga at 0630 the next morning.

"Shit!" she exclaimed, looking at her own watch. "I haven't even packed yet!"

"Are you going somewhere?"

"I have to be at Arlanda at half past four."

"Then there's no point even thinking about going to bed," he said cheerily.

"I don't think so," she said, and fumbled for her bag.

The undersecretary of state asked for the bill and paid it in cash. He asked the waiter to call a taxi, then helped her on with her jacket.

Outside it had started to snow, hard little flakes of ice swirling through the air and hitting her face like needles. The sign over the door creaked in the wind. A group of young men with slicked-back hair and wearing English oilskin coats were marching down the middle of the street, waving wine bottles and mobile phones. Annika turned away.

A taxi came gliding down Österlånggatan. Jimmy Halenius stepped out into the road and the door closed behind him.

He wasn't particularly tall, maybe ten centimeters taller than her.

"Where are you flying?" he asked.

"Málaga," she said as the taxi got closer.

"Ah, España," he said. "*Entonces, vamos a saludar como los españoles!*"

He took hold of her shoulders and pulled her toward him, then gave her an air kiss on the left cheek, then one on the right.

"The Spaniards kiss twice," he said, with his lips close to her ears. "It's worth remembering when you're there."

He let go of her and smiled so hard that his eyes narrowed to slits.

The taxi pulled up alongside them and stopped.

"I'll be in touch," he said, and opened the car door for her.

Annika got in without thinking and let him close the door behind her as well. She saw him turn away and walk off toward Järntorget, fold up his collar against the wind, and disappear round the corner.

"Where to?" the taxi driver asked.

And only then did she realize that she knew absolutely nothing more about the Kitten than she did when she arrived.

TUESDAY, JANUARY 4

The light was so bright that she had to close her eyes. She stood there swaying on the steps of the plane for several seconds before she could open her eyes enough to make her way down the steps to the ground.

Her knees and back ached. The low-cost airlines weren't joking when they said you get what you pay for. The local buses in Stockholm were a utopia of personal space compared to the sardine tin that had flown her to Málaga.

It was warm, almost twenty degrees. A smell of aviation fuel and burned rubber hovered over the cement apron. She was shepherded onto a huge bus that swallowed all the passengers and realized it had been a mistake to put her padded jacket on. Helpless as an insect on its back, she tried to wriggle out of it. Impossible. Instead she sweated and suffered as the bus jolted its way along the endless terminal building and over toward the entrance.

It looked like the entire airport was a huge building site.

The deafening sound of cement mixers and earth movers reached all the way into the baggage hall. There were lots of different conveyor belts, close together, and they rattled and creaked as they spat out suitcases and sports equipment in an endless torrent.

"Do you know where I can hire a car?" she asked an elderly man with a large stomach and an even larger golf bag.

He gestured toward customs, then to the right.

She squashed her jacket into her bag and went with the flow.

On the floor below the baggage hall another equally large hall stretched out, full of nothing but car-hire companies. She walked hesitantly along the row of counters. All the usual names were there, Hertz and Avis, as well as some cheaper options with enormous queues. At the far end were a few local companies.

She found herself at the far end of the row, standing indecisively at the end of the hall.

Tucked away in the corner was a shabby desk with a tired girl who was sitting half-asleep under a sign that read *Helle Hollis*.

What the hell, Annika thought, and hired a Ford Escort.

It took quarter of an hour to find the car in the huge garage. It was small, blue, and anonymous. She threw her case in the boot and put her bag, notepad, mobile, camera, the guidebook she bought earlier from the bookshop at Arlanda, and the map from the hire company on the passenger seat.

She squeezed into the driver's seat and switched on her mobile.

She had read Clobbe's worthless article online at Arlanda. The headline was "Death in Paradise." The short text was piled so high with clichés that it could have won a prize: The sun is shining in the sky, but there is a chill in people's hearts. They wanted nothing more than to live a peaceful life, but instead they got a brutal, early death.

She had decided there and then not to bother with any sort of handover with Clobbe.

"You have . . . four . . . new messages," her electronic voicemail told her.

The first was from Patrik, telling her to call the newsroom as soon as she landed.

The second was from Patrik, wondering if she was there yet.

The third was from Patrik, shouting excitedly that the Spanish police had confirmed that Sebastian Söderström and his family had died of gas poisoning, and how come she hadn't managed to find that out, seeing as she was there on the scene?

The fourth was from Berit.

"We've divided it up like this," her colleague's message ran. Annika could hear her leafing through some notes. "I'll put together Sebastian Söderström's life story from old cuttings. Sport will take care of his ice hockey friends in the NHL and get comments from them. You can have three articles: 'All about the gas murders,' 'The life of the family on the Costa del Sol,' and that old classic, 'Idyll in shock.' Let's catch up this evening. Good luck!"

And with that she had hung up.

A man came over waving both arms, shouting something at Annika inside the car. She presumed he wanted her to drive off so he could have her space.

She locked the door and picked up her notepad and mobile.

The man banged on her windscreen.

She wound the window down a centimeter.

"What?" she said.

He was waving his arms and shouting, and she pretended not to understand.

"Sorry," she said. "*No comprendo.*"

The man started yelling that he'd call the police.

"Go ahead," Annika said, closing the window again. "Good idea!"

She dialed the number of the first of the two Scandinavian police officers whose names Berit had given her, a Knut Garen, who turned out to be Norwegian.

"My name's Annika Bengtzon, I'm a reporter on the *Evening Post* newspaper. I was given your number by . . ."

"I know, I spoke to Berit Hamrin yesterday," the policeman said. "She said you'd be in touch. Are you in Marbella now?"

"I'm on my way."

"Let's meet at La Cañada at two o'clock."

"Lackanyarda?" Annika said.

"Outside H&M," the policeman said, and ended the call.

Lackanyarda, she wrote on her pad, started the engine, and came close to running down the gesticulating man as she wove her way through the garage toward the exit.

The traffic was terrible. She understood perfectly well why the Spaniards were European champions at knocking over pedestrians on road crossings. Car horns blared and drivers shook their fists and waved their arms.

"Calm down before you have a heart attack," she muttered, trying to make sense of the road signs. She failed.

The reconstruction of Málaga Airport looked like a massive project. Immense concrete skeletons stuck up into the sky in every direction; there were great piles of reinforced steel along the side of the road, lorries and forklift trucks and diggers fighting for space with cars and mopeds and the courtesy buses that carried people into the terminals from the long-stay car parks. All the roads were provisional, painted with a mess of lanes and arrows.

There was no logic to the places she was supposed to aim for either; the girl at the Helle Hollis desk had warned her about that. In order to get to Marbella, she should aim for Cádiz or Algeciras, and take the toll motorway to start with, but then she had to head for San Pedro de Alcántara; that was important, she mustn't forget that, because otherwise she'd end up in Estepona.

"And that's a terrible place, I've heard about it," Annika said, thinking of Julia.

The girl gave her a blank look.

"I live there," she said.

Annika passed Torremolinos far below on her left, an endless grotesque chaos of shabby white buildings strung out along the Mediterranean coast. She overtook several VW camper vans with French plates that seemed to have all their occupants' belongings strapped to the roof, and was herself overtaken by a German-registered Merc. A Spanish BMW was weaving between the lanes and came close to hitting a SEAT. She clung onto the wheel tightly and wondered what *lackanyarda* was.

When she reached the toll-paying section of the motorway, the traffic decreased radically. She could relax a bit and admire the dramatic scenery.

Thousand-meter-high mountains stretched all the way to the sea. The four-lane motorway, broad and smooth, clung to the mountainsides and leaped across valleys. Large advertising hoardings for nightclubs and estate agents lined the road, sometimes right next to the abandoned ruins of old farms. Newly built residential areas with boldly colored villas with huge terraces started to pop up as soon as she passed the tollbooth. She had to dig her sunglasses out of her bag, the colors were so bright they hurt her eyes: the clear blue sky, the green of the valleys, the pastel colors of the houses, and the sea glittering like a shattered mirror.

Just outside Marbella, next to a shopping center that reminded her of the one at Kungens Kurva outside Stockholm, the motorways merged once more, and the traffic became just as crazy as before. She kept to the right and managed to be in the correct lane when they split again. She didn't want to end up in Estepona, after all.

By the slip road to something called Istán the motorway made a broad sweep toward the sea. There were more houses. She thought she should probably turn off soon and try to find a hotel. The next moment she saw one off to her left. HOTELPYR.com, she read on the sign that stood out against the sky.

What the hell, she thought, and turned off toward a bullfighting arena.

*   *   *

The Pyr was in the middle of Puerto Banús, and had plenty of vacant rooms. She got a corner room on the third floor with a glorious view of the motorway.

"Do you know something called lackanyarda?" she asked the receptionist.

"La Cañada? It's a shopping center. It's huge, on the way to Málaga. You can't miss it. Turn off toward Ojén."

Ah, she thought. The thing that looked like Kungens Kurva.

She looked at the time, half past one.

She went back out to the car.

Naturally, she missed the turning.

She saw the development flash past on her left just as she realized that she'd gone too far. After a moment of panic she managed to avoid ending up back on the toll motorway. She searched the jungle of incomprehensible Spanish advertising slogans and road signs and electronic messages lining the motorway for a slip road that would let her turn round and head back the way she had come. She found one just after the Costa del Sol hospital.

It was only as she was pulling into the jam-packed car park of the shopping center that she noticed her shoulders were hunched up somewhere near her ears. She forced them back down into their normal position, squeezed the car past a British-registered Jaguar, and parked right next to the exit.

Inside, the mall was thick with people. The days before *El día de Reyes,* Epiphany, were among the busiest shopping days of the year, she had read that in the guidebook on the flight down. Most Spanish children didn't get their Christmas presents until the Twelfth Day, and it looked like every single last-minute present in the south of Spain had to be bought here.

The temperature was the same inside as out, she noted as she headed off across the polished granite floor. The sun was shining through the glass ceiling several floors above, only reinforcing the impression that you were still outdoors. She was forced forward by the flow of people, past exactly the same shops as in the shopping centers back home in Stockholm: Mango, Zara, Lacoste, and Swatch. She found a floor plan and realized that she was standing just beside the entrance to H&M. She couldn't see anyone who looked like a policeman in the mass of people, so she stood with her back against the plate-glass window to stop herself from getting trampled.

In front of her a huge Christmas tree reached up toward the roof, its bright green color giving away the fact that it was plastic. Christmas baubles, two meters across, hung from the beams in the roof, and a few palms leaned against a concrete pillar. They were so ugly that she presumed they must be real.

She looked at the time. They ought to be there soon.

"Annika Bengtzon?"

There were two of them, and their appearance screamed plain-clothes Scandinavian police so loud that it practically echoed off the plate-glass windows. One was very fair, the other ash blond. They were both wearing jeans and comfortable shoes, and were very fit, exuding the confidence that only men in positions of un-questionable authority possessed.

She shook their hands with a smile.

"We're in a bit of a hurry," Knut Garen said, "but there's a tapas bar upstairs with an excellent view of the car park."

His colleague introduced himself as Niklas Linde, and it sounded like he was from northernmost Norrland.

They took the escalator up and pushed their way through to a window table, where, as promised, they were treated to a magnifi-cent view of ten thousand cars.

"Thanks for taking the time to see me," Annika said, putting her pen and notepad on the table.

"Well," Knut said, "this is the way it works. All contact between the Spanish police and the Swedish authorities has to go through us. We're the ones who coordinate communication."

"To begin with, I was wondering if you know of a good interpreter?" Annika said. "Preferably Swedish to Spanish, but someone who could translate from English would be fine."

"You don't speak Spanish?" Knut Garen said.

"*No mucho,*" Annika said. "*Comprendo un poquito.*"

"Carita," Niklas said. "She's Swedish, lives with her family down here, works with translations and stuff when she's not interpreting. I'll give you her number."

Knut took out his mobile.

"This whole business with the Söderströms is just tragic," he said as he looked up the interpreter's number in his phone book. "Break-ins involving gas have been getting more and more common, but we've never seen one go this badly wrong. Here you are, Carita Halling Gonzales, have you got a pen?"

She jotted down both her home number and what she assumed must be a mobile number.

"Will you be working on the case?" she asked.

"The Spanish *policía nacional* will be in charge of the investigation," Niklas Linde said. "We're not actually operational here."

"We're working on a different case at the moment," Knut said. "You might have reason to write something about that in the future. Greco and Udyco seized a shipment of 700 kilos of cocaine in a warehouse in La Campana last week, and we think there's a Swedish connection."

"Greco?" Annika said.

"The specialist Spanish unit that deals with narcotics and organized crime. We work with them a lot."

Knut looked at his watch.

"I've just got a few general questions about crime down here," Annika said. "I've read that the Costa del Sol is also known as the Costa del Crime. Is that an exaggeration?"

"Depends how you look at it," Knut said. "There are four hundred twenty criminal organizations here, involved in everything from growing hash and smuggling cocaine to car theft, people trafficking, and illegal gambling. It's estimated that there are about thirty contract killings in Málaga alone each year. The sex industry is huge—it employs over forty thousand people. There are at least a hundred known brothels . . ."

"How common is the use of gas in break-ins?"

"Extremely common," Niklas said. "The victims are often foreigners, as well as rich Spaniards, of course. It's believed that the gangs identify their victims at the airport, follow them to their villas or apartments, then knock them out with gas when they're asleep. There've been cases of people waking up to find their homes stripped bare, including the rings from their fingers. It often leaves people in a very bad way, and I don't just mean the consequences of the gas itself."

"Can I quote you on that?"

"Of course," he said, "but not by name. I'm fairly incognito here."

She let her gaze linger on him: What exactly was his role?

"And I understand that Swedes have been the victims of gassings before this?" she said.

"We have a hundred or so Swedish cases each year," Knut said, waving over another dish of *jamón serrano*.

"What do you think about this particular break-in?" she asked.

The police officers looked at each other.

"I mean," Annika said, "didn't they have a gas detector? I've heard that everyone in Nueva Andalucía has a gas detector these days . . ."

"There are indications that this wasn't an ordinary gas attack," Niklas said.

"I don't know if we should . . ." Knut said.

Niklas leaned across the table and lowered his voice.

"The victims weren't in their beds when they were discovered," he said. "The woman was lying dead just behind a door, the man was found lying across a desk. The gas detector had been set off, and that probably woke them up. Someone switched it off."

"And the children?" Annika said, and had to swallow.

"They were found on the landing outside their parents' bedroom. Their grandmother, a pensioner, was the only one found in bed. Maybe she couldn't move too well, we don't actually know."

Annika was thinking hard. She didn't bother asking about details like the victims' names and ages; the news agencies would have all that sort of thing.

"How did the gas get inside the house?"

"Through the ventilation unit at the back of the building. The thermostats in the house were set at twenty degrees and it was cold last night, no more than eight, nine degrees. When the temperature outside fell, the heating came on and the whole house was gassed at the same time."

Annika looked down at her notes.

"This might sound like a strange question," she said, "but what was . . . the man doing on the desk?"

She couldn't bring herself to say his name.

"The desk was right under the air vent," Niklas said. "When he was found there was a duvet beside him. It looks like he actually noticed the gas pouring into the house and tried to stop it with the bedclothes, which only makes this case even more unusual."

He fell silent, and the two policemen looked at each other.

"What?" Annika said. "Why?"

"Normal knockout gases like hexane, isopropanol, and carbon dioxide are transparent," Niklas said. "If any of those had been used, he wouldn't have been able to see it."

She made a note of the gases, guessing at their spelling.

"So this time something else was used? What?"

Niklas shook his head.

"The gas must have been stronger than normal, seeing as it

killed them when they were awake and trying to escape, and it looks like it was visible somehow. Like mist, or smoke."

Annika shuddered.

"So they died pretty quickly?"

"Well, they were left paralyzed more or less instantaneously."

"The children too?"

The policemen didn't answer, and Annika could feel nausea rising in her throat. Was there anything else she needed to know?

"Who found them?" she asked, looking through her notes as she tried to suppress the urge to throw up.

"The home help, she worked there five days a week and had her own key."

"And she definitely wasn't the one who gassed them?"

"If she'd wanted to rob them, she could have done it last week when the family was away in Florida for Christmas."

"So things were stolen as well?"

"Everything of value. The safe's missing. The thieves—or killers, rather—smashed down the wall that the safe was cemented into and took it with them, presumably unopened. All the artwork's missing, along with computers and televisions and other electronic equipment, as well as any jewelry and cash. It looks like they took their time."

"What does 'took their time' mean?" Annika asked.

"At least twenty minutes for the safe, and the same again for the rest of the job."

"Any idea what time of night it happened?"

"The killers got into the house at 0334."

Annika's eyes opened wide.

"How do we know that?"

"That's when the alarm on the gate was disconnected."

"How do you mean, 'disconnected'?" Annika said. "Did they cut the power? Pull out the cables?"

Knut looked at his watch again.

"The only explanation I can come up with is that the killers knew the code," he said, standing up.

Annika remained sitting at the table after the police officers left and took her phone out of her bag.

She began with Carita Halling Gonzales's home number.

No answer.

She dialed the mobile number, and after four rings a woman's voice answered with "*Sí, díga?*"

"Carita Halling Gonzales?"

She could hear children shouting in the background.

"*Soy yo.*"

"My name's Annika Bengtzon, I was given your name by Knut Garen. I'm a reporter for the *Evening Post,* and I could do with an interpreter for a few days. Is it right that you interpret from Swedish to Spanish?"

"Will you please be quiet?" she said away from the receiver, and the children's laughter died down. "Yes, I'm an interpreter, but things are a bit crazy today. I mean, it's Twelfth Night tomorrow . . . no, now listen to me!"

Annika pressed the bridge of her nose between her thumb and forefinger and tried to summon up some patience.

Obviously, she ought to have asked for some other names, how silly . . .

"What sort of job is it?" Carita asked.

"*Está libre?*"

Annika looked up and saw three fat women pointing hopefully at the empty chairs round her table.

"*No,*" Annika said, lowering the phone. "*No libre.*"

The women started to sit down regardless.

"*No libre!*" Annika roared, waving her hands, and the women looked at her indignantly and made their way off toward the other end of the bar.

When in Spain, speak the way the Spaniards do, she thought as she raised her phone again.

"I'm here looking into a number of deaths," she said. "A Swedish family, a Sebastian Söderström and his wife and children. Maybe you've heard about it?"

"Goodness, yes," Carita said. "I only found out this morning. It's awful. We've been expecting something like this to happen, there have been so many break-ins using knockout gas down here."

Annika was making notes to help her remember the quote.

"Did you know the family?"

"The Söderströms? No, I can't say that I did really. I've met them, of course. Our children go to the same school."

"Which school is that?"

"Marbella International College. What would the job entail, what would you want me to do?"

Annika scratched her head. She didn't like traveling and had always avoided it as much as she could. She'd never worked with an interpreter before.

"My Spanish is too poor for me to make myself understood," she said, "and I've never been here before. I need help with the most basic things, talking to people and finding my way to where I want to go . . ."

"I'll check with Nacho," she said, "see if I can get hold of him. He's probably got patients now, of course . . ."

"Nacho?" Annika said.

"My husband, he's a pediatrician. Can I call you back?"

Annika leaned back in her chair and put her mobile down on the table. She ought to ring Patrik, even though there would be absolutely no point to the call.

She closed her eyes and leaned her head against the wall.

She really was horribly tired. When the alarm clock went off at 0315 that morning she had almost thrown up. Now she could feel her neck relax as her head lolled to one side and her chin dropped.

Her entire body was heavy with sleep, and she sat up with a start, blinked several times, then picked up her mobile again.

Patrik answered at once, of course.

"I'm doing a couple of pieces," she said. "I'm writing the details of the gassing—I've got quite a lot of new information. I've spoken to a mother who's got kids in the same school, and I'm going to do a piece about the family and their lives here as well."

She closed her eyes and held her breath in the hope of avoiding the clichéd "idyll in shock" piece.

"What about the idyll in shock, then?" Patrik asked. "That's what you're there for, after all, to describe the panic in the Swedish colony."

Is it? Annika thought.

" 'Idyll-in-shock' is my middle-name," she said. "Every word will be dripping with shock. *No te preocupes*."

"Hmm," Patrik said, not sounding convinced.

Two bleeps on the line told her she had a call waiting.

"I have to go," she said, and took the other call.

It was Carita.

"Hi," she said, "it's all okay. I can take the job. I charge forty euros an hour, plus expenses."

"Er, okay," Annika said, presuming that was a regular rate for interpreters. "What does 'expenses' mean?

"If I'm going to be driving you around, I'll charge for petrol, that sort of thing."

"I've got a car," Annika said. "Well, it's only a Ford. Can you start straightaway?"

"Oh, hang on, a police car . . ."

There was a crackle on the line followed by a long silence.

"Carita?" Annika said tentatively.

"Sorry, they've gone now. You're not allowed to use your mobile when you're driving. Nacho got a sixty-euro fine last week. Where are you now?"

"Lackanyarda," Annika said.

"Poor you, on a day like today. Do you want to meet there or somewhere else?"

"I'm staying in a hotel called the Pyr. It's . . ."

"Let's meet up there, in fifteen minutes or so? See you soon!"

"Wait!" Annika cried. "Can you bring the latest school year-book?"

Carita looked exactly like the women shopping in La Cañada: thin and blond and suntanned, slightly older than her. Gold earrings and rattling bracelets. A tight low-cut top and a leopard-skin pat-terned bag.

"Nice to meet you," the interpreter said, shaking her hand warmly as she dropped a gold-cased lipstick in her bag. "What do you want to do first?"

"Head out to the villa where they lived. Do you know where it is?"

Carita raised her eyebrows.

"Somewhere in Nueva Andalucía," she said. "You haven't got a more specific address, or a *supermanzana*?"

Annika stared at her: a what? A super apple?

"Block, district," the interpreter said.

"Oh," Annika said, pulling out her notepad. She leafed through it until she found the details Berit had got from the Páginas Blancas.

"Las Estrellas de Marbella," she read out.

"The stars of Marbella," the interpreter said, shaking her head. "No idea. We'll have to call Rickard."

"Marmén?" Annika said.

"Do you know him?" Carita said in surprise.

"Doesn't everyone know Rickard?" Annika said, digging out the number from her notes.

Oh yes, Rickard knew where Las Estrellas de Marbella was, all right. He'd run a decorating business sometime in the not-too-distant past and managed to make a few deliveries to Las Estrellas before the company went bust.

Carita wrote the directions on Annika's pad.

"Thanks, big kiss," she said, then handed the phone back to Annika.

"Do you want to drive or shall I?" Annika asked.

"You drive, I'll have my hands full trying to make sense of these directions."

They got in the car and passed beneath the motorway.

"Go past the bullfighting arena," the interpreter said, pointing a varnished fingernail. "What sort of articles are you going to write?"

"I've already met a couple of police officers who told me some of the detail about the actual murders," Annika said. "Now I want to have a look at the house, so I can describe the area it's in, maybe talk to some neighbors. Then I was thinking of trying to meet up with some of the Swedes living down here, see if they can tell me how this sort of event will affect their lives, if at all . . ."

"Murders?" Carita said.

Annika glanced at the woman beside her, who was looking in a compact mirror and picking something off her teeth.

"The police don't think this is an ordinary break-in. The thieves used some strange kind of gas that killed the family almost instantly."

She thought for a moment.

"They didn't actually call them thieves, but murderers."

"How awful," the interpreter said. "Left at the roundabout."

The roads meandered between high concrete walls, dense cypress hedges, and thickets of hibiscus and bougainvillea. Behind the walls and vegetation they could make out roofs of terracotta-colored tiles, paved gardens, and close-cut lawns.

"What huge houses," Annika said, looking out of the windscreen.

"Expensive too," Carita said. "That one up ahead, for instance, that's on the market for nine and a half million."

Annika peered at the black wrought-iron gates as they drove past.

"That's a lot, of course," she said, "but that's what villas out in Djursholm cost."

"Not kronor, euros," Carita said, looking down at the directions. "Right here, I think."

They drove on for another kilometer or so. The interpreter was looking round, very alert.

"That part up there must have only just been finished," she said, pointing up to the left. "I don't think I've seen it before. Oh, watch out for that pothole . . ."

Annika had to swerve sharply to avoid hitting a large hole in the middle of the road.

"Bloody hell," she said. "How can they leave the roads in this state?"

Carita sighed.

"A few years ago the whole of Marbella local council was arrested. That hole has probably been dealt with and paid for several times over, but the work probably took the form of renovations on the home of the head of the highways department . . . Ah, here it is."

A grand gateway that looked like something from an old Western appeared as they drove alongside a large hedge. *Las Estrellas de Marbella,* it said in curling gold lettering above the gate. An angel with marble wings was playing a harp right at the top. Two pink stone lions with their mouths wide open roared silently at the world.

"Fuck," Annika said. "That's the most tasteless thing I've ever seen."

"It'll pass," the interpreter said. "After a couple of years down here you're pretty much immune."

She opened the passenger door and got out of the car.

"I wonder how you get in?"

There was a post containing a keypad in front of one of the stone lions. Annika pointed at it. Carita skipped over and tapped in a few numbers at random. Nothing happened.

"We'll have to wait for someone to go in or out," she said.

Annika switched off the engine, grabbed the camera, and went out into the afternoon sun.

"What weather," she said. "Is it always like this?"

"From November to March," the interpreter said. "Then it gets warmer again."

Annika took a few shots of the grand gateway.

"Have you lived here long?"

Carita frowned and counted on her fingers.

"Almost seven years now," she said. "My husband's Colombian, and we couldn't live there for a number of reasons, so we moved to Sweden first, but that didn't work at all. Do you know what happens in Sweden?"

Annika shook her head and listened to the wind. She could hear a car approaching.

"Nacho, who's obviously a qualified pediatrician, couldn't even get a job delivering papers. The government employment agency wanted to send him on a course so he could work as a hospital cleaner. Have you ever heard anything so ridiculous?"

A silver Jaguar Cabriolet swung in toward the gate and a man with a very high hairline pressed a remote control and the gates started to glide open. Annika and Carita both jumped back in the car. Carita waved cheerily at the man in the Jaguar as they drove in.

"So we moved here instead," she said. "Nacho got a job at the hospital straightaway. We're very happy here. It's a bit like Southern California."

She looked at the directions again.

"Down here," she said. "It's supposed to be on the left-hand side of the road, a little way down the hill."

The house loomed up above them, heavy and solid. It stood on its own in a cul-de-sac, facing south toward the sea, with a mountainside to the west. The drive was blocked, partly by a large gate, and partly by a police cordon.

Annika parked next to the pavement farther down by the turning circle, next to an overgrown plot with some abandoned foundations in the middle. They got out of the car, and Annika took the camera from the backseat. They walked rather solemnly toward the house.

The drive carried on climbing behind the gate and swung off left toward a carport. There were two cars parked there, an urban jeep and a smaller soft-topped car. Annika raised her camera and took a few pictures.

The house itself was right in front of them. It stretched up toward the sky, a mixture of two and three floors, in an irregular and elaborate design. It was all terraces and balconies, bay windows and pillars, and various types of arch, curved balcony rails, and ornate iron railings. At the top was a tower with arched windows in all directions. The garden was full of fruit trees and large palms. In front of the house was a paved pool area.

The whole plot was in shadow. Annika suddenly became aware that there was a cool breeze from the mountain. She fired off a series of shots of the house against the sun in the evening light.

"Have you any idea how long the family lived here?" she asked, folding her arms to keep warm.

Carita looked up at the house.

"It can't have been long," she said, "the area's so new."

"But the trees?" Annika said. "They look very mature."

"Down here you buy palm trees when they're ten meters tall.

They deliver them on lorries with articulated digger attachments. Do you think this is a bell?"

She pressed something that looked like a switch on one of the gateposts.

A few seconds later the terrace door opened and a uniformed police officer came out onto the sundeck. Carita waved frantically. Annika hid the camera behind her back. The uniformed man came down toward the gate and stopped a reasonable distance away.

Carita rattled off something in Spanish and the policeman sounded irritated when he answered. Carita pointed at Annika and said *Suecia* and *amiga* in a pleading tone of voice, as well as a lot more that Annika couldn't understand. The policeman looked more friendly now but shook his head sadly, *Hoy no, imposible, mañana sí.*

"You can get inside the house early tomorrow morning," Carita said, taking her sympathetically under the arm and giving her a consoling pat on the shoulder with her other hand. "I told him you were a friend from Sweden and that you're devastated by the tragedy and that you'd like to go in and say a last farewell to your friends here, in their home . . ."

"I don't usually lie about what I'm doing or who I am," Annika said, feeling ill at ease.

"I don't think the constable reads the *Evening Post,*" Carita said, heading back toward the car.

Annika had put the camera back in its case and was about to get in the driver's seat when her mobile phone rang. She looked at the display.

Bosse calling.

Bosse?

"Hello?" she said hesitantly.

"Annika? This is Bosse. Bosse Svensson."

The reporter for the other evening paper, the one she'd

done some serious flirting with. She still had his number in her phone.

She turned away from the car and took a few steps into the abandoned plot.

"What do you want?" she asked quietly.

"Okay," he said, "it's about work. In my hand I'm holding a picture that I was wondering if you'd like to comment on."

Silence.

"What?" Annika said. "What sort of picture? What are you talking about?"

"I've got a picture of you, outside a restaurant, where you're standing cuddling the undersecretary of state at the Department of Justice."

Annika stood perfectly still and let the words sink in.

"Cuddling?" she said. "What do you mean?"

"Well, snogging, then."

Annika's jaw dropped as she stared at the derelict foundations.

"Snogging? With Halenius?"

"And I'm giving you the chance to comment."

She shut her eyes and put her hand to her forehead.

The Spanish air-kissing just before she got in the taxi.

The group of noisy rich kids with their mobile phones in their hands.

She let out a deep sigh.

"And you're thinking of publishing the picture? In the paper?"

"Yes, that's the idea."

"And you're wondering if I'd like to comment?"

"Obviously, you have to have the chance to explain yourself."

She snorted, then spat on the pavement.

"Okay," she said. "This is my comment: I'm so relieved I never fucked you, Bosse. I've heard you're completely useless in bed. Otherwise I have to refer to source confidentiality. Who I talk to, what we talk about, and how we do it, all of that is protected by the constitution. I have no intention of breaking the constitution simply because you can't handle rejection, Bosse."

There was a long silence. Annika could hear the sounds of the newsroom on the other end of the line. She knew Bosse was recording what she said. She wasn't about to say anything in such a way that he could edit her words and replay them online or to his bosses.

"I've been told that you drank a great deal of wine. Is that true?"

"I didn't want to drink wine with you, did I, Bosse? Has that left you feeling insulted?"

"So you don't want to comment?"

"You're married, aren't you?" Annika said. "A wife and three kids in Mälarhöjden?"

Another silence.

"Annika," he said. "I'm serious. We're going to write about this. We've got information that Halenius was on duty that evening, but instead of doing his job he was out at a restaurant, drinking and flirting. As for you, who always make such a big deal of your high morals and journalistic integrity, can't you see what this will do to your credibility?"

"Did you volunteer to make this call, Bosse, or were you ordered to do it?"

He sighed and Annika heard a click. Presumably he was switching off the recorder.

"You realize that we'll request to see the receipt from the department?" he said. "Credit card receipts, taxi receipts . . . It'll all come out."

"If it was your idea to call, that means you still haven't got over me, and you want revenge. If you were ordered to do it, you have remarkably little backbone, seeing as you didn't refuse. Are we done?"

"You're not going to get away with this," Bosse said.

She cut him off.

"Problems?" Carita said.

"Not really," Annika said, unable to help herself imagining Thomas's face when he opened the other evening paper the next day. "Shall we try knocking on the neighbors' doors?"

Hardly anyone came to the door.

No one had seen anything.

No one wanted to say anything.

"Where are we going now?" Carita asked as they reached the first roundabout on the way back down to the motorway.

"Somewhere where there are plenty of Swedes who'd be happy to talk to a reporter from one of the evening papers," Annika said.

"The La Garrapata restaurant or the Los Naranjos clubhouse," Carita declared. "Left here, then."

Annika pulled out, but the interpreter put a warning hand on her arm.

"Watch out," she said, pointing at a red Land Rover approaching from the right. "That looks like a Brit, they're lethal. They always look the wrong way at roundabouts. They're used to driving on the left."

Sure enough, the driver pulled out right in front of Annika without looking in her direction. Annika braked hard and blew the horn, and the driver of the other vehicle spun round and gave her the finger.

"Their driving doesn't get any better when they've been drinking wine all day long," Carita said. "Right here. The golf club or the restaurant?"

"Preferably not the golf club," Annika said.

She recalled Sven's description of golf: "The easiest sport in the world, hitting a ball that isn't moving."

The interpreter guided her through winding roads past several golf courses and massive villas and huge apartment complexes. In one way or another they all bore similarities to the Söderström family home. Nothing understated or tasteful. Annika stared in fascination at a four-story building in gold and white that looked like a cream cake. There was an entrance from a road above the house that meant you could park in the attic. Right next to it was a pistachio-green house with a pink roof and five gold-colored onion domes.

"Is this what Southern California looks like?" Annika asked.

"The flashier parts of Los Angeles," Carita said. "I grew up in Beverly Hills. This is the closest we get to the USA in Europe. Did the police say anything else about the break-in? Have they got any leads?"

Annika realized that she hadn't actually asked that, which was ridiculously sloppy.

"Nothing they wanted to tell me about," she said quickly. "What sort of people are we likely to see at the restaurant?"

Carita thought for a moment.

"Ordinary people," she said. "Some who got fed up with the Swedish climate, some who moved here for their children's sake, and others who've sold their businesses and spend their time drinking wine and playing golf. What's the ground clearance on this car, by the way? Oh well, it's probably okay. Head down onto the riverbed."

Annika stopped the car.

"What?"

"Down into the river. There's cement at the bottom. That way we won't have to fight our way up to the N340. There are terrible holdups at this time of day because of the roadworks."

She saw the skeptical look on Annika's face.

"It's not deep."

Annika drove cautiously over the edge, through a clump of reeds and down onto the riverbed.

Sure enough, the water was only a few centimeters deep. She followed the river for a few dozen meters and emerged on the other side of the motorway.

"You do seem to be building an awful lot of new roads," Annika said, looking at the dormant roadworks in the rearview mirror.

"The N340? New? It was built by the Romans and has hardly had any work done on it ever since. Okay, here we are. You can park here."

"On the pedestrian crossing?" Annika asked, but Carita was already out of the car.

They were in an older residential area with chalk-white row houses. Annika picked up the camera and flash and followed the interpreter toward the restaurant.

La Garrapata, Annika read from the sign above the entrance, where the menu was given in three languages: Swedish, English, and Finnish. "Does the name mean anything special?"

Carita was adjusting her hair.

"Yes," she said, "it actually means *tick*. Why anyone would want to name a restaurant after a blood-sucking insect is beyond me, but that's what they did."

La Garrapata was an extremely modest establishment. The glass door facing the street had an aluminum frame that rattled when you opened it. There was condensation on the inside of the windows. Carita stepped inside and immediately let out a little squeal. She set about air-kissing all sorts of people, first the right cheek, then the left, just as Jimmy Halenius had demonstrated.

The pictures couldn't be that bad, Annika thought. It had been dark, and she hadn't noticed any flash, and there certainly hadn't been any tongues.

She looked around.

They were in a dining room with about thirty tables and a bar with space for maybe twenty guests. A large screen on the wall was showing Swedish television.

"This is Annika Bengtzon," Carita said, pointing at Annika. "She's been sent down by the *Evening Post* to write about the poor Söderström family, and she was wondering if any of you would like to talk to her about them . . . Lasse, you knew Sebastian! Tell us!"

There was deathly silence in the restaurant. Annika could feel herself blushing. This wasn't the way she usually worked. She took pride in the way she approached her interviewees, slowly but unambiguously. She always made sure to explain the purpose of the interview as clearly as possible, so that no one could feel they had been tricked into anything afterward. They usually did anyway, because they didn't think Annika had portrayed them generously enough.

But Lasse cleared his throat and came over, and started to talk about his friend Sebastian, loudly and with feeling, in front of the whole restaurant.

All very un-Swedish, Annika thought, writing so hard that her arm started to ache.

"Sebbe could have picked any sport at all," Lasse said. "He was just as good at all of them. The fact that he ended up in ice hockey was mainly just chance; he was almost as good at golf and tennis. And he knew it, he knew he had a gift, he was aware of it and wanted to give something back to the world."

Lasse sniffed, and several of the guests nodded and dabbed at their eyes with napkins.

"He wanted to do something worthwhile with his money and time," Lasse said, "not just sit at home polishing his trophies. That's why he got all those talented poor kids into the tennis club, that's why he employed Francis to train them. He'd been given the chance to develop his talent when he was young, and he wanted to give other kids the same chance."

Lasse started to cry.

"I remember the last time we were there with Leo and My, it must have been just before Christmas. Sebbe had organized a club tournament where the winner got not only a cup and a new tracksuit, but also a place at Marbella International College until they took their International Baccalaureate exams at eighteen."

There was a murmur among the guests, and Lasse nodded.

"Yes," he said, "a place at MIC. The girl who won was ten years old. That prize cost Sebbe a cool half million, but he was over-joyed. 'She's great,' he said, 'she'll go far. Imagine, being able to fol-low her progress over the years, watching how she develops, being there when she graduates' . . ."

Several of the women were crying loudly by now.

Annika wondered about taking out her camera, but decided to wait until they weren't crying quite as much. She looked down at her notes—who were My and Leo? The dead children?

She glanced at the time, this mustn't take too long. She was going to have to call Niklas Linde again and ask if they had any leads on the murderers, and she had three articles to write. She also had to make sure she got to bed at a sensible hour, seeing as the following day was bound to be pretty tough as well.

So she said in a loud, clear voice: "Sebastian's wife, did anyone know her?"

A woman in a blond page-cut and designer jeans stood up.

"Vivve was a Swea," she said, "so we all knew her."

Almost all the women nodded in agreement.

Vivve was a *Swea*—what the hell did that mean?

Annika make a note in her pad and kept her eyes down to mask her confusion, waiting for the woman to go on.

"Even though she was so busy with the children and the school and Sebastian, Vivve always made time for her committee work, and we should remember that she looked after her mother, and Suzette as well whenever she was down here . . ."

"Did she have a job?" Annika asked, and the woman stopped short. Then she pursed her lips slightly.

"Yes, Vivve had a job, but having a job isn't as important down here as it is up in Sweden," she said, then sat down.

Oops, Annika thought. I just trod on someone's toes.

"I appreciate that the Söderström family were well known and very popular in the Swedish colony on the coast," she went on, hoping that she'd expressed herself correctly. Evidently she had, because everyone murmured their agreement.

"Veronica has been here ever since she was a little girl," said an older woman who was sitting alone at the table closest to the kitchen, with an almost empty bottle of wine in front of her. Annika had to crane her neck to see her.

"Did Veronica Söderström grow up in Spain?" Annika asked.

The woman fingered her glass, and her eyes fluttered.

"I came here at the same time as Astrid, her mother. Astrid made everyone feel happy, somehow. And Veronica was the most beautiful little child you ever saw, and then she went on to become a model, of course . . ."

The old woman seemed to lose herself in her memories.

Astrid had to be the dead mother-in-law.

"How long have you known Astrid?" Annika asked.

The woman refilled her glass.

"Almost forty years. She was my bridesmaid when I married Edgar, and she sat next to me when I buried him last year. Here's to you, Astrid!"

The woman drained her glass and Annika felt her throat tighten, and had to cough to clear it. She stood up, went over to the woman, and sat down beside her. The guests took this to mean that the group interview was over and started to talk among themselves at their tables.

Annika asked the woman her name, how old she was, and whether she could take her picture.

Her name was Maj-Lis, she was sixty-nine, and she was happy to have her picture taken if that was really necessary.

Annika took several pictures using the flash, from the front, no artistic flourishes. Then she put a consoling arm on the woman's arm before moving on to Lasse and repeating the process.

He had known Sebastian for five years. They had met when

Lasse started playing tennis at Sebastian's club, a fairly small setup, just five courts but with a fantastic view, up in El Madroñal. Lasse's own children were the same age as My and Leo, eight and five, but Lasse was divorced these days, and his ex-wife had moved back to Sweden, so he only had the kids occasionally during the holidays.

The woman who was a *Swea* like Veronica, whatever that meant, didn't seem to know the dead woman terribly well. Nor did any of the others.

Annika took pictures of some of the *Sweas,* then gathered the guests together for a sad group picture. With that, she was almost done.

"Is this going to affect your lives down here at all?" she asked.

A large, blond man who hadn't said anything before stepped forward and spoke up.

"I think this just emphasizes the importance of fitting a gas detector," he said. "As you all know, I sell top-class alarms in my ironmonger's down in San Pedro, so I'd advise anyone who hasn't already got one to fit one now. We're open till two pm tomorrow . . ."

All of a sudden Annika felt she couldn't do any more of this.

She went over to Carita. The interpreter was deep in conversation with two men in light knee-length shorts, and Annika tapped her gently on the shoulder.

"I'm done," she said, and the interpreter stood up at once.

They thanked everyone, waved, and left the restaurant.

"That seemed to go well," Carita said when they were back in the car. "Where are we going next?"

"Now I need to write this up," Annika said, starting the engine. "Shall I drive you home?"

"It's kind of you to offer, but you'd never find your way back to the hotel. Straight ahead, the Hotel Pyr is just round the corner. Anyway, my car's in the Corte Inglés car park. Here's the school yearbook, by the way. Just drop me off outside. I'll invoice for the cost of the car park, if that's okay?"

"Sure," Annika said.

She took the neatly bound book printed on glossy paper.

"Oh, what does the fact that Veronica was a *Swea* mean?"

"She was a member of the Swedish Women's Educational Association, SWEA. They're all over the place. One of my mum's friends started it in Los Angeles in the late 1970s."

"Are you a member?"

"Who, me? No, I don't have time. Turn off here."

A minute later Annika pulled up in front of the hotel.

"Just one more thing," she said. "Do you think the death of the Söderström family will have any effect on the lives of Swedes on the Costa del Sol?"

"Definitely," Carita said. "Everyone will be a lot more careful after this. See you tomorrow!"

She slammed the car door and tottered off along the pavement in her high-heeled boots.

Annika let out a deep breath. Everyone will be a lot more careful after this.

There was the last quote of the day.

Darkness fell quickly. There was a faint rumble from the motorway. The bright yellow lamps lining the roadworks cast harsh shadows across the room.

Annika put her bag and the camera and the plastic bag with all her books and maps on the bed and went to close the curtains.

But instead of shutting the shadows out she stopped at the window, looking out at the cluttered view.

There was a solitary, sad little tennis court below her window. Two of the floodlights were broken, leaving the far end of the court in darkness.

On the far side of the motorway, buildings clambered up the

valley toward a massive cliff face. She could see lights from windows, neon signs, and streetlamps glowing and shimmering in the darkness. Then the mountains took over, off in the distance lay the Sierra Nevada, with twenty peaks over 3,000 meters, and she could see the foothills standing out like black giants against the starry sky.

She opened the window and got the wind and exhaust fumes in her face. The evening was still mild. She shut her eyes.

The children would have eaten by now. They had probably sat down to watch their favorite children's program, but it would be over now. Ellen had probably been on the point of falling asleep, and if she did it would be difficult to get her off to sleep in bed, and then she'd be impossible tomorrow morning.

She closed the window, took out her phone, and dialed Thomas's number. His tone was abrupt when he answered.

"Are you in the middle of eating?" she asked apologetically.

"Sophia and I are having a glass of wine," he said. "The children are watching a kids' program. Did you want anything in particular?"

She sat down on the bed and pulled her knees up under her chin.

"I'd just like to talk to them," she said.

He sighed theatrically, then shouted, "Kalle, Mum's on the phone," and Annika heard the boy call back, "But the sport program's on."

"You've got stiff competition," Thomas said down the line, then a moment later she heard running footsteps and clattering.

"Hello, Mummy," Ellen said.

Annika's shoulders relaxed, and a smile rose up from her heart.

"Hello, darling, were you asleep on the sofa?"

A hesitant pause.

"Maybe a bit," the girl said. "Can we have a dog?"

"A dog? Oh, we can't have a dog. We only live in a small flat, we can't have a dog there."

The girl sounded genuinely surprised when she replied.

"Anna's got a dog, a brown one, and it's much smaller than a flat."

Annika stifled a sigh. This debate arose every time any of the children at preschool got a new pet.

"It's lovely that you like animals, I do too, but we have to think about what's best for the animals as well. And you get to play with Zico when you visit Grandma and Grandad in Vaxholm, that's good, isn't it?"

"Zico's nice."

"He's very nice. What did you do at preschool today?"

The little girl, who had evidently been fast asleep in front of the television, sounded full of energy as she related everything she had done during the past day. Once the two-time world boxing champion Ara Abrahamian had finished talking and handing out prizes in the television studio Kalle came over and joined in. No disasters, no crises, no nasty little sods taking out their own low self-esteem on her kids today.

She said good-bye with lots of kisses and good-night hugs, then sat there for a minute or two with a warm, sad lump in her chest.

It was now completely dark outside the window. An ambulance drove past on the motorway, its siren blaring. She got up from the bed and closed the curtains, then turned on the main light and the lamp on the desk and got out her laptop. She felt utterly exhausted.

How many times had she plugged in this computer?

Every time she arrived at work, every time she got home.

The base of her spine ached when she sat down. The chair creaked.

She logged into the hotel's network, 15 euros a day. She leaned her forehead in her hands for a minute or so before she got going. Then she took out her mobile and called Patrik Nilsson.

"Annika," he cried, "where have you been all day?"

"Oh, just sitting around drinking coffee," she said. "I'm going to send you three articles: the fatal gassing and break-in, the family, and the idyll in shock. There are pictures for everything. How much do you want me to write?"

"I don't know what you've got," Patrik said.

"How much space have you kept?"

"Three double-page spreads and the centerfold, although Berit's doing that with sport."

"I'll send things through as I finish them so you can start work on them," Annika said. "You'll have the first in an hour or so."

They hung up, and Annika rang Niklas Linde's mobile.

He answered on the fourth ring, and there was the sound of club music in the background.

"A quick question," she said. "Have the Spanish police got any leads on the perpetrators?"

Thud, thud, thud.

"Now I'm disappointed," he said, and Annika bit her cheek. What had she done wrong now?

A woman was laughing so hard somewhere in the bar that she was practically howling.

"There was me hoping you were after my body," Niklas said, "but you only want me for my brains."

Okay, so he was one of those.

"I wonder if Constable Linde might have had a few glasses of vino tinto since we last met?" Annika said, looking at the time: half past eight. At that moment her hunger kicked in. She hadn't eaten since that awful sandwich in the sardine tin that morning.

"And a few cavas," he added. "Do you want to come down and have a glass or two?"

Thud, thud, thud.

"Not tonight," Annika said. "I've got articles to write. That's part of the deal."

"But some other night, maybe?"

Thud, thud, thud.

"Maybe, who knows. Any leads in the case?"

"Just a moment," he said, suddenly sounding completely sober.

There was a banging and crashing on the line, and she had to take her earpiece out.

"Hello?" he said. The thudding was gone, now he had the sound of traffic in the background.

"I was asking about leads," Annika said.

"They've got quite a lot to go on," Niklas said. "Tire tracks from two different vehicles, both types identified. Footprints from three suspected perpetrators, shoe sizes confirmed. There's also other evidence that I can't divulge at the moment."

"So the police are fairly confident of solving this crime?"

"It's just a matter of time," Niklas said. "Have you eaten?"

"Er," Annika said, "no, but . . ."

"Where are you staying?"

"In a hotel called Pyr, it's . . ."

"Bloody hell, are you in the Pyr? I'm at the Sinatra Bar down by the harbor, it's only three hundred meters away. Do you want me to bring you an emergency sandwich?"

She couldn't help laughing.

"Ha, not a chance!" she said. "Sleep well."

She clicked to end the call, picked up the hotel phone, and called reception.

The hotel didn't have room service, thank you very much.

The minibar was full of ridiculously expensive miniature bottles of spirits, but at the back she found two bars of chocolate and a dusty tub of roasted almonds. She ate the lot as she wrote the article about the murders.

She referred to anonymous sources inside the police investigation and described how the thieves, three people in two vehicles, opened the gate to the road leading to the Söderström family home at 0334 in the morning, made their way round to the ventilation unit at the back of the building and released an as-yet unidentified gas into the system. She outlined the police theory about the family's panic-stricken actions when they realized they were being gassed: how the gas detector woke them up, how the father tried to stop it using the duvet, while the mother rushed to open the door for the children, then their instantaneous paralysis and death. Then how the thieves, or murderers, had smashed the wall and taken the safe away with them, stripped the house of valuables, and drove off.

She described the positions of the bodies when they were found by the home help, the police leads on the perpetrators, and how it was "just a matter of time" before the culprits were caught.

She added some facts about gases used in break-ins:

Hexane: a common industrial solvent, and a constituent of petrol and oil. Smells. Large quantities required to knock someone out.

Isopropanol: a solvent used in sprays such as de-icers, windscreen washer fluid, and detergents. Has a characteristically strong smell. It would take several hundred grams of isopropanol to knock someone out.

Carbon dioxide: a natural constituent of air, forming about 0.03 percent by volume. Large amounts are required to render someone unconscious, several kilograms, which would cause a fair amount of noise if it was pumped into a room quickly.

Narcotic gases: gases used as medical anesthetics, such as efrane and isoflurane. Fast-acting and capable of knocking someone out in very low percentages. More than 2 percent by volume can be fatal.

Laughing gas: used for medical purposes and as an oxidizer in finely tuned engines. To knock someone out would require a relatively high percentage, 65 to 70 percent by volume.

She wondered what the thieves did to avoid dying from the gas themselves. They must have worn gas masks.

Then she wondered what the other evening paper was doing, as the article vanished over the Internet. She ought to have bumped into one of their reporters somewhere along the way. The fact that she hadn't done so suggested one of two things: Either she was a long way ahead and had found better material, or else she was on the wrong track entirely and had missed the real story.

Time will tell, she thought grimly, loading the photographs from the camera onto the computer.

Her mobile rang.

It was Anders Schyman.

"I've just had a strange phone call from a reporter on the other paper," he said. "Have you been snogging some bigwig from the Ministry of Justice in some restaurant?"

"No," Annika said. "We had dinner. He gave me some information about something, then gave me a Spanish air-kiss when we left. Are you worried?"

"Not at all. Is everything going okay?"

"Fine, although I've got a lot to do."

"I won't disturb you any longer."

The pictures of the house were good. They made it look the way it was, big and flashy, with long shadows over the garden.

She even offered a suggested headline: *KILLERS KNEW THE CODE.*

Then she set to work on "idyll in shock."

She described the residential area, how scared the neighbors were, the air of sadness in the Swedes' regular bar, and then Carita's quotes, albeit anonymized:

"It's awful. We've been expecting something like this to happen, there have been so many break-ins using knockout gas down here," and "Everyone will be a lot more careful after this."

She attached a picture of the grand gateway to the residential area, then the photographs of the Swedes, with their names and ages.

That just left the hardest piece of all: the article about the family.

She went into the *Evening Post* website. The main article was about an argument between a television presenter and a politician, followed by a piece about a reality television star being insulted in a live broadcast. The rest of news came below that, in order of importance. The fatal gas attack was in seventh place on the page.

There were pictures of the five victims: Sebastian Söderström, 42, Veronica Söderström, 35, My Söderström, 8, Leo Söderström, 5, and Astrid Paulson, 68. The photographs were of variable quality, and none seemed very recent.

She started by going through the school yearbook, or rather annual report, that Carita had lent her. The Marbella International College yearbook beat most Swedish coffee-table books in terms of size and quality. It included a presentation of the school, a run-through of all the subjects, courses, and premises, then finally photographs of all the classes, neatly lined up in their pale-blue school uniforms.

After a few minutes she managed to find both Leo and My's school photographs.

Leo was much older than in the picture on the paper's website, with unkempt blond hair and a gap between his front teeth. He looked as if he could easily turn out to be a bit of a troublemaker. My was wearing a pale-blue school dress and had her hair in plaits.

Annika swallowed hard and called reception to ask them to scan the pictures and send them to her computer. A weary young man with acne collected the book and promised vacantly to do as she requested.

It certainly looked as though the Söderström family lived an idyllic existence. But was it really? Wasn't it a bit rigid and confined? Veronica had been active in a women's association, and Sebastian had been involved with kids who were good at sports. Leo looked a bit of a troublemaker, and My was pretty and sweet. The stench of stereotypical gender roles was so strong, it was all she could do not to hold her nose.

She put her hands over her eyes, so tired that everything was spinning.

Then she started writing. She wrote about Sebastian and his desire to give something back in return for having been given so much, about the tennis tournaments in the sun where poor kids won the chance for a better life, about how involved Veronica had been with her friends and family, about how cheerful and support-ive the grandmother had been, in good times and bad.

As she finished it, she realized that she was actually in tears.

She emailed the final article and the scanned photographs, then went to bed without even brushing her teeth.

The last thing she thought about was Jimmy Halenius and the picture of them that was going to be published in the other eve-ning paper the next day.

She tried to work out if it bothered her at all, but fell asleep before she came to any sort of conclusion.

It was raining. Annika was standing at the gate to the Söderström family's villa. She could hardly see the house through the sheets of rain, sweeping over the garden like dancing curtains, dense as waterfalls.

"Costa del Downpour," Carita said, walking up beside her under a huge golf umbrella. "It doesn't sound quite as catchy, does it?"

She flicked the switch that acted as a doorbell and peered up at the house.

"Do you really think it'll be the same policeman as yesterday?" Annika asked. "And that he's really going to let us in?"

Carita took a firmer grasp of her handbag, a check-patterned one today.

"Oh yes," she said, "he's here, you can be sure of that."

She turned to Annika.

"You can't take that big camera in," she said. "He'll know straightaway that something's not right."

The terrace door of the house opened, and Annika ran back to the car and tossed the camera onto the backseat.

"Can I leave everything here?" she called. "Or do you think it'll get stolen?"

"I should think this road has had its share of crime for this year," Carita said, waving at the policeman.

Annika watched as the police officer approached the gate, a

blurry figure through the rain. She checked that her mobile was in her bag. She'd taken pictures with it before. Pretty poor, admittedly, but publishable.

"Are you coming, Annika?" Carita called.

She jogged back toward the interpreter as the policeman pushed the heavy gates open.

"*I'm sorry,*" he said in rough English, and shook Annika formally by the hand.

She nodded and wiped the rain from her face.

The pool in front of the house was huge. The dark wooden loungers looked black in the rain. She couldn't get any sense of the view; everything beyond the garden was hidden by curtains of rain.

"This is how they got in," the policeman said, showing them the broken terrace door.

"Do you want me to translate?" Carita asked.

"I'm fine with English," Annika said.

They stepped inside the house, and the policeman closed the door behind them. The silence surrounding them was as dense as the rain. Suddenly Annika felt she couldn't breathe.

"The gas?" she said, turning toward the policeman. "Is it gone?"

"Long gone," he replied.

They were standing in a large hall that stretched all the way up to the roof on the second floor, at least six meters, maybe more. Two staircases, one on either side of the hall, led upstairs. From the center of the ceiling hung a huge wrought-iron chandelier. The floor, creamy-white marble, was shiny and ice-cold. There were alcoves in the walls containing replicas of classical statues.

She couldn't shake the feeling that it was hard to breathe. The air seemed damp and stale.

"Where do you want to start?" the policeman asked, and Annika jumped.

She felt in the bottom of her bag and pulled out one of Ellen's stuffed toys that had ended up there by accident. It was a little yellow dog that her daughter had won at a stall promising prizes for everyone at the fun fair in Stockholm.

"My daughter," she said, "she wanted me to give this to My."

"You have a daughter?" the policeman said.

"The same age as Leo," she said, as the policeman led the way up the marble staircase.

Annika followed the policeman as softly as she could, with Carita a few steps behind her. There was a cold draft blowing through the house; there must be an open window somewhere. She didn't want to ask again, but she couldn't help wondering if all the gas had really disappeared.

Upstairs, a corridor led off in each direction. The rain clattered against the tiles. The policeman turned left. The sound of their footsteps echoed on the stone floor. There were two doors on each side of the corridor, and an ornate double door at the end.

The policeman pointed at the double door.

"That's where the children were found," he said.

Annika felt her throat tighten.

The parents' bedroom, she thought, trying to force herself to think clearly and sensibly.

"And this was the little girl's room, but of course you know that," he said, opening the door to the first room on the left.

Annika stopped in the doorway.

The room was fairly small. The color scheme was pink and gold. A pair of French doors led out onto a large terrace with a view of the pool, and she could just make out the golf course down below through the rain. In one corner stood a pink desk with a leather top and curved legs, covered in paints and brushes and paper. There was a glass of dirty water alongside the one the girl had dipped her brush in when she changed colors. The bed in the other corner was unmade, left as it had been when the girl got up, woken by the gas alarm.

Annika coughed, walked into the room, and went over to the bed. At its foot sat a doll with curly brown hair. She crouched down and picked it up.

"*Creo que la señora quiere estar sola,*" Carita said to the policeman, and Annika got the drift of it.

(I think the lady would like to be alone.)

The policeman closed the door behind her. There was a deathly hush in the room. The rain was still drumming on the marble terrace outside.

She clenched her teeth and got out her mobile. She aimed it at the bed, saw the mess of covers on the screen, and took a picture. Then she went over to the picture on the desk.

It was of a girl riding a brown horse. The sun was shining and the grass was green. The girl and the horse were both laughing. Tears welled up in Annika's eyes, and she had to bite her cheek, then held out the mobile phone and took several pictures. She put the phone back in her bag, glanced at the door, then picked up the painting, rolled it up, and put it in her bag. Then she put the little yellow dog on the pillow at the top of the bed, looked at the room for a moment, then went back out into the corridor. She closed the door carefully, but a little sign on the door saying *My lives here* still rattled slightly.

Carita and the policeman had gone into the parents' bedroom; she could hear their voices talking quietly. One of the double doors was ajar, and the gray daylight was illuminating the far end of the passageway.

Annika took out her mobile. Her hand was trembling as she took a picture of the door behind which the mother and children had been found dead.

She walked slowly along the corridor, putting her mobile away again. The next door had a sign similar to My's: *Leo lives here*. She felt round the bottom of her bag again and found one of Kalle's broken toy cars. She opened the door and went into the boy's bedroom.

The room was in complete chaos.

The bed was unmade, in the same state as the little girl's. She could almost smell the lingering warmth in the bed from the sleeping child, that special smell, the dampness in the sheets. On the floor there were clothes and cars and dinosaurs all mixed up. There was a large bookcase full of all sorts of sports equipment, tennis rackets and golf balls and baseball gloves.

On the desk, the same as the girl's only green, stood a plate with a half-eaten sandwich and a glass containing dried-up chocolate milk. The edges of the cheese were hard and yellow. There was a skin on the chocolate.

She opened her mouth to get some air, pulled out her mobile, and took several pictures: the bed, the chocolate milk, a teddy bear on the floor.

"Señora?"

The policeman was standing in the doorway. Annika spun round. She still had her mobile and the racing car in her hand.

She gulped.

"For Leo," she said, putting the car on the pillow.

Then she went out of the room, turned left, and walked straight into the parents' bedroom without a backward glance.

This room was several times the size of the children's. A heavy desk, the sort the British upper class would have, dominated the right-hand wall. Her eyes were automatically drawn upward to the air vent.

"Señora, I must ask you to hurry. The detectives are on their way. Do you want to leave anything for the eldest girl as well before you leave?"

The eldest girl?

She turned to the policeman and nodded.

The man gestured for her to leave the room first.

"Just one moment," Annika said, putting a hand to her forehead.

"Of course, naturally," the policeman said, and stepped out into the corridor.

She looked around. The bed was big, with a two-meter-high headboard made of dark wood. The covers with which the father had tried to stop the gas were no longer on the floor. The police had bundled them into a heap in the middle of the bed.

That's where they spent the last night of their lives, where they woke up to the howl of the gas detector, where they died, unable to get to their children . . .

She took a picture of the bed. Then she aimed the mobile at the desk and air vent and took a couple more.

Then she hurried out into the corridor. The constable made sure the door was closed properly behind her. They went back down the stairs together. Carita was waiting by the terrace door.

"Just one more thing," the policeman said, turning left through the hall.

They passed the kitchen, a rustic affair with a heavy wooden table in the middle and dark shelves along the walls, covered with all manner of painted ceramics.

The policeman stopped outside a door next to the entrance to the kitchen. A sign similar to those on the children's rooms hung on it, this time: *Suzette lives here*.

Who's Suzette? Annika thought, but obviously she couldn't ask.

"Where is Suzette?" she said instead. "She wasn't here when it happened, was she?"

The policeman opened the door. Annika looked in at a tidy teenage bedroom. The bed was made, the bedspread arranged neatly. A laptop like hers was out on the desk, but switched off. Beside the door was a sun-bleached poster of Britney Spears.

The policeman looked at the time and started to look worried.

"Señora," he said, "I must ask you to leave now."

Annika nodded.

"Thank you for being so kind," she said, walking off quickly toward the kitchen again.

When she got back to the big hallway she glanced at the other rooms. She could see a large living room with dark-brown leather furniture and a library with built-in bookcases.

"*Muchas gracias,*" Annika said, then she and Carita stepped out onto the terrace again.

The downpour had stopped abruptly, leaving the ground steaming, with trickling streams running off the stonework.

They walked slowly back toward the road, the policeman opened the gate for them, then they were out.

"Did you get what you wanted?" Carita asked.

Annika leaned against the car and closed her eyes.

"Your powers of persuasion are astonishing," she said. "How did you do it?"

"I was thinking of invoicing for it under 'sundry expenses,'" the interpreter said, looking in surprise at the look of incomprehension on Annika's face. "You didn't imagine that he let us inside the house just because we were nice and he was so kind?"

I really am incredibly naïve, Annika thought.

"One hundred euros was enough," Carita said. "After all, you were only a grieving friend. He'd never had let a reporter in, but no one's ever going to know the difference. The evening papers might be available down here, but their sales are hardly impressive. Where are we going now?"

"Do you know anything about a Suzette?" Annika asked.

The interpreter shook her head.

"Suzette? Who's that?"

"There was another child's room, a teenager's, next to the kitchen. It said 'Suzette lives here' on the door . . . Hang on, didn't someone mention a Suzette yesterday? That woman who was a Swea with Veronica?"

"Another child?" Carita said, looking almost pale.

"I need to check this out," Annika said, opening the car door. "How do we get back to the hotel?"

She dropped the umbrella on the floor, tossed her bag on the bed and her jacket on the floor, and practically leaped at her laptop. With her fingers trembling she opened the other evening paper's website.

Before she had set off, they hadn't managed to post anything about either the gassings or her and Halenius, but now both stories were near the top of the page.

The gassings were at the top, and even though she knew it was egocentric, she felt obliged to start with herself and the undersecretary of state.

The picture taken outside the Järnet restaurant looked worse than she had imagined. It wasn't very clear, thanks to the darkness and low resolution of the camera, but you could definitely see it was her in the light from the restaurant windows. Her hair was blowing in the wind, standing out like a cascade behind her. It looked like Halenius was holding her, hugging her, his lips close to one of her ears. He was either kissing her on the cheek or whispering something tender.

Star Reporter and Hotshot Politician's Big Night Out! the headline shrieked.

Oh well, at least she was a star reporter.

She settled down and read the start of the article:

Schyman: I have complete confidence in her.

Evening Post crime reporter Annika Bengtzon spent last night partying with the Justice Minister's right-hand man.

"They were drinking wine and kissing in public," a source told us."

She straightened her back, affronted. What was this rubbish?

Somewhere over by the bed her mobile started to ring. She glanced over at her bag: Carry on reading, or answer?

In the end she leaped for the bag, pulled out her mobile, and checked the screen.

"Hello?" she said, and noticed that her voice sounded very high.

"I've seen the picture," Thomas said.

"Er, okay?" Annika said.

"Did you do it just to embarrass me?"

Her eyes opened wide in unfeigned surprise.

"Oh, Thomas," she said, "you're not jealous?"

"For fuck's sake, Halenius is one of my bosses. Can't you see what an awkward position you're putting me in? Can't you see what people are going to say?"

Her teasing attitude vanished.

"*You're* lecturing *me* about putting people in an awkward position?"

Thomas snorted.

"Don't you ever think about anyone but yourself?"

She was so angry she had trouble saying anything.

"You fucking hypocrite! You left me and the kids in a burning house and ran off to your little fuck buddy, I've been homeless for six months, falsely accused of arson, at risk of losing my children because *you're* trying to take them from me, and now you're the one who feels all upset. You make me feel totally fucking sick!"

She was about to end the call, the way she usually did, but changed her mind.

Instead she waited, taking quick, shallow breaths.

"Annika?" he said.

She coughed slightly.

"Hmm, yes, I'm here," she said.

"How can you say that? That I left you in a burning house?"

"You did."

"You're being very unfair. I went round to Sophia's because you and I had a row, and when I came back to talk to you the house was in ruins. How do you think that felt? I didn't know if you were okay, if the children were still alive . . ."

"There, you see, it's always about you!" she said. "Poor Thomas!"

He sighed deeply at the other end.

"You always manage to make everything my fault . . ."

"You were unfaithful to me," Annika said. "I saw you. I saw you together outside NK. You were holding her and kissing her, joking and laughing with her."

Now it was Thomas's turn to be silent.

"When?" he finally asked.

"The autumn before last," she said. "I was on the other side of the road with both the children, we'd just bought Kalle some Wellington boots, we were on our way home, and . . ."

Suddenly she started to cry. The tears welled up and she couldn't stop them, trickling between her fingers and onto the phone, like a burst dam. She cried for a long while, messily and uncontrollably.

"Sorry," she said when the sobs had started to subside.

"Why didn't you say anything?" he asked quietly.

"I don't know," she whispered. "I was probably scared you'd leave me."

The silence that followed echoed with surprise.

"But," he said, "you drove me away. You stopped talking to me, you wouldn't let me touch you . . ."

"I know," she said. "I'm sorry."

They were silent for a long while.

"So now you tell me," he said.

She laughed and wiped away the last of her tears.

"I know," she said.

"The children say you've got a new flat," he said. "Have you bought it?"

She blew her nose on a tissue that she found in her bag.

"I'm renting," she said. "But I didn't have to pay for a sublet, I got it through contacts."

"What, your new friend Halenius, or someone else?"

Defiance bubbled up again, but she swallowed it.

"No," she said. "Not through him. And that picture in the paper is utterly misleading. We had dinner and he gave me . . . information about something I'm working on, and when we said good-bye he gave me a Spanish kiss on the cheeks, because I was flying to Spain early the next morning. And I didn't drink any wine. I don't like red, you know that . . ."

"God, the things you journalists do," he said.

She wiped the mascara from under her eyes on the tissue.

"Mainly it just feels ridiculous," she said. "But it's probably worse for Halenius."

"It says he was on duty that evening."

"I haven't had time to read the article," Annika said. "And if Jimmy Halenius has committed some kind of work-related offense, that's really not my problem. More like yours, actually . . ."

They both laughed, with a warmth that surprised Annika.

Then Thomas sighed.

"God, I'm going to get some stick on Monday," he said.

"You won't be the only one," Annika said.

They laughed again, then fell silent.

"Can I come round with the children on Sunday evening? Then I could have a look at the new flat."

He'd never made that sort of offer before. He had never once visited the office in Gamla Stan where she had lived for six months.

"There's not much to see yet," Annika said. "I haven't even had time to unpack."

"Where is it?"

"Agnegatan 28."

"But . . . that's . . ."

" . . . our old block, I know."

They sat in silence for a few moments.

"How are the children?" Annika asked.

"Good. We're in the park, they're chasing each other. Do you want to talk to them?"

She shut her eyes for a few seconds.

"No," she finally said, "let them play."

"So, shall I come round about six o'clock? On Sunday?"

They ended the call, and Annika was left standing there with the phone in her hands.

Then she slumped onto the bed and crept under the bedspread. The sharp-edged brick that she had got so used to carrying around in her chest was suddenly less noticeable. It felt smaller, lighter, and the edges weren't quite as sharp. Just a little while, just a few minutes, just long enough for her to enjoy . . .

She was on the point of falling asleep and sat up with a jolt.

She had to read the article about her.

She straightened her back and cleared her throat, as if she were about to give a speech.

"By Bo Svensson," she read.

Bloody gorilla, she thought.

"Annika Bengtzon's day job is to keep watch on those in power in Sweden," the article began. "Today we can reveal that she goes much further than that. The night before last she was seen in the Järnet restaurant in Stockholm with the Justice Minister's right-hand man, undersecretary of state Jimmy Halenius, a Social Democrat.

The picture shows the couple enjoying their night out together, kissing and cuddling.

A statement from the *Evening Post* says that her employers have full confidence in their reporter.

"Yes, I have every faith in her judgment," says editor in chief Anders Schyman.

Does this damage Annika Bengtzon's credibility?

"Absolutely not."

But other commentators don't agree.

"Annika Bengtzon crossed the line when she kissed her source," says political journalist Arne Påhlson.

How will this affect Annika Bengtzon's credibility as someone who reports on those in power?

"Clearly, that's going to look a bit threadbare now . . ."

She had to get up and take a walk around the room.

Who the fuck was Arne Påhlson to sit in judgment on her? An overhyped dime-a-dozen reporter who was being wheeled out as some sort of fucking expert on ethics and morals. Like fuck!

She returned to the laptop.

> At the Ministry of Justice, where Jimmy Halenius is one of the most senior officials, the significance of the pictures is being downplayed.
>
> "The fact that politicians and journalists are in contact with each other is hardly news," the Justice Minister's press secretary said.
>
> The department is reluctant to confirm whether or not Jimmy Halenius was on duty on the evening in question.
>
> Annika Bengtzon herself has referred to the confidentiality of sources and has declined to comment.

She pushed the computer aside and stood up. She realized that her heart was pounding in her chest.

It was incredibly unpleasant to read about herself in the third person. She herself as a human being had no value at all. She was merely a symbol, a punching bag, being set up in a version of reality that wasn't actually true.

She realized how impotent she was in the face of the paper's sweeping generalizations. It didn't matter if what they wrote was either wrong or irrelevant; the only thing that mattered was the media's judgment, the newspaper's worldview, its redacted truth.

She picked the laptop up, but resisted the urge to throw it at the wall.

She sat down, took three deep breaths and rubbed her eyes in an attempt to find a more professional way of looking at it.

Then she read the article again.

It really wasn't a very good piece of writing.

Admittedly, every article like this followed a ridiculously formulaic template, but this one felt particularly clichéd. Bosse had clearly had trouble expressing himself.

She felt rather embarrassed at her first reaction, to feel sorry for herself because the journalists were so mean.

Was this what she herself did? Riding roughshod over other people in her articles?

Of course. Absolutely. It probably happened on a daily basis.

What was the alternative? For her to start using her very own journalistic frame of reference? Not to put any spin on anything, stop looking for headlines and pictures, just report but never reflect?

She walked around the room and thrust the thought aside.

Then she sat down again and scrolled through the rest of the other paper's website to see what they had written about the gassings. The reporter was their Madrid correspondent, a stylish woman in her fifties who presumably spoke fluent Spanish. They had a picture of the house from the road as well, but with the shadows at a different angle. The photographer had his own byline, a Spanish name. So they were a team, and they must have been there earlier in the day.

The article contained the same facts that Annika had got from Niklas, just from sources within the Spanish police.

Then the competition's reporters had evidently gone to the Los Naranjos golf club to speak to grieving Swedes there. They had ended up with the same sort of quotes that Annika had got from La Garrapata.

A dead heat between her and the Madrid stringer, in other words.

It was always a relief not to have been outdone . . .

Her mobile rang again, and sounded somehow angrier this time. She let it ring twice before reaching out for it. She looked at the screen, and let out a deep sigh.

"Hi, Patrik," she said.

"The golf club in mourning!" Patrik shouted. "The tennis club in mourning! See if you can't get together a group of old ice hockey stars standing for a minute's silence for Sebastian Söderström on some green somewhere. Bollocks, why limit it to old players? Get any sports stars you can find!"

"I've got a number of other angles," Annika said. "Pictures from inside the house, from the scene where they died. There might be another child in the family, a girl who survived. I need to look into that a bit more."

"The sports stars is a much better story. Make sure they all look fucking miserable."

Annika closed her eyes.

"I don't have a photographer with me," she said.

"You've got a camera, haven't you? Call once you've sent the picture. By the way, what sort of behavior do you call that, hanging out with the undersecretary of state and snogging his face off in public?"

Then he was gone.

Annika let her mobile fall to the floor.

This was crazy.

She got up and walked over to the window looking out onto the motorway.

It was a long time since she had been in this situation. During her years as an independent reporter she had been excused jobs designed to reflect the worldview of the head of news. Instead she had reported her own truth, or rather the one she thought was proper and important.

There was a difference between creating reality and reporting it.

If a gang of former sports stars took it upon themselves to mourn their colleague with a minute's silence, she wouldn't have had any problem reporting on the event, but actually staging the image was something completely different.

She went back to the computer and opened the website of Spanish directory inquiries, and looked up the numbers for Sebastian Söderström's tennis club and the Los Naranjos golf club. She rang them both.

The tennis club was closed, a man said in English with a Spanish accent. No, nothing was planned to commemorate the deceased owner. Yes, he'd call her if they changed their minds.

Nor had the Los Naranjos golf club planned any sort of ceremony to mark Sebastian Söderström's death, but he had been a member, so perhaps that wasn't a bad idea. In fact, it was an extremely good idea. They'd actually been thinking of something along those lines that morning. Round about four o'clock, they were thinking . . .

She bit her lip as she hung up.

So, she had adapted reality to make it fit her five-column-tabloid format.

She went over to the window again.

The clouds were hanging so low that they were surrounding the large mountain in front of her with thick gray cotton wool. The traffic was moving sluggishly along the old Roman road.

Whom could she call to find out more about Suzette?

She went over to the minibar and found that the cleaner had

restocked the supply of chocolate, so she took a Snickers bar and went and threw herself on the bed with her mobile.

Knut Garen answered at once; it sounded like he was standing close to running water.

"I'm in Granada," he said. "You'll have to call Niklas Linde about that, he's still down on the coast."

She swallowed her question about what he was doing in Granada and dialed Niklas's number. He answered after four rings.

"Now isn't a good time," he said in a low voice.

"Quick question," Annika said. "Do you know anything about a girl called Suzette who lived in Sebastian Söderström's villa?"

"Negative. I've got to go . . ."

Annika ended the call. She felt oddly indignant.

Did they really have that much to do, or did the two police officers simply not want to talk to her?

She licked her fingers clean after the chocolate, tossed the wrapper in the wastepaper basket, and sat down at the computer.

The Spanish directory inquiries website was still on the screen.

She typed in the name of the Swea woman, whose name was Margit. She wasn't listed in the Páginas Blancas, so she couldn't call her.

Maj-Lis, the older woman, was there, however. She lived in an urbanización called Los Cuervos in Estepona. It sounded like she was asleep when Annika called.

"What's this about?" she croaked, then cleared her throat loudly. "Why are you asking about Suzette?"

"She's got a room in the Söderström family home," Annika said. "Who is she?"

"Can you hold on just one moment?"

The woman put the phone down without waiting for an answer. Annika heard her shuffling off somewhere, then coughing and hacking and spitting. A toilet flushed. Then she came back to the phone.

"Oh, that Suzette," the woman said with a sigh. "She's Sebastian's daughter from his first marriage. A proper little storm cloud. What do you want to know?"

"What was she like? How old is she?"

The woman coughed.

"Time isn't constant, have you noticed that yet? It goes faster and faster the older you get. What would Suzette be now? Fifteen, sixteen, I should think."

"She wasn't in the house during the break-in. Do you know where she might be?"

"Well, I suppose she's with her mum in Sweden."

"So she doesn't live here?"

"Just sometimes during the holidays, if that. Suzette isn't very easy to deal with."

Annika was clicking her ballpoint in frustration. If there was one thing she was allergic to, it was generalizations about teenage girls not being "easy to deal with." That was exactly the way they had described her at school in Hälleforsnäs.

"In that case, why did she have her own room?"

"Oh, Astrid probably insisted. Astrid always kept an eye out for the girl. Sometimes I thought she was the only person who actually liked her. Suzette actually used to call her Grandma."

"Even though she wasn't her grandmother?"

Maj-Lis fell silent, then sniffed. When she spoke again her voice sounded weak and broken.

"It's so hard to accept that she's gone. How can people just disappear? Where do they go? God, I wish I were Christian."

She blew her nose loudly.

"Of course it's terrible about Veronica and Sebastian and the children, but I was so close to Astrid. I can still feel her here, right next to me, as a sort of warmth, a vibration in the air. Hold on . . ."

Annika heard the sucking sound of a cork being pulled from a bottle.

"Cheers, Astrid . . ."

Maj-Lis took an audible gulp of wine for the sake of old friend-ship.

"So Suzette lives with her mother," Annika said. "Do you know where? You don't happen to know what her mother's name is?"

"Sebastian's first wife was a real mistake, according to him. I can't actually remember her name, but it's something pretty plain, reminded me of an actress in a seventies porn film. She was his childhood sweetheart from somewhere out in the suburbs, if I'm not mistaken. I never met her."

She took another audible gulp of wine.

"And they were married? Do you know if she's still called Söderström?"

"Oh yes, they were certainly married," Maj-Lis said. "It was a really messy divorce. She demanded half of all Sebastian's earnings from his time in the NHL, but he was about to use that money to buy the tennis club . . ."

"And Suzette, is her name Söderström?"

"Veronica took his name at once, didn't hesitate at all. She wanted a large family, lots of children, and she wanted them all to have the same surname, like a proper, settled, real nuclear family . . ."

Dear old Maj-Lis was starting to get a bit drunk on the other end of the line.

"Well, thanks very much indeed for your time. Would you mind me calling again if . . ."

"Veronica never forgave her. Never!"

"Thanks, good-bye," Annika said, and clicked to end the call.

She hesitated for a moment, then dialed Berit's mobile.

Her colleague was at home, not in the newsroom.

"I'm on a rota these days, you know. I get all evenings, week-ends, and holidays off from now on unless I'm told otherwise at least two weeks in advance," Berit said ceremoniously.

It sounded as if she was standing and peeling something.

"Oh," Annika said. "In that case I'm not supposed to be working either."

"Not according to the locally negotiated agreement, no," Berit said. "Congratulations!"

Annika heard a tap being turned on, then running water.

"I could have spent today unpacking the children's toys."

"Wouldn't it be better to do that together with them?" Berit said. "Otherwise they might get the feeling that they live in a hotel."

Annika sat up straight.

"Of course," she said. "Why didn't I think of that?"

"Let's try to learn from each other's mistakes," Berit said. "How are you getting on?"

"Have you got a few minutes to go through a couple of things with me?"

The running water stopped.

"Of course," Berit said, and it sounded like she was pulling out a chair and sitting down.

"I got inside the family's house this morning and took some pictures on my mobile," Annika said. "I'm about to load them into the laptop and see how they turned out. And I've uncovered another child, a teenage girl who evidently survived the gas attack."

"What?" Berit said. "How?"

"She wasn't there," Annika said, "so it's not quite as dramatic as it sounds. But someone should still try to talk to her. She lives with her mother somewhere in Sweden."

"That's brilliant. Who's dealing with that in the newsroom?"

"No one," Annika said. "Patrik just shrugged it off. He wants grieving sports stars."

"That's a bad call," Berit said calmly. "Of course he can have his grieving sports stars, but a child who survived mass murder is considerably more important."

Annika breathed out. Of course she knew that, but it was still a relief to hear someone else say it.

"Have you got the passwords for the national ID database with you?" Berit asked.

"Of course. I'll have a look myself from here."

"If that doesn't work, I'll be back on duty on Friday," Berit said. "What sort of weather are you having?"

"Very gray," Annika said. "One more thing."

"Halenius," Berit said.

"Hmm," Annika said.

"Were you really kissing? It looks like it in the picture."

"Actually we weren't, not in the slightest," Annika said. "Does it matter?"

Berit thought in silence for a moment.

"From now on it's going to be difficult for you to look into any-thing that Jimmy Halenius does," she said. "But of course there are other people who can do that."

"So you don't think I've blown my credibility?"

"A bit, maybe, but it'll pass."

"Thanks," Annika said quietly.

"Remember to make a note of the overtime," Berit said. "You won't get paid, but you take it as time owing."

They hung up.

Annika's chest felt warmer and lighter.

She opened the national ID register, logged in, and waited while the site loaded.

Investigative journalism had largely stopped being a competi-tive sport the moment the database went online. Subscriptions were horribly expensive, but it was extremely effective. Thanks to the newspaper's subscription Annika had access to all the details of every Swedish citizen: their name, age, ID number, current and previous addresses, taxable income, directorships, the color of their car, details of any property, their credit rating, and any debts they might have. It also included all the details of every business, organization, and official authority in Sweden and fourteen other European countries: their annual accounts, financial state, and creditworthiness.

She clicked to get into individual records.

A search form appeared on the screen. She could search either by name or ID number, so in this instance she moved the cursor to name: Söderström, Suzette. Gender: female.

She left the rest blank.

The results came up, showing that there was just one person with that name in the whole of Sweden.

A Jannike Diana SUZETTE, born sixteen years ago and a resident of 77 Långskeppsgatan in Bromma, in the region covered by Stockholm council.

So what might her mother be called? The facility that enabled you to search for relatives in the database had been removed after September 11, 2001, so now it was considerably harder to find that information.

Annika clicked to see local registration details, which gave her the postcode of Långskeppsgatan. Then she did a new search of individual records, with slightly different information. She filled in three boxes: gender, the postcode for Långskeppsgatan, and the surname Söderström.

The computer searched to find any woman called Söderström within the same postcode. If Suzette was registered at the same address as her mother, and her mother's name was Söderström, she ought to show up here. The only reason why she might not was if she was one of the nine thousand or so Swedes whose records had for some reason been protected and concealed by the authorities.

Direct hit!

Söderström, LENITA Marike, forty-two years old and registered as living at number 77 Långskeppsgatan. She had four bad debts registered, according to Svensk Handelstidning Justitia, and a current debt outstanding with the national enforcement service for 42,392 kronor. She wasn't active in any businesses, wasn't self-employed, and wasn't registered as owning a motor vehicle.

The debts consisted of unpaid television licenses, outstanding tax, and a payment plan with Ikea that had fallen into arrears.

She switched to a free website that listed every phone number openly registered in Sweden, along with a map identifying where the number was located, even including pictures of the buildings in question.

Annika filled in Lenita Söderström's name and address, but there were no results.

Suzette Söderström's mother either had an ex-directory number, or just a pay-as-you-go mobile.

She removed the name and searched for the address alone.

Number 77 Långskeppsgatan turned out to be between Blackeberg and Råcksta in the west of Stockholm. She clicked to look at a satellite image of the area and saw that the postcode covered several blocks of flats at the end of a street containing several different types of building. The old madhouse, Beckomberga, was just around the corner, she noted, although these days all the nutters had been discharged and rehabilitated to lives they were in no fit state to handle.

She went over to the minibar and took out the other chocolate bar, a small Toblerone.

So how was she going to get hold of Suzette's mother, Lenita Söderström?

Maybe she was active in some association or other? Listed as a contact person for something on the net?

She went back to the laptop and googled her.

The list of results was short but categorical.

Lenita Söderström, Facebook.

Annika clicked and opened a Spanish page with a picture of a blond woman on the screen. With the help of the flag in the top right corner she switched language and got the page to appear in English.

Sign up to Facebook to connect with Lenita. Already a member? Log in!

She clicked on a sentence on the right-hand side of the page, *Send a message.*

A page containing a long form appeared.

In order to contact Lenita Söderström, she would evidently have to register on the site.

Okay, so she'd heard of Facebook. She knew there were several people at work who seemed to spend all day on their Facebook pages. They appeared to be competing about how many "friends" they had, and they got terribly excited if anyone "poked" them. The sort of thing she had grown out of when she was eight.

What the hell, she thought, and filled in the form.

She typed her name, said she worked for a company, date of birth, email address, then she thought up a password. Finally she ticked the box saying she had read the *Terms of Use and Privacy Policy,* which she obviously hadn't, then clicked *Sign up.*

Well, that all seemed fairly painless.

Confirm your email address.

Oh, so it wasn't done yet?

She clicked on *Go to Hotmail now.*

There was a message in the inbox of her Hotmail account, containing a link for her to click on.

A new message appeared on the screen.

Welcome Annika! Your account has been created.

She clicked on *Search for friends,* typed in Lenita Söderström, and found herself on a page where she could send a direct message to Suzette's mother.

She explained who she was and what she wanted, said she

wanted to contact both Lenita and Suzette, that it was important and urgent. She ended the message with her mobile number.

What a ridiculously elaborate way of getting hold of someone, she thought in irritation as she was obliged to fill in a *Security check* before the message could be sent.

She looked at the time.

She was going to have to hurry if she was going to have time to eat anything before the golf club got started with its act of remembrance for its deceased member.

'Here it is," Carita said.

Annika braked in the middle of a roundabout and pulled in next to several recycling containers for glass and plastic. The clouds had broken up, and a hesitant sun was casting wary shadows. She locked the car and looked up at the sky.

Four flags were flying on tall flagpoles next to the car park of the golf course: Spanish, Andalucian, Swedish, and one with a yellow, red, and green emblem on a white background.

"What's the Gais flag doing here?" Annika asked.

Carita squinted up at the sky, then switched her attention to the little pocket mirror she had in her hand.

"The what flag?" she said, taking her lipstick out of its gold case.

Annika pointed.

"That last one. Is the owner a mackerel?"

The interpreter looked up, thoroughly confused.

"Gais is a football club in Gothenburg," Annika said. "Their supporters are called mackerels."

"Percy Svensson has just sold the club to four Swedes. One of them might be one of those fish. The entrance is over there."

Carita put her lipstick back in her bag, a silver-colored one this time.

A brick staircase led up to an overelaborate gateway surrounded by huge orange trees.

Annika pushed the door open and gasped.

"So this is how the other half live," she said. "Talk about an escape from reality!"

White marble terraces stretched out in front of her. Some ducks were swimming around gently in an artificial lake below. Bright green lawns rolled off toward the horizon, smooth as women's legs in adverts for razors. Little golf buggies were driving about on dusky pink cement paths. Men with neat haircuts and dark-blue sweaters draped over the shoulders of their white polo shirts were sitting relaxing at round tables.

"Is that someone you know?"

Carita pointed at a middle-aged woman and a very young man who were waving in their direction.

The other evening paper's Madrid correspondent and her boytoy photographer.

"I know who they are," Annika said, "and they probably recognize me."

From today's paper, she thought, but didn't say so. Carita probably didn't keep up to date with the Swedish media. There was no reason to tell her about that picture.

The door behind them flew open, and a crowd of people surrounded them and filled the marble terraces in just a few moments. The way they behaved and how they were dressed were so different from the other guests that everything stopped.

"And are these colleagues of yours as well?"

"The Swedish broadcast media," Annika said in a low voice as the men began noisily setting up their cameras and tripods, and laying out long cables and microphones with furry socks on them.

The rumor about the minute's silence had obviously taken flight.

The guests who had been eating and drinking in the club's restaurant came streaming out among the tables on the terrace, enticed by the cameras and the looks of concentration on the television crew's faces. As soon as a television crew showed up anywhere, everyone's attention immediately focused on them.

"Can you see any sports stars here?" Annika whispered to Carita as she made sure that her camera had enough charge.

"Those would probably be your mackerels, I suppose," the interpreter said, pointing at several bald, overweight men in dark-green blazers with the yellow, green, and red emblem on the lapels.

People were still pouring out of the restaurant. Soon the staircase was crowded with people.

"What's all this circus about?" a man in a pale-blue polo shirt asked just behind Annika.

"A minute's silence for Sebastian Söderström," Annika said, looking intently at the man to see if he might be an old celebrity.

The man stiffened and adjusted his sunglasses.

"Really?" he said. "That's going to be pretty gloomy, then."

Annika pulled her pen and notepad out of her bag.

"So you think it's going to be a moving act of remembrance?" Annika asked politely.

The man laughed and shook his head.

"People will be mourning all the money they're never going to get back. Half the people standing here have at some point invested in Sebastian Söderström's crazy fantasy projects."

Annika's pen stopped after just a few words. Her brain wasn't quite registering their meaning.

"How . . . what do you mean?" she asked.

The man tucked his shirt neatly into his golf trousers and looked at his watch.

"Söderström was a persuasive bastard. A few seasons in the

NHL meant people thought he was capable of shitting gold. The most tragic thing of all is that he believed it himself."

He stopped a man wearing yet another polo shirt, pale green this time, who was on his way down toward the golf course.

"Sverre, have you heard? They're having a little memorial for Söderström; we're supposed to stand for a minute mourning him in silence."

Sverre's face turned red.

"That bastard," he said, turned on his heel, and went back inside the restaurant.

Annika watched him go in surprise.

"What sort of fantasy projects?" she asked.

The man smiled in amusement.

"Like the introduction of the new global sport of stickball, for instance. You've never heard of it? Funny, that. Or the racetrack that was going to be built up in the Sierra Nevada, but which turned out to be right in the middle of a national park? And then there was that tennis club . . ."

"I got the impression that Sebastian Söderström was pretty well off," Annika said, noting that several other guests were leaving the terrace.

"It wasn't his own money he lost; it was everyone else's, otherwise he wouldn't have been able to carry on for as long as he did. And that tennis club was a financial disaster. I mean, giving away millions in prize money just for club tournaments, can you imagine . . . Sonja!"

The man in the pale-blue polo shirt hurried off down the terrace steps and stopped a woman in a pink cap. Annika watched as they exchanged a few words, and saw the woman get annoyed. She turned on her heel and walked back toward reception.

"Excuse me," Annika said, standing in the woman's way as she tried to get past. "Did you know Sebastian Söderström?"

"You bet I bloody did," the woman said, attempting to get past. Annika took a side step and blocked her.

"Could you tell me what he was like?" she asked.

The woman called Sonja took off her sunglasses. Her face bore the traces of numerous surgical interventions, mainly around her eyes.

"Sebastian Söderström was a fraud," she said. "He wanted to be a star. He was addicted to applause, but he didn't want to work for it, he just wanted the rewards."

"I don't quite understand what you mean," Annika said.

"He'd get an idea, trick people out of a load of money, live the high life on other people's investments until he got bored, then he'd start something new. He'd find new investors, borrow money, polish the façade a bit, and pretend to be a big star."

"But he really wasn't?" Annika said.

"Listen," the woman said, poking her surgically enhanced nose close to Annika. "That was all a fuck of a long time ago."

Then she shoved Annika aside and left the golf club.

Annika looked out across the lawns and the ducks and the little golf buggies.

How should she handle this? Pretend she hadn't heard anything? Or should she write the truth, that people would rather leave their golf club than participate in the minute's silence for Sebastian Söderström?

Ice hockey heroes, she thought. That's why I'm here.

She gulped and searched the crowd.

"Can you see any sports stars?" she asked Carita. Then at that moment she caught sight of one of the NHL's biggest stars, a lad from Norrland, who had just signed a contract with some club in the American Midwest that landed him quarter of a billion kronor.

"I have to get him," Annika said, forcing her way through the crowd.

The ice hockey star had some friends with him. Two of them had been in the team that won bronze in the Football World Cup in 1994, and a third one had made several distinctly average Swedish films.

"I'm from the *Evening Post*," Annika said. "Can I have a picture?"

The ice hockey star looked round.

"What's going on? Why are there so many people?"

"Minute's silence for Sebastian Söderström," Annika said, raising the camera and taking several shots.

Click, click, click.

"Oh shit," one of the football players said.

"Did you know him?" Annika asked.

"Course I did," the ice hockey star said. "I played in the national team with him one season."

"What are your memories of him?"

The ice hockey player scratched his head.

Click, click, click.

"Well," he said slowly, "he was a good defender, in his day. I know he had a house down here somewhere, but I don't really know where."

"Somewhere called Las Estrellas de Marbella," Annika said.

The star shook his head.

"Don't know where that is."

"What about you?" she asked the footballers. "Did you know Sebastian?"

They both mumbled that they didn't.

"I play at his tennis club," the almost-unsuccessful film director said. "Sebbe was great. If everyone was like him, the world would look very different."

That's the one, Annika said, firing off a few last shots.

A group picture of the four stars, all casual clothes and sunglasses, and the quote: "If everyone was like Sebastian, the world would look very different."

She'd done it.

"Thanks very much," she said, and walked back toward Carita.

"I recognize that man," the interpreter said, pointing at the ice hockey star. "Isn't he . . ."

"Yes," Annika said, putting her hand over her finger. "Let's just wait until the minute's silence is over, then we can go."

Suddenly a man with thick white hair and a bulging stomach was standing in front of her, smiling enthusiastically.

"Annika Bengtzon?" he asked, and there was no mistaking the Gothenburg accent.

"Rickard Marmén?" Annika said. "How nice to be able to put a face to the voice."

They shook hands, warmly and at length. Then he air-kissed Carita on the cheek.

"Listen," Annika said, pulling him a few steps in the direction of the car park. "There are a couple of things I'd like to ask you. Did you know the Söderström family?"

"I'm not sure if I'd say I really knew them, but I knew who they were."

"Did Sebastian Söderström owe people a load of money?"

Rickard Marmén smiled.

"Yes, quite possibly. But only people who could afford it."

Annika's feet were shuffling about.

"I'm sorry if I'm being blunt, but it seems like a lot of people are angry with him. Have they got any reason to be?"

The white-haired man shrugged his shoulders and smiled.

"In general, people have far too little to do down here. Which means they have a tendency to get hung up on details."

"Did you have any dealings with him yourself?"

Rickard Marmén laughed.

"No," he said, "certainly not. I don't have that sort of money."

Annika looked intently at the man standing in front of her. His face looked like old leather, his eyes were small and bright blue. He had a week's worth of chalk-white stubble. His hair stood out like a sort of halo around him.

"You've been down here for a while now, haven't you?"

"Since my twenty-third birthday."

"Did you know that Sebastian had another child? A teenage daughter called Suzette?"

"Yes, she was down here sometimes. Why?"

"When was she last here, do you know?"

Rickard Marmén stroked his beard.

"She used to go riding with Vibeke at the Cancelada Club," he said. "I think the idea was that she was supposed to help out up there."

Annika moved a bit closer to the man and lowered her voice.

"So she's here, or was here, recently?"

Rickard Marmén scratched his nose.

"I don't know," he said. "It's probably best that you talk to Vibeke."

He saw the questioning look on her face and went on:

"Jensen, she owns the club. They've got a house just above it. It's . . ."

"I know where the Cancelada Club is," Carita said, stepping up to Annika. "I can show you the way. It's not far, it's just on the other side of that mountain over there . . ."

The murmuring around them died away. There weren't many people sitting on the terrace now. A man in a black jacket and pale trousers who was standing at the top of the steps leading down to the artificial lake began to speak.

"Dear members, dear guests . . . we're gathered here today to honor the memory of a good friend and dear colleague, a man who was an example to us all . . ."

"Who's that?" Annika whispered to Rickard Marmén.

"The new owner. He got here on Saturday, I doubt he ever even met Sebastian."

Annika took a few pictures of the gathering. She would have to crop them later to make it look as if there were more people than there actually were.

The minute's silence began. The ducks went on swimming on the lake. A motorbike roared past the roundabout outside the club. The television cameras rolled. People glanced at each other and tried to look sad.

Annika looked at her watch. After forty seconds the new owner had had enough and clapped his hands.

"Well, thank you, guests and members, and representatives of the media" (here he actually waved at the television cameras). "I'd just like to point out that the restaurant is open until . . ."

"Let's go," Annika said, thanking Rickard Marmén and heading off toward the exit.

The road wound up the mountainside like a fat snake. It was lined with broad pavements and ornate lampposts, and every so often there was an electrical junction box or some other small building. Occasionally side roads would slice off into the greenery of the valley.

Otherwise there was nothing but overgrown bushes and big thistles.

"Where are all the houses?" Annika asked, staring up at the mountain in fascination.

"This is one of the developments that never got going," Carita said. "They had grand plans, and the view's amazing, but somewhere along the way everything ground to a halt. They never got further than building the roads. Be careful . . ."

Annika braked.

Ahead of her half the road had slid into the chasm below. The area around the landslide was cordoned off with a few cones and a bit of red-and-white tape.

"Bloody hell," Annika said. "Is it really safe to drive here?"

"Just not too close to the edge, that's all," Carita said.

The carriageway had been washed away in a couple of other places. It carried on winding over the mountain, sometimes very close to the big toll motorway, sometimes several hundred meters above it. The rainy weather had blown off toward the Atlantic, leaving the view clear in all its dizzying glory, with the sea a bright blue carpet off to the left and the iron-gray Rif Mountains of Africa on the horizon.

As they got closer to the riding school the road was surrounded by a half-finished golf course. Diggers, bulldozers, and lorries were laying the foundations for the same sweeping grass lawns and artificial lakes as at Los Naranjos.

"Do rich people really have nothing better to do than walk around a make-believe world trying to hit a static ball with a little metal stick?" she asked.

"They don't walk," Carita said. "They use a golf buggy."

She pointed at a sign saying *Club Hípico* and Annika indicated and turned off to the right. The car park was full of expensive cars. They parked behind a Range Rover Sport and walked up toward a low white building with ornate iron railings in front of the windows. Off to the left lay the stables, big open boxes made of dark wood with beautiful green wrought-iron detailing, shaded by huge trees. Girls with blond ponytails walked among glossy brown thoroughbreds. A stable lad pushing a wheelbarrow said something to one of the girls who laughed.

Annika stopped short.

"This can't be happening," she said. "I recognize this place. I've been here before."

"Are you a horsey girl?" a woman asked in Danish. She had short, gray hair and red-rimmed eyes.

Annika looked at her, bewildered.

"Hööks and Kingsland both do the photography for their summer catalogues here," the woman said.

She held out her hand.

"Vibeke Jensen," she said.

"Annika Bengtzon," Annika said, tearing her eyes from the backdrop of those fantasy catalogues, the brochures of equestrian equipment and clothing that she and her friends had stared at endlessly when they went riding every week.

"I understand that you want to ask me about Suzette," Vibeke Jensen said.

Annika saw that she was leaning heavily on a crutch. Not the sort you get from A&E when you have an accident, but a beautiful if rather worn design made of dark wood. The woman had been using it for a long time.

"Do you want me to translate?" Carita asked.

"I can handle Danish," Annika said. "Yes, I understand she used to ride here?"

The owner turned round with jerky movements.

"We can go into my office," she said.

They walked past another block of stables, as Annika had another shiver of déjà vu. A skinny girl of about fourteen with long legs and shiny riding boots was leading an Arabian Thoroughbred up toward the riding ground where jumps had been set out, at least one and a half meters high. She felt a rush of something unpleasant, envy or malice, possibly just sadness at something that might have been if everything had been different.

She'd loved riding. And she'd been very good at it.

"Can I offer you something?"

Annika asked for a little water. Carita took a glass of red.

They sat down in a small room behind a combination of shop and café. Vibeke sat down heavily, leaned her crutch against the desk and stretched her bad leg out in front of her. She looked up and met Annika's gaze.

"A riding accident," she said. "More than forty years ago now. I've got used to it, and I can still ride."

Annika lowered her eyes.

"Suzette was supposed to have started working here," Vibeke said, folding her hands in front of her on the desk. They were callused and chapped with work.

"But nothing came of it. In retrospect, of course, it was a blessing that she flew home."

The woman looked out at the stables, and her mouth quivered slightly.

"So Suzette was here very recently but went back to Sweden?"

Vibeke Jensen nodded.

"She called last week to say she'd changed her mind. She was going to give school another go. I have to say, I thought that was a good idea."

She put her hands to her mouth.

"You'll have to forgive me," she said.

"So you knew the family well?" Annika asked gently, not bothering to take out her notepad.

The woman looked out of the window, her eyes roaming over the stables and yard and the eucalyptus trees beyond.

"Not really," she said. "My's pony is here; I don't know what we're going to do with it. But I didn't know Sebastian, nor Veronica very well either. She used to come riding before she had the children, but after that she was always so busy with work that she never had time for anything else. Astrid, on the other hand . . ."

She feel silent for a while.

"I got to know Astrid when I was a little girl. She and Mother used to go off to *juergas* together. She let me go on outings with her. I liked her a lot."

"Was it Astrid who arranged for Suzette to work here?"

Vibeke nodded.

"Astrid was very fond of the girl. I didn't have any objections; the girl's a decent rider and is good with the horses . . ."

The phone on the desk rang, and Vibeke answered curtly in Spanish.

"I'd quite like to be heading home," Carita whispered in Annika's ear. "It is Twelfth Night, after all . . ."

Annika picked up her bag and stood up. She wasn't going to get any further here.

Vibeke put the phone down.

"Do you know when Suzette went back to Sweden?" Annika asked.

The stable owner got laboriously to her feet, leaning on her crutch.

"She called last week, Thursday, I think it was. She said she was going back home. I assumed she was going at once."

Annika shook her hand.

"Thanks for taking the time to see us. Is it okay if I use some of your quotes in an article about the family?"

Vibeke nodded.

"Could I take a picture as well? Outside the office, with the stables in the background?"

Vibeke ran her fingers through her hair and hesitated.

"With me looking like this," she said.

They went outside into the evening sun. The horses and stables were glowing in the slanting light.

Annika took several pictures of the woman leaning heavily on her crutch and looking across the field down toward the road. She thanked her again and turned toward the car.

"Oh, by the way," Annika said, stopping suddenly. "You said that Veronica was busy working. What did she do?"

"She was a solicitor," Vibeke said. "She worked in an office in Gibraltar. She was the family breadwinner."

"What about Sebastian?" Annika said, then held her breath.

Vibeke shook her head.

"She must have earned a lot of money," Annika said, thinking of the size of the house.

At that moment her mobile rang.

A number she didn't recognize. She excused herself and answered it.

"Annika Bengtzon?" an unfamiliar woman's voice said. "You emailed me. What do you want?"

"Er," Annika said. "Who are you?"

"On Facebook. Lenita."

Söderström, bloody hell!

"Yes, of course," Annika said, taking a few steps toward the car park. "Thanks for getting back to me. Well, I'm a reporter for the *Evening Post*, and I was trying to get in touch with you and Suzette to ask a few questions about events in Marbella . . ."

"I don't know anything about that," Lenita said. "No one tells me anything. You'd think I'd be told, seeing as I was actually married to the man once upon a time."

"It must have come as a terrible shock," Annika said sympathetically.

"God, yes," Lenita Söderström said. "It's just lucky that Suzette had come home, or who knows what might have happened."

"How has she reacted to everything that's happened?"

"Well," Lenita Söderström said, "you'd think she could answer her mobile, but apparently that's too much to ask. I suppose she's not bothered to charge it, as usual."

Annika looked over at the riding ground. The girl with the shiny boots was just going over a combination jump on her beautiful Thoroughbred.

"So you haven't spoken to your daughter since the deaths?"

"How am I supposed to have done that? She's in Spain, isn't

she, and she's not answering her mobile. And I haven't got a number for that Jensen woman."

Annika looked at the diminutive Danish woman, who was slowly walking back to her office again.

"Vibeke Jensen?" she said. "Why . . . What does she have to do with anything?"

"Suzette lives there. She couldn't stand the witch, that Veronica, so she moved out to go and live with her employer."

Nothing was making any sense in Annika's head. Carita was staring at her intently.

"So you're telling me that Suzette is staying with Vibeke Jensen, the Danish woman who owns the Cancelada Club?"

"She called me the day before New Year's Eve and said she was going to be moving in with the woman who owns that riding school. It doesn't matter to me where she lives, as long as she looks after herself and doesn't cause any trouble."

"The day before New Year's Eve," Annika said. "That was last Thursday, wasn't it?"

"I said to her, if you don't want to study, you have to get a job. She can't go on thinking she can live off me forever."

Annika began striding back toward the office of the riding school.

"Can you hold on a moment?" she said down the line. "There's someone here I think you should talk to . . ."

She pulled the office door open, and Vibeke looked up at her in surprise.

"Lenita Söderström," Annika said, holding out her mobile. "She thinks Suzette is living with you."

The search parties gathered at dusk. They set out from a dried-up riverbed just behind Las Estrellas de Marbella, the area where the Söderström family had lived. The blue lights of the police cars swept across the wild oleanders and dead olive trees. People moved like shadows between the vehicles, as a man in a reflective jacket held his arm out and directed the silhouettes in different directions.

Annika was sitting beside Niklas Linde in his big BMW watching the scene. She was lucky to be allowed to be here. She had given the police officer an ultimatum: She would only tell him what she knew about Suzette if she could join in the search. Niklas hadn't been able to argue.

They had stopped on a hill overlooking the riverbed. Annika took the camera out of her bag and opened the car door. Using the door as a support, she took several long-exposure pictures. She could hear voices and the bleeping of the search team's portable police radios.

"Do you think they're likely to find her tonight?" she asked in a low voice.

"They have to try," Niklas said.

"She's been missing six days," Annika said. "If she's been out here the whole time, she must be dead."

"Do you want to talk to the officer in charge?"

"Maybe just to get a quick comment on what he thinks of the situation," Annika said.

They rolled down toward the river. Niklas parked, got out of the car, and marched up to the man in the reflective jacket. She saw them talking and gesticulating. She headed slowly toward them, past groups of people with sticks and lamps tied to their foreheads, about to set off searching for the missing girl. The ground was still warm and smelled of herbs. The wind coming off the sea was damp.

"Our man isn't an optimist," Niklas said, coming back to her. "The toll motorway's just above here. On the far side there's the start of a huge national park that covers a vast area. I was thinking of going along for a while. Do you want to come?"

Annika looked up at the stars.

"Has Suzette been formally declared missing yet?" she asked into the darkness.

"Her mother reported it to the Western District in Stockholm an hour ago. Interpol circulated it at once. The moment Suzette Söderström goes through passport control, takes money out at a cashpoint, or makes a call on her mobile, the alarms will go off."

"Is Interpol really that effective?" Annika asked skeptically.

"If she's still alive, we'll find her."

"Do you think she is?"

The police officer didn't answer. He stopped beside her and looked out at the moonlit riverbed. Annika concentrated on looking straight ahead and not at him. She couldn't make him out.

"Has anything new happened in the murder investigation?" she asked.

"Actually it has," he said. "We've got a preliminary cause of death."

"Gas?" Annika asked.

"Not just any gas. Fentanyl."

He nodded in emphasis at the darkness.

"Means nothing to me," Annika said. "Should it?"

"The Dubrovka Theater," Niklas said. "It's the same sort of gas Russian special forces used to knock out the terrorists and hostages during the storming of the Dubrovka Theater in Moscow a few years ago."

Annika stared at him.

"Loads of people died there," she said.

"At least one hundred seventeen of the hostages were killed. Some sources claim it was even more than that. Seven hundred survived. The interesting thing is that fentanyl is spread in aerosol form, as vapor."

"Which fits with the details of this case, from the position of the man on that big English desk . . ."

He glanced quickly at her.

"How do you know it was big and English?"

She looked straight ahead again.

"Another interesting detail from the Moscow siege is that the special forces soldiers didn't need gas masks," Niklas went on. "Each of them was injected with the antidote, a derivative of naloxone, before entering the theater. It blocks the effects of opiates for several hours."

Annika looked at the police officer quizzically.

"It's used to treat addicts," he said. "It makes it impossible for heroin users to get a kick out of their gear. Are you coming?"

She looked off toward the search party, which was just disappearing beneath the concrete pillars of the toll motorway.

She had three articles to write.

First the description of the interior of the House of Death, her visit to the Söderström family home, illustrated with the poor-quality photographs from her phone. They were only publishable because they were exclusive; otherwise they were useless.

"You can't sell them on," she had told Patrik. "They *mustn't* reach the Spanish papers. I pulled a lot of strings to get in, and I don't want to get anyone into trouble."

"They're not that fucking brilliant," the head of news had replied.

Then she had the main story of the day: "Where Is Suzette?"

Now that the girl had been reported missing, she was being encouraged to contact her family or the nearest police station, but according to her mother she didn't speak Spanish and could hardly speak English, and she never listened to the radio, never read the papers, and never watched television.

"The best way of reaching her whenever she takes off is usually through MySpace, MSN, or Facebook," Lenita had said.

Suzette's mother had booked a flight early next morning with the same cowboy outfit Annika had flown with, and they had arranged to meet up for an interview that afternoon.

"So Suzette has taken off before?" Annika had asked, but Lenita had pretended not to hear her.

She hadn't even researched the third article. It was about what she had just been told, about fentanyl gas, what it was made of, what its effects were. Maybe she could put the facts about the gas together with the pictures from inside the house, and come up with something that way.

She looked at Niklas and nodded.

"Yes," she said. "I'd like to come along for a while."

THURSDAY, JANUARY 6

In a country far away, in a strange moonlit landscape, Annika was walking with Niklas, looking up at the stars. The bushes around her were prickly and tall, but she wasn't scared. They were looking for something, she just couldn't remember what, and she turned to ask him if he liked horses . . .

She woke up to find her mobile ringing. It sounded muffled and enclosed, as if it were being suffocated. She pulled herself up in bed, got tangled in the sheets, and tumbled out onto the floor, then grabbed for her bag and pulled her phone out just before voicemail took the call.

It was Carita.

"I can work this morning," she said, "but after that we're going to be celebrating Epiphany here at home. Did you want to go to the tennis club?"

Annika sat up on the floor and managed to disentangle her feet from the sheets. The dark night was still lingering within her. Niklas was still sitting beside her.

"Mm," she said, "that would be great."

She saw it was already full daylight outside but had no idea what time it was.

She took the phone from her ear for a moment to check the time—0947—so she missed Carita's next sentence.

". . . in reception."

"Okay," Annika said. "When?"

"Hello! In fifteen minutes! Were you asleep?"

"No, no," Annika said.

She clicked to end the call.

Good grief, Carita certainly took her work seriously. She must really need the money.

She put her mobile back in her bag, and that was when she saw the painting.

It had got a bit crumpled, but not too badly.

She smoothed out the girl and the laughing horse on the desk, the last thing eight-year-old My painted before she died.

Then she hurried away to have a shower, to stop herself crying.

The tennis club was high above the sea, at the edge of a cliff. An enormous gate of the usual overelaborate sort blocked the entrance, and was closed and locked.

Annika parked on the road, blocking the traffic in one direction, but she had come to realize that this was perfectly normal.

There was no bell on the gate, and no one answered when they shouted.

"But you're sure that this is the place?" Annika said.

Carita tied her belt tightly around her waist and headed off beside the wall surrounding the property. Annika followed her with her bag and camera. On the other side of the wall the ground was considerably higher. With a distinct lack of grace they managed to heave themselves up onto the wall and down onto one of the stands.

The club was fairly small. There was one grass court and four clay. In the middle stood the clubhouse, the customary palatial affair with pinnacles and turrets and bay windows and terraces. The doors facing the sea were open.

"Hello?" Annika called, sticking her head through one of the windows.

"*Oh God!*"

A man with a mane of black hair stuck his head up from behind a desk.

"Where did you come from?"

He spoke good English.

"From a Swedish newspaper," Annika said. "We spoke yesterday, I asked if you were going to be having any sort of ceremony here, in light of what's happened . . ."

"Ah," the man said, getting up and brushing the dirt from his knees. "I remember. What are you doing here?"

"I'm writing about the Söderström family for my paper. I know that Sebastian put a lot of effort into his club. Can I come in?"

The man put down a sheet of paper that he must have just found in one of the bottom drawers. He hesitated.

"We're actually closed today as well," he said. "In fact I don't know when I'm going to open up again. I don't know who to ask."

"Didn't Sebastian have a solicitor?" Annika asked.

The man looked away.

"Yes," he said. "His wife."

Annika nodded, of course.

Then the man let out a deep sigh, walked round the reception desk, and opened one of the terrace doors for her and Carita.

"My name's Francis," he said, holding out his hand. "Come in."

Annika and Carita stepped into the clubhouse and introduced themselves properly. He gestured to them to walk over to the desk. There were large piles of documents heaped on top of it.

"Would you like something to drink?"

Carita asked for a beer. Francis went off to the bar and got one for Annika as well. She took a sip and it went straight to her head. She put the glass down on the counter.

The whole of the large building was one single room, open up to the eaves. On the left-hand side was a long bar counter with stools and little round tables in front of it. The reception desk dominated the middle of the room, and off to the right lay a shop selling tennis clothes and rackets.

"Do you know if Sebastian had any sort of legal representation in Sweden?"

Annika and Carita both shook their heads.

"I've been looking everywhere," Francis said, gesturing toward the piles of paper on the reception desk. "I can't find any deeds to the property, nothing about any debts, no indication of what he wanted to do with the club. . . . He must have kept all his legal papers somewhere else, maybe in the villa . . ."

The man's hands were trembling on the counter as he picked up a beer mat, then dropped it again. Annika realized that he was still in a state of shock.

"So what's your role here?" she asked. "Are you the manager?"

"I'm a tennis coach," Francis said. "Sometimes I book people onto the courts as well if I'm not doing anything else. Sebastian's the manager."

"How many people normally work here?"

"There are ten of us. I've told them all to come in on Monday. Do you know if they've found any sort of will? I suppose Suzette owns the club now?"

His eye fluttered round the room.

"The gym's downstairs," he said, pointing off toward the shop.

"Do you know Suzette?" Annika asked.

Francis looked at her in surprise.

"Of course I do," he said. "I'm her coach."

"Coach?"

"She doesn't want to put in the work needed to get really good. I've tried to increase her motivation, but she's not focused enough."

Annika blinked.

"Are we talking tennis here? Suzette plays tennis?"

Francis leaned across the bar and said in a low, confidential voice:

"Suzette's world is governed by her emotional life, with about a minute's warning, which is why it's so hard to book coaching sessions. If she can't be bothered to train, she can't be bothered, but she only knows that just ahead of each session . . ."

Annika nodded.

"Is she . . . good?"

"I recognize myself in her. She could have made it as far as me, at the very least."

Annika was feeling stupid.

"And how far was that?"

"I was ranked thirty-eighth in the world when I was nineteen."

Annika's eyes opened wide and she looked more closely at the man.

Why hadn't she ever heard of him? Mind you, she probably hadn't heard of anyone ranked thirty-eighth in any sport . . .

"And now you work here," she said.

Francis gave a sad little smile.

"I got fed up," he said. "It doesn't matter how good a player you are if you're not happy with your life. I was sent away to boarding school in the USA when I was eleven. Of course it was a huge opportunity for me, but it meant I had to be away from my family. It wasn't worth that. I gave it all up when I was twenty."

"And Suzette could be that good? Among the best in the world?"

"She's a lot like her dad, very athletic. Sebastian's a very talented tennis player as well."

Annika didn't bother to correct his use of the present tense.

"But it's too late now," Francis said. "She should have focused more on her training when she was younger."

"Have you heard that she's missing?"

Francis nodded.

"Do you know where she is?"

He shook his head.

"When did you last see her?"

He thought for a moment.

"It must have been last Thursday. She turned up and canceled her session, said she was going to a New Year party at a friend's, that she'd be spending the night there."

"Did she say which friend?"

The tennis coach looked out over the courts.

"Amira? Was that her name? Or Samira? It's hard to keep track of those girls. It might have been Akira . . ."

"Do you know where this . . . friend lives?"

He walked round the bar and over to reception and sat down on the chair. Annika followed him.

"Do you think she's likely to contact you? She must have had a mobile?"

Francis picked up a few sheets of paper and put them in a file.

"She tried to make a call on her mobile while she was here, but she said it was broken, it wasn't working. It made her very angry."

"Do you think she could have been playacting?" Annika asked.

Francis put the file down without closing the chrome clasp in the middle and looked up at her.

"Playacting? What do you mean?"

"Could she have made up that business with the phone so that you wouldn't wonder why she wasn't answering it?"

The coach thought for a moment.

"No," he said, clicking the file shut. "Suzette was never calculated in that way. She was far too impulsive. She'd never be able to keep up the pretense."

"Do you have any idea where she could be hiding?"

Francis let his hands fall onto the piles of paper.

"Have you tried the stables? She used to spend hours there. If there was anything she obviously cared about, it was the horses."

They drove back toward the Hotel Pyr in silence.

"So she's with an Akira Amira Samira?" Carita eventually said.

"I doubt it," Annika said. "If she was planning to run away, she wouldn't have told her dad's coach where she was going to stay."

"Do you really think she's run away?" Carita said. "You don't think something's happened to her?"

Annika braked in the middle of a roundabout. She had started to recognize the Brits who always looked the wrong way.

"For someone who's supposed to be so impulsive, she seems very devious. She calls her mum and says she's going to stay with Vibeke Jensen, and she tells Vibeke that she's going back to Sweden. She tells her tennis coach that she's going to a party and is going to stay with a friend, and also demonstrates that her mobile doesn't work. Sounds like running-away-from-home plan A to me."

"So what did she tell her dad?" Carita asked.

"Well," Annika said as she pulled out onto the motorway, "we're never going to know, are we?"

"What if she doesn't turn up soon? Are you going to tell the police?"

"I'm going to write about it in the paper," Annika said.

"By the way, do you want to come round to ours this evening? We're going to a big lunch in Estepona at two o'clock, but we were thinking of doing something smaller this evening with a few neighbors, have some tapas . . ."

Annika took a moment to answer as she turned off toward the harbor. If she went, would the food appear on the invoice?

"I've got a lot to write," she said, "and I think . . ."

"But you still have to eat, and we'll be starting late. Come at half eight, nine, something like that. You don't have to stay the night."

Annika smiled as she pulled up in front of the hotel.

"How do I find you?"

"You need to get the right exit from a total of seven round-abouts. I'll email you detailed instructions."

The interpreter opened the door, jumped out onto the tarmac, and walked off on her high heels.

Annika parked and went up to her room, glancing at the time. She'd just have time to eat lunch and write up the interview before Lenita Söderström was due to arrive in Puerto Banús.

Annika, or rather the *Evening Post,* had come to an arrangement with Suzette's mother. The paper was going to pay for her stay in the Hotel Pyr for three nights, under the condition that she didn't speak to any other media in that time.

She switched on her laptop and went to the paper's home page.

The online edition was dominated by a web-TV item about a man whose nose was fourteen centimeters long.

She moved on to the second most important news of the day, her article about Suzette. The murder of the Söderström family had been given its own little section of the website: "Costa del Sol Murders." The newsroom in Stockholm had managed to dig out an old school photograph, but presumably Suzette looked rather different now. In the picture she was smiling uncertainly at the camera, with brown curls framing her face. In the description circulated by Interpol, her hair was described as short and jet-black.

Annika skimmed her text; it was pretty thin.

The picture of the search party which obviously hadn't found anything was, on the other hand, rather good. The blue lights were reflected in the looks of concentration in people's faces. The picture reeked of night and panic.

The second piece, about the House of Death, was considerably better.

Using the pictures from her mobile and facts about fentanyl gas and the storming of the Russian theater, she had managed to come up with a fairly credible reconstruction of the family's last minutes alive.

There was the doorway where they were found, the two young children on one side and the mother on the other. One important physical effect of fentanyl is apathy, she had written. Which meant that victims became lethargic, and even though they could see and register everything, they didn't react. That could be one explanation of why the terrorists in the Moscow theater hadn't fired their weapons when the building was stormed.

So the mother and children had been on either side of the closed door, unable to call out to each other or open the door, but still fully aware that something terrible was happening.

Then they had simply gone to sleep.

Their final seconds hadn't been full of anguish. Fentanyl was a strong narcotic. It didn't cause hallucinations, anxiety, or any similar response. Muscle control simply declined and finally ceased altogether. Victims lost consciousness, then their breathing stopped. The whole process was very rapid, and would have been over in a couple of minutes.

There were the pictures of the children's rooms, and the desk where the man was found, and the bed with the duvet he had used to try to save his family.

Dreadful pictures, but they were exclusives.

The minute's silence at the golf club was the third item under the Costa del Sol Murders heading. The picture of the three and a half celebrities in sunglasses was perfectly okay, with the caption "If everyone was like Sebbe, the world would look very different."

She took a quick look at what the competition had got.

They were leading with the Söderström family, but with a different heading: *The Gas Murders*.

The Madrid correspondent hadn't got anywhere near as far today. She had fewer facts about Suzette's disappearance, and obviously she didn't have any pictures from inside the house. But she had already spoken to Francis, which was fairly typical.

Oh well. She'd have to try to squeeze Francis into the article about Suzette's mother somehow.

In an attack of despair she went over to the bed and threw herself down on it. The best thing about staying in a hotel was that someone else cleaned up after you. It would have been nice if they could have brought up a bit of food every so often, but of course Officer Linde had offered to do that for her.

She remembered her dream, of them walking side by side through the pitch-black national park, the prickly thorns, the mild breeze . . .

Her mobile started to ring.

It was Niklas.

"Hello," she said. "I was just thinking about you."

"We've found the burglars," he replied abruptly. "Can you find your own way to La Campana?"

"Found them? Not arrested them?"

"They're dead," he said. "Have you been to La Campana?"

"No idea," Annika said. "How do you mean, dead?"

The police officer groaned.

"Okay," he said. "I'll pick you up. Ten minutes."

She heard a shriek of car tires before he ended the call.

The BMW had mud splattered up the side windows.

"Have you been driving off road?" Annika asked as she pulled on the safety belt.

Niklas didn't answer, just handed her a local Spanish paper and headed off toward Nueva Andalucía.

"What's this?" Annika said. "I can't read Spanish."

"Take a look at page seven," the police officer said.

She turned to it and found herself staring at her own pictures from inside the Söderström family home in Las Estrellas de Marbella.

"Fuck," Annika said, crumpling up the paper. "I told them not to sell them to anyone else."

"I'm thinking of doing a deal with you," Niklas said, maneuvering the car between Porsches and cars rented for Sunday outings. "I'll take you to the place where the Söderström burglars were found, and you write an article about a case we're working on."

"You're *thinking of doing a deal* with me," Annika repeated. "What makes you think I'll agree?"

"Because that way you'll get two good articles instead of none," Niklas said. "And I've done my research and found out that you're the sort of person who likes doing deals."

She looked at him in horror.

"What do you mean?" she said. "What's that supposed to mean, *the sort of person* . . . ? Who have you been talking to?"

He glanced at her.

"What is it you lot usually say, 'my sources are protected by the constitution'?"

"You've been talking to Detective Inspector Q," she said.

He grinned and turned off left, into a run-down working-class district. He was heading for an industrial area, a *polígono,* on the edge of the community, and stopped outside a warehouse with shutters pulled down over its doors.

Apits Carga, Annika read on a sun-bleached sign above the entrance.

"What's this?" she asked.

"In here the Spanish police found seven hundred kilos of cocaine less than two weeks ago," he said, pointing at the shuttered building. "It was concealed in a cargo of melons from Brazil. We know that some of the shipment was intended for Scandinavia, mainly Malmö and Stockholm."

Annika nodded.

"Your colleague mentioned something about this when I met you out at that shopping center."

"Things have moved on since then," Niklas said. "Now we need to pour oil on troubled waters up in Stockholm."

"You need an article," Annika said, "to calm down the intended recipients."

"*Exactemente*. You can interview me about a big drug-smuggling operation being cracked on the Costa del Sol. A big raid has been carried out and the final arrests will be made before you write the article."

"That's not enough," Annika said. "I need a Swedish angle, otherwise my editor won't take it."

"One of the men who's been caught is a Swedish citizen," Niklas said. "Will that do?"

She hesitated, trying out the headline: *SWEDE ARRESTED IN SPANISH DRUG RAID*.

"That's not going to sell many copies," she said. "Definitely not a lead."

"It doesn't have to be the lead, as long as it gets in the paper."

"Then I'll need details."

"You'll get them."

"Can I take a picture?"

"Go ahead."

She pulled out her camera, opened the door, and got out of the car. She quickly took three pictures of the peeling façade in portrait format and four in landscape. Then she got back in the car. Niklas put the car in gear and drove off.

The street was narrow, the houses small and pretty shabby. Washing was hanging from the balconies. The pavements were full of rickety plastic chairs and advertising hoardings and doormats. Men in caps were drinking coffee from shot glasses. Large Spanish women were carrying vegetables in flimsy plastic bags. Workmen blocked the traffic as they loaded their tools.

"Looks like real people live here," Annika said.

Niklas waited as two young women crossed the street with their prams.

"The construction workers who were ordered to build Puerto Banús in the 1950s came from the north. They had to start by building their own homes. That's what we're looking at here."

"And this is where the thieves were found?" Annika said, fishing out her notepad. "Is it spelled the way it sounds, La Campana, with a C?"

"The truck's over there," Niklas said, turning into a large vacant plot. The furrowed ground and mass of tire tracks indicated that the plot was used as a general parking lot.

A police cordon surrounded the whole of the far end of the plot. An old truck was parked with its back doors facing the wall. One of the rear doors was open, creaking in the wind. A car from the Policía Local was parked beside the cordon.

"Are they . . . still there?" Annika asked with a gulp.

"The bodies were taken off to the mortuary early this morning."

"And this is where they were found?"

"In the driver's cab, to be precise. Shall we take a look?"

Niklas switched off the engine, grabbed a torch, and got out of the BMW. Annika followed, hoisting her bag up onto her shoulder. The policeman went over to his Spanish colleague, shook his hand, and exchanged greetings in Spanish. She could see Niklas waving and pointing, toward both the car and her, then he beckoned her over.

"We can go in as long as we don't touch anything," he said, holding up the tape so that Annika could get underneath.

The ground was uneven and hard, and she stumbled a little in her boots. A few clumps of grass were clinging to life between the potholes and clods of earth. Patches of cement suggested some old foundations or a roadway.

She stopped a couple of meters from the truck's rear door. Niklas took a couple more steps, lit the powerful torch, and directed the beam inside the vehicle. It reflected back toward them off a large flat-screen television. Niklas moved the beam and Annika watched as it moved over the frame of a painting, a statue, a large globe, and a rolled-up rug. He moved the beam downward. On the floor of the truck sat a jewelry box and several game consoles; Annika recognized a PlayStation 3 and an Xbox.

She pulled out her camera and took some pictures.

"Five lives," she said. "For this."

"Seven," Niklas said. "The thieves were killed as well, of course."

He walked over to the left-hand side of the driver's cab, where he was out of view of his Spanish colleague.

"Is this everything that was taken?" Annika asked, following him on unsteady feet.

"The list of what was taken isn't definite; it was put together by the home help going from room to room, and she hasn't got much idea of what the art was or who it was by."

"How did the thieves die?" Annika asked. "Were they shot? Beaten to death?"

He shook his head.

"There were no external injuries on the bodies."

"Could it have been the gas? Fentanyl?"

"Probably."

"Who found them?"

"A man who lives on the other side of the street, above that lunch restaurant. He'd seen the truck standing here for several days and thought it was odd that it was still here over Epiphany. He came over to take a closer look, and that's when he found them."

Annika looked up at the cab. She could only see a dirty side window and the pattern of the roof.

"They couldn't have been visible from the outside," she said, "otherwise someone would have noticed before."

Niklas stopped beside the cab and inspected it, keeping his hands by his sides.

"The cab was unlocked," he said. "The old man opened the

driver's door. One of the thieves was in the passenger side, the other in the driver's seat. The driver tumbled out when the door was opened. The old man had a minor heart attack and had to be taken off to hospital by ambulance."

Annika looked up at the door of the truck. She could do with a picture of the inside of the cab.

"Can we open the door?" she asked. "If it's still unlocked?"

Niklas shook his head.

"We can't touch the handle."

"But if I climbed up?" Annika said. "And took a picture through the side-window?"

"Without touching anything?"

Annika looked up at the cab. There were steps beside the wheel arch that she could stand on. She turned to the policeman.

"Can you lift me up?" she asked.

He looked amused.

"How much do you weigh?"

She hit him on the arm.

"Come on, then," he said.

Annika let go of her bag, took a firm grip of the camera with her right hand, and stood in front of the policeman. He put both hands round her waist, breathing on the back of her neck.

"Okay," he said. "Now."

And with a powerful thrust he lifted her up into the air. She put one foot on the steps of the cab and looked in through the dirty side window.

A narrow driver's seat and a wider passenger seat in cracked vinyl, hamburger wrappers above the dashboard by the windscreen, a map of Marbella, mud on the floor, two half-empty beer bottles in the cup holder by the radio.

She raised the camera and fired off a series of pictures of the interior of the cab.

Then he put her down.

"Quite some place to die," he said, still holding onto her.

She stood still, breathing into his shirt. He smelled of soap and grass.

"What are you doing this afternoon?" he asked.

At that moment her mobile started to ring in the bag by her feet.

She pulled free, her cheeks glowing, and grabbed the hands-free lead.

It was the presenter of the radio program Studio Six.

"I'd like to have you on for a debate on Monday afternoon," the man said.

She looked up at Niklas. The way he was looking at her was more than she could handle. She turned away.

"I see," Annika said. "Who with, and what about?"

"With Arne Påhlson among others, about journalists' credibility, about how easy it is to hold those in power to account when you're sitting in their lap, about . . ."

She screwed her eyes shut: Don't get angry, don't feel insulted, don't do anything stupid, don't give them the chance to play her outraged response on the radio.

"I'm in Spain on a job," she said, "I can hardly hear you. What did you say?"

"Er, about journalists' credibility, about how easy it is to . . ."

"Hello?" Annika said. "Hello?"

"Hello?" the man from Studio Six said.

"Oh," Annika said, holding the microphone some distance away. "He disappeared."

Then she ended the call and switched off her mobile.

"I've got a date," she said, looking up at Niklas again. "With Lenita Söderström, Suzette's mother."

"You didn't want to talk to the caller?" the police officer said.

"Can you drop me back at the hotel?"

They climbed back through the cordon, and Annika took a few pictures with the police car and cordon in the foreground.

She could already see the headline in tomorrow's paper: *Sebastian's Killers Died Here.*

Then the story would be on its way off the front page.

Lenita Söderström checked into the hotel without Annika realizing who she was.

The small woman stepped into the lobby with a brown suitcase on wheels, a coat over her arm and a slight limp, as if her shoes were chafing. She walked up to reception and said something in labored English, and Annika went back to the English-language edition of the local paper, *Sur.* They too had reprinted her pictures from inside the house. Photos: *Evening Post.*

"Annika Bengtzon?"

She'd been expecting a blonde who'd gone to seed, with tortured hair and low-slung jeans.

The little woman standing in front of her had reading glasses on a cord round her neck and a slightly pilled top. She was fifteen years older than her picture on Facebook, and introduced herself as Lenita with a sturdy handshake.

"Can we go and get some lunch?" she said. "I'm starving."

Annika folded the paper and left the interior shots of the Söderströms' villa on the table beside her.

"I don't actually know where to eat round here," Annika said. "We can ask at reception."

"No need," Lenita said. "I've been here before."

The woman led the way through the doors, turned left on the street outside, past the entrance to the El Corte Inglés department store, then down the steps in the Marina Banús shopping center. There she stopped and looked around curiously. Little fashion boutiques and two trendy cafés filled up the whole of the ground floor of the small shopping center.

"Well," she said, "I know it was here somewhere . . ."

"This will do fine," Annika said, heading toward one of the cafés.

Lenita followed her with somewhat hesitant steps.

"Isn't it funny how the small, reasonably priced places never last?" she said. "They always lose out to the big chains."

She sat down opposite Annika at a small, round café table. Annika glanced at the woman as she skimmed the menu. The café specialized in organic smoothies, freshly roasted coffee, and salads "made with love." She knew Lenita Söderström was forty-two; she was born the same year as Sebastian, but she looked older. Her hair was ash blond; she had the beginnings of a double chin and a boyish figure.

"These new places always seem to overcomplicate things," Lenita Söderström said, putting the menu down. "I'll have lasagne if they've got it, otherwise just a muffin. And a glass of red."

Annika ordered two chicken stir-fries in her hesitant Spanish, plus two *agua con gas* and *una copa de vino tinto*.

Lenita sighed, and it sounded like it came from a bottomless chasm.

"If you only knew," she said, looking up at Annika. "It's so terrible, not knowing where she is. It makes me so angry, so upset. The least she could do is call!"

Annika took her pen and notepad out of her bag.

"Is this the first time Suzette has disappeared? Or has she left home without saying where she was going before?"

Lenita Söderström squirmed on her chair.

"Don't all teenagers do that? And she only does it because she knows how worried I get. I can't eat, can't sleep . . ."

Their food arrived, and Lenita tucked into the stir-fry without asking where her lasagne was.

"Suzette doesn't think of anyone but herself," she said as she chewed. "Since she was four years old, it's been nothing but 'me, me, me' with Suzette."

She drained her glass of wine and gestured for another.

Annika couldn't think of anything to say. The woman was stressed and wound up. This was going to take time.

"And Sebastian was off playing ice hockey the whole time. Stuck in America, unable to understand what anyone was saying, how much fun do you think that was? And with a kid that did nothing but cry."

She took a gulp of wine.

"Where do you think Suzette might be?" Annika asked.

Lenita leaned over the table.

"All these years I've had to look after her on my own," she said emphatically. "Now Sebastian finally agrees to take a bit of responsibility, and what happens? She disappears after just two weeks. It's incredibly irresponsible!"

She groaned and leaned back against the rather too fashionable chair.

"When did you last hear from Suzette?"

"She called and said she was going to be moving in with that woman who has the stables up in the mountains."

"And that was last Thursday, then?"

"After we spoke yesterday I had a look at her Facebook page. She hasn't added anything since then."

"Do you think something might have happened to her?" Annika said gently.

The woman's eyes filled with tears.

"I found out about Sebastian in the paper," she said in a small voice. "Imagine, finding out your ex-husband is dead in a headline in the gutter press. Do you have any idea how awful that was?"

Annika nodded and wondered if the gutter press in question was her own paper.

"I tried calling Suzette's mobile straightaway, but it wasn't switched on. I left a message, but she hasn't called back. I can't understand why she's treating me this way."

"You didn't talk to her on New Year's Eve," Annika said. "No text message at midnight, nothing like that?"

"I was on a mini-cruise with my work colleagues, so I didn't have a very good signal," Lenita said.

"What's your job?" Annika asked.

"I'm in the hotel industry," Lenita said, ordering a third glass of wine. "I deal with the accounts, budgets, payroll. It's a very demanding job."

She mentioned a hotel that Annika had never heard of.

"When Suzette has gone missing before, how long does it usually take before she gets in touch?"

Lenita closed her eyes, her shoulders slumped; the wine was making her calm down slightly.

"A day," she said. "Once she was gone overnight, she slept at a friend's, Polly, without telling me. After that we talked about all this. About how worried it makes me."

Annika looked down at her notes. She'd been hoping for a different answer. She'd been hoping that Suzette had got into the habit of going missing for several days before getting in touch, that she was experienced and competent when it came to running away, able to cope in all weathers.

But that evidently wasn't the case, and it was now a week since she had disappeared.

"Has Suzette ever mentioned a friend called Amira, or Samira?" she asked.

"She never tells me anything."

"When did you realize she was missing?"

"When I spoke to that Danish woman who owns the stables," Lenita Söderström said.

In other words, when Annika had passed her mobile to Vibeke Jensen.

"And then you booked a flight down here at once?"

"It's expensive, flying abroad, but what can you do when something like this happens?"

"What are you planning to do down here?"

"Look for my daughter," Lenita said, and her tears overflowed.

Annika let her cry for a few minutes. Then she put her hand on the woman's arm.

"This is what we'll do," Annika said. "I'll write an article for the paper in which you say you're here to look for Suzette. We'll encourage Suzette herself and anyone else who might have had any contact with her to get in touch with the police and tell them whatever they know. I'll say that she's never gone missing like this before, because that's correct, isn't it?"

Lenita blew her nose on a napkin and nodded.

"I understand that Suzette was good at sports," Annika said. "She was good at horse riding and a promising tennis player ... ?"

The woman opposite snorted.

"Do you know what it costs for a kid to go horse riding regularly? And when I said I couldn't afford it, that Astrid showed up waving her purse. But what about getting there and back? To start with, I had to go with her, it took more than an hour each way, then, when she started to go on her own, I had to keep forking out for underground tickets and bus tickets and ..."

"You said she slept at a friend's that night when she didn't come home. What are the names of her best friends?"

Lenita gave Annika four names, four girls who were all in the same class as Suzette at middle school in Blackeberg.

"Did she have a boyfriend?"

"Suzette was wary of boys," Lenita said, gesturing to the waiter. "She could see what had happened to me, after all."

"Is Suzette happy with her friends? Is she happy in Bromma?"

"Bromma's a nice suburb," Lenita said. "I know it isn't Marbella, but I work hard to keep things together financially, so we can stay in Långskeppsgatan."

"Why would she want to move down to Marbella and live with her dad?"

"Suzette was fed up of school, but I told her the truth: that if you want to make anything of your life, you need an education. I can't support her for the rest of her life. And her dad won't either, even if he's rolling in money."

"But she did start high school?"

"Yes, the one specializing in sport," Lenita scoffed. "What sort of an education's that, I asked her, playing tennis all day long? I don't get it. I thought she should have studied economics, then she could have got a good job. She might have been able to get into the hotel branch, maybe as a temp to start with; we always need people over the summer, and for Christmas and New Year . . ."

"But she moved down here to her dad so she could . . . what? Play tennis? Work?"

Lenita leaned toward Annika as the fourth glass of wine appeared between them.

"If you knew what he's done to me. The way he's treated me!"

Annika put her pen down on her pad.

"Lenita," she said in a low voice. "Can we stop talking about you, and concentrate on Suzette instead?"

It didn't end up as much of an article. Fortunately she had Francis's description of Suzette to bulk out the text with, because Lenita's quotes were next to useless.

The picture was even worse.

Lenita Söderström was standing outside El Corte Inglés, looking absolutely furious. With a good deal of wishful thinking you could just about interpret her expression as upset and desperate rather than affronted and half-cut.

After Annika's pertinent but clumsy remark that she would rather talk about Suzette, Lenita had clammed up. She didn't want to have her picture taken, and it was only when Annika threatened to tear up the paper's agreement to pay the hotel bill that she finally relented.

She decided to wait a while before sending the text off to Stockholm. Full of Thai chicken, she concentrated on writing the article about the dead thieves instead. She emailed that to the newsroom together with the pictures, and pointed out that her pictures from inside the Söderström house were in all the Spanish papers even though Patrik had promised they wouldn't be. Then she looked at the time.

Only half past six.

Maybe she should try to get hold of Suzette's friends from middle school. None of them had their own flat or a listed phone number, but if she kept trying with various combinations of surname and postcode, she ought to be able to dig out their parents, and then their home phone numbers.

She tried the first girl, Polly Sandman.

No results.

Maybe her real name was something completely different, and not Polly at all.

The second name, Amanda Andersson, produced 618 results in Stockholm alone. Too many to choose from; Annika couldn't assume the girl lived in Bromma and was born in exactly the same year as Suzette.

The third one, Sandra Holgersson, lived on Aladdinsvägen and had the same surname as her parents, and they were all registered at the same address. There was a phone number listed, but no one answered.

Mind you, it was Twelfth Night.

The fourth girl was called Klara, but Lenita hadn't been sure of her surname. Something double-barreled, she thought, Hermans-son-Eklund or something like that. That particular combination drew a blank.

Annika got up from the computer and walked round the hotel room.

Dusk was starting to fall. The big mountain on the other side of the motorway was turning dark red in the dying rays of the sun, and the streetlamps had come on. The cars snaked slowly but relentlessly in both directions.

Maybe she should go round to see Carita and her family after all. She had no great desire to spend another evening sitting here. She looked at the time again.

One hour left. Maybe she should have a shower? Go for a walk? Call the children?

She picked up her mobile and called Thomas's mobile, unable to bring herself to call Sophia Fucking Bitch Grenborg's home number.

The call bounced around the satellites, one ring, two, five, six, and with each ring the loneliness in the room echoed a bit louder. Finally the call went to voicemail. She clicked to cut it off without leaving a message. She went back to her laptop and stared at the screen.

Suzette hadn't been active on Facebook since last Thursday.

Annika remembered the computer on the desk of the teenage bedroom next to the kitchen out in the villa in Las Estrellas de Marbella. It must have been Suzette's.

Mind you, she could get into her account from any computer.

Annika opened her own Facebook profile.

0 Friends.

She moved to *Search* and typed in "suzette söderström."

There, a direct hit.

Name: Suzette Söderström

Network: Sweden
Matches: Name

On the left-hand side was a picture of Suzette that was presumably fairly recent and carefully selected. Her eyes were heavily made up and open wide, her head was slightly tilted, and her black hair was sticking up. The angles were slightly odd, it had probably been taken with a webcam.

On the right were four options: *Send Message, Poke!, View Friends,* and *Add to Friends.*

She clicked on *View Friends* and let out a whistle.

Suzette had 201 friends. They filled five pages, with names and photographs in alphabetical order, with a short description of each of them. They were all young, and they were all from Sweden. On the first page Annika found Amanda Andersson. Seeing that she herself was now part of the big fat Facebook community, all she had to do was click on the picture of the young Amanda Andersson and send her a message. Whoosh, off it went into cyberspace, and with a bit of luck it would result in a phone call or email.

Then she carried on through the list of friends, and found both Klara, whose surname was Evertsson-Hedberg, and Sandra Holgersson, and sent them messages as well. On the next page she found someone who really was called Polly, actually Paulina Sandman, with identical jet-black hair and the same expression and tilted head as Suzette.

They took the pictures at the same time, Annika thought, on the same webcam. Maybe they set up their accounts at the same time, and gathered friends together. This was Suzette's best friend.

She wrote her a message as well, slightly longer and more explicit than the others. She explained who she was, that she was writing about Suzette for the paper, that she didn't want to get anything wrong, and that it was important that her friends were given the opportunity to voice their opinion.

Then she looked through the list of friends once more.

No Amira, Samira, or Akira.

She tried calling Niklas but got no answer, so she rang Knut instead.

The police didn't have any leads on Suzette, the Norwegian explained. The physical search area had been expanded to cover a four-kilometer radius from the Söderström family home, which included parts of a rugged national park with deep ravines and steep waterfalls. They were also following up other lines of inquiry by going through her computer, speaking to her friends and neighbors, as well as the staff in the bars of Nueva Andalucía.

She added a few lines to her article about the unsuccessful police search, explained that Suzette was a promising tennis player and that she trained a lot at her dad's club, that her coach had once been ranked thirty-eighth in the world, and Suzette had been expected to have a career at least as successful as that.

Then she emailed her text and the terrible picture of Lenita to the newsroom of the *Evening Post*.

Then she opened the email with Carita's directions to her house. They consisted solely of advertising hoardings and various bars and restaurants, seeing as there didn't seem to be any road names. "Turn left after Mercadona, drive past OpenCor and follow the road round to the left . . ."

On the way out to the car she stopped at reception and asked for the number of Taxi Marbella.

Just as backup, in case she got lost.

The gate wasn't quite as showy as the one to Las Estrellas de Marbella, but it wasn't far off.

Carita's development of row houses lay high up a mountainside with a golf course immediately below. The streetlamps formed a river of light down toward the sea, where Puerto Banús spread out like an intense thousand-watt bulb in the moonlight. She pressed the security phone for house number 6 and waited in the car as the obligatory gates slid open.

Inside, a world opened up that felt as natural and genuine as the Los Naranjos golf club. The buildings huddled together in groups of three or four. They were all different, pink or pale blue, ochre yellow or deep red, with balustrades and terraces and decking. A swimming pool with two waterfalls and large stone terraces faced the valley. There were ornate streetlamps, like old London gas lamps, lighting up the roads with yellow energy-saving bulbs.

"Welcome," Carita said, kissing her on both cheeks. Annika realized that she was kissing back a bit too hard, seeing as Carita ended up with red lipstick on both cheeks. She didn't feel able to point it out.

"Come in, come in, no, no, there's no need to take your shoes off, you're in España now. Come on, I'll introduce you to everyone . . ."

Having "a few neighbors" around turned out to involve practically everyone in the area.

"You see that couple standing over there laughing?" Carita said. "She's a math teacher at Marbella International College, and he captains one of the yachts down in the harbor. They've got two children and live just a bit farther up. Nice people, but they're Brits. The people going up to them now are Swedes. Do you remember the adverts for Diesel clothing back in the nineties? He was the one who did them. His wife was an international model in those days. Now they live in a neighboring development. They've got two children as well, a son who plays football and a daughter who's a Spanish horse-jumping champion."

Annika looked at the beautiful woman with the long, glossy hair. She was laughing as she put her hand on her husband's arm. And she had a horse.

Carita gestured toward the other end of the room.

"That woman there, she's Swedish, she's a partner in a law firm in Frankfurt. And he's from New Zealand, he works with boats as well. The young man with the dog, he's an estate agent from Jamaica. That older man used to run a bank in Kenya, but now he plays golf full-time. The couple having cava poured in their glasses are from Värmland, they moved down here when they sold their tire company. But dear me, you haven't got a drink yet . . ."

She bustled off and Annika was left standing beside a group of expensively dressed people holding glasses of wine. She tried talking Spanish for a short while, but after saying *soy sueco* she stuck to English. She'd managed to introduce herself as a Swedish man. Great.

She went out onto the terrace and stood there looking out across the harbor. The neon sign of El Corte Inglés was clearly visible all the way up here.

"Ah, so you found your way all right."

Annika spun round when she heard the thick Gothenburg accent. She felt her face crack into a smile as if she'd just met her oldest friend.

"Rickard Marmén," she said. "I thought you lived in Marbella."

"I do, but my business partner has a house up here. What do you think, do you feel like investing?"

He pointed at a sign on the next house, *Se vende,* for sale.

"It's all a bit too model village for my taste," she said.

He laughed heartily.

Annika nodded toward the for-sale sign next door.

"How much do you want for that house, then?"

"Depends what the owner needs. He's a professional poker player from Liverpool and he puts the sign up whenever things aren't going well. The next time he wins he takes it down again."

"You're kidding," Annika said. "I thought everyone who lived here was rich."

Rickard Marmén smiled.

"That depends on what you mean by 'rich.' Most people here have a lot more time than people in Sweden, for instance. The tempo's much slower."

"Naturally," Annika said. "If everyone spends all day playing golf, things don't have to move quickly."

Rickard Marmén moved closer to her and nodded toward the crowd by the bar.

"I'd say most of them have worked hard in their lives, if they aren't still doing so."

"So why have they moved here? For tax reasons? Or is everyone just here for the weather?"

"A lot of taxes are lower in Sweden than they are in Spain these days," Rickard Marmén said. "I think it's more to do with wine, women, and song . . ."

Carita came sailing out onto the terrace and tucked her arm under Annika's.

"My dear," she exclaimed, "you still haven't got anything to drink, have you? Nacho, *una copa de cava, por favor . . .*"

Then she leaned toward Annika and lowered her voice.

"How did you get on today? Did you get a good interview with Suzette's mother?"

Annika was given a glass of sparkling wine, which she put down at once.

"I don't think the girl's run away from home," she said. "I think something terrible has happened to her."

"What makes you think that?" Carita asked.

Annika hesitated.

"She hasn't shown any sign of life in seven days. A girl with no connections in the area, who hardly knows her way home, and who can't speak the language, what are her chances?"

"She could be with a man," Carita said.

"Of her own free will? When she's never even had a boyfriend? She's only just turned sixteen."

"I was sixteen when I met Nacho," Carita said, beckoning over a tall, thin man with a receding hairline and sensitive hands. "Annika, this is my husband."

She was clearly very proud of her husband. They greeted each other properly, in the Swedish manner, by shaking hands.

"I understand that you're a doctor," Annika said in English, but the man replied in Swedish.

"Pediatrician," he said. "It's an incredible career, taking care of the future."

Annika smiled.

"And you work at the hospital here in Marbella?"

The man nodded.

"It's a first-rate hospital. It's just been completely renovated. I'm in the neonatal department, working with premature babies. To my mind that's the most important type of care of all. It repays you for decades to come. Will you excuse me . . . ?"

And he slid away.

"Unbelievable," Annika said, "to think that we haven't got space for a man like that in Swedish society. Where did you meet?"

"At a party in Beverly Hills, at the home of a girl whose father was a scriptwriter on one of those never-ending soaps that never make it in Sweden. Nacho was so different from all the other boys, so much calmer, so much more . . . masculine."

"And he's from Colombia?"

"From Bogotá. Victor, his father, was chief of police there. We spent a few years living there in the early 1990s, in Chía, the university city twenty kilometers north of Bogotá, on the way to Zipaquirá . . ."

She fell silent and twirled her wineglass.

"Why did you move?" Annika asked.

Carita hesitated for a moment.

"We couldn't stay," she said in the end. "Victor, Nacho's father, led a big raid against one of the big drug syndicates that ran cocaine factories in the jungle, and he was murdered immediately after the raid."

"That's terrible," Annika said.

Carita took a large gulp of wine.

"The Colombians are a bit unusual," she said. "They're not content just to kill their enemies, they wipe out whole families. There mustn't be anyone left alive to inherit anything."

She smiled, a quick, sad smile.

"Nacho survived," she said, "because we were visiting my parents in Sweden. Have you had any food? The children and I spent all afternoon preparing kebabs . . ."

She took hold of Annika's elbow and made her way back in among the guests.

"I thought you were just going to be having a few neighbors round," Annika said. "This must be everyone in the neighborhood."

"Certainly not," Carita said firmly. "Can you believe it, one in five households won't pay the fee for our little association, the one that pays the gardener's wages, and for pool maintenance and the cost of the satellite television dish. Isn't that just dreadful?"

She drank some more wine.

"They're not welcome here, and do you know what?"

She leaned over and whispered in Annika's ear:

"They're all Brits."

She was running along the beach at sunrise. The sand was firm and pale gray. Large flocks of birds she didn't recognize took off, shrieking and crying, toward the light. She had the wind in her face and salt from the sea in her hair.

I could get used to this, she thought.

Afterward she took a long shower and decided to have a proper breakfast, for the first time in a whole week.

The breakfast room had a tiled floor and spotlights set into the ceiling. The walls were yellow, the chairs blue, and the curtains striped. She ate a slice of white bread with some ham, and a yogurt, and drank coffee and a glass of juice.

Then she went up to her room and called the newsroom.

Berit wasn't there yet, so she asked to talk to Patrik.

"What's happening today, then?" he said in a tone of voice that suggested he'd already been up and running for many hours.

"I told you I didn't want the pictures to be sold on," Annika said. "Despite that, they showed up in every Spanish paper yesterday."

Patrik's reply sounded affronted.

"For fuck's sake, I'm not the one who sits here trying to sell pictures abroad."

"But I told you . . ."

"Do I look like a messenger? You'll have to take it up with the picture desk. What are you writing for tomorrow?"

"The burglars are dead, and the stolen property's been found, and Suzette's still missing, so I'm starting to run out of new angles," she said.

"The whole story has gone cold," Patrik decided. "Get the first plane home tomorrow morning. You can spend today tidying up anything that's left."

"I've got something about a Swede who just got picked up in a big drugs raid down here," she said, thinking of her deal with Niklas.

"Write it up and we'll have to see if we can use it. What I want for tomorrow is a summary of what life is like for the Swedes down there. Are they all tax dodgers, by the way?"

Patrik's voice sounded wistful, four thousand kilometers away up in the newsroom.

"'Swedes flee Costa del Sol,'" he said, and Annika could imagine him making a sweeping gesture with his hand to illustrate the headline. "Death in paradise. End of an era. Truckloads of possessions heading north again."

He took an audible gulp of something, probably coffee.

"I've heard there's a Swedish estate agent down there who knows all there is to know about the Costa del Sol. His name's . . . hang on, I've got it here somewhere . . . Rickard Marmén! Do you think you can find him yourself or shall I try to get a phone number for him?"

Oh, so Mr. Marmén was an estate agent as well, was he? Of course he was.

"I think I can manage," Annika said, leafing through her notepad until she came to his number.

"Get some really doom-laden quotes that show that the whole thing's about to go under," he said, and hung up.

She called Rickard Marmén's mobile number from the hotel phone, but got his voicemail.

Must have been a late night out at Carita's, she thought, and left a message asking him to call her.

Then she dialed Niklas Linde's number.

He picked up at once.

"The Swede in the drug raid," she said. "I need more details."

"I'll pick you up from the hotel at eight o'clock this evening," he said. "See you then."

Her mobile rang.

"Sorry I didn't answer in time, love. How are you today?"

Rickard sounded bright as a lark.

"Fine, thanks. My bosses up in Stockholm have just asked me to interview you, in your capacity as an estate agent. What do you think?"

"I think we could probably sort something out, don't you, my dear? Call in at my little boutique at lunchtime. It's opposite El Corte Inglés in Puerto Banús, you know, the big department store that . . ."

"I know where it is," Annika said. "And lunch, that's at . . . two o'clock?"

"Say half past," Rickard said.

She looked at her watch.

She had four hours to kill.

The yachts were packed in along the jetties in the harbor. The lower the number of the jetty, the bigger the boats. So jetty number 0 had boats that looked like miniature versions of the ferries that sailed between Sweden and Finland. She walked slowly past them, licking an ice cream. There weren't many people about. A few men were carrying tools on a huge boat; a woman was walking about with a rag on a different one, polishing it.

There was a sharp breeze from the sea. The sun was cold and the light harsh.

She went and ordered a coffee in the Sinatra Bar, the place where Niklas had been the first night when she called him. It was decorated in pale blue and white, with a maritime theme. The coffee wasn't particularly good. She didn't like these silly little cups with two centimeters of tar at the bottom. At home she used to brew a whole liter every morning in her French *cafetière* and warm cups of it up in the microwave throughout the day.

She was actually looking forward to getting back to her flat. To the rooms she hadn't even moved into properly yet, to the cafetière in the austere kitchen, to the stack of unread paperbacks on the living room floor, and the children's scent in their bedclothes.

She had really understood how homeless she had felt in her temporary accommodation in the office in Gamla Stan. And she was happy to be living back on the island of Kungsholmen again.

For some reason an image of Julia Lindholm popped into her mind.

Julia had been homeless for exactly the same amount of time as she had.

The night Annika's house burned down, Julia was arrested and locked up for the murder of her husband.

She looked out at the boats and the sea beyond them. They were bobbing about slowly and irregularly in the sharp wind.

Julia and Alexander were going to be stuck in that cloying rehabilitation center at Lejondalssjön for several more months yet. And how would it feel when they finally got back to the three-room flat on Södermalm where David was shot?

Like moving back into a nightmare, Annika thought. As if I could have moved back into the burned-out ruins out in Vinterviksvägen.

She shivered. The bar was starting to fill up. Four blond women were taking the first *tinto verano* of the day at one of the window tables. A few British football fans were drinking Spanish beer straight from the bottle. Two young girls were giggling over a newspaper farther in.

Annika stood up to pay at the counter. She handed the man

at the till a fifty-euro note, then turned to watch the people going past.

The man put a few coins in change by her elbow.

She looked at the pile of shrapnel.

"Hey," she said, pointing at the coins. "Shouldn't I get a few notes as well?"

The man looked at her and shrugged his shoulders.

"Maybe, maybe not," he said, and turned away.

A flash of fury went through Annika's head.

"Hey," she said, louder this time. "I paid with a fifty-euro note."

The man was absorbed in doing something with his back to her. His muscular shoulders moved under his black T-shirt. He probably needed the money for anabolic steroids.

"Give me my change," she said, loudly and angrily.

The bar had fallen completely silent now. A couple came in through the door and looked round for somewhere to sit.

"Don't come in here," Annika said loudly. "They cheat people out of their change."

"Shut up," the man behind the counter said, tossing two twenty-euro notes at her.

"Fucking crook," Annika said in Swedish, picked up the notes, and walked out.

When she got out onto the quayside her mobile rang.

It was Berit.

"How's life in the sun?"

"Do you know," she said, "someone just tried to cheat me out of four hundred kronor in change in some shitty bar."

She was marching away from the Sinatra Bar now.

"You give them what for. How's it going with the missing girl? I saw the mum's down there with you now. Is there anything we can use to move on with this?"

"Her friends back home in Bromma, maybe," Annika said.

"But I've already contacted them through Facebook. They haven't got back to me."

"Facebook?" Berit said. "I read in the business pages that Facebook's on the way out."

"Well, of course it is," Annika said, "seeing as I've finally joined. Listen, I was thinking about Julia Lindholm; has anything happened with the review of Filip Andersson's case?"

"That'll probably take months," Berit said. "They've got a lot to check through. The preliminary report alone ran to over a thousand pages. It was woolly and circumstantial and full of holes and things that weren't clear. There were people shouting about a miscarriage of justice even when the first verdict was announced."

"Did you know Filip Andersson has a sister in the police?" Annika said. "Nina Hoffman, that one who's Julia Lindholm's best friend . . ."

"She's Filip Andersson's sister? I didn't know that."

"Don't you think it's odd that two such criminal individuals as Filip Andersson and Yvonne Nordin should have a sister who's a cop?"

It sounded as if Berit was leafing through a paper.

"I don't know," she said. "To me it seems more like different sides of the same coin. Opposite reactions to the same sort of up-bringing, so to speak."

"So Nina's the white sheep of the family?"

"Stranger things have happened. Bill Clinton has a brother who's a petty crook, for instance. And my cousin Klas-Göran's done time as well."

"Bill Clinton's brother's done time?"

"Clinton pardoned him on his last day as president, January 20, 2001. Him and one hundred thirty-nine other criminals. It's the custom for American presidents to do that. What's your sister doing these days, by the way?"

Annika was taken aback midbreath.

"Birgitta? No idea. I don't even know where she lives."

The silence that followed spoke volumes.

"Do you think I should try to contact Suzette's friends?" Berit eventually asked.

"It might be more use to try Sebastian Söderström's Swedish relatives," Annika said, breathing a sigh of relief. "See if they have any idea where the girl might be."

"We've already tried, no one wants to talk."

"What about Astrid Paulson, then? Everyone seems to be saying that she was the only person who got on well with Suzette. Maybe she's got family who might know something?"

"I'll give it a try," Berit said. "Have you been able to do any work on that series of articles that Patrik keeps going on about?"

"The Costa del Cocaine? I haven't actually seen a single rolled-up euro note, let alone any drugs . . ."

They arranged to meet on Monday and ended the call.

Annika had reached the end of the quayside. She was outside a shop selling bags where even the cheapest, smallest cloth bag cost 500 euros.

She turned her back on the shop window, took out her mobile, and looked up "Nina H, police" in the phone book. She clicked *call* and waited as the phone call was put through; then everything went quiet. The voice that came on instead was metallic.

Telefónica le informa que actualmente no es posible connectar al número llamado. Telefónica le informa . . .

She clicked to end the call.

Telefonica was one of the big Spanish telecom companies, but why was their message cutting in on Nina Hoffman's Swedish mobile? Was Nina in Spain, or was there something wrong with the signal on her own mobile?

She tried again.

Telefónica le informa que actualmente no es posible . . .

She gave up and looked at the time. Twenty past two.

Time to pay a visit to Rickard Marmén.

The estate agency was hidden behind a British bookshop. It wasn't much more than a hole in the wall. A dozen fairly faded advertisements for various properties were stuck up in the window.

Rickard was sitting behind a desk and typing at a computer when Annika walked in.

"Ah, here you are, my dear," he said, getting up and kissing her on both cheeks. "Is the *Evening Post* thinking of buying an apartment in Puerto Banús?"

"Not exactly," she said. "How's business?"

"Fucking awful," he said. "There's no movement at all. It's this damn Operation Malaya."

He saw the look of incomprehension on her face and settled back in his chair.

"One hundred and two people have been arrested for corruption in the property market down here, including the whole of Marbella's previous town council. The bribes for illegal planning permission were astonishing. The place was awash with money. The head of the highways department turned out to have three farmhouses, each of which was the size of Stockholm City Hall. He had over a hundred racehorses and a genuine Miró above his Jacuzzi."

Annika laughed.

"And we thought it was a scandal when our old prime minister used the wrong sort of scaffolding at his country house."

Rickard leaned back happily in his chair.

"The mayor was arrested in her bedroom where she was recuperating after her latest liposuction. Ten council workmen were busy fitting a new kitchen for her. Now every application for planning permission over the past twenty years is being gone over with a fine-tooth comb. Until that's done, the banks are refusing to authorize any mortgages. Talk about putting a damper on the market. It'll take at least a year before things pick up. A glass of wine, perhaps?"

She shook her head and smiled.

"Tell me about the way the Swedish colony has reacted to the death of the Söderström family," she said. "Do you think it's going to scare Swedes away from the Costa del Sol?"

"They've already been scared off," Rickard said. "Not by crime, but by the price of property. Operation Malaya has stopped prices going up even more, but you still won't find a flat in Marbella for less than three million kronor, or a row house for less than four. The smallest detached houses cost at least six million, and you won't get a normal family villa for under thirteen. Around Alicante you can get the same properties for around half the price."

"Why's everything so expensive at the moment?" Annika asked.

Rickard threw out his hands.

"Because Marbella is exclusive and Alicante is common. People pay for the address. Sometimes it gets really ridiculous. Look at this!"

He opened a website and turned the screen toward Annika.

"This is a vacant plot with no view on the hill just below Carita's house. The owner's asking 5.6 million euros for it."

Annika looked at the picture. There was a rusty lamppost by the side of the road. A tarmac drive, cracked with thistles and thorns, led down to an abandoned set of building foundations in a hollow. Beyond it the undergrowth took over.

"Fifty million kronor," Annika said skeptically. "That must be some sort of joke."

"It's not," Rickard said, turning the screen back again. "Mind you, the owner hasn't managed to get shot of it."

"So people aren't scared of crime?"

Rickard turned serious.

"Even if break-ins involving gas are common, this is the first time anyone has died," he said. "My experience is that people carry on living in the same houses, even after they've been gassed. A lot of them are in a bad way, a lot worse than after an ordinary break-in, but they still stay. And I don't think there are as many muggings or as much street crime down here as there is up in Stockholm. I've got no figures for that, but it hardly ever happens."

"But there are so many criminal gangs here," she said, remembering Knut Garen's statistics: 420 gangs carrying out more than thirty contract killings each year in the Málaga area alone.

Rickard thought for a moment.

"Nobody notices them," he said. "What you see out in the street are a lot of police cars, a lot of Guardia Civil, a lot of police officers on the beat, or on motorbikes. That means people feel safe, not scared. That's the way it works, you know . . ."

Annika put her pen down on her pad. This wasn't going to make much of an article.

"Am I disappointing you?" the estate agent asked.

She laughed.

"Not me," she said. "My head of news, maybe. He wanted the headline 'Swedes Flee Costa del Sol.'"

"I don't think he's likely to be proved right," Rickard said. "So how are things going for the big papers these days—do they still pay for lunch?"

"Definitely," Annika said.

She fell asleep that afternoon. She was lying on the bed in her hotel room reading a Harlan Coben thriller when sleep swept her away. She dreamed about Kalle and Ellen: They were both missing, and she was searching for them in a sterile lunar landscape with no water or vegetation.

She felt incredibly thirsty when she woke up.

As she showered and got herself ready for the evening, she tried calling Nina Hoffman twice. The message from Telefonica didn't come back. The phone just rang and rang until the call was cut off automatically.

She called Carita and thanked her for being so great to work with, gave her the details for the invoice, and said she would be flying home the next morning.

"We can stay in touch, can't we?" Carita said. "Maybe you'll be down here again?"

Annika said, "Sure," remembering Patrik's series of articles.

She was standing outside the hotel in good time.

Niklas was almost half an hour late.

"Sorry, sorry," he said with a grin. "I'm starting to get a bit Spanish."

She got in the car without smiling. She didn't like being made to wait.

"Okay," she said, slamming the door. "How many arrests, how many suspects, where, when, and how were they arrested, what does the prosecutor say, and what about the defense?"

"First I'm going to make sure you get something to eat," he said, as he steered the car under the motorway.

She folded her arms on her chest.

"I'm not hungry," she said, then realized she was lying.

Niklas smiled at her. He turned off into a narrow street that led to an even narrower road that carried on up the mountainside. After just a couple of minutes the car was surrounded by total darkness, which made Annika both relieved and nervous. She couldn't see the drop from the edge of the twisting road, but the drawback was that the view ahead was almost as bad.

"Have you been through the stolen property in the thieves' truck?" Annika asked, holding onto the dashboard as the car went round a right-hand hairpin.

"Everything seems to be there apart from the safe."

Annika stared into the darkness to the side of the headlights' beams.

"Apart from the safe," she echoed. "Now where could that have got to?"

"If it was brought out in the back of the truck along with everything else there'd have been some evidence of that, but there was nothing."

"What sort of evidence would a safe leave?"

"It was cemented into a brick wall in the villa. The thieves knocked the wall down to get it out. There'd have been grit and cement dust and fragments of brick somewhere in the back of the truck if it had ever been in there."

"Maybe they put the safe in a bag?" Annika suggested.

Niklas looked away from the road to stare at her instead.

"Please, the road," Annika said, pointing in front of her.

The police officer sighed and looked back at the road again.

"It wasn't a huge safe," he said, "but it wasn't the sort of thing you could just chuck around. It would take two people to move it. I think there's another explanation."

They drove round a jutting cliff, and a moment later a built-up area appeared on the mountainside in front of them. Row after row of white houses clung to the slope, lit up by streetlamps and small neon signs. The glow from televisions flickered in the windows.

"Where's this?" Annika asked.

"Istán," Niklas Linde said.

"What-istan?"

"That's what it's called, the village. Istán. It means 'spring.' It was founded by the Moors, it's been here since the thirteenth century. I know the woman who runs the restaurant in the square."

They parked on a hill above the little town and walked slowly down through the cobbled streets. There was a slight wind, a mild breeze that smelled of herbs. Annika could see the lights of the coast twinkling in the distance, in another age, another world. The sound of running water followed them. There were drinking fountains dotted around, fed by water brought along underground channels from the springs up in the mountain.

Suddenly Annika stopped halfway down a steep slope.

"I know what happened to the safe," she said.

Niklas stopped a few steps below her, looked up at her, and smiled.

"Let's hear it."

"The first time we met you told me you'd found evidence of two vehicles and three people outside the Söderström family house. The third person didn't die in the truck. The third person wasn't interested in the stolen property, just the safe. The third person took it with them, in the other car."

"That's probably correct," Niklas said, walking on down the street, then pushing open a saloon-style door. He ushered Annika in ahead of him, and she stepped through and found herself in a brightly lit neighborhood bar.

A radiantly beautiful Spanish woman with swirling tresses and a low-cut top let out a happy cry when she caught sight of Niklas. She rushed over to him, put her hands on him, and kissed him warmly on both cheeks. Their Spanish sounded like the water in the channels running beneath the streets.

"This is a friend of mine, Annika," he said in English, and the woman turned to her. Her smile faded slightly.

"*Una mesa para dos,*" she said, spinning round and heading farther into the restaurant.

Annika and Niklas followed her.

They were shown to the table in the far corner. The woman lit a candle with a yellow Bic lighter, gave them two dog-eared menus in Spanish, and sailed off toward the bar.

"How well do you know her?" Annika asked.

The policeman's eyes twinkled.

"Fairly well," he said, then set to studying the menu.

Annika was feeling strangely subdued. She picked up the laminated menu and looked at the Spanish words without seeing them. She didn't like the beautiful Spanish woman.

"What's been happening in the search for Suzette?" she asked, trying to sound laid back and unconcerned.

"It's like she's been swallowed up by the ground. According to her mobile operator, her phone hasn't been switched on since last Thursday. Would you like me to order for you?"

Annika put the menu down on the tablecloth.

"*Por favor.*"

The police officer ordered a long list of small dishes that flowed out onto the table whenever the kitchen finished preparing them. Niklas drank beer, Annika *agua con gas*.

"Shall we talk about this drug raid?" she asked as the dishes started to empty. "I need some meat on the bones if I'm going to write a whole article."

Niklas picked at his teeth with a toothpick and thought for a few moments.

"If you tell me what happened to your finger," he said, pointing at her left hand.

She hesitated but saw no reason not to tell the truth.

"Two men dragged me into an alleyway and cut it open last winter," she said. "They told me not to snoop about in a story I was working on."

"Do you know who they were?"

She shook her head.

"Do you want me to find out for you? Catch them and beat them up?"

She smiled at him.

"Have you got a flash on that camera?" he asked.

"Of course."

He looked at his watch.

"Maybe you can come along on something, if you want," he said. "We're going to try to pick up one of the men later tonight. You'd have to stand well back and not show any identifiable police officers in your pictures."

Her pulse rate went up slightly.

"A raid?" she said. "Tonight?"

He leaned closer to her.

"Okay, this is how it is," he said, lowering his voice, even though they had to be the only people in the restaurant who understood Swedish.

"Greco, the drugs unit of the Spanish police, had been tracking two shipments of coke that were being delivered simultaneously to the harbor in Algeciras. They were both in refrigerated cargoes of fruit from South America: One was the melons in the Apits warehouse in La Campana, and the other was a container load of oranges from Argentina."

"And where are the oranges now?"

Niklas gave her a wry smile.

"Exactly," he said. "The oranges are on a lorry, on their way to Malmö."

"And you've switched the contents?" Annika said.

Niklas clenched his jaw.

"We've got a transmitter on the lorry, but we haven't been able to switch the cargo. It's a gamble. My colleagues in Greco in Málaga can locate the exact position of the lorry down to ten meters. The problem is that the prospective recipients are getting nervous. They know that half the shipment has been seized, and they think there's something dodgy about the other half."

"Okay," Annika said, opening a fresh page in her notepad. "Tell me what you want the article to say."

"That Greco had been following the impounded shipment for several months . . ."

"Remind me, what does Greco stand for again?"

Niklas Linde looked annoyed.

"Does that matter? They made their move when the cargo had been unloaded and was ready for distribution, which meant they could catch both the recipients and the suppliers."

"And when did this happen?"

"Early morning, Thursday, December 30."

"How?"

Niklas took a sip of beer and told her how the police had rented several units in the same *polígono* as the fruit warehouse in question. They followed the shipment from the moment it was unloaded in the large harbor in Algeciras, a city some way west of Marbella, until it arrived in La Campana by lorry. Officers from Greco were lying in wait in the rented units, with additional support from the riot police and police marksmen, and watched as the fruit was unloaded. They waited until the recipients showed up, then they made their move.

Annika was taking a lot of notes, writing quickly without looking up.

"How many arrests?"

"Five in the warehouse. The lorry driver was arrested in his home in Estepona later the same morning. Tonight we're going to pick up the last member of the gang, one of the minor players. He usually acts as a courier, he was supposed to be driving the shipment up to Malmö via Berlin."

Annika put her pen down.

"But how were they able to just unload a whole container full of cocaine and pretend it contained melons? Doesn't anyone check that sort of thing in customs?"

Niklas looked at her, then burst out laughing.

"The cocaine wasn't inside the container," he said. "That was full of melons. A hell of a lot of melons, several tons, in fact. You can't begin to imagine the smell."

"It was a refrigerated container, you said. That ought to keep them for at least a week."

The policeman pointed at her with a finger, like it was a pistol.

"Bull's-eye," he said. "It wasn't a refrigerated container. There were seven hundred kilos of cocaine inside the walls of the container instead of insulation."

"And all the paperwork was in order?"

"Pure as driven snow."

He glanced at his watch, then waved to the Spanish waitress. She sent one of the men behind the bar over with the bill.

"Let me," Annika said, taking out her credit card.

"Carmen only takes cash," Niklas Linde said.

"You're kidding," Annika said. "Her name's Carmen?"

He stood up, put his jacket on and grinned.

They walked back up the hill toward the car in silence. The sound of Spanish television, laughing voices, and the clatter of crockery followed them. The cacophony leaked out onto the pavement along with the light from tapas bars and open living-room windows. Two teenage boys on a moped passed them with just a few centimeters to spare, and four cats leaped up, startled, from a large bin. The wind was chilly now, and Annika wished she had brought a jacket.

"Are you cold?" Niklas Linde said, and before she had time to answer he had put his arm round her and pulled her toward him, stroking her upper arm with his other hand to warm her up.

She let herself be held, leaning into him, her hip bumping against his thigh with every step. The exhaust fumes of the moped lingered on the cobbles. He pulled her closer, and his steps became slower, until in the end he stopped completely. He turned to face her, with his arms round her shoulders. She let her own hands, which she had been holding folded to her chest, fall, then put them round his back, feeling their way over the rough cotton of his jacket, pulling him to her.

Yes, she thought. I want this.

He leaned forward and kissed her.

His mouth was warm and salty and tasted of garlic.

She realized that his leg had slid between her thighs.

Her breathing quickened, and she let go of him.

His eyes were twinkling.

"Shall we go and catch some bad guys?" he asked, taking a step back from her but keeping his arm round her shoulders, and they carried on walking.

She let one arm slide down his back and take hold of his waist. Their hips bumped against each other all the way up the long slope.

SATURDAY, JANUARY 8

The house was on a backstreet in the neighboring town of San Pedro. It was in a corner, beside a little square lined with orange trees, two stories high, originally white but discolored by damp and pollution. All the windows were covered by rusty black bars. The balcony on the upper floor was hung with toweling nappies put out to dry.

"The drug runner has children?" Annika asked in a low voice.

"He rents a room on the ground floor from the family that owns the house," Niklas replied, then left her in a doorway on the other side of the square. She pulled up the zip of the rough, over-sized jacket she had been lent.

She watched the police officer walk off slowly and silently along the pavement, toward his Spanish colleagues, who were gathered in a side street. The movement of his muscles was visible under his loose clothing.

He can have anyone he wants, she thought, and he knows it.

The suspected drug runner wasn't home. Right now he was in a nightclub called Dreamers down in Puerto Banús. He had himself informed the Spanish police of his whereabouts, albeit unwittingly, of course. He had called a woman named Betty and tried to persuade her to come down to Dreamers and meet him in the bar, but Betty was tired and cross and had rejected the offer. Because the officers from Greco had been bugging his mobile for four months, they knew perfectly well that Betty wouldn't go. She hated it when he called her up, drunk, from various bars and hangouts. It made her feel "cheap." She didn't think he showed her enough "respect."

Niklas had told her all this while they were sitting in the car outside one of Greco's safe houses, while the officers inside planned the impending arrest.

Annika pulled her hands up into the jacket sleeves and stamped her feet. She stared at the drug runner's window and thought about Betty.

Had they had sex in there? How had that made Betty feel? Valued and respected?

She stifled a yawn.

Her flight to Stockholm would be taking off in eight hours.

Then she heard stumbling footsteps approaching the square. They were a mixture of dragging and tottering, as if someone was trying hard not to fall.

She retreated deeper into the doorway and took out the camera. She switched it on, holding it with the lens pointing down. She had been given strict instructions not to test out the distance to the door in the darkness until the man had been arrested, because the red dot of the distance gauge could be mistaken for the laser sight on a rifle.

Then she saw a skinny person come stumbling down the street on the other side of the square. He was a fairly young man with spiked hair that looked almost blond in the faint light of the square. He took a few steps forward, then a couple to the side, seriously drunk. He stopped outside the door and swayed.

It was a good thing Betty had stayed at home.

He spent a long time fumbling with the key before he got it into the lock. Evidently he couldn't be bothered putting any lights on, because the door was about to close without any lights going on.

Then she saw a series of shadows emerge from the alleyways and streets around the house.

She raised her camera.

Several plainclothes police officers and two in uniform

reached the door just before it clicked shut. A moment later the drunk man was outside again with a Spanish policeman holding him under each arm. His feet were dragging along the ground, and his face showed an expression of total surprise. He kept twisting his head from one policeman to the other, then he started to protest in a pronounced Stockholm accent.

"What the fuck's all this? Eh? Come on, lads, what the fuck are you playing at?"

Annika touched the camera button lightly to get the image in focus. The man was sharply depicted in the middle of the picture, then she pressed the button down fully. The flash lit up the whole square for a sixteenth of a second. She waited a couple of seconds, then took another picture.

"What the fuck . . .? *Joder!*"

The drug runner had decided he didn't want to go with the policemen. He started waving his arms and kicking his legs, but to little effect.

"*Cabrones! Imbéciles!* Let go, for fuck's sake. . . . *Fucking hell!*"

A few moments later he was in the backseat of a guardia civil car, handcuffed, with one policeman beside him, one in front of him, and another behind the wheel.

The car disappeared down the road with a quiet rumble.

Niklas appeared beside her.

"You said the Swede had already been arrested," Annika said.

The police officer grinned.

"He is now," he said, then leaned over and kissed her.

His mouth was wonderful.

"What's his name?" Annika whispered at his teeth.

"Jocke Zarco Martinez. Are we going back to yours or mine?"

She pulled away and looked down at the camera.

"I'm flying home in a few hours."

"You can do a lot in a few hours."

She shook her head and looked up at him.

"No," she said.

He lowered his head for a moment, then looked up and laughed.

"Come on," he said. "I'll drive you back to your hotel."

He didn't hold her on the way back to the car.

They got in the BMW without a word, and drove in silence.

Far too soon he pulled up in front of the entrance.

"I wouldn't tell anyone," he said, looking straight ahead through the windscreen.

She looked at him.

"It's not that I don't want to."

He glanced at her.

"What is it, then?"

She decided to be completely honest.

"I daren't," she said. "It's been so long that I don't even know if I could."

He laughed again, raised his hand, and stroked her cheek.

"You don't have to worry," he said. "It's like riding a bike."

"How long are you going to be down here?"

"Don't know. I travel back and forth quite a bit. Why?"

She had been about to ask if he was on his way back to Sweden, where he lived when he was at home, if he had anyone waiting for him. If he would still be here if she was sent back down to write about Patrik's Costa Cocaine.

But she just picked up her bag, opened the door, and climbed out of the car.

When the taillights disappeared round the corner of El Corte Inglés she had to bite her lip to stop herself from crying.

She wrote a piece about the Swede's arrest, uploaded the photographs, sent it all off to Stockholm, and slept for two hours. Then she got to her feet again, packed her clothes and laptop, then went down to reception and paid for her and Lenita Söderström's rooms with her personal Visa card. She left a note for Lenita saying that she had gone back to Stockholm. Just in case anything happened, she left her mobile number again.

She pulled out onto the motorway, which was now practically empty of vehicles, drove past the roadworks and the big shopping center, La Cañada, and turned up onto the toll road.

Just before Torremolinos she passed a road accident. A lorry with French plates had turned over, spilling its load onto the carriageway, and she had to crawl past slowly on the hard shoulder. In the rearview mirror she could see a Muslim woman wailing and beating her hands on her knees. Then the woman vanished behind a lorry.

She arrived at the airport two and half hours before her flight.

She spent an hour and a quarter trying to find the car hire company's depot. She was sweating by the time she reached the check-in desk. In the security control they went through the whole of her bag, finding things that she'd completely forgotten about, including a shriveled, half-eaten apple and a letter opener with the advertising slogan "Evening Post—sharp and to the point." They took the letter opener off her, and forced her to put her lip gloss in a see-through plastic bag.

"Are you serious?" Annika asked, looking skeptically at the security guard when he handed her the little bag. "Do you really think I'm *not* going to blow the plane up just because my lip gloss is in here?"

"*No comprendo,*" the guard said.

"Exactly," Annika said, taking her deadly lip gloss and putting it straight back in her bag. "You really don't understand anything."

The plane took off almost on schedule, and she fell asleep at once.

She woke up at Arlanda when the wheels hit the runway. Her

Harlan Coben book was on the floor and the bottle of water she'd bought from Upper Crust in the departure lounge had leaked in the seat pocket in front.

Confused and slightly giddy she was swept out of the plane and into the terminal building, through deserted corridors, past the empty passport control, and off toward the baggage hall. She had to wait over an hour for her case.

It was dark by the time she finally emerged from the arrivals hall. Anxious snowflakes were dancing in the air, unsure whether to rise or fall. Taxi drivers from several independent companies threw themselves at her, trying to grab her case, but she snapped at them and struggled off with it toward a Taxi Stockholm car. Over the years she had tried to be open-minded and liberal, trying out all sorts of obscure little taxi firms, but after being shouted at and turfed out once too often because she wanted to pay by card or couldn't tell them the way to her destination, she had given up.

The Taxi Stockholm driver took her case, opened the door for her, then didn't say a word. Perfect.

She tried reading the evening papers in the backseat, but started to feel sick and gave up.

At five o'clock in the afternoon she unlocked the door to her as yet unfurnished flat. The rooms were big and black, and there was a faint hiss from an air vent somewhere.

She put her case and bag down on the floor and hurried round turning on all the lights in the flat. In every window she could see her own reflection, a hollow-eyed woman with unkempt hair and skinny arms.

She turned away from her many selves, threw herself down on the bed, and grabbed the phone. She dialed the head of news's direct number in the newsroom, and sighed quietly when Patrik answered.

"I thought Sjölander was supposed to be working," Annika said. "Isn't this your day off?"

"Just sorting out a few loose ends," he said. "What have you got?"

She shut her eyes and rested her forehead against the palm of her hand.

"I've been sitting in a plane all day, and got home three minutes ago. What do you think I've got?"

"The search for Suzette, you can check if anything's happened, can't you? Anything new about how the thieves died? A picture of the mother sitting on her missing daughter's bed hugging a stuffed toy?"

Her tiredness gave way to anger. She stood up beside the bed, holding the phone.

"At four o'clock this morning I sent an article and photographs of a Swedish citizen being arrested in a drugs raid in San Pedro, outside Marbella. I think I've filled my quota of exclusives on this particular day off. If you think your new job means you can treat me like some nineteen-year-old temp, you're seriously mistaken."

There was silence on the line.

"Hello?" Annika said.

"Just so you know," Patrik said, "I've got this call on speakerphone."

"Excellent," Annika said. "In that case, your friends can note that I'm taking next week off as time owing. I've been working twenty hours a day for five days in a row. I'll be in on Monday to put in a claim for expenses."

"What do you mean, expenses? Your ticket was bought for you."

"Fuck you," Annika said, and hung up.

She slumped onto the bed again, picked up the evening papers that she'd thrown on the floor, and leaned back against the pillows to read them.

Her piece about the raid was in the paper. It probably hadn't made it into the earlier regional edition, but Niklas had said that wouldn't matter.

She studied the pictures. They were certainly dramatic.

The two uniformed officers were in the foreground, the reflexive strips on their jackets shining like lasers in the flash. The Swede was waving his arms and kicking in protest, and his face was more or less obscured. Niklas had his face turned away and was pretty much unidentifiable.

The text was short and to the point, and said that the Spanish police had crushed a cocaine-smuggling operation shipping drugs from the Costa del Sol to large parts of northern Europe. She had listed the facts about the raid in La Campana, 700 kilos found in a warehouse, melons from Brazil. Last night's arrest was the final one pending; now the charges would be laid and the trials prepared.

She let the paper fall to her lap and wondered how she felt about writing an article to order like that.

Nothing much, she realized. There was always someone who stood to gain from a piece of journalism. The only difference this time was that she was fully aware of the manipulation, although of course she would never admit that to her bosses at the paper.

She looked through the rest of the paper. A UN helicopter had crashed in Nepal. Sweden's first bed-and-breakfast for nudists was due to open in Skåne. A singer with silicon breasts had turned down the opportunity to appear in the Swedish heats of the Eurovision Song Contest, which had led to crisis talks at Swedish Television last night.

She dropped the paper onto the floor and picked up the other evening paper.

The first thing that struck her when she reached the editorial was her own picture byline from the *Evening Post* and a portrait of Jimmy Halenius. Between them hovered the picture taken outside the Järnet restaurant.

"In the hands of power," the headline read.

The text was a piece of indignant bluster, full of insinuating questions such as "How much did they really have to drink?" and "Should those in power and those holding them to account really have an intimate relationship?" as well as "Did Halenius neglect his duties?"

She picked up the phone and called her editor in chief.

"Have you seen the opposition's editorial?" she asked without bothering to say hello.

"I've spoken to their editor in chief," Anders Schyman replied. "If they don't drop this now, we're going to lay siege to every bar in the vicinity of their offices and take pictures of all their reporters and reveal all their sources. I'll be replying in our editorial tomorrow. We will never reveal our sources, we will never surrender our expense receipts, and we will never go into any detail about what the two of you discussed."

"Good," Annika said.

"What did you discuss, by the way? And how much did you drink? And who the hell paid?"

She collapsed into a little ball.

"Okay," she said. "To take them one by one: None of your business, I drank water, and Halenius paid. Not his department."

"How do you know him?"

She hesitated for a moment.

"I grew up with his cousin."

"I heard you on the speakerphone a little while ago. You really should watch your language, you know."

The editor in chief hung up.

She stayed on the bed for a while, struggling against an almost overwhelming feeling of self-pity.

She did nothing but stand up for that fucking newspaper, and what did she get in return? Apart from demands, criticism, and public humiliation over her choice of dinner partner?

She cried for something like thirty seconds, then got up and went out into the hall for her suitcase. The bathroom was equipped with both a washing machine and a tumble dryer, so she emptied her case straight into the machine and started the quick-wash program. She took her laptop with her into the kitchen, plugged the modem into the phone socket, and prayed to God there was an Internet connection.

There was.

She sat down on one of the kitchen chairs and surfed out into cyberspace.

Apart from the usual disasters, gossip, and political squabbling, it didn't look like anything much had happened in the world.

Instead she went onto her Facebook profile.

She had eleven new messages.

One was from Amanda Andersson, one from Sandra Holgersson, two from Klara Evertsson-Hedberg, and seven from Polly Sandman.

So, all of Suzette's friends had replied to her. Her pulse quickened as she opened the most recent message, the one from Amanda.

"I think your a gutter reporter who likes wallowing in other people's mizery," she read.

"Learn to spell first," Annika said out loud, and clicked to open the next message, from Sandra.

"Do you really work for a newspaper? Can you get tickets for X Factor?"

For a moment she considered replying, then decided against it.

Klara was the financially minded sort. She offered to give an interview for 10,000 kronor. In her second message she lowered the fee to 500.

Annika didn't answer her either.

Polly was the literary type, as the seven messages suggested without her even opening them properly. There were poems and reflections and thoughts about Suzette, about school and boys and life in general. Annika read through them and then composed a reply.

"Dear Polly, what lovely poems and thoughts. Thanks for letting me read them. If you feel like writing anything longer, I know my newspaper runs a short-story competition for teenagers up to eighteen years old. I understand that you haven't heard anything from Suzette. If you do, please feel free to contact me again."

She signed off with both her first and last name, to maintain a professional tone. She was careful not to give her mobile number; she didn't want anyone shouting at her about her ethics, or asking about X Factor tickets either, for that matter.

She was about to shut down the laptop when her mobile rang.

The number was withheld and didn't show up on the screen.

"Annika? Hi, this is Nina Hoffman."

She stood up so quickly she hit her head on the lamp.

"Hello," she said, rubbing the bump. "Hello, Nina."

"You left a message on my voicemail a few days ago. It sounded urgent. Has something happened?"

Annika stopped the lamp from swinging with one hand and remembered the crackly Telefonica voice on Nina's mobile.

"Yes, I've tried calling you a few times. Have you been in Spain recently?"

"Er, yes, I've just had week's holiday on Tenerife. Why?"

"I went to see Julia and Alexander," Annika said, going out into the hall and over toward her bedroom. "We got to talking about you, and Julia told me something I didn't know."

Nina waited.

"Oh?" she said eventually.

Annika sat down on the bed.

"Filip Andersson is your brother," she said, and noticed that her heart was beating faster. "Why didn't you say something?"

"Like what?"

"And Yvonne Nordin was your sister. Why on earth didn't you say?"

"You mean I'm under some kind of obligation to tell you who I happen to be related to?"

Annika tried to focus. She could see Nina in front of her, the police uniform, the brown hair in a ponytail, the straight shoulders and stiff creases, the feeling of restrained power, her efficient calm that night when they stumbled upon the murder scene in Sankt Paulsgatan. *"Annika, get out of here. 1617 to Control, we have a code 23, possibly 24, and need reinforcements. I can see two, correction, three injured, possibly deceased . . ."*

"But we've talked about that night so many times," Annika said. "I kept going on about Filip Andersson, the murders, about the fact that I thought he might be innocent, about whether he knew David Lindholm. You listened to all my theories about David's women, Yvonne Nordin among them, you even helped me get hold of a photograph of her, and throughout all that you didn't say a word about the fact that they were your brother and sister. Don't you see how odd that looks?"

Nina was silent for a long while.

"Would you have mentioned it, if they'd been your brother and sister?"

"Of course I would have!"

"So if you had any criminals close to you, or if you yourself had committed a crime, you'd have told me all about it straight-away?"

"Absolutely."

"You've killed someone. Why haven't you ever mentioned that?"

Now it was Annika's turn to be silent.

"That's hardly relevant," she said at last.

"Yes, it is, in the same way that it's relevant that my siblings are criminals."

They sat for a while without saying anything.

"This changes everything, don't you see?" Annika said. "It feels like you've been deceiving me all along."

"Well, I haven't been," Nina said. "I've never lied to you."

"You must have known that David and Filip knew each other, for instance. How long for?"

Nina let out a sigh from the depths.

"They grew up together," she said. "David and Filip and Yvonne and little Veronica, they were more like brothers and sisters than anything else. More than they ever were with me."

Annika screwed her eyes shut and tried to fit the pieces in place.

David Lindholm, the most famous policeman in Sweden, married the girl from Södermanland, Julia Hensen, who grew up next door to her friend Nina Hoffman. David himself had grown up alongside Filip Andersson, who had two sisters, the insane killer Yvonne Nordin, and police officer Nina Hoffman, whose best friend Julia he went on to marry, even though he was simultaneously having an affair with Yvonne Nordin, and got her pregnant . . .

"How long had you known David Lindholm?" she asked.

"The first time I met David was when he came to give us a lecture at Police Academy."

"So you didn't grow up with him?"

"I suppose I must have bumped into him when I was little, and of course I knew who he was, but I didn't know him. Mum and I moved to Tenerife when I was three, and by that time Filip and Yvonne were already grown up. Then I ended up outside Valla when I was nine, and that's where I got to know Julia."

"You once told me," Annika said slowly, "that David came up

to you and Julia after that lecture at the Police Academy. Did he know who you were?"

"Obviously. I think he was extremely curious to see what had become of me."

"But he pretended to be more interested in Julia?"

"He didn't have to pretend. I mean, he went on to marry her."

There was a subtext of bitterness, unspoken, but it was there. Annika rubbed her head.

"The murders on Sankt Paulsgatan took place nearly five years ago. When did you realize that Filip and Yvonne were involved?"

"When Filip was arrested. That was the worst moment in my life."

"And Yvonne? She was the one who did it, after all. When did you realize that?"

"When Filip told me, after she was dead. But I hadn't spoken to Yvonne for years before that. I lost contact with her after the abortion. She withdrew, became a bit peculiar."

"The abortion?" Annika said, putting her hand on her forehead. "You mean when she aborted her and David's child?"

"The same time that Julia was pregnant with Alexander," Nina confirmed.

Then she fell silent for a few moments.

"It's not like you think," she said finally. "I never meant to hide anything, but my family and childhood are a bit of an open wound for me."

Annika didn't know what to say. She waited in silence.

When Nina went on, her voice sounded thin and distant.

"I really loved my mum, but she was hardly capable of looking after herself. Filip and Yvonne slipped away from her; she couldn't take care of them. I was lucky, because of course I had Julia's family. It's always felt like . . . like an obligation, somehow. As if I have some kind of duty to put everything right . . ."

Was that why you joined the police? Annika thought, but didn't say so out loud.

"Somewhere I believe in people's innate goodness," Nina continued, her voice stronger now. "I think everyone can change, if we're just given the chance. Mum tried, and it worked for a while, but she was too damaged for it to last in the long run . . ."

"Is your mum dead?" Annika asked cautiously.

"Nine years ago. She died the day after David and Julia got married. Now all the others are gone too, apart from Filip."

Annika was making an effort to keep up.

"You said there were four of them who were like a family?" she said. "David, Filip, Yvonne and . . . who was the fourth?"

"Little Veronica. Veronica Paulson. But she's dead too."

"Did you know her as well?"

Nina sighed deeply.

"Not exactly. She and her mum came to visit us on Tenerife a couple of times, but I haven't seen her since I moved back to Sweden."

"She can't have been that old. How did she die?"

Nina sounded surprised when she replied.

"But you've just been writing loads of articles about that. She was murdered a few days ago."

Everything around Annika stopped. There was total silence inside her head and time stood still.

"What do you mean?" she said, scarcely able to breathe.

"She married that ice hockey player," Nina said. "Sebastian Söderström."

PART 2

After Easter

THE LITTLE TROLL GIRL WITH THE MATCHES

––––––––––

She arrived at Gudagården with no shoes and wearing a tattered dress. The lady from the Child Welfare Commission shoved her out of the car. The gravel on the drive was sharp as glass beneath her feet.

"Curtsy to your foster mother and foster father," the lady said, driving her forward toward the wall of people.

She stared down at the ground. The people stared at her.

"She looks like a troll," Foster Mother said.

The lady kicked her on the back of her knee and forced her head down. Quick as a polecat she spun round and bit the lady on the hand, then she ran away across the gravel, cutting the skin on the soles of her feet.

Foster Father pulled her down from the haystack after night had fallen. She fell to the stone floor and landed hard on her hip.

"Let's see if we can't whip the Devil out of you," he said, raising his riding-crop.

And he beat her and beat her and beat her until the skin on her thighs and buttocks was in ribbons, then he blocked the door. She fell asleep in the hay and dreamed that she was lying on an anthill. The insects were busy eating their way into her legs and backside, constructing passageways under her skin, a whole society with paths and storerooms and nurseries and everything else the ants needed, everything that Sigrid had told her about the amazing life of ants.

When she woke up day had already broken. The hay had got stuck to the scabs on her legs. She knew she needed to wash.

She found a loose plank at the back of the hay shed. The hole was narrow. The hardest thing was getting her head through, but her body slid through like she was a little worm.

She had seen a lake out of the car window. It must be very close by.

She took a long detour round the farm. There was nobody in sight.

She found a small beach with white sand under a large oak. She got in the water, still wearing her dress and underwear. Her legs stung like fire.

A walleyed boy caught sight of her when she was creeping back toward the farm. He called for Foster Father, who came rushing out, his big boots flapping. He was quick, and she was weak with hunger and pain.

He tore her dress off and flayed the skin off her back as well.

"You are never, ever to run away from this farm again," Foster Father hissed in her ear. "If you do, I'll kill you."

But she ran away, and he beat her, and she ran away, and he beat her.

In the end he got tired of beating her, and then she stopped running away.

She was given a room in the loft, along with the baby swallows and wasps' nests. From the crack of dawn the swallow parents would start flying in and out, bringing food to their young, gathering the food in their own mouths and stomachs, and then vomiting it up for their young. Sigrid had told her about the amazing life of birds.

Sigrid had told her fairy tales as well. She had told her about other girls who also had a hard life, like the Little Match Girl.

"So the little girl wandered along with her naked little feet red and blue with cold. She was carrying a great pile of matches in an old apron and she held one bundle in her hand as she walked. No one had bought a thing from her the whole day, no one had given her a halfpenny; hungry and frozen, she went her way, looking so woebegone, poor little thing! The snowflakes fell upon her long fair hair that curled so prettily at the nape of her neck, but she certainly wasn't thinking about how nice she looked . . ."

The girl herself had no fair curls. She had black, unruly hair that the Child Welfare Committee had cut short, so short, to get rid of all the lice.

She wasn't a pretty girl, she was a little troll girl. She knew that because Foster Mother had told her. She was the Troll Girl with the matches, even though she hadn't actually sold matches but illicit home brew, and it had all been going so well, so well, until Mother ended up in prison and the Child Welfare Committee came to take her away.

At night she could see out through a crack in the roof, and once she saw a falling star.

The little match girl had also seen a falling star in the fairy tale.

"Her old granny, who was the only one that had been kind to her, but who was now dead, had said that when a star falls a soul goes up to God . . ."

She wondered who it was going up to heaven this time, and she clasped her hands together and prayed to the Lord: O Father, let it be Foster Father next time, and then Wall-Eye.

And she thought that one day she herself would be a grandmother, the sort who was kind to troll girls that nobody liked.

But as time passed and the darkness came, and the cold, and the harvest was brought in, and she thought her back would break, her prayers changed.

O Father, let it be me next time.

She repeated this prayer until the day the Princess came to the farm.

It was a wonderful day. The little Troll Girl had never seen anything so beautiful.

The Princess had blond curls that hung down to her waist, and a pale blue dress that swayed around her calves, and a doll like a fairy in her arms.

But Foster Father, who saw the temptations of the Devil in everything that was pure and loveable and beautiful, tore the dress off the girl, and her coat with the fur collar, and the lovely doll, and poured paraffin over the lot, and as the flames rose up into the autumn sky he screamed that the sinner must burn in hell.

The little Troll Girl was standing right at the back, watching in amazement at the Princess's despair. She lay on the gravel drive weeping so hard that she was shaking, in just her vest and pants, and her hair tumbled across the gravel, until Wall-Eye walked up and kicked her, and Foster Mother grabbed her by the arm and dragged her inside the house.

They installed another bed in the loft.

The Princess looked scared and looked at the little Troll Girl and said something to Foster Mother in a language she didn't understand, and Foster Mother replied in the same language.

Then Foster Mother came over with her stone face and said to the little Troll Girl:

"You leave her alone, do you hear? You're a bit simple in the head, and you don't say a word."

But that very first night the little Troll Girl got into bed next to the Princess and kept her warm when she was shaking, and told her fairy tales that Sigrid had taught her by heart, about the Ugly Duckling and Thumbelina and the Little Match Girl, and the Princess lay there, clear-eyed, listening, and that was how she learned Swedish.

SUPREME COURT REPORT

Case no. Ö 3490-11
Stockholm, April 26

PLAINTIFF
Filip Andersson
Representation: Sven-Göran Olin, barrister

OPPOSING
Prosecutor's Office

CASE
Appeal for retrial regarding murder and other convictions

SUPREME COURT VERDICT

*The Supreme Court authorizes a retrial in Stockholm
Appeal Court case no. Ö 9487-01, and orders that this case
be reconsidered by the appeal court.*

The Supreme Court's decision to suspend sentence stands.

The rain was beating against the windows.

Annika was standing in the kitchen stirring a saucepan of hot chocolate. Under the grill two slices of bread with tomato and cheese were toasting, one with ham and one without. The cheese was spitting ominously, and she took the saucepan off the ceramic hob and pulled the grill pan out.

Another thirty seconds.

She peeled two mandarins and opened two small pots of coconut yogurt. She took the toasted sandwiches out and put them on separate plates, then the fruit and yogurts. She put the plates on the kitchen table, poured the hot chocolate into two mugs, one red, one blue, then went out through the windowless living room toward the children's rooms.

Ellen still slept with her thumb in her mouth. Thomas was seriously worried about that and kept saying the little girl would have to have braces when she was bigger, but Annika found it hard to feel worried. There would be worse things to wrestle with when the children reached their teens. Having braces wouldn't count as a major disaster.

She crept into bed beside the little girl, took her in her arms, and snuffled her neck.

"Darling," she whispered. "It time to wake up now, it's a new day."

The girl stretched like a cat, reaching the ends of the bed. She yawned loudly, then curled up into a little ball beside her mother.

"I've made breakfast for you," Annika said, stroking the hair from her daughter's forehead.

"Mmm," the little girl said. "Coconut yogurt?"

"And toasted sandwiches," Annika said. "And hot chocolate. Don't go back to sleep, or it'll get cold."

"Mmm," Ellen said, as her thumb drifted into her mouth again. Annika pulled it and it came out with a little plop.

"You know what Daddy says about your teeth," she said.

"Daddy doesn't live here," the little girl said, turning away, still curled into a little ball.

Annika got out of the bed and went in to see Kalle.

"Hello, little man," she said. "Are you wide awake or still tired?"

"Tired," the boy said, and yawned noisily.

"There's a toasted sandwich for you in the kitchen," she said, pulling him to her.

The boy hugged her back; he was warm and a bit clammy.

"Has it got ham on?" he asked.

"Not on yours," she said.

"Good," he said.

She kissed him on his forehead, hair, and ear, laughing when he pretended to fend her off, then went back in to Ellen, who had fallen asleep again.

"Come on, you," she said, shaking her gently. "Your hot chocolate's getting cold."

"Carry me," the child said, holding her arms out.

She lifted the little body up in a single swift movement, spun round on the wooden floor with her, then jumped out into the kitchen with her feet together. Her daughter was laughing. Annika put her down on one of the four chairs round the table. Kalle stumbled into the kitchen in the pajamas that were too big for him, sleepy and half blind. Annika steered him to the table, pulled out his chair, and tucked him in at the table.

Their morning rituals had their foundation in her fears about how vulnerable the children were. She wanted to wrap them up in something pink and fuzzy, force the world around them to show them mercy. If she gave them enough love and confidence during the first hour of the day, she liked to imagine that it gave them some sort of protection, a confidence that would make them less susceptible to the evil and cruelty of the world.

Now they were sitting at the kitchen table in their pajamas, eating their toasted sandwiches and licking the spoons of coconut yogurt and eating pieces of mandarin. She herself was drinking a mug of coffee. Seeing them sitting there, so unaware of their own vulnerability, so open and malleable, was almost too much for her, sometimes she had to turn away and go and do the washing up or wipe the worktop so that her chest didn't burst.

"Daddy's going away," Kalle said, pushing the empty yogurt pot aside. "He's going to Málaga and we're going to stay with Sophia."

Annika stared at the wall.

"Yes," she said, "I know."

"Why can't we stay with you, Mummy?" the boy said. "I don't want to be with her, I want to be with you."

She stroked his hair, and he leaned back instinctively and pushed her hand away. He was a big boy now.

"It's Daddy's week," she said. "You know that. And I have to go to work too. I'm going to Málaga as well."

"Are you going to work with Daddy?" Kalle asked in surprise.

"No, not really. We're just going to be in the same place."

"Why can't we come?"

"Daddy and I are both going there to work, just not together. We've got different jobs, you know that."

She stared down into her mug of coffee and clenched her jaw. She didn't want to show how furious she was about Thomas's decision to leave the children with Sophia while he went away on business.

Then she realized that Ellen was sitting quite motionless. The girl was holding her spoon completely still on her plate. She looked down at the toasted sandwich and the cheese that had gone cold and solid. Her little body started to shake with sobs.

"Oh, darling, what is it?"

She took her daughter in her arms and rocked her slowly. The little girl didn't say anything, just curled up into a fetal position and put her thumb in her mouth. Annika felt reality seeping into the kitchen and clutched the child tighter, fighting to maintain the illusion of warmth and love.

"Daddy's going to pick you up today," she said. "He'll be at home with you tonight, and if you eat your tea quickly you might have time to watch a film together afterward."

"*Spiderman!*" Kalle said, lighting up.

"That might be a bit too rough for Ellen," Annika said. "But you could take *Desmond and the Swamp Barbarians* with you, what do you say?"

"But we've seen that," Kalle said.

"It's so good it's worth watching lots of times," Annika said, and blew into Ellen's hair. "Then you'll be staying with Sophia on Tuesday, Wednesday, and Thursday, and on Friday Grandma and Grandad are going to come and take you out to the island, and then you can play with Zico, and then on the day before May Day Daddy will be home, and on Monday I'll pick you up from school and you'll be able to tell me all about what you've been doing, won't you?"

"She's horrid," Ellen said, wiping her nose on Annika's T-shirt.

"No, she isn't," Annika said, feeling the hypocrisy echo through her body. "Sophia's really nice. She likes you ever such a lot, and she's very pleased that she's going to be able to look after you."

"She only likes Daddy," Kalle said.

Annika could feel panic building. She wiped her daughter's nose with a bit of kitchen roll and stared out at the persistent rain.

At certain moments everything she said was a lie. She lied to justify her own choices in life, making the children pay the price for her own failures, dragging them between one home and the other. But instead of two homes they had none; instead of two complete parents they had two mutilated halves.

She had to bite her lip to stop herself crying.

"I know it's hard," she said. "I miss you too when you're not with me."

"Why can't we be with you all the time?" Kalle asked.

"I want to be with you all the time," Ellen said, clinging to Annika's neck so hard she had trouble breathing. Gently she loosened the girl's arms.

"All children have a mummy and daddy," Annika said, "and the best thing for children is to grow up with both of them, but if that isn't possible people have to find another way . . ."

Kalle was looking at her obstinately.

"Why do only the grown-ups get to decide?" he said. "Why aren't children allowed to make the decisions?"

She swallowed her pain and smiled at him.

"When you get bigger you can make your own decisions."

"I'm big now."

"You're eight years old. That's not really that big."

"When's big, then?"

"Big enough to decide where to live? When you're twelve, maybe."

The boy slumped.

"That's four more years."

He'd learned to subtract.

"I don't want to stay with Sophia," Ellen said.

Annika looked at the time, then stood up, still holding her daughter in her arms.

"Okay, leave your sandwiches, I'll deal with them later. Kalle, off you go and get dressed. Ellen, go and put on the clothes we picked out last night. You've got your bags packed, haven't you? You've got everything you're going to need?"

The children wandered off into the hall and off to their rooms.

Annika stood in her minimalist kitchen and watched them go, feeling her heartbeat burning in her veins like acid.

They managed to leave with a quarter of an hour to spare. Annika knew that she was a fascist when it came to punctuality, a characteristic that had been accentuated during her marriage to Thomas, seeing as he was a hopeless optimist when it came to timing.

Having fifteen minutes in hand gave them time to sing as they walked. To stop and look in shop windows and pick out things they would like. To buy two packs of sweets at the kiosk on Kungsholmstorg and promise, promise, promise not to open them before the film that evening.

The rain had eased and almost stopped. It was chilly, just a few degrees above freezing, but there was no wind. The clouds were resting thick and heavy on the rooftops and spires, the streets became canyons where you could breathe pretty much okay. Some of the pink fuzziness returned, some of the defenses strengthened again.

Annika had the children's overnight bags over her shoulders, plus her own heavy bag with her papers and laptop. There were more and more things that had to go with the children when they shuttled between homes, and up to now Annika hadn't made them choose what to leave behind. It was no longer enough just to move new Poppy and new Chicken for the children to feel at home (old Chicken and Poppy had gone up in flames in Vinterviksvägen); now there were the favorite jeans and favorite jackets and best shoes and a few films and books that also had to go with them.

Annika dropped Kalle off in the school playground with a quick good-bye hug.

"See you in a week's time. I'll pick you up as usual from after-school club, okay?"

The boy nodded and ran off.

Then she and Ellen went off to the after-school club and left the heavy bag containing all Kalle's things on the shelf marked with his name.

"Can you carry me?" Ellen asked, holding her arms up.

"No," Annika said, adjusting Ellen's hat. "You're too heavy, you're a big girl now. Here, hold my hand."

They walked side by side through the underpass that connected the south and north of the island. Ellen was frowning as if she were thinking really hard about something.

"Mummy," she said, looking up at Annika as they passed the City Boule club. "Will I be a mummy one day?"

"Maybe," Annika said. "If you want to."

The child thought for a few moments.

"But," she said, "if I'm a mummy, what will you be?"

"I'd still be your mummy, but I'd be a grandma as well. For your children."

Ellen nodded thoughtfully.

"That's right," she said. "And then I'll get old, and then you'll be little again, and then I'll be your mummy."

"Will you?" Annika said in surprise.

"Because when I get old, you'll be dead, and then you'll come back."

"Ah," Annika said.

She had a child who believed in reincarnation.

They emerged into the gray daylight next to the Hotel Amaranten and walked down Pipersgatan toward the preschool in the White House, slipping in past the entrance to Radio Stockholm and making their way down to the third floor. Annika's shoulders were aching when she finally put the heavy bag down on Ellen's shelf.

The little girl took off her outdoor clothes, her scarf and boots and overalls. Then she put on her slippers that looked like mice and adjusted her skirt.

"I want you to have a really lovely time until I see you next Monday," Annika said, leaning over and hugging her daughter.

Ellen nodded. Her tears from earlier that morning were forgotten.

"Mummy?" she said. "Isn't it funny? God, he exists, but he's invisible. But Father Christmas, he's visible, but he doesn't exist."

Then she ran off to assembly.

The clouds had lifted a little and were now hovering a few meters above the rooftops. It felt as though Annika hadn't seen blue sky for several weeks.

In February Sweden had been hit by record-breaking high temperatures. Snowdrops and crocuses came into bloom all the way up in Ångermanland, but then the cold returned. March had been cold and windy, with several snowstorms. Eight people froze to death in Jämtland when a bus got stranded in the snow outside Trätgärde. On one of the weeks when Thomas had the children she was sent up to Östersund to write about the "City of Death," but otherwise she had been in Stockholm. She had hunkered down, running between home, school, and the newsroom, and hadn't had time for anything but everyday matters.

She didn't mind. Having a functional life with the children and work and flat wasn't something to take for granted.

She went down the hill at the end of Barnhusbron, breathing the exhaust fumes of Fleminggatan into her lungs. She jumped on a number 1 bus out toward Stora Essingen, and managed to get a seat halfway through the journey.

She reached the main entrance of the newspaper's offices at twenty past nine. She stopped at the bus stop for a few moments, looking in through the gates of the Russian Embassy on the other side of the road. A guard wearing a hat with earmuffs was standing by the gate stamping his feet and looking frozen. He couldn't be a day over twenty.

Does anyone ever really appreciate how fortunate they are? she wondered as she went into the building.

She always used to try to sneak into the newsroom without being noticed, walking with her head down and her shoulders hunched, slipping off toward the desk used by the day-shift reporters with her back to everyone. Then she would try to come up with something to fill her own schedule, a story to chase up, an old article to reexamine.

Now, in this new age, that sort of thing was just a waste of effort.

Patrik always had a long list of things for her to go through when she arrived at work. It could be anything from rewrites of articles about British nurses who had set about systematically murdering their patients, to interviews with football stars who had just had their second child. As soon as the head of news caught sight of her over by the caretaker's desk, he would set off toward her. She usually found herself with a whole bundle of notes in her hand before she had even had time to take her jacket off.

The children's sense of calm, which came from their inability to feel stressed, was still somewhere within her as she stepped into the newsroom and saw him slam the phone down and come racing toward her.

"Hello, Berit," she said as she headed for the chair opposite her colleague.

"The Costa Cocaine," Patrik yelled. "We need to sketch the outline of the series."

She brushed the hair from her face and took a deep breath.

"Looks like it's time to go traveling again," Berit said, glancing up over her reading glasses before going back to her morning paper.

Annika put her bag down at her place at the news desk, took off her jacket, and pulled her chair out.

"This is what we're going to do," Patrik said, sitting down on her desk with a handwritten sheet of paper in his hand. "Four human interest articles, two factual pieces, we'll start with the human stuff . . ."

He left a dramatic pause and let his hand outline the imaginary headline in front of him.

"One: 'Costa del Sol, Europe's money-laundering machine—where dirty money comes out clean.' Gibraltar, down there on the Costa del Sol, is apparently a real tax haven. You'll have to find a Swedish solicitor in Gibraltar who can explain how you turn drug money into reputable business profits."

Annika took out her pen and notepad and started making notes.

"Two: 'Cocaine parties in Europe's Beverly Hills—the yachts, luxury cars, jet-set lifestyle.' You'll need to dig out a young Swedish girl to talk about drug-fueled parties in Puerto Banús. Ideally she'll have been arrested in a drug raid and bitterly regret what she's done. Breast implants would be an advantage."

Annika looked up.

"How important are the breasts?"

Patrik lost his train of thought and lowered his hand.

"What? How do you mean?"

"On the priority list. How important are the breasts compared with, say, how much she regrets her jet-set lifestyle?"

The head of news shuffled on the desk in annoyance.

"You'll have to make a decision on that when you get there. Three: 'My life as a drug-runner.' Get in touch with that Swedish bloke in prison in Málaga and get him to talk about being a drug runner."

Jocke Martinez, Annika wrote in her pad, she remembered his name.

Niklas Linde had kissed her as he said it.

"Four: 'The hero who's going to put a stop to the money laundering.' There's a seminar on international financial crime starting in Málaga tomorrow, Wednesday, and the Swedish government's going to be represented by some civil servant who's supposed to bring back everything he's learned to Stockholm. Dig him out and do some sort of glamorous article about him and how vital his work is."

Annika put her pen down.

"That could be tricky," she said.

Patrik stared at her.

"Of all the possible protests I expected to hear, this one was way down at the bottom of the list."

"Your heroic Swede is my ex-husband," Annika said. "I know you think incest is good, especially if it's kept within the family, but this feels a bit much."

"There must be someone else, some Swedish policeman down there or something, some liaison person . . ."

She looked down at the desk and forced her voice to sound neutral.

"He's there incognito," she said.

"There's usually someone there in a official capacity."

"He's Norwegian."

Patrik stood up, irritated.

"God, it's all getting fucking complicated. The factual articles are easy: 'This is how the drug trade works.' You'll need to cover production, transport, smuggling routes, distribution, and sales, but don't write too much. Keep it short and snappy. And then the second one: 'How money laundering works.' You describe the tax haven, the methods, the companies. Same thing there, short and sharp. You'll have Lotta with you, so we get some pictures that are actually publishable."

He dropped a bundle of printouts in front of her computer.

"Plane tickets and hotel rooms?" Annika asked.

"You'll get the plane tickets by email today. You'll have to sort out rooms when you get there. Find somewhere cheap this time."

"What about the gas murders?" Annika asked. "Suzette's still missing. The third killer is still on the loose, the safe hasn't been found."

"That story's dead," Patrik said.

"A missing girl?" Annika said, realizing that her voice sounded animated. "How can the story be dead?"

"She was hardly a girl, she was a fucking *emo*. Just drop it."

Annika gulped hard. He wasn't worth arguing with.

"Who's Lotta?" she asked instead.

"New photographer, a temp," Patrik said, walking back to his desk.

The chair of the local journalists' union, Eva-Britt Qvist, came marching across the newsroom, heading straight for Annika.

"Oh, what does she want?" Annika whispered to Berit, who shrugged.

"Annika," Eva-Britt said. "I want a word with you."

"Sure," Annika said. "What about?"

The union rep held a printout toward Annika, and she took it and saw that it was the same article that she had at the top of her bundle of printouts.

"Swedish government prepares to get tough on money laundering," she read, then lowered the sheet. "Yes, and?"

"This article has been written to order at the request of the Ministry of Justice," Eva-Britt said. "We really have to make sure that this newspaper doesn't become an uncritical mouthpiece for government propaganda."

Annika raised her eyebrows.

"But Eva-Britt," she said. "Surely you don't think I look like a megaphone?"

The union rep blushed.

"Well, someone has to try to maintain the ethical rules," she said, and grabbed the printout.

"This is a good and important series of articles," Annika said. "It puts a new perspective on the drug trade in Sweden, shows how global finance and international crime affect us here."

"In that case, why aren't we doing it on our own initiative? Why let the Justice Ministry commission it?"

"They're just opening doors for us. As a reporter out in the field, you need friends you can call on. You know that as well as I do."

Berit pulled a face behind Eva-Britt's back: That one hit its target. The fact was that Eva-Britt had never worked as a journalist, and that was a particularly sore point. She'd started in the archive and then worked her way up to become a secretary, before being elected union rep.

She turned on her heel and sailed off through the newsroom.

"I thought you had serious doubts about this series of articles?" Berit said.

Annika smiled.

"I've changed my mind," she said, logging into the national database. "What are you working on today?"

"The Supreme Court has granted Filip Andersson's right to appeal," Berit said. "I suppose I'll have to put together a short piece about that."

Annika lifted her head from her screen and looked up at her colleague.

"Why do you sound so skeptical?"

Berit hesitated.

"I don't know," she said. "I just don't think he's innocent. I think he did carry out those murders."

"You can't mean that," Annika said, stopping with her fingers poised above her keyboard. "They've identified Yvonne Nordin's fingerprints and DNA at the crime scene, they found the meat cleaver buried behind her cottage, right where Filip Andersson said it would be. Filip's description of how Yvonne shot the victims in the legs fits as well. How can you doubt that?"

Berit took of her reading glasses and looked at Annika.

"It could just as easily have been Filip who buried the meat cleaver. And the fact that he knew about the shots could be because he was the one who fired them."

"But it still doesn't make sense," Annika said. "He refused to tell the truth while Yvonne was alive, that would have meant signing his own death warrant. But as soon as she was gone he could tell the truth."

"Or else he could begin to lie," Berit said.

Annika shook her head.

"It was Yvonne," Annika said. "It was Yvonne who killed David and kidnapped Alexander. And it was Yvonne who killed those people on Sankt Paulsgatan . . ."

She stopped herself and swallowed.

"Remind me, they never found the amputated body parts, did they?"

Berit sighed and put her reading glasses back on.

"Two hands and a foot are still missing," she said, picking up the phone to call the Supreme Court.

Annika stared off toward Sports, and the image from Sankt Paulsgatan emerged from her memory.

Nina Hoffman had been first up the stairs, then Julia, and lastly Annika, first one floor, then another.

Annika had stopped on the stairs, but she still saw the scene.

Her memory was dominated by the smell, sweet and heavy and thick. In the fragmented images she couldn't see any blue-trousered police legs in the way, just the dying woman, the blood on the walls, the arm without a hand. The woman, who was really little more than a girl, had crawled out into the stairwell, blood pumping from the stump of her arm, pouring over the floor and onto the stairs, splashing up at the walls. The blood bright red, the walls yellow. Her hair was dark and her skull had been smashed in, white fragments visible through her thick hair. Julia had thrown up in a window alcove, and Nina had driven Annika out onto the street with the words *"Get out of here!"*

Annika shuddered.

She turned back to her screen, and went into the national ID database. She selected Gender: male, Name: Joakim Martinez, Check phonetic spellings: yes.

One result, a young man in the south of Sweden who didn't call himself Joakim and who was eighteen years old. It couldn't be him.

She blinked at the screen.

There must be something wrong. Every Swede was in this database, the official national register. Either Niklas Linde had got the wrong name for the drug runner, or else he wasn't a Swedish citizen.

She tried male and Martinez.

Too many results (820). Refine search.

She screwed her eyes shut.

Niklas had mentioned another name, a middle name, hadn't he?

Jocke Something Martinez.

Damn, why hadn't she written it down?

"Are we going back to yours or mine?" he had asked, then kissed her, and that was when he had said the name.

The whole name.

Jocke Zarco Martinez?

Could that be it? How was that spelled?

She tried "male" and "Zarco Martinez."

Two results, but the first was completely clean.

Johan Manolo Zarco Martinez, twenty-six years old, registered in Skärholmen in the south of Stockholm, *deregistered.*

She leaned toward the screen.

Deregistered?

She clicked to bring up the man's full details.

"This individual has emigrated or been transferred to the register of untraceable persons."

Of course. He'd emigrated to Spain, and his name wasn't Joakim but Johan.

Then she was struck by a thought from a dusty corner of her unconscious. She stared at the screen.

Zarco Martinez.

She'd seen that name before. Not heard it, because she didn't know how it was pronounced, Sarco or Zharco or Charco, but she'd seen it on a screen, just like now. She leaned closer. She was quite sure of it.

Zarco Martinez, Zarco Martinez. When, where, how?

She couldn't think of anything, and let it go.

How was she going to get in touch with Johan Manolo Zarco Martinez in some Spanish prison? Through his lawyer? And what might their name be?

She took a deep breath and smiled.

She took out her mobile and opened the address book.

Niklas Linde, Spain.

She loosened her shoulders, then pressed *Call*.

He answered at once.

"Hello," she said in a high-pitched voice. "It's Annika. Annika Bengtzon, from the *Evening Post* in . . ."

"Hi, Annika," he said easily. "How are things?"

"Oh, fine, thanks, how about you?"

"The sun's shiny, and I'm bright-eyed and bushy-tailed."

"Are you in Spain, by any chance?"

"Puerto Banús, baby."

"Great, because there's something I need help with."

"Oh, I see, what?"

She could hear laughter and the rattle of crockery in the background. She could see him before her, suntanned and in a loose sports shirt, sunglasses, and stubble.

"That bloke," she said, "the one who was arrested that night in San Pedro . . ."

"When you didn't want to play?"

She felt her face glowing and lowered her face toward the keyboard.

"Hmm, that's right," she said. "His name is Johan Manolo Zarco Martinez, isn't it?"

"Absolutely right."

"I'd like to interview him."

An espresso machine was making a noise somewhere behind Niklas down there in the sun. The police officer waited for it to stop. There was the sound of wind down the mobile. So he was outside. It was probably hot, the wind warm and dry.

"That's going to be tricky," he said. "He's in prison in Málaga, and I presume you're in Stockholm."

"I'm coming down tomorrow," Annika said, suddenly blushing even more furiously when she heard Niklas laughing.

"Really, that's interesting," he said.

"Is he under any restrictions, or can he have visitors?"

"I think the restrictions have been lifted. He's elated. Unfortunately he doesn't know very much. He's spilled the beans on the rest of the gang who are already under arrest, but he hasn't told us anything new."

"Do you think he'd talk to the *Evening Post*?"

Annika heard a woman's voice say something quietly in Spanish close to Niklas's mobile. The police officer replied, "*vale*" and "*hasta luego*." Then she heard something that sounded like a kiss.

She put her hands over her eyes.

"I doubt he'd want to be depicted as the grass of the gang, if I can put it like that," the police officer said lightly when the woman had gone.

Annika looked at the time. Was he eating breakfast? Just having coffee? Who was the woman? Something serious, or just for the night?

"I'm not expecting any long confessional," Annika said, making an effort to sound professional. "I want to conduct a personal interview with him, about how he ended up in this position, about his life on the Costa del Sol . . ."

"I can check with his lawyer, if you like," Niklas said. "When are you coming down? Do you want to be picked up at the airport?"

She had to exert herself not to sound too happy.

"Thanks, but don't worry," she said. "I'll be heading straight to the international seminar about money laundering in Málaga. There's some sort of press conference at the Palacio de Congresos at two o'clock . . ."

"Oh, okay, then I'll see you there. I'm going as well."

She felt a peculiar sensation in her stomach.

"Great," she said. "Maybe you could help with a few other things as well. Do you know if there's a Swedish lawyer or solicitor of some sort in Gibraltar who could explain how dirty drugs money gets turned into clean business profits? Or some Swedish girl with silicon tits who'd like to tell me all about her crazy jet-set life in Puerto Banús?"

"The lawyer might be difficult, but I ought to be able to find you a few girls. How important are the breasts?"

"Absolutely vital."

"Splendid, consider it done," he said and laughed.

She smiled down the phone.

"See you tomorrow," he said, and ended the call.

He was going to be there. She was going to see him. He'd offered to pick her up from the airport. Maybe he'd kiss her again.

"Earth calling Annika," Berit said, waving a hand in front of her face. "Who was that you were talking to?"

Annika cleared her throat and hurriedly shuffled a pile of papers.

"A policeman in Málaga," she said.

"Knut Garen?" Berit asked in surprise.

"No," Annika said. "His Swedish colleague."

Berit looked at her intently over the top of her glasses.

"Policemen are usually good in bed," she said. "It's something to do with how masculine they are, it's all so unquestionable, somehow. Same thing with senior ranks in the armed forces."

Annika realized her jaw must have dropped.

"Just a little tip," Berit said, then went back to her computer screen.

Annika wrote an article about a man who had sex with a bicycle, a note about a miracle wrinkle cream from Britain that had just gone on sale in Sweden, and then she did a quick follow-up piece about a company director who had just been acquitted of aggravated tax avoidance in the Court of Appeal.

"This just goes to prove what I've been saying all along," the former executive thundered. "I'm completely innocent! This verdict proves it!"

"Well," Annika said, "it doesn't really. It just means that the evidence wasn't sufficient to secure a conviction. There's a significant difference."

She ate a baguette with Camembert cheese and ham for her lunch and drank two cups of coffee from the cafetière that she and Berit had clubbed together to buy for themselves.

She checked out a rumor that a famous television celebrity had hit his girlfriend. Both the girlfriend and the celebrity were denying it vehemently. Annika drew the conclusion that the rumor was perfectly true but let it go.

A security van was robbed on Sveavägen in the center of Stockholm.

A fourteen-year-old was raped by her coach.

A high-jump star said something nasty about a long-jump star. The long-jump star replied with something even nastier.

This last item was deemed to be the most important thing that had happened all day, and was given a huge amount of space on the website. People were encouraged to write in and comment on the "star quarrel," and were asked to tick a box and vote for which one they supported, and could email in their best pictures of the stars, and were asked to suggest other sports stars who could do with a serious dressing down.

Once Patrik had gone off to the editorial conference and was unable to throw any more notes in her direction for a while, she took the opportunity to read up about money laundering on the Costa del Sol.

She found a fresh article from one of the morning papers in the archive. It was about "Operation White Whale," described as the largest police crackdown in Spain to date against international money laundering and the mafia behind it. After eighteen months' surveillance and bugging the police had raided several locations on the Costa del Sol, according to the paper. More than forty people had been arrested: Spaniards, Moroccans, Russians, Ukrainians, Frenchmen, and Finns. Seven of them were lawyers, and three public clerks. A Russian oil company was also involved. They had seized 251 apartments and villas, forty-two luxury cars, two planes, a luxury yacht, as well as numerous works of art and jewelry. The amount of money that had been laundered was estimated to be at least a quarter of a billion euros, more than two billion kronor, thanks to fake companies in various tax havens, mainly Gibraltar. The money had then been filtered back into Spain and invested in construction and property companies on the Costa del Sol, described as "the biggest tourist paradise in Europe, and its hottest property market."

The spider at the center of the money laundering and fake

companies was said to be a firm of solicitors in Marbella. Its founder had taken care of the legal side of things and the formalities surrounding the establishment of the companies, including finding stooges to run them.

She googled a bit more and found a company at Stureplan, in the center of Stockholm, specializing in "taxation law for the global economy." It explained to her why Gibraltar in particular was so practical for "international investors."

Companies in Gibraltar had been free from taxation since 1967, she read. When Spain joined the EU in 1985, the number of companies registered there exploded. The regulations were tailor-made for foreign proprietors who didn't want anyone to know what was going on.

Annika got up restlessly, wondering at the amount of effort these people were prepared to put in. She fetched another cup of coffee.

She called Carita but reached the interpreter's cheery trilingual voicemail. Annika left a message asking if Carita would be available to interpret for her for the rest of the week.

Then she printed out maps of the Costa del Sol, and took the virtual tour of the Palacio de Ferias y Congresos de Málaga, the congress hall that would be the venue for the press conference, and booked two rooms at the Hotel Pyr, which seemed to be the cheapest on the Costa del Sol.

She stopped and wondered where all the people attending the conference would be staying, and what plane they would be taking.

Finally she looked up break-ins involving gas, which she had learned were called *robos con escalamiento,* as well as *nueva andalucía* and *soederstrom.*

Nothing new had been written about the gassing or the dead family in the Spanish papers.

She packed her laptop away and left the newsroom with Berit at quarter past five.

"Do you know who Lotta is?" she asked as they emerged from the lift on the ground floor.

"The temp photographer? Pale and blond, the artistic type."

Annika groaned.

"I've never worked with her," Berit added quickly. "She might be efficient and focused on news."

"In the best of all possible worlds," Annika said.

They went their separate ways outside the main entrance. Berit turned right toward the garage, Annika headed left toward the bus stop. Her mobile rang just as the number 1 bus pulled up at the pavement.

"Annika? Hi, this is Julia."

Julia Lindholm had got into the habit of calling every so often.

Annika felt strangely pleased about that, as if she were being allowed to look behind the scenes of reality. She had paid another visit to Julia and Alexander out at the home at Lejondalssjön. And on another occasion Annika and Julia had gone to the cinema to see *La Vie en Rose*, about Edith Piaf.

"Hi," Annika said, making an effort to sound cheerful as she held up her monthly travel pass and climbed onto the bus. "How are you?"

"Oh, fine, thanks. Alexander and I are in the city having a look round. We've been to Södermalm and had a look at the flat; Mum's been there and made it look really nice. Flowers everywhere, pelargoniums and African violets. We're just going to get some coffee. Do you fancy coming along?"

The bus set off with a jolt, and Annika had to grab onto an elderly man to stop herself falling over.

"Sorry," she said, looking round for a seat, only to be met with rows of blank gray stares. At home her minimalist kitchen awaited her, with its leftover toasted sandwiches, as well as the unmade beds. And she didn't even have any food in, seeing as she was about to go to Spain.

"Sure," she said. "Where are you now?"

"The Central Station. We're meeting Henrietta in an hour. Shall we meet up at the coffee shop upstairs?"

Alexander had grown. He was taller and heavier and his face was darker somehow, maybe because his blond curls had been cut off.

"Hi," Annika said, crouching down next to the boy. "My name's Annika. I don't know if you remember me? That's a nice car you've got there. Can it drive on the floor?"

The boy turned away and hid the toy car in his arms against Julia's legs.

"So you've started coming into the city?" she said, standing up and giving Julia a quick hug.

"We've done a bit of shopping, been to museums, and once we went to the children's theater," she said. "They say we're making good progress. Next week we're leaving the home to live on our own, in a little house a bit closer to the center of the village. What would you like? Something to eat?"

Julia had ordered juice for her son and two slices of Princess cake.

Annika suppressed a grimace.

"Chicken salad, please," she said to the waitress, "and a mineral water."

Julia asked for a cup of tea.

Annika looked at her from the corner of her eye. She looked completely different now compared to just a few months ago. Her hair was thicker and glossier, her movements more assured. There was a sense of depth in her eyes, something to reflect reality against. She was starting to look like the police officer she had once been.

"I've finished, Mummy," the boy said, licking his spoon.

"Do you want to play with your car for a bit? You could go over there near the toilets, but watch out for people's legs."

They watched the boy as he walked slowly toward the back of the café.

"So he's talking properly now?" Annika said.

"Only with me and Henrietta, but apparently that's 'normal' as well."

They laughed.

"But things are moving in the right direction," Annika said.

The waitress came over with the salad, water, and tea. Annika unfolded a napkin and put it on her lap. Julia looked down at her hands, picking under one nail.

"You know," she said, "I miss him."

She nodded toward her hands, and gulped as if she had something in her throat.

Annika put her knife and fork down, unsure of what to say.

"I know he treated me like shit and all that, but I really do miss him."

Julia looked up at Annika, a quick glance with moist eyes that soon moved on to Alexander and his toy car.

"You should see the pictures of him when he was little; Alexander looks just like him. It's almost unnatural. We went to see David's mother a few weeks ago and had a look in some old photograph albums."

"Does Alexander realize that his dad's dead?"

Julia nodded and blew her nose in a napkin.

"He's started drawing pictures of him in heaven. The clouds look like potatoes and the angels are stick figures with wings."

Annika couldn't help smiling, and Julia laughed.

"Those albums," Annika said. "They contained photographs of when David was little?"

"He looked so sweet, and Hannelore was a real beauty."

"Were there any pictures of David's playmates as well? Any of the other kids he grew up with?"

Julia rested her chin on her hand and looked off toward her son. He was pushing the toy car carefully around the grimy floor in front of the toilets.

"They had such a lovely house out in Djursholm," she said. "Well, it was Torsten's, of course. One of those big merchants' villas, with an ornate veranda and rose beds and raked gravel paths . . ."

"Were there any pictures of Filip Andersson?"

Julia blinked and let her hand fall to the table.

"Filip Andersson? Why would he be there?"

"He and David were childhood friends," Annika said.

She didn't mention Yvonne Nordin.

Julia shook her head.

"Did David ever mention anyone called Veronica?" Annika asked. "Veronica Paulson or Veronica Söderström?"

Julia leaned back in her chair and looked down at the checkout on the floor below them.

"No, I don't think so," she said.

"Does David's mother ever mention a Veronica? Or Filip Andersson?"

Julia sighed loudly.

"Hannelore isn't well," she said. "I don't really know what's wrong with her. It must be some sort of dementia, but there's something else as well. She'll soon have been in that home for twenty-five years. No, Alexander, not there. Stay between the tables . . ."

Annika waited in silence as Julia went over toward the toilets to show her son where he could play. Then she sat back down again and warmed her hands on the teacup.

"How does David's mother treat you and Alexander?" Annika asked. "Does she realize who you are?"

There was a chink of porcelain as Julia stirred her tea.

"I don't know if she recognizes us. I sometimes wonder if she's ever really understood that I'm David's wife, and Alex his son. She used to recognize David, and she asks after him all the time. She doesn't seem to understand that he's dead."

"So what do you do? Explain that he's no longer alive?"

Julia nodded.

"Every time. She just stares at me, for ages, then she starts talking about something completely unrelated. About things that happened in the sixties, old films, and radio shows. Do you remember something called the Breakfast Club with Sigge Fürst?"

Annika shook her head.

"She can still sing the whole theme tune. She idolized Sigge Fürst. She seems to think he was German, which of course he wasn't at all."

"But Hannelore was German, wasn't she?"

Julia nodded.

"Jewish?"

Julia tilted her head.

"Why do you ask?"

"Nina once said she came to Sweden on the white buses full of refugees after the war. And David's middle names, Zeev and Samuel, well, they could hardly be more Jewish . . ."

"She refuses to talk about it. She's never said a word about what it was like in the concentration camp."

"Did David have any cousins or other relatives?"

Julia wrapped her cardigan more tightly round her.

"Hannelore was the only member of the family who survived."

Annika was chewing on a lettuce leaf that seemed to be swelling in her mouth. She took a gulp of water and managed to swallow it.

"David's father," she said, "what happened to him?"

"He's been out of the picture for the past forty years. David grew up with Torsten, Torsten Ernsten."

"Who was he?"

"A Finland-Swedish businessman. He and Hannelore weren't married. He used to come and go pretty much as he liked."

"Okay," Annika said, "that sounds complicated, particularly out in Djursholm in the sixties. Do you have any contact with Torsten these days?"

Julia shook her head.

"He disappeared when David was eighteen. That was when things started to go wrong for Hannelore."

"Disappeared? What do you mean, 'disappeared'?"

"He went off on a business trip and never came back. Soon after that Hannelore was put in the home."

"What sort of business trip, where to? What business was he in?"

Julia shrugged.

"Don't know."

Annika looked intently at Julia. What was this peculiar family Julia had married into? A German Jewess, alone in the world, who had a son who was childhood friends with a famous financier and an international glamour model. The son gets murdered, and then the model gets murdered, and the others all either join the police or turn into murderers.

Annika leaned across the table.

"When you lived down in Estepona," she said, "when David was working undercover on the Costa del Sol, did you ever meet Sebastian Söderström and his family?"

Julia looked up at her, wide-eyed.

"The ice hockey player?" she said. "The one who died? No, just because David was famous from television didn't mean we socialized with other famous people. We spent all out time down there on our own, when David wasn't away for work, of course. When he was away I was left all on my own . . ."

She shuddered and looked quickly at her watch. Annika did

the same. Ten minutes left until Julia was supposed to meet Henrietta down in the Central Station.

"We probably ought to get going," Julia said, standing up and taking her son's outdoor clothes from the back of his chair and heading over toward the toilets. She put them on him as if he were a helpless doll.

"It was lovely to see you," she said as they walked past Annika on their way to the stairs. "In June we're going to start spending daytime in our flat. Maybe you could call in and visit?"

"Of course," Annika said automatically.

Julia took a pen and a scrap of paper out of her handbag.

"This is our home phone number," she said, writing something on what looked like an old bus ticket. "We went ex-directory when David started appearing on television, when everything went completely mad, calls at all hours of the day and night . . ."

She gave Annika a hug, took her son by the hand, and led him down the stairs.

Annika watched her ponytail bounce gradually toward the ground floor before it disappeared altogether. She looked down at her almost untouched chicken salad and realized how hungry she actually was. She gulped down the chicken and vegetables but left the pasta: After all, these days you were supposed to watch out for carbohydrates more than fat.

Then she walked home along crowded pavements with an intangible sense of anticipation in her gut.

Annika gasped for breath as she emerged onto the steps of the plane. The heat and the stench of aviation fuel made her lungs burn and her eyes water.

Lotta, the photographer, appeared beside her.

"Oh!" she said in delight. "It reminds me of Tehran. Did I mention I used to work there?"

"Yes, you did mention it," Annika said, hoisting her bag onto her shoulder and going down the steps toward the bus that would take them to the terminal building.

The air above the cement apron was quivering, quite literally. The planes a little way off looked distorted, as if they were behind uneven glass. Annika was breathing through her mouth; how hot was it? A hundred degrees?

"Everything in Tehran was extremely photogenic," Lotta said, squeezing on board the bus and pushing the rucksack containing her photography equipment in the face of an old lady. "Things seem much more rigid here. I mean, you want to try to capture the expressions, the character of the buildings and people . . ."

She took a deep breath and closed her eyes.

"Oh!" she said happily. "Other cultures are so wonderful!"

Annika looked around. She had already worked out that Thomas wasn't on the flight, but she checked again just to make sure. Civil servants didn't fly with low-cost airlines when they traveled abroad on government business, she should have realized that.

They got their bags after just a ten-minute wait, and headed off toward the car-hire hall. Annika made her way along the row, aiming for Helle Hollis at the far end. She was almost there when she realized that the photographer wasn't following her. Taken aback, she stopped and went back the way she had just come. She found Lotta at the Avis counter.

"Large companies are great," Lotta said. "They know what they're doing, they operate everywhere, and they offer a sort of continuity that I think is important when so much else around you is new . . ."

"Oh, I see," Annika said. "I thought I'd be doing the driving."

"As a photographer I'm used to being the chauffeur."

Annika raised her hands in a gesture of capitulation.

Lotta hired a Ford Escort, the same model Annika had last time. They went down into the garage to find the car. Annika switched her mobile on, and found one message on voicemail. Carita, saying she was busy Tuesday and Wednesday, but that she could work on Thursday, and possibly Friday, and asked Annika to leave her a message, which she duly did.

"Let's go and check in first," Lotta said. "It always feels good to get unpacked and settled in before you start work."

Annika looked at her watch.

"The conference center is only five minutes from here," she said, "and the press conference starts in three quarters of an hour. We won't have time to get to Puerto Banús and back before then."

Lotta looked down at her and raised her eyebrows.

"Who arranged such a tight schedule?"

Annika shrugged.

They found the car after fifteen minutes or so, and squeezed their luggage into the small boot. Lotta got behind the wheel, started the engine, and headed off toward the exit. Annika opened the glove compartment and pulled out the contract that Lotta had tucked away in there. Avis was three times the price of Helle Hollis.

The sunlight outside the garage was blindingly white, eroding all shapes. Annika and Lotta were both left fumbling for their sunglasses.

"Where do I go?" Lotta said, braking.

Annika put her glasses on and peered out through the windscreen. Either Avis used an entirely different *salida* to Helle Hollis, or the building work had proceeded at such a pace that her earlier frame of reference was all gone. The only thing that was the same was the chaos of cars and people and trucks and cement mixers. Temporary signs in yellow and red shouted directions from gantries and pillars.

"Do you want me to drive?" Annika said.

"Just tell me where to go!"

Annika clenched her teeth.

"Aim for Málaga," she said, turning on the air-conditioning. "Try to get up onto the A7, northbound. It should be the first or second exit."

The driver of the car behind them sounded his horn. Stressed, Lotta found the wrong gear and the engine stalled. Annika turned her head away and shut her eyes, determined to swallow her frustration.

It took them half an hour to find the way.

The Palacio de Ferias y Congresos de Málaga turned out to be smaller than Annika had expected from the pictures on the website. The building had been thrown up in a rundown industrial area and was a futuristic affair in glass, steel, and aluminium. The roof was shaped like a wave, and the walls looked like the folds of a concertina. Annika remembered the virtual tour and aimed for the smaller conference hall where the press conference was due to take place.

"What a clichéd building," Lotta said behind her. "It strikes me that it personifies some sort of Mediterranean macho idea, with an excess of style and elaborate construction methods . . ."

"There's plenty of that down here," Annika said as she walked under the series of multicolored pipe work hanging above the entrance.

Lotta was right, she thought as she entered the building. It was overblown, all cladding and lamps and orange-colored pillars. She had to stand in a disorganized queue, then identify herself and undergo airport-style security checks.

The conference hall was on the floor above. She heard Lotta's footsteps tail off, and by the time she reached the doors they had come to a complete halt.

"What is it?" Annika said, turning round.

"Press conferences are never very photogenic," the photographer said. "I think I'll go out again, try to capture the soul of the building."

Annika looked out across the hall. Blue chairs. Irregular walls of cherry-colored wood, sharp angles, and a blue podium with four chairs. The ceiling was heavily ornamented. Would anything from inside the press conference ever be published? Men in suits sitting in a row? Hardly. A picture would only be useful if anything completely unforeseen happened, if something caught fire or the participants started fighting among themselves.

She checked that she had her mobile handy. If anything did happen, it would probably do the job.

"Okay," Annika said, taking a copy of the press release from a pile and walking into the hall.

She took a seat right at the back, switched off her mobile, and looked out at the sea of people who were filing into the rows of seats.

There were media representatives from all over Europe, but the order of precedence seemed to be the same as at press conferences back home in Stockholm.

The television teams installed themselves right at the front with the unquestioning authority of people who knew they were most important. The radio reporters buzzed about in the row behind them, making a huge song and dance of putting their microphones out on the podium and adjusting their little digital recorders to get the sound levels right. The newspaper photographers hung around in the gangways between the seats. Behind the radio reporters sat the newspaper editors who wanted to be seen, she could tell from their studiously relaxed posture and self-important expressions. They found their purpose in life demonstrating to their colleagues just how important they were, in cases like this by shouting muddled and uninteresting questions at the podium once the radio reporters had finished.

She looked around for Thomas but couldn't see any sign of him.

Four men walked up behind the table on the podium: an EU commissioner, a Spanish lawyer, a Dutch lawyer, and a moderator.

She groaned inwardly.

Lotta had made the right decision.

The press conference was a very long-winded affair. At the sentence "about coordination and other measures to counteract crime as outlined in the following statement," Annika nodded off for a minute or so.

The press conference was basically about the coordination of legislation covering financial crimes throughout EU member states, everything from accounting offenses to tax evasion, VAT fraud, credit card fraud, and a duty of disclosure for banks and *bureaux de change*. To do that, the various countries first had to sit down and compare their existing legislation, work out what the differences were, and then discuss who was going to change what so the bad guys couldn't get away just by moving from one country into the next.

There must be a way of expressing that more simply, Annika thought, as she stood up with everyone else. She turned and looked over the room. No sign of Thomas.

Then she felt a hand at the base of her spine.

"Hello," Niklas said in her ear. "Would you mind accompanying me?"

"Am I under arrest?" Annika asked.

"Definitely," the police officer said.

They stepped out into the vestibule outside the conference room. Niklas put his hands on either side of her neck and kissed her, first on one cheek, then on the other.

"Welcome back," he said in a low voice.

She laughed and put her right hand up to her neck, placing her palm over his fingertips.

"Is Knut here as well?" she asked.

"He's sitting over at the tapas bar."

"Annika?"

The voice came from behind her. She took a deep breath. Niklas let go of her. She turned round.

"Hi, Thomas," she said.

He was wearing one of the new suits he had bought after the fire, dark, a bit shiny, Italian. Red tie, Rimowa briefcase, freshly polished shoes. She smiled at his tousled hair and blue eyes, but he didn't see. He was staring at the policeman beside her.

"Have you met Niklas Linde?" she said. "A narcotics police officer, he works down here."

The policeman took a step forward, held out his hand, and said, "Good to meet you." Thomas took his hand as his gaze flickered back toward Annika.

"Thomas Samuelsson," he said.

"Thomas is representing the Swedish Ministry of Justice," Annika said. "We used to be married; we have two children."

"Bloody hell," the policeman said, "that's great. Was he the one who didn't like playing?"

Annika felt like jabbing him in the ribs with her elbow.

"Good to see you," she said to Thomas, then to Niklas, "Shall we go and sit down?"

Niklas put a hand on her shoulder, not taking his eyes off Thomas.

"One floor down," Niklas said, moving his hand to her neck and showing the way along the paneled corridor.

They turned round. His palm ended up at the bottom of her back. She could feel contentment burning through her body as she felt Thomas's stare on the back of her head.

"Recently divorced?" the police officer asked, standing close to her on the escalator.

"Not particularly," Annika said, not moving away.

Knut had installed himself at one of the tables, with chicken wings, fried baby octopus, and prawns in a strong garlic sauce. He greeted her warmly.

"It's brilliant that we can do this straightaway," Annika said, sitting down opposite him. Niklas Linde sat down beside her.

She put her pen and notepad on the table, ordered *agua con gas* and a *tortilla* with *albóndigas* from the waitress.

"You know why I'm here?" Annika said, and the police officers nodded. "Why have drug smuggling and money laundering become blurred on the Costa del Sol?"

"Look at a map," Knut said. "An hour by boat to Morocco, Europe's very own hash plantation. Three quarters of an hour to the Atlantic coast, where the ships turn up from South America with their cargoes of cocaine. And slap bang in the middle of it all is Gibraltar, a tax haven with no intrusive restrictions."

He popped a baby octopus in his mouth and threw his arms out.

"It's all here," he said. "The raw materials, the transport network, the distributors, the tax haven, serious corruption, and customers."

"Customers?" Annika said.

"Spain has overtaken the USA as the biggest users of cocaine," Niklas said. "One in four Spaniards over fifteen has tried it."

"But hash is still the main drug of choice," Knut said. "It's estimated that one hundred and twenty thousand families in Morocco derive the whole of their income from growing hemp and producing cannabis. Do you know how they go about it?"

She shook her head. The police officer wiped his greasy octopus fingers on her napkin and picked up her pen and notepad.

"They plant the seed in the spring and the plants grow through the summer," he said, drawing a plant with deeply lobed leaves. "Here, right at the top, is the seed, hidden in little pods. Between the pods and the seeds themselves is a fine yellow powder, a form of pollen. When the plants are harvested in the autumn they're laid out on finely woven cloths on the floor and covered with plastic. Then they're beaten with sticks to crush the seed heads. The pollen filters through the cloth and gets collected underneath."

She looked at the drawing of a seed head. It looked like a fried egg.

The police officer looked over toward the entrance hall with an almost dreamy expression.

"In October and November, nights in Morocco echo to the sound of sticks beating the ground, *da-dunk, da-dunk*. That's the hundred and twenty thousand families crushing the seed heads of their hemp plants. Obviously, outsiders have no idea what's making the sound."

He drummed his fingers on the table.

"All night long," he said in a low voice, "until the plants have been beaten three times. Then they're done, and that's when the buyers show up."

He took his fingers from the table.

"The gangs that deal in cannabis handle about twenty hash farmers each. The pollen and plants are taken off to the coast, where they're dried and packed into hard blocks. It's been going like that for as long as anyone can remember."

He drank the last of his beer and looked at her.

"What do you know about hashish?"

Annika took a sip of her mineral water.

They used to meet up for a smoke behind the snowdrifts next to the sports ground back home in Hälleforsnäs. Sven was always the one who got hold of the hash, Sylvia Hagtorn brought the tobacco to roll it with, and Roland Larsson would bring his grandfather's pipe. Annika always thought the pipe was a bit disgusting, sucking up the remnants of the old man's saliva. And she didn't think much of the effect either. It just made her feel sluggish and a bit silly. Grass was much more fun. A bit of marijuana sprinkled on a cigarette paper just made her giggly and desperate for sweets.

"Well, I know you smoke it," she said, looking down at her pad.

"The pollen from the first beating is made into top-grade hash, the highest quality. We hardly ever get that in Sweden, it gets bought up along the way. The hash that reaches us is category three, the worst sort, the remnants from the last beating."

Maybe that's why it never really worked for me, Annika thought.

"How does the hash get to Europe?" she asked.

Niklas shifted on his chair. His leg ended up pressing against her thigh.

"It gets shipped out of two small coastal towns, Nador and Asilah, in February and March," he said.

She nodded and suddenly noticed how dry her mouth felt. She didn't move her leg.

"The latest development is the use of what are known as go-fast boats."

She was greedily gulping down the mineral water.

"Go-fast boats are really just big barges with somewhere between three and five 225-horsepower Yamaha motors on the back. Half the boat is full of fuel, the other half drugs. They go so fast that they can outrun helicopters. They dock out at sea with ships that refill their fuel tanks, then they can just carry on, sometimes as far up as Barcelona."

Niklas held out his mobile toward her with one hand. He rested the other on her knee. She took his mobile and looked in surprise at the screen, which was showing a shaky film clip of a cheerful dark-skinned man standing in the middle of a load of shipping pallets, holding onto a wheel. The wind was pulling hard at his hair. The cameraman, whoever he was, moved the camera away from the man and did a 360-degree turn. She realized the film had been taken on board a huge barge that was crossing the sea at very high speed. The prow was full of countless square pallets, while the stern contained several hundred cylindrical drums full of fuel. Then the film returned to the black man again and the screen went dark.

"He doesn't look so happy anymore," Niklas said, putting his mobile back in his pocket. "What you saw in the prow was three tons of hash. Both him and the cameraman are in prison in Granada now."

He let go of her knee.

She laughed.

"The EU have done a deal with the Moroccan government," Knut said. "The state has marched in and destroyed millions of hectares of cannabis plants. What do you think that means for the families who depend on growing hash? No bread on the table. So what do they do?"

He threw out his hands and leaned back.

Annika realized the question was a dramatic rhetorical gesture and waited in silence for the answer.

"Their plants are gone," he said, "but everything else is still there."

He leaned forward again.

"The whole logistics, completely intact: staff, buyers, sellers, transportation, boats, vehicles, ships, containers, the network of contacts and distributors . . . so what do they do?"

"They start transporting and selling something else," Annika said.

"They start transporting and selling cocaine," the police officer said. "Morocco and the Western Sahara have taken over as the transit countries for the cocaine trade, and here, right where we're sitting, this is the doorway to their customers. All the cocaine comes from the coca plantations in South America, and almost all of it comes through here on its way to the European market."

"How much gets seized?"

"About ten percent, an average of ninety kilos a day. It's estimated that a ton of cocaine reaches Europe via Spain every day."

"Bloody hell," Annika said, noting the figure.

Knut leaned toward her.

"And do you know what the drug gangs' biggest problem is?" he said.

Annika waited.

"What?" she said. "Bribing customs officials? Finding runners? Creating new markets?"

Knut shook his head.

"All that's easy. The hardest thing is knowing what to do with all the cash."

Annika looked skeptically at the policeman.

"Hard?" she said. "Just using notes?"

"Money laundering is the most complicated thing they do. And we're making it harder. That's why we have seminars like this one."

The police officer ate the last of the garlic prawns and looked at his watch.

"I have to get off to Granada," he said. "Are you happy with that?"

Annika looked through her notes. There were several things she was wondering about, but he had to leave and her head felt terribly tired. She smiled at the Norwegian.

"Thanks very much," she said. "This has been a huge help. I'm just wondering if you've got any ideas of people I could interview. For instance, I'd like to get in touch with Jocke Martinez's lawyer . . ."

"I've looked into that," Niklas said. "We can take that afterward."

"Excellent," Knut said, getting up. "Well, I'll leave you to it."

He kissed Annika on both cheeks and headed for the exit.

"I guess I'm picking up the tab," she said.

Lotta was close to a breakdown. She'd called Annika at least a hundred times but there was something wrong with her mobile. It wouldn't connect the calls; she kept getting a Spanish voice saying something unintelligible.

"You need to dial 46 before you dial my number," Annika said.

The photographer stared at her.

"Do you think I'm stupid or something? Of course I dialed the country code first. Is your mobile even on?"

Annika dug around in her bag and fished her mobile out on the end of the hands-free earpiece.

"Hmm," she said, "sorry."

"How could you just leave me like that?" she said. "We're supposed to be doing this series of articles together."

"Calm down," Annika said, switching her mobile on. "You haven't missed anything important, I've just been getting some background information. Did you get any pictures?"

"Of what? This overblown building? Or the picturesque surroundings?"

She gestured toward the windswept expanse surrounding the conference center, the thundering motorway, the shabby industrial buildings in the background.

"We need to sit down and try to book up some interviews for tomorrow," Annika said. "A drug dealer, a solicitor specializing in money laundering, a few jet-set Swedes . . ."

Lotta looked at her uncomprehendingly.

"This has been really hard for me," she said. "Getting up so early, and then you just disappearing like that. I want to go to the hotel now and get unpacked, and then I need something to eat."

Annika stared at the woman before her, her mane of blond hair and hurt expression, her long legs and angular shoulders.

"Unpacked?" she said.

Then she remembered Anders Schyman's words of wisdom: Choose your battles carefully. It was Wednesday today. They were flying home on Saturday. They had two full days in which to complete the entire series of articles.

"Sure," she said. "You go ahead. The Hotel Pyr is in Puerto Banús; you can see it from the motorway."

She put her mobile in her bag.

"What?" The photographer said. "Aren't you coming?"

"I've got loads of work to do."

"But . . ."

"With a bit of luck I'll be able to get hold of the Swedish drug runner in prison in Málaga. One of us needs to sort that out. Shall we meet up over breakfast in the hotel early tomorrow morning? Eight o'clock?"

Lotta was about to say something else, but Annika turned away and walked toward Niklas's car. Not the BMW this time, but a smaller model of Jaguar.

"Is that your photographer?" the policeman said, looking with interest over at Lotta.

"No," Annika said as she opened the car door. "She's not mine, she's the *Evening Post*'s. You're welcome to borrow her."

He grinned.

"I prefer reporters," he said, getting in the car.

Annika waved as they drove past her in the car park.

The traffic was heavy, almost static. Niklas closed his window and switched the air-conditioning to internal circulation. The thermometer on the dashboard said the outside temperature was twenty-nine degrees.

"Is it always this warm?" Annika said, realizing that the sweat under her breasts was starting to show through her T-shirt.

"It'll be like this until October," he said. "There's never a drop of rain during the summer months."

The white light was thinner now and seemed more pink. She took off her sunglasses and peered out at the sea.

"Has anything happened in the Sebastian Söderström case?"

He frowned.

"Have you heard what the postmortem report said?" he asked, glancing at her. "About the thieves?"

She shook her head.

"They weren't gassed. They died from respiratory failure caused by a morphine overdose."

Annika looked at the police officer. His arms were chestnut brown.

"A morphine overdose? They were addicted to morphine?"

"The morphine was in their bottles of beer."

Annika stared out at the road, remembering the inside of the cab of the thieves' truck: the dirty windows, the split vinyl seats, the hamburger wrappers on the dashboard by the windscreen, the map of Marbella, the mud on the floor, the two half-empty beer bottles . . .

"I remember," she said. "They were in the cup holder next to the radio."

"One-liter bottles of San Miguel," he said. "Screw-top."

"So someone doctored them," Annika said. "That means . . ."

". . . that someone killed them. Exactly."

"But who? And why?"

"Why do you think?"

She fell silent and looked straight ahead again.

"It's actually pretty smart," Niklas said. "You can get morphine from any hospital. The cupboards are supposed to be kept locked, but they're not hard to break into. The liquid forms have flavorings in them, so in this instance the pathologist thinks we're dealing with morphine in tablet form."

"But wouldn't it take loads of pills to actually kill someone?" Annika said.

"Someone who's not used to it would die from sixty milligrams of morphine chloride. That's either three or six tablets, depending on their strength. The amount of poison left in those beer bottles would have knocked out an elephant."

Annika held onto the dashboard as Niklas overtook a bus full of golf-playing pensioners.

"So what happened during the actual break-in, then?" she said. "Didn't the thieves have those injections to counteract the gas . . . ?"

"A naloxone derivative, yes, that's right, traces were found in their blood."

"They opened the gate by using the right code. How did they know it?"

"The code that was entered was the emergency one, not the one chosen by the family. Those sorts of codes get sold fairly often. There have been several cases of security companies being behind large-scale break-ins; they did one in an apartment complex in Nueva Andalucía."

Annika scratched her cheek.

"So they gassed the family," she said, "went inside without gas masks, smashed down the wall around the safe, carried it out to one of the vehicles, then looted the house and put everything into the truck, and drove away."

"More or less."

"And when they thought they were home and dry they opened the bottles of beer to celebrate."

Niklas nodded.

They left the crowds on the public motorway and headed up onto the toll road.

"But didn't those injections mean they weren't susceptible?" Annika said. "I thought they were supposed to block the effect of tranquilizers? So how could they die of a morphine overdose?"

"The naloxone derivative only lasts an hour or two. Then the morphine kicks in. They must have got tired and parked up in La Campana for a rest."

"I presume there are no fingerprints on the beer bottles apart from the thieves'?"

"Correct."

They sat in silence for a while. Mountains, sea, and greenery flashed past outside the windows. Annika shut her eyes and saw the little girl's bedroom in front of her, the unmade bed, the paints, the doll with the curly brown hair. She recalled the corridor leading to the closed door of the parents' bedroom, the floor where the children had died.

"There's something very odd about this crime," she said. "Don't you think?"

Niklas was staring straight ahead, and didn't answer.

Then it struck her, a sudden, terrible realization.

"No one laces beer with a fatal dose of morphine in advance unless you're determined to kill the people drinking it," Annika said.

"Quite right."

She shivered, and he noticed and turned down the air-conditioning.

"So this was a meticulously prepared mass murder camouflaged as a break-in," she said. "Do you have any idea why?"

The police officer shook his head.

"They cleaned up very carefully after them. The thieves who carried out the break-in were a risk, and they were eliminated. Presumably the explanation was inside the safe, but we're unlikely ever to see that again."

She looked out across the landscape.

"What are the Spanish police doing?"

"Nothing," Niklas said. "The case is regarded as officially closed from a police perspective. The thieves are dead. There are a few loose ends, but there usually are."

"You sound critical?"

He shrugged.

"I'm not formally involved in the investigation," he said. "I'm here to deal with the international drugs trade, not break-ins in local residential properties."

"But you think the Spaniards were too quick to drop this?"

He shuffled in his seat and cleared his throat.

"There must be some motivation for this crime that we haven't identified," he said. "Executing an entire family is an expression of serious fucking brutality. The killer was making a point. We don't know which one of the victims was the real target. Was it the whole family, or just one of them?"

"It could hardly have been the children," Annika said, "so that must mean one of the adults. Have you checked them out?"

Niklas sighed.

"Not very thoroughly. Sebastian Söderström was a charming slacker, completely incompetent when it came to money. Veronica Söderström was a well-regarded solicitor, Astrid Paulson was practically retired, and Suzette was a schoolgirl who was about to start work at a stables."

"Could there be something there, in Sebastian's shaky finances?"

"Of course, but if you don't ask any questions, you don't get any answers."

"And what about Suzette? Have you heard anything from her at all?"

He shook his head.

"Not a thing. It's like she went up in smoke on December 30 last year."

"Is there still any kind of active search for her?"

"Now? No."

"Do you think she's alive?"

Niklas hesitated before he replied.

"There's been no sign of life from her for four months. She hasn't crossed any national boundaries, hasn't withdrawn any money, hasn't made any calls, hasn't logged onto the Internet. If she's alive somewhere, she's locked up, unable to contact the outside world. So the worst of it may not be that she's dead."

Annika sat in silence, staring out through the windscreen for a long minute. She thought of the picture of the girl with the sullen demeanor, her black hair, and fragile face. *The worst of it may not be that she's dead.* How utterly appalling.

"But there are still things to follow up," she said. "Aren't there?" Niklas nodded.

"The person who doctored the beer."

"He set the whole thing in motion," Annika said. "Hired the thieves, got hold of the gas and naloxone derivative, paid to get the villa's alarm codes, poisoned the beer, took the safe and drove off."

"If it is a he."

Annika looked at Niklas, her mouth open.

"What do you mean?"

"The footprints found at the crime scene," he said. "Three pairs, two of which match the thieves. The third were shoe size thirty-seven."

Few men have feet that small.

"Do you have any idea who she could be?"

He looked up and smiled.

"Oh, little Annika, you're so serious," he said. "I'm glad you're here again. Shall we put the gas attack behind us and talk about something more pleasant?"

"Just one last question," she said.

He raised his right hand and brushed the hair from her face.

"There were no fingerprints and no DNA to go on. No vehicle and no witnesses."

She could feel his touch, like scalding water.

"Just footprints," she said.

"Just footprints," the police officer said.

She looked down at his feet. They were huge.

"You know what they say about men with big feet," she said.

He glanced at her quickly, with a twinkle in his eyes.

"No," he said. "What?"

She relaxed and laughed, feeling her face getting warm. She looked out at the concrete skeletons lining the motorway, and felt anticipation radiate from her stomach.

"That Swedish drug runner," she said, trying to sound normal. "Does he want to talk to the *Evening Post*?"

"I spoke to his lawyer this morning. You've got an appointment to visit him in prison in Málaga at eleven o'clock tomorrow morning."

He braked as they reached the toll station in Calahonda, and joined one of the queues, ending up behind a lorry from Morocco.

"What do you think the cargo is?" Annika asked.

Niklas stretched out his hand again, took a gentle hold of the back of her neck, leaned across the Jaguar's central console, and kissed her. The effect was electrical. The hair everywhere on her body stood on end. She kissed him back as if she were drowning, putting her hand on the back of his head, running her fingers through his hair, then tightening her grip and holding him there. She kissed him until she felt she was getting short of breath and the cars behind them started to blow their horns.

"Are you staying at the same hotel?"

Annika nodded, feeling giddy. The car behind overtook them, its tires squealing, and the driver gave them the finger as he passed.

"Are you in a rush to get somewhere?" she asked in a low voice. "Or have you got time to see me to my room?"

Niklas put the car in gear and drove up to the toll booth.

It was much easier than she had expected. There was no embarrassment, no performance anxiety. Their clothes ended up on the floor just inside the door, he looked at her with a mixture of laughter and seriousness in his eyes, and she found she felt okay looking back at him. He kissed her intensely. He tasted different from Thomas. His body was harder but the tempo calmer.

He stayed with her afterward.

Lotta was already installed at one of the window tables when Annika got down to the breakfast room. The photographer had a tray laden with eggs and bacon, cereal with pink yogurt, one glass of orange juice, and another of tomato juice, bread, cheese, and peppers, and two chocolate croissants.

Annika got a cup of coffee and an English morning paper and sat down beside her. From the corner of her eye she saw Niklas cross the vestibule toward the main doors. They were going to meet up again that afternoon and go through what the Swedish police were doing on the Costa del Sol to combat drugs and money laundering.

"You've got no idea what you missed last night," Lotta said, chewing energetically on a bit of tough bread. "I had a wonderful Spanish meal at a really authentic tapas bar down by the harbor."

She seemed to have got over the fact that Annika hadn't had her mobile on during her interview with the two police officers.

"And you know those mountains you can see over there?" she went on. "They're actually in Africa!"

Annika looked at the photographer for a moment to see if she was joking. She wasn't.

"Really?" Annika said, opening her paper.

She still felt warm inside, and could feel Niklas's arms round her back. They had showered together that morning, something she had never done with Thomas. He always wanted to be left in peace in the bathroom.

"Mind you, the amount of crime down here is terrible," Lotta said, as she set about ladling the yogurt into her mouth. "A man in the bar said they've got the mafia here."

"Four hundred twenty different versions of it," Annika said as she leafed through the paper.

Lotta opened her eyes wide.

"What? How can you say that?"

"Police information," Annika said. "They told me during my meeting with them yesterday, when you were having trouble with the phone."

"Well," Lotta said, "I think you have to take figures like that with a pinch of salt. The police say things like that to justify their budget. What we really need is proper journalism, based on facts that we find out for ourselves. That sort of thing gets badly overlooked in newsrooms these days."

Annika looked at her watch.

"I think I'm going to go back up to my room, and find out a few basic facts for myself," she said. "Shall we meet down here in an hour?"

She went over to the buffet, grabbed a bit of bread, cheese, and ham, which she wrapped in a napkin and put in her bag.

Then she went up to her room, called Carita and told her about the planned series of articles. They arranged that Carita would go with them to Málaga, and agreed to meet in the hotel lobby at nine o'clock.

She ate the bread, cheese, and ham as she read the Swedish morning papers online. Then she switched off her laptop and looked up at the room, before getting up and walking slowly over to the unmade bed and curling up on it. She could still detect his scent on the sheets.

This isn't love, she thought. This is just because I want to do it.

*　　　*　　　*

The prison was located in a *polígono* not far from the airport. The building was a plain single-story construction of concrete blocks, covered with what had probably once been whitewash. Now it was peeling off, gray-green from pollution and damp. It was surrounded by a wall topped with barbed wire and an electrified fence.

"Not exactly the Hilton," Carita said from the backseat as she peered through the windscreen.

Annika looked at the time: quarter of an hour before their allotted visiting time.

They had parked in the shade, on the road that led north from the prison. According to the thermometer on the dashboard, the temperature outside was thirty-two degrees.

"Why does this man want to talk to a newspaper?" Carita asked.

Lotta was looking out of the side window. Annika turned toward the backseat so she could look Carita in the eye.

"That's one of the things I want to ask him. He's obviously got some sort of motive."

"Do you think he's going to reveal something to you in exchange for something else?"

Annika shrugged.

"There's not much I can do for him, except write about his case."

"What do you know about him?" Carita asked.

"He's got a Swedish-Spanish mother and a Spanish father. He was arrested just after New Year as some sort of courier for the drugs that were seized in La Campana. I want his life story, his background, how he ended up as a drug runner, a bit of an insight into that world . . ."

"The light's completely wrong," the photographer said. "It's far too flat, soon there won't be any shadows at all."

Annika looked at Lotta. The photographer was staring intently out through the windscreen, as if she were evaluating what she was looking at with millimeter precision.

"You have to get going much earlier to get any depth into the pictures," she said. "We should have been here at dawn."

Annika took a deep breath. Lotta was basically uninterested in anything to do with their work; she hadn't asked a single question about the drug runner or any other aspect of the articles.

Annika turned back to Carita.

"He speaks Swedish," Annika said, recalling the drunken swearing when he was arrested that night in San Pedro. "But none of the guards do, so you'll have to do the talking before we get in. We've got authorization, but Niklas Linde warned me that they might kick up a fuss."

Annika turned to the photographer.

"We won't be allowed to take anything into the visitor's room," she said. "No bags or cases. They'll check our pockets for mobile phones and pens and notepads and so on, but you can try smuggling a mini camera inside your trousers. If we're lucky, they won't have metal detectors."

Lotta's eyes opened wide.

"But that's unethical!"

"The Spanish justice system doesn't decide what we publish," Annika said. "Anders Schyman does. We provide the material, and he makes the decisions. Shall we go?"

She opened the car door and stepped out onto the street without waiting for an answer. It was like walking inside a hair dryer. The wind swirled round her legs, blowing yellow sand around her skirt.

"This couldn't have been a prison to start with," Carita said, raising her hand to screen the sun as she looked at the mold-stained façade. "This must be some sort of adapted industrial building. A slaughterhouse, maybe. Well, he'll probably be here for a while.

The Spanish judicial system is renowned for being slow. People sometimes have to wait several years before they get to trial."

She took the opportunity to touch up her lipstick, then trotted off toward the entrance round the corner. Her blond locks bounced rhythmically on her shoulders. Annika had left her sunglasses in the hotel room and couldn't keep her eyes open when they stepped out into the full sun. It wasn't quite eleven o'clock, and they had to stand and wait out in the dust for several long minutes before the electronic lock on the gate whirred and they were let through to walk the few meters up to the actual prison building itself.

"*Buenos días, señores,*" Carita chirruped, pushing her sunglasses up onto her forehead. Annika wiped the sweat from her face with her palm and followed her in. The cool of the air-conditioning enveloped her like a blanket and she shivered and wrapped her arms around her. The door closed behind her with a metallic clang. She could sense Lotta close behind her.

They were in a cramped reception area. In front of them was a tall veneered counter, and to the left was the arch of a metal detector. Four uniformed guards with batons and leather belts were staring blankly at them. The only light in the little room came from a small window beside the door.

Carita started talking to one of the men. He had a peaked cap on although they were inside, and a large ring of keys on his belt. Annika heard the name "Manolo Zarco Martinez" several times; here he evidently wasn't Jocke but Manolo. Carita took her passport from her handbag. The man with the cap waved both hands dramatically and raised his voice, and Carita shrugged and began to do the same.

"We've only got authorization for two visitors," Carita said. "Not three."

Annika put her passport on the counter and looked at Lotta.

"I find things like this difficult," the photographer said. "It doesn't feel natural for me to force myself on people in tough situations. I'll wait outside."

Annika hesitated, then nodded. They'd never manage to smuggle a camera past the metal detector anyway, and even if they did, they wouldn't be able to show the man's face. His condition for agreeing to the interview was that he would be anonymous. The best they could have got would be a silhouette from inside the cell, facing the window, if there was one, or a view of the back of his head as he faced the wall.

"Okay," Annika said in a low voice. "Take a few shots of the prison in the meantime, something that makes it look really awful, that'll do almost as well. You can imagine the headline, 'This is where the Swede is being held,' something like that . . ."

Lotta put her hands on her hips.

"Well, I'm the photographer," she said. "There are loads of factors that determine whether a picture turns out well."

"Of course there are," Annika said. "That goes without saying."

"We're signed in," Carita said, putting her leopard-skin-patterned handbag on the counter. Annika stepped up, put her outsized bag beside it, and signed her name on a form she didn't bother to read.

"I need to keep my pen," she said. "And a notepad."

Carita shook her head.

"You can't take anything in," she said.

"Can't I borrow one? That's what usually happens in Sweden."

"*Bienvenido a España,*" Carita said, stepping through the metal detector.

Annika's belt set off the alarm so she had to take it off and leave it next to the bags on the counter.

"Do you think they'll go through our things?" Annika asked quietly, glancing at the bags as she and Carita walked past the back of the counter toward the cells.

"Bound to," Carita said, smiling at the guard in the cap.

They went through a narrow doorway into a long, tunnel-like corridor that was even darker than the reception area. A single strip light flickered weakly at the far end. On each side of the corridor was a row of metal doors, the same brownish-red color as the floor. The air-conditioning rumbled and rattled. The man with the cap held out his hand.

"*Celda numero seis.*"

Carita took the lead and set off into the tunnel. The floor was slippery and she held one hand up to keep her balance. Her high heels echoed hesitantly. Annika's sandals clattered and slipped. The guard's keys jangled.

"*Aquí.*"

Slowly he identified the right key and unlocked the cell door in two different places, at shoulder and waist height.

"*Sesenta minutos,*" he said, opening the door.

They had an hour.

The cell had no window. The floor was the same color as out in the corridor, but the walls were darker, grayer. Annika stared into the room, at first unable to see the prisoner in his gray clothes, sitting on his gray bed. She stopped short when she met his gaze over in the far corner.

"Good morning," Carita said, going over to the man and shaking him by the hand. "My name's Carita, I'm an interpreter, but I understand that you speak Swedish?"

Johan Manolo Zarco Martinez got up slowly and reluctantly. He shook Carita's hand with a distinct lack of interest and didn't look away from Annika.

"You the reporter?" he asked.

His accent was from the suburbs with a large migrant population. Annika held out her right hand. He took it and looked at her dubiously.

"My lawyer said you were pretty," he said. "He hasn't met you, has he?"

"Sorry to disappoint you," Annika said. "I'm afraid he was going on hearsay."

"You didn't bring a beer or anything with you? They don't check that closely."

Carita sat down at the end of the bed.

A low-energy bulb in the ceiling was casting a bluish light from above, throwing deep shadows under the man's eyes and nose. Annika looked away and glanced round the cell. There was nowhere to sit apart from the bed. A faint whining sound was coming from the air vent by the door. It was cold, but not as cold as out in the corridor. She stayed on her feet, with her back against the door. An hour suddenly felt like an eternity.

"Your name's Johan?" she asked.

"Jocke," Jocke Zarco Martinez said, slipping back into the shadows at the corner of the bed again. "But you're not going to print my name, right? I don't want my picture in the paper. Mum still lives in Sweden, you know. My sister too."

Annika looked at the man. She knew he was almost twenty-six, but he looked younger. There was something naïve about him, something rather touching, or possibly just a bit crazy.

"What would you like me to call you in the article?" she asked. "You can suggest a name."

He lit up.

"Any name I like?"

Annika nodded.

"Steel Bollocks!" he yelled, then burst out laughing so hard he could hardly breathe.

She sighed to herself and waited for the laughter to stop.

"Are you okay with . . . Andreas?"

He stopped laughing and pretended to throw up.

"No, fuck it, that's totally fucking uncool."

He thought hard for a few seconds.

"Call me Bobby."

"Bobby? That's not a Swedish name. It's English."

He straightened his back indignantly.

"What the hell . . . ? You said I could choose!"

"A Swedish name."

He slumped back against the wall with his arms folded.

"Fredrik," he said.

"Fredrik," Annika confirmed, unable to see why Fredrik was so much cooler than Andreas.

Jocke pulled his sleeves down over his hands and tucked his knees up under his chin.

"Have you got any idea how long I've been in here? I've told them I was supposed to drive the gear to Stockholm so I could get a quick trial, but the bastards tricked me. I said I wanted to be transferred to Sweden, but now they're going to take me to the provincial prison in Alhaurín de la Torre. I know a bloke who spent three years there before his trial. You've got to help get me out of here!"

"You're really going to have to talk to your lawyer about that," Annika said. "I don't have any influence over the Spanish judicial system. I'd like to interview you about how you ended up here, that's why I'm here."

"I want guarantees," the young man said.

"Of what?"

"That I can serve my sentence in Sweden."

Annika shook her head.

"I can't give you that sort of guarantee. All I can do is write about you in the paper, try to influence opinion . . ."

He lit up and held his arms out.

"Yes," he said, "That's good. Influence opinion. So they get me home again. Fuck, I can't stay here."

Annika breathed out and sank down onto the floor. She had thirty-five minutes left.

"Shall we take it from the beginning?" she said.

She asked some general questions about his childhood and youth. It didn't sound much worse than anyone else's. The third floor of a concrete block out in Skärholmen, parents divorced, an older brother and younger sister, mum and sister still living there. He talked animatedly about his school days and the gang he had been in, hanging out in the shopping center and competing to nick things; whoever nicked most was best. They used to sell their haul at the flea market in the basement of Skärholmen shopping center on Saturday mornings. His brother, who was ten years older, had started dealing hash while he was in high school. He was the one who introduced his little brother to the job of drug running, a career choice that had been extremely profitable until just a few short months ago.

"I started when I was too young to be charged," Jocke said. "It was perfect. I couldn't be charged even if I was caught, but I never got caught."

"How did it work? What did you smuggle?"

"Coke, mostly. That's where the money is. It went really well."

He looked genuinely happy.

"Shouldn't you have been in school?"

He shrugged.

"My brother used to call and say I was ill. They probably just thought I was a very sickly child."

He grinned brightly.

"What about your mum? What did you tell her?"

He shifted a bit and suddenly looked uncomfortable.

"That I was with Dad, and Dad thought I was with Mum. They never talked to each other."

Annika stiffened. In a flash she saw her own children in twenty years' time, sitting in a windowless cell in some foreign country, explaining how their lives had gone wrong in a similar way: I'm here because my parents never talked.

She dropped the subject and noticed that her voice sounded rasping.

"How did it work? How did you find your employers?"

He shrugged.

"First through my brother," he said. "Then just contacts."

"People you knew, or people they knew, or through the employment service?"

He grinned broadly again.

"Not the employment service," he said. "Mates. Friends of friends."

"Do you use drugs yourself?"

"Not much. Just occasionally. I prefer beer."

Annika wished dearly that she'd managed to bring a pad and pen with her. Her head was starting to ache with the concentration.

"Did you always run the route from Spain to Sweden?"

"Not just that," he replied. "I did Holland and Germany as well. The market's better there."

"Do you remember the first time you did it?"

He laughed.

"Oh yeah. Mind you, to start with it was easy. I used to go by train, with the gear in a sports bag. The first time with rubbers was worse. It's tough when you don't know how to do it."

Annika blinked.

"Rubbers?"

He put his head to one side and smiled. In another setting she would probably have found him quite charming.

"You think coke looks like it does in the films, then? Powder in little white bags, something like that? That's such bollocks. Coke's hard. Comes in blocks. Big as your thumb, pretty much."

He held up his left hand to show the size he meant.

The small of her back was aching. She adjusted her position against the concrete wall.

"You practice with grapes," he said. "Big grapes. You have to swallow them whole without breaking the skin. They put us in a hotel room. There were eight of us. We were there two whole days, just practicing. Then we moved onto swallowing rubbers and lumps of coke."

She felt the urge to vomit rise in her gullet.

"So you swallowed condoms full of cocaine? How many?"

"I know a bloke who took a whole kilo once. That's probably the world record. I used to take half a kilo, that's pretty normal."

"Isn't it dangerous?"

"You can't fly into Stockholm Arlanda anymore; they're too thorough there. You go to Skavsta or Västerås. It always went okay for me; it's the West Africans who get picked up."

"I meant in terms of your health."

"You just have to be careful when you swallow. It's only dangerous if a rubber breaks."

"Because then you die?"

The young man just smiled.

"But you got caught in the end," Annika said. "How did that happen?"

The smile disappeared as if he'd been slapped.

"It can't have come as any surprise when you got caught," Annika said. "All your friends had started to disappear around you. You were the last one arrested. Why didn't you run while you had the chance?"

"I shouldn't have had to," he said. "People ought to keep their mouths shut."

"Are you quite sure that someone betrayed you?" Annika said. "You don't think you could have been bugged or watched?"

He laughed, a hard, sharp sound.

"Of course I was bugged! No one ever says anything over the phone."

"So how did you hear about your jobs?"

He fell silent.

"Anyway, you've been talking as well, haven't you?" Annika said. "I mean, now, afterward? So you can get back to Sweden?"

Jocke sat up, annoyed.

"But I've only said obvious things, the things they already knew! I haven't said anything about Apits. They want me to talk about the whole fucking lot, but I don't know anything!"

"Apits," Annika said. "That's the freight company that owns the warehouse where the raid happened, isn't it?"

"I'm not saying a fucking word about Apits, or about the Colombians," the young man said, huddling up in the corner of the bed again.

"Not even if it gets you a ticket home to Sweden?" Annika said.

He hunched his shoulders and wrapped his arms tight around his legs.

"My mum and sister," he said. "Everyone knows where they live."

He looked up at Annika, and there was genuine fear in his eyes. She felt the hairs on the back of her neck stand up.

"What?" she said. "What do you mean by that?"

He shook his head. Annika tried to hold his gaze.

"What do you mean, everyone knows where your mum and sister live? You're worried about their safety if you say what you know?"

"I don't want to say anything else," the young man said.

A heavy silence descended on the little cell. The ventilation unit rattled and groaned. Jocke scratched his head hard with one hand. Carita was fingering the buttons of her blouse. Annika looked at the time. Five minutes left.

"Do you know anything about other activities?" she asked. "For instance, do you know anything about using gas in break-ins?"

The young man raised his eyebrows.

"What do you mean, using gas in break-ins?"

"Do you know anyone who does that sort of thing?"

"That's those fucking Romanians," he said. "I don't work with Romanians."

"You haven't heard anything about the break-in at the Söderström family home? Just after New Year, gas was used, they all died, just before you were arrested?"

There was a noise at the door. The guard was cutting the visit short by a few minutes.

The young man sat up on bed.

"When's your article going to be in the paper? When can I get out of here?"

Annika got up from the floor on stiff legs. Carita smoothed out her skirt and stood up from the bed. Only Jocke didn't move.

"Vamos," the guard said bluntly.

Annika went over to the young man and held out her hand.

"I hope things sort themselves out for you," she said, and realized that she actually meant it.

And before she knew what was happening, the young man had jumped up and leaped over to Annika, to give her a proper bear hug.

"Help me," he whispered in her ear. "Help me get away from here."

Lotta was sitting in the car, with the engine idling and the air-conditioning on.

"Málaga's a really authentic city," she said. "There's proper street life, a genuine tradition of work and siesta."

"Have you taken any pictures of the prison?" Annika asked.

The photographer looked at her in surprise.

"It's not remotely photogenic," she said. "And the light is far too harsh."

Annika shut her eyes for a few seconds. Pictures had to be taken, and she had an interview to write up. She dug around in her bag and took out her mobile, noting that she had three missed calls, then went back out into the blinding sunlight. She switched on the mobile's camera function and walked right round the building, squinting as she took pictures every ten meters or so. When she got back to the car she opened the passenger door and leaned inside.

"There's a bar down on the left," she said. "I'd like to sit down and write up an outline of the interview. Do you want to come along and get something to drink?"

"I was just about to suggest that," Lotta said. "This heat makes you so thirsty."

Carita came up to her and said in a low voice:

"What did he whisper to you?"

Annika looked at her in surprise.

"What do you mean?"

"Just before we left, when he hugged you. What did he say?"

Annika searched her memory.

"Nothing special," she said. "That he wanted help to get out."

Carita smiled and shook her head sadly.

"Poor lad," she said.

The bar was dark and reeked of smoke. The EU ban on smoking in bars and restaurants evidently hadn't hit home in Spain the way it had throughout the rest of Europe, because there were people smoking everywhere.

They got a table toward the back of the room. Carita ordered a *café cortado*, Lotta a glass of wine, and Annika pushed the boat out with a Coca-Cola.

"When in Rome," Lotta said. "I like the Spanish tradition of having a glass of red with lunch. It's very civilized."

"Don't worry," Annika said, taking out her pen and notepad. "I can drive us back."

Lotta raised her eyebrows.

"Why? We're in Spain. They're not so strict as they are in Sweden."

Annika looked up at the photographer.

"If there are three of us in the car, two sober and one tipsy, who do you think should drive?"

Lotta shrugged in annoyance.

"That's so uptight," she said. "Anyway, you know you don't get tipsy after one glass of wine."

Annika bit her tongue.

She was on the point of declaring open warfare, not about anything important, but just to let out some of her frustration.

She forced herself to smile.

"Of course," she said.

Then she leaned over her notepad and began to structure her article with keywords, scrawled notes, and arrows. She put together a quick sketch of the cell and the young man, describing the smell and the damp and the shadows, then moved on to a chronological account of his life.

"The people seem a lot more genuine here than in Puerto Banús," Lotta said. "I took some pictures of some women leading their goats to market while you were in there, their whole lives etched in their furrowed faces."

"Yes," Carita said, "you won't find any of them in Puerto Banús. They can't afford to live there."

"Mind you, I wasn't expecting to find anything genuine on the Costa del Sol," Lotta said. "It's nothing but golf-obsessed pensioners and tax evaders. That's why it's such a nice surprise to find something real here in Málaga. It could make a really good exhibition."

"Have you worked at the *Evening Post* long?" Carita asked.

Lotta chuckled.

"Well," she said, "this whole tabloid journalism business really isn't my thing. I'm an artist deep down, but everyone has to eat."

Annika took her Coke and moved to the next table to get away from the sound of their voices. She started sketching out Jocke Zarco Martinez's offenses when he was younger: the gang, the shoplifting contests, the winner being whoever stole most. The flea market in Skärholmen, his brother dealing hash, then he himself starting to smuggle drugs while he was still legally a minor.

"It's got terribly expensive down here," Carita was saying. "Not just property. Food costs a lot more, and the restaurants are more expensive. Ordinary people can't afford to go out and eat Sunday lunch anymore."

Lotta sighed.

"It's so sad when tradition is forced out by commercialism. It's the same where I live, on Södermalm. Do you know Söder?"

Annika tried to shut out their conversation and concentrated on trying to listen to the young man in the cell.

Smuggling coke in sports bags on the train, his brother reporting him sick to the school, his mum thinking he was with his dad.

"It was lucky I bought my flat in time," Lotta was saying. "I'd never be able to afford it today."

"Same here," Carita said. "I inherited some money from my parents; that was how we were able to afford the house in Nueva Andalucía."

"So your parents are dead, how sad," Lotta said. "Was it long ago?"

"Eight years now. I inherited a biotech company that they set up . . ."

Annika looked up.

"A biotech company?" she said. "What was it called?"

She remembered her former neighbor out in Djursholm, Ebba Romanova, who had set up and been bought out of a biotech company, and who got 185 million kronor for her trouble.

Carita looked at her in surprise.

"Cell Impact," she said. "Why?"

"Have you ever heard of a company called ADVA Bio?" Annika asked. "One of my neighbors used to own it."

Carita laughed.

"I don't know anything about that business, that's why I sold the company straightaway."

"You should always focus on what you know," Lotta agreed. "I'm going to concentrate on exhibitions from now on. That's where I feel I belong."

Carita began to gather together the things she had spread out on the table.

"Have you had many exhibitions?" she asked, putting her sunglasses, powder, and lipstick in her handbag.

"Four," Lotta said. "All with everyday life as their theme. I sold several works from my series of women's portraits from Tehran."

"Shall we go?" Carita said.

She stood up without waiting for an answer.

Annika looked down at her notes.

"Two minutes," she said.

"We'll get the car," Carita said.

Quickly Annika thought through the end of the interview, the details about drug smuggling, practicing with swallowing whole grapes, the hard blocks of cocaine, the problem of security at Arlanda.

Her pen paused when she remembered the look of fear in the young man's eyes.

I'm not saying a fucking word about Apits, or about the Colombians. My mum and sister. Everyone knows where they live.

She gathered together her things, drank the last of the cola, and went out into the sunshine.

The missed calls were from the newspaper, Thomas's mobile, and the central exchange of the main government offices in Stockholm.

She waited until she had got up to her hotel room before calling back.

The room had been cleaned and the bed made. Every trace of Niklas Linde had been swept away.

She decided to return the calls in the order they had been made.

"How's it going?" Patrik snapped.

She sat on the bed and rocked on the mattress.

"I've met the drug runner who's been arrested. He's not having much fun."

"What pictures have we got?"

She took a couple of deep breaths before replying. There was no point complaining about the photographer; she'd only get told off for not being able to work with other people.

"We couldn't take a camera inside the prison," she said, "but we've got the outside of the building. It looks like shit."

"That works," Patrik said. "'This is where the Swede is being held.' What else are you doing today?"

"I'm meeting a Swedish police officer who's working on a massive seizure that was intended for the Swedish market."

"Hmm," Patrik said. "Sounds pretty cold. What pictures will you have?"

"He's not here officially, so we'll have to sort something out."

"Just make it fucking dramatic. What else?"

"I was at the press conference about international cooperation to stop cross-border financial crime, and I've got a decent long interview with two Scandinavian police officers about the Costa del Crime and drugs and money laundering. I've got a good source in the police down here who can help me sort out the rest of the interviews we want."

She refrained from saying that one and the same policeman fulfilled most of those roles.

"What about the girl spilling the beans about her jet-set lifestyle?"

"I'm still hoping to find her."

"And she's not allowed to be fucking anonymous."

No, Annika had got that. Close-ups from the front were the order of the day.

One of Patrik's other phones began to ring and the head of news hung up abruptly. She sat there with her mobile in her hand, slightly taken aback, hesitating over whether to dial the next number.

What could Thomas want with her? They hadn't talked about meeting up.

She pressed *Call* and listened to the phone ringing. No answer. Disappointed, she let the phone sink to her lap. The room was completely silent. She could hear her own pulse rushing in her ears.

They had to learn to talk to each other. Their failure to communicate was what had caused their marriage to break down, she could see that now, not his unfaithfulness or her sniping, not because he worked too much or because she asked too much of him. She hadn't talked, and he hadn't listened.

Her head felt heavy as lead when she recalled their phony conversations about things that were actually completely irrelevant, when they would shout at each other about terrorism and integrity and proposed new legislation instead of what they really meant, when they would circle each other in a destructive spiral that led nowhere but into the darkness.

She put her mobile down and went into the bathroom. Just as she was about to sit down the phone started to ring out on the desk. She pulled up her underwear again and stumbled out into the room.

"Annika Bengtzon? Hello, this is Jimmy Halenius. Are you busy?"

She was taken aback. They hadn't spoken since that infamous evening at the Järnet restaurant, with the ensuing pictures.

"I was on the toilet," she said, adjusting her pants and still needing a pee.

There was a short, surprised pause on the line.

"What?" Annika said.

"Was that something you'd rather carry on with, or can we talk for a minute?"

"I'll manage," Annika said.

He cleared his throat.

"How's the series of articles going?"

So he'd been informed about it.

"Don't worry," she said breezily. "It'll be the perfect publicity brochure for the Justice Department."

"Excellent. Listen, I've got some information about our friend, the Kitten."

She raised her eyebrows and adjusted her skirt, as though anyone could see her on the third floor of the Hotel Pyr with nothing but the tops of palm trees and the motorway outside.

"Really, what's she done now?"

"As you know, she was charged with three individual murders and one double homicide in a court in Boston. The trial was pretty quick, the verdict was announced yesterday. She's been sentenced to eighteen years in prison."

Annika blinked.

"Eighteen years? That's all?"

"She had one of the best lawyers in the States. He got the three counts of murder discounted on some technicality, and she wriggled out of the double homicide by claiming self-defense."

Annika sank onto the bed.

"So what does this mean?"

"That we can request her extradition, under suspicion of arson on your house."

She stared down at the stone floor.

"Extradition? There'll be a trial? And my name will be cleared? Will I get my insurance money?"

"Our extradition request won't be granted by the American authorities, so there won't be a trial, but the fact that charges are laid against someone else means that you'll be formally discounted from the investigation. The insurance company has already been informed. You'll get the full amount."

The insurance company. Get the full amount.

She tried to identify some sort of emotion inside her, relief or delight, but nothing came. She was just aware of the low murmur of the air-conditioning and the background rumble of the motorway, and the questions that were piling up inside her head. Will they take the flat away now? Will they let me buy it from them? When will I get the money? Thomas will get half. Or will we have to rebuild the house? Oh no, I don't want to rebuild it! Can we sell the plot?

"Annika?" Jimmy Halenius said over the phone.

"Er, yes?" she said.

"Did that picture in the paper cause you any trouble?"

She took a deep breath, forcing the background noise and all the questions to one side.

"I survived," she said. "How about you?"

He paused before replying.

"Only just," he said. "There was a big fuss in various parts of the building."

Presumably he meant Rosenbad, seeing as that was where he was calling from: the building in the center of Stockholm that housed the prime minister's office, the cabinet office, the Justice Department, and a few sections of the Foreign Office.

"Shit happens," she said, without feeling particularly embarrassed.

"So what lessons do we learn from this?"

She got up and headed toward the bathroom.

"Not to kiss in public places, and especially not when you're on duty?"

"Exactly!"

"Listen," she said, "I really need to go to the toilet."

"Okay," he said, "I'll wait."

She stopped midstride.

"You're going to stay on the line while I pee?"

"Well, you don't have to hold the phone next to the bowl."

She shook her head, put the mobile on the floor, went in and peed, washed her hands, then picked the phone up again.

"Are you still there?"

"So where were we?"

"Lessons for the future."

"Right. So, I was wondering if you'd like to come round to mine next time?"

She sat down gently on the edge of the bed.

"What makes you think there's going to be a next time?"

"I don't think. I'm asking. Next Friday?"

"I'll have the children," she said.

"Tomorrow, then, or Saturday?"

She looked up at the ceiling and breathed in the smell of the room: dust, disinfectant, insecticide, and something unidentifiable, could that be a lingering trace of Niklas?

Did she want to? Did she want to meet him?

She closed her eyes and all the questions and men blurred.

"I don't know," she said. "I don't know what I want."

"Can I call you at the weekend?"

She opened her eyes.

"Sure."

She ended the call and curled up on the bedspread, pulling her knees up toward her chin and wrapping her arms around them. She thought about dead children and ruthless women and powerful men. She let herself be swept off into something that was warm and dangerous.

Lotta was standing waiting in the lobby a few minutes before four. She had all her photographic equipment with her, the rucksack, and a clumsy tripod and a flash so big it had its own bag.

"It's good you've got everything with you," Annika said, "because this is going to be a difficult shot. The police officer in question can't be recognizable, but the picture still has to be dramatic. The question is whether we doctor it instead of fussing about with shadows and backlighting and screens . . ."

Lotta looked at her in surprise.

"Okay, I'm the photographer here," she said. "I thought we'd agreed on that."

Annika put her bag on the floor. She'd fallen asleep on the bed and woken up with a headache. The limit for what she was prepared to put up with had moved considerably closer. The fact that she was going to be meeting Niklas along with a colleague from the paper was making her tense and nervous.

"This series of articles is being published in the *Evening Post,*" Annika said curtly. "There are certain guidelines that need to be adhered to, and they're there because they work."

"That may be true for you," the photographer said. "I'm here to do a good job."

Annika picked up her bag again.

"I'll be waiting outside," she said.

Niklas arrived fifteen minutes late, true to form. Annika hurried to sit in the front seat while Lotta put her things in the boot.

"Hi," he said, putting his hand briefly on her thigh. "How are you?"

She took a deep breath, terrified that Lotta would see, but overjoyed at his touch.

She managed a smile as he looked at her.

"Great," she said.

Lotta closed the boot; Niklas removed his hand. She got in the backseat and leaned forward between the front seats the way that Kalle and Ellen did when they weren't strapped in.

"Lotta Svensson Bartholomeus," she said, holding her hand out and smiling broadly at Niklas.

He took her hand for a moment and looked at her in the rear-view mirror.

"Niklas Linde," he said. "I know this doesn't look like a police car, but I can assure you that it is. So I'll have to ask you to put your seat belt on."

Lotta actually giggled. Annika turned her head and glanced at her from the corner of her eye as she fastened her seat belt. Then she looked ahead, through the windscreen, and avoided looking at the police officer beside her.

Mustn't give anything away, she thought. Lotta won't notice anything if we don't give her any reason to.

She folded her arms on her chest.

He'd changed his clothes. The sports shirt had been replaced by a short-sleeved shirt of some rough material. His hair curled down onto his shoulders; she had been the one who washed it. She imagined she could still detect the smell of the cheap hotel shampoo.

"How was Jocke?" Niklas asked.

"Not too good," Annika said. "He's homesick."

"That particular prison in Málaga usually has that effect on people," the police officer said as he pulled out into the traffic.

She braced herself as they went round a bend by holding onto the dashboard. The best defense was actually to act perfectly normal.

"I've been thinking about something," Annika said. "The name Zarco Martinez can't be terribly common?"

"You'd be surprised," Niklas said. "It's not Andersson, exactly, but it's not Bartholomeus either. I know a few people called Zarco Martinez here in Marbella, one of them's a bloody good solicitor."

"I've seen the name somewhere before," Annika said. "Before I ever heard of our little drug smuggler."

"Jocke's got a brother," Niklas said. "He must be in prison somewhere, because we haven't seen him for a while. His name's Nicke Zarco Martinez. They used to work together."

Ah, the big brother who started dealing while he was still at school. But where would Annika have come across his name?

She shook her head.

"No," she said. "That's not right. Not Nicke Zarco Martinez. It was something else."

She looked out of the window, watching as a large bullfighting stadium slid past on the right.

"Oh!" she said. "I recognize this, I've been here before."

"You wanted pictures of the warehouse in La Campana."

Annika turned to Lotta.

"What do you think? Do you think there's any point trying to get pictures of an old drug dealers' warehouse?"

"There's not really much to see," Niklas said. "The container's been taken away as evidence."

The photographer thought for a moment.

"Is it in an authentic neighborhood?"

Niklas glanced at her in the rearview mirror.

"I think you could safely say that."

Lotta nodded enthusiastically.

"Let's go, then."

Annika looked at his profile.

"My head of news wants a heroic portrait of a Swedish police officer on the Costa del Crime. Can I write about you, or is there anyone else down here at the moment?"

He was steering the Jaguar hard and fast through the narrow streets.

"Knut Garen is the official Nordic representative here."

"Yes," Annika said, "I know. But sometimes the Swedish police conduct operations down here, don't they, without actually being stationed here?"

She was thinking about David Lindholm and Julia's terrible description of Estepona while David was working undercover, infiltrating some drug gang.

Niklas braked and blew his horn at a cement mixer that had stopped in the middle of a roundabout.

"At the moment I'm the only one here."

"So what do you do, then?"

He drove up onto the pavement and passed the cement mixer on the inside.

"I'm a coordinator. An observer, you could say. I'm the link between the police in Malmö and the Spanish police on a particular case affecting both countries."

Ah, so he was stationed in Malmö.

"How active are you?"

"I follow the surveillance and am involved in the decision-making process: Do we go in now? Do we wait? Shall we let the shipment through and try to get the recipient as well?"

"Like you did with the second shipment at New Year?" Annika said. "That one with the oranges, the one you put a transmitter on?"

The police officer's face assumed a grim expression.

"They ditched the truck in Karlsruhe. The sides of the container had been broken open. They threw the transmitter in the Rhine."

"Oh," Annika said.

"A serious fuck-up," Niklas Linde said. "And I was the one who insisted that we should let it through."

She didn't say anything for a minute or so. The streets were climbing upward, the gates were getting more ornate and the walls higher.

"God, how tasteless," Lotta said from the backseat. "Who on earth would want to live like this?"

People willing to pay ten million euros, Annika thought.

"Is it common to have Swedish police officers working under-cover here?" she asked.

"I wouldn't say that."

"But when it does happen, how does it come about?"

"We'd be talking about an agent who's extremely active. He in-filtrates an organization, probably as a buyer. Under Swedish law we're not allowed to incite people to commit crimes, unlike most other countries. That makes the situation a bit tricky."

"But we do have agents like that?"

"All countries do."

"Did you know David Lindholm?"

He cast her a quick glance of surprise.

"The guy from TV? No. Why do you ask?"

"He was down here a few years ago on a fairly long undercover job."

"David Lindholm? Down here? When was this?"

Annika thought for a moment. Julia had been pregnant with Alexander, and the boy was four and half now.

"About five years ago," she said. "He lived in Estepona with his family for a while."

Niklas shook his head.

"Not a chance."

"Yes," Annika said. "I'm absolutely certain. His wife hated it.

David was gone for weeks at a time, and he couldn't tell her a thing about what he was doing."

Niklas frowned.

"I spent all that year traveling back and forth, and I can assure you that we didn't have any independent agents from Stockholm stationed in Estepona. That's not to say that he wasn't here, of course, but he wasn't working for the Swedish police if he was."

Annika frowned and looked out through the window. Could she have misunderstood Julia?

"Maybe he was so secret that no one knew about him?" she tried. "Not the Nordic coordinator nor the Spanish police . . ."

"That's not how it works. Everyone is always kept informed of what we're doing."

He turned left, and the road started to slope downward.

"Suppose we were driving down from Malmö to Holland for some reason," he went on. "We'd have to have approval from both the Danish and German police, simply in order to cross their territory. Being so deep undercover that no one knows about it is completely out of the question. Do you recognize where we are?"

Annika looked round in surprise. They were in an industrial district with low buildings and narrow streets.

"Yes!" she said. "I've been here before!"

Niklas sighed.

"You must have the worst sense of direction in Europe. Yes, you've definitely been here before, with me. You even took a picture of that doorway."

He leaned across her, resting his lower arm on her thigh, and opened the glove compartment. His touch made Annika stiffen. What if Lotta saw? The police officer fished out a large bunch of keys, then sat back up in his seat again. Annika could feel his arm burning through the fabric of her skirt.

"What a charming place," Lotta said, opening the door.

"Hang on," Niklas said. "We can't stop here."

He put the car in gear and drove off.

"Aren't we going in?" Lotta said, looking at the closed shutters as they disappeared behind them.

"I'm fond of this car. So it's a better idea to leave it round the corner."

Niklas parked on a pedestrian crossing on the next block, switched the engine off, and turned to face Lotta.

"I'd appreciate it if you only took a fairly discreet camera with you. We'll all benefit from being a bit incognito."

"Oh," she said. "Of course."

"Good," he said, taking the key from the ignition and getting out of the car.

Lotta took a camera and a small flash from the boot, then they started to walk up toward the warehouse. Annika and Niklas were walking next to each other, close but without touching, up the long slope. The workshops and carpenters and wholesalers had opened up again after the siesta. The sound of saws cut through the air, and they had to jump to avoid a cascade of sparks from a metal-work lathe, and two men were shouting something farther up the street. It was hard to tell if they were angry or happy.

"So what's going to happen to this particular gang?" Annika asked. "How far have you got with the investigation?"

"Let's talk about that when we get inside."

He stopped beside the entrance to the warehouse. Annika studied the façade. The faded sign saying *Apits Carga* was hanging crookedly. The metal shutters had probably been blue once, but the paint had peeled off through weather and heavy use. The building was fairly tall compared to its neighbors, she guessed about six meters.

Niklas looked round, then crouched down, unlocked a small padlock by the wall, and pulled up the metal screen. Behind it was another door, which he quickly unlocked and slid open.

"Please," he said, gesturing for them to hurry inside.

She stepped into the darkness, closely followed by Lotta, and Niklas closed the door behind them. It went pitch-black.

"Scared of the dark?" he asked.

"Actually, yes," Lotta said.

Annika didn't answer, just breathed in the smell of sawdust and rotten fruit.

A moment later there was a click over by the wall and the warehouse was bathed in light. She raised her arm to her eyes instinctively, blinked a few times, and saw that the warehouse was equipped with the same sort of halogen floodlights you normally see in sports stadiums or building sites.

The warehouse was bigger than it looked from the outside. The walls had been whitewashed, with the exception of a gray rectangle of cinder blocks on the long wall at the back. Dust and spiderwebs hung in the air. Chunks of wood and fragments of plywood lay scattered around the walls. A rusty saw was leaning against one of the end walls. There was a pile of tools, or rather fragments of tools, in the far left-hand corner. In the right-hand corner there was a meter-high pile of sawdust.

Niklas Linde let go of the circuit breaker and came over to her.

"You can't refer to me as your source for this," he said. "Not even anonymously. You can write something opaque, 'the police investigation indicates,' something along those lines."

She pulled her notepad out.

"Okay," she said, and wrote "reliable sources within the Spanish police."

Lotta had pulled out her camera and was heading enthusiastically toward the pile of tools in the far left corner.

The police officer took a few steps across the concrete floor, and the sound echoed in the empty space. His hair curled at his neck and his jeans were tight on his thighs.

"Apits is a haulage company," he said. "They ship fruit and vegetables from South America to Europe. There's no big apparatus behind it, it's all fairly small-scale. Apits Carga is the actual freight part of the business; we assume that Carga owns the containers and pays the shipping costs. Apits Depósito is the storage side of things, and that's the part of the business that rents this warehouse, for instance. Apits Transporte owns the articulated lorries that carry the containers north from here."

"What does Apits stand for?" Annika asked.

"Don't actually know," Niklas said. "There's nothing that resembles 'apits' in English, Spanish, or any other language. 'Apios' is the plural of celery in Spanish, that's the closest we've managed to get. We don't think it's got any significance, even if celery is a type of vegetable. The domain name apits.com has been registered, but isn't in use. It's not a first name or surname, so we're assuming it's an acronym."

"A Place Indoors Thwarts Storms?"

"Or Airport Passenger Intelligent Transport Systems. That's a Japanese setup for streamlining passenger check-ins at large airports. Or Analogue Proprietary Integrated Telephone System. Together with Dpits, Apits forms an integrated telephone system developed by Panasonic."

"Not very likely, then?" Annika said.

"Not really," Niklas said.

"So it stands for something completely different?"

"Anna Petter Ines Tore Sigurd. Your guess is as good as mine."

"This is brilliant," Lotta said. "Good light, and great atmosphere. You really get a sense of workers toiling at their machinery."

This is good, Annika thought. We sound completely normal. Not like we spent half the night fucking.

Niklas walked past her, off toward the gray rectangle on the far wall.

"There used to be an entrance at the back as well," he said, pointing, "but they bricked it up. They wanted control over anyone coming or going."

"Who are 'they'? Who owns Apits, or rather, who's behind it?"

Niklas let out a deep sigh.

"Gibraltar," he said.

"So how much do you really know?"

Niklas held out his hands. Annika knew perfectly well that they were hard and strong. She looked down at her notepad.

"We know that the warehouse was rented on a two-year contract to Apits Depósito. We found that out when we searched the offices of the owners of the building, a company in San Pedro."

"But this has nothing to do with oranges and melons."

"In part it does. The company ships fruit and vegetables, but only as a smokescreen for their real business."

"Which is cocaine from South America."

"Which is cocaine from Colombia," Niklas Linde said.

Annika walked around the walls, looking up at the exposed roof. She could feel him following her with his eyes.

"Are the owners of the building under any suspicion?"

"Discounted from the investigation entirely."

He stopped in the middle of the floor.

"This is where the container was," he said. "Checked through customs in Algeciras on December 29 last year, with Apits Carga listed as the owner. Your little friend Jocke was supposed to have driven the contents up through Europe in a small lorry leased on a one-year contract by Apits Transporte. And that's all we know."

She walked over to him. He didn't move.

"So how did you catch them?"

He had shaved. He smelled good.

"Surveillance," he said. "The boys talked among themselves. Jocke seems to have been at the center of the web. We've reevaluated his status. It looks likely that he was the link between the distributor and the rest of the men who were arrested."

"He told me he never said anything important on his mobile."

"True," Niklas Linde said with a grin. "But only if you count his conversations in Spanish. One of the lads used to live in Rinkeby and Jocke didn't think we'd be able to understand what he was saying if they spoke Swedish to each other."

"Is there any way to lower the lighting?" Lotta called from over by the saw.

"Lower it?" Niklas Linde asked, turning toward her. She was lying on the floor with her camera pressed to her nose, photographing a broken pair of plate shears.

"A dimmer switch or something?"

"Er, no."

He turned to Annika and ran his finger quickly down her cleavage.

Annika opened her eyes wide and pulled a face telling him to stop.

They couldn't start any rumors that she was having sex with her sources, not after the picture with Halenius.

"So the distributor is Apits and its filials," she said, checking over Niklas's shoulder to make sure Lotta hadn't seen anything. The photographer was engrossed in the plate shears.

"Correct."

"And the men under arrest are . . . what, small-time gangsters?"

"Right again."

"And the supplier is . . . ?"

"The Colombians."

Annika looked over to the photographer again. She recalled what Carita had said about her murdered father-in-law: The Colombians wipe out whole families. No one must be left to inherit anything.

"Does the Colombian mafia have a presence here on the Costa del Sol at the moment?"

"Obviously they have representatives who make sure that the deliveries work."

"Is it okay if I move the saw?" Lotta called from the corner.

"Not really," Niklas Linde said.

She wanted to touch him. She wanted to put her hand on his stomach and stroke downward, over his jeans.

"How big was the seizure?" she asked.

"What do you mean by 'big'?"

She stared down at her notes.

"Did everyone get all excited and start cracking open the champagne?"

"Seven hundred kilos is a lot, but on average the Spanish police seize a ton a day. So it's not going to go down in the history books."

Lotta got to her feet and brushed the sawdust from her summer dress.

Annika took a step back.

"And Apits isn't a particularly big player," Niklas said. "But they have been established and active on the Costa del Sol for a long time. We've found information about rental contracts for trucks and warehouses going back to the mid-sixties. In other words, this is a small but very well-organized drug-distribution company. And obviously it's a good thing if such an established syndicate gets smashed, particularly from our Swedish perspective."

"Why?"

"Because their main customers were in Holland, Germany, and Sweden."

"And this is the first time they've been caught?"

"They're bound to have had smaller shipments seized before, but nothing on this scale."

"What will it mean for them? Is this the end of the business?"

"We don't know anything about their internal state of affairs, so it's very difficult to answer that."

"Will they get trouble from the Colombians?"

"They'll have to replace what was lost, and usually both parties share the hit. Every tenth shipment is lost, and the Colombians bear that in mind in their planning. Anyway, it's like a piss in the Nile for them. But for a setup like Apits it could be make or break."

He took a step forward, so that he was standing right next to her, and put his lips to her ear.

"I won't be able to spend tonight with you."

She stiffened and her pen slipped, drawing a long line across her notepad.

"Why not?"

"I have to be somewhere else."

He walked past her toward the door, carefree and untroubled.

She stayed where she was, immobile. He's got someone else, she thought. The woman in the background at the terrace where he was having coffee when I called. *Hasta luego*, then a kiss. Or Carmen at the restaurant up in that mountain village. Or one of the girls who were laughing so hysterically when he called me from the Sinatra Bar the first night I was here last time . . .

"Is there anything else you want to know?" he asked.

Who is she? Annika thought, looking down at her notes.

"Jocke Martinez," she said. "How did he get his information from the distributors?" The police officer opened the door a crack and looked out, then he closed it again.

"That's one of our biggest stumbling blocks," he said. "We don't know how Martinez communicated with his employers, and we don't know how Apits communicated with the Colombians."

"If they didn't use the phone, what did they do? Write letters? Emails? Did they meet at various tapas bars and exchange coded messages in folded newspapers?"

"We had Martinez under surveillance. He didn't meet anyone we can link to the supply chain. We haven't found any written evidence, and nothing on the hard drive of his personal computer. But he could have gone to an Internet café and received messages under the alias Horny Finnish Housewife, on some online message board that we don't know about."

"Did he often go to Internet cafés?"

"This was a really great place," Lotta said, stopping beside the police officer with a smile.

"Never," Niklas said. "By the way, I've found you a party girl. She says she wants to speak out in the paper as a warning to others."

"Great," Annika said, forcing herself to smile. "Thanks a lot."

"Come on, I'll drive you back to your hotel."

Lotta dashed to sit in the front seat. She was talking enthusiastically to Niklas about how much she had appreciated the bare setting of the warehouse, the harsh shadows, the worn tools.

Annika sat in the backseat trying to get a grip on her feelings.

Somewhere else.

Obviously.

What had she been expecting?

That he was going to move into the flat on Agnegatan?

She stared out of the window. Gates and walls and rooftops rushed past.

No, she thought. I wasn't expecting him to move in with me, but I did think he'd be with me for the few nights I'm actually down here.

Then a terrible thought:

He didn't think I was any good in bed.

She shut her eyes. Tried to pull herself together, console her-self.

I thought it was good, and that's what matters. He can think what he likes. I don't regret it.

She stifled a sob.

"What do you say, Annika?"

She met his gaze in the rearview mirror.

"What?" she said.

"Do you agree that art is much more real than journalism?"

She looked out of the window again.

"That's an impossible question," she said. "What does 'more real' mean? That's like asking, 'What's special about a fish?' and getting the answer: 'It can't ride a bike.'"

Niklas burst out laughing.

"What I mean is that art creates an experience inside you as a viewer, whereas newspapers only report other people's experiences," Lotta said.

"That's crap," Annika said. "Do you mean you never experience anything when you read a newspaper or watch the news on television? When children are gassed to death? Or teenage girls vanish without a trace? Or dictators are toppled and people get democracy?"

"That's not what I meant," Lotta said, sounding hurt.

"So what did you mean? That people will be more affected by your photographs of those plate shears than reading about little children dying of fentanyl gas poisoning on the floor of the land-ing outside their mother's bedroom door?"

The silence in the car was deafening. The only thing she could hear was her own agitated breathing.

Bloody hell, she thought, I'm doing it again. Going into battle for the most ridiculous things instead of talking about the real problems. There must be something wrong with me.

"Sorry," she said. "I've got the most awful headache."

"Here in Spain there are lots of fun pills," Niklas said. "Do you want me to stop at a *farmacia*?"

"I've got some paracetamol in my room," she said.

Lotta was sitting there trying to blink back tears. Niklas looked irritated.

They passed the bullfighting arena on the left and Annika could just make out the motorway below. Thank God they were nearly there.

They sat in silence until they pulled up in front of the Hotel Pyr.

"Give me a call before you leave," he said with a smile though the open window.

She slammed the back door shut and forced herself to smile back.

Lotta went straight up to her room without looking at Annika.

Fine, Annika thought, and went back out onto the street and off toward the big department store. She turned right toward the harbor and went into McDonald's. She'd had enough of spending the evenings sitting in her hotel room starving. She ordered a Quarter Pounder with Cheese, carrot sticks, and mineral water, then went and sat at a window table.

It was relatively calm around her. A few Spanish kids were laughing over toward the counter. Two smartly dressed Spanish women were talking confidentially over a couple of muffins. At the table in front of her sat a man in a suit, white shirt, and tie, next to a teenage boy in a wheelchair. The child seemed to have some sort of cerebral palsy. His arms, hands, feet, and legs were contorted, and were jerking uncontrollably. Annika made an effort not to stare at him, which was hard seeing as the boy was sitting right in front of her. She picked at her carrots and drank the water.

The dad in the suit was talking to his son in low, soft Spanish, feeding him fries and holding a cup with a straw for him to drink from. The boy tried to say something that his father evidently understood, because he laughed conspiratorially.

"*Sí, sí, claro,*" the dad said, feeding him another fry.

The door opened and an elegant woman and a girl of about five walked into the hamburger restaurant. The woman looked round the room for a moment, then lit up when she caught sight of the father and son in the wheelchair. She skipped between the tables, holding the little girl in one hand and shopping bags from D&G and Versace in the other. She went over to the table and kissed the man on the lips and the boy in the wheelchair on the cheek, and said something that made all four of them laugh, including the boy in the wheelchair.

Without thinking Annika got up from her table and walked toward the door. She bumped into tables on the way, and could feel the bruises on her legs, but they didn't hurt, because all her pain was in her chest.

There was so much love in the world, if you only knew how to find it. And what did she choose to do? Fight pathetic little battles with everyone, obsessed with the idea of winning, of being *right,* of showing off and getting recognition.

Some teenage British girls were coming along the pavement toward her, with loud voices and Zara bags in their hands, and their noses peeling. She wiped her tears with the back of her hand and walked quickly, head down, toward El Corte Inglés. She stopped outside the department store and looked up at the hotel. She didn't want to sit up there, alone in her room, waiting for someone to call.

I have to be somewhere else.

She looked in the other direction, and remembered that Rickard Marmén's estate agency was just round the corner. Maybe he was still open?

She turned right, past the British bookshop, and saw that the lights were still on. She tried the door, but it was locked. She stood in front of the shop window and cupped her hands round her eyes to escape her own reflection.

The office was empty, but a bluish reflection on the wall behind the desk gave away the fact that the computer was still on.

She knocked on the glass with her knuckles.

Rickard Marmén poked his head through a doorway at the back of the room. He seemed to say something, but Annika couldn't make out what.

He disappeared again, but reappeared a moment later with a key in his hand.

"Annika Bengtzon, our favorite representative of the Swedish press," he said, holding the door open. "Welcome!"

Annika smiled and air-kissed him on both cheeks.

"And what can we do for you this evening?" the man asked.

"I don't suppose you've any new lives for sale?" she said, walking into the shop.

"But my dear, we don't sell anything else here. Dreams and new lives, that's our speciality. Did you have anything particular in mind? Marble floors, or wild vines on the terrace? Four bathrooms, each with a sea view?"

She laughed, and with the laughter her spirits rose. She sat down on one of the chairs in front of his desk. There was a large dust ball by the desk leg. The window looked smeared. Rickard Marmén locked the door again and came and sat next to her on the other chair.

"So what's wrong with the life you've already got?"

Annika looked down at the floor and decided to blank the question.

"I'm here to write some articles about drug trafficking and money laundering," she said, "so right now things aren't too bad. The title of the series is 'The Costa Cocaine.'"

"How exciting," Rickard Marmén said. "Glass of wine?"

Annika shook her head.

Rickard Marmén stood up anyway. He went and fetched a bottle of red wine and two glasses.

"You can keep me company," he said. "So how are you getting on with the cocaine?"

Rickard Marmén poured some rioja into both glasses.

"I've got a bit more to do before I go back home," she said.

"I can't help you there, I'm afraid," he said. "Drugs are one of the few things I've never dealt in. I've got no contacts at all there. Cheers!"

He drank with his eyes closed.

Annika tasted the wine. It tasted of vinegary alcohol. She put the glass to one side.

"Has business picked up?" she asked.

"If it was static before," he said, "it's going backward now. The mortgage companies are now demanding that buyers have fifty percent of the cost in cash, even if there's already planning permission. Only the drug barons have that sort of money, and although there are a lot of them, they can't keep the whole market afloat. Prices are falling, so people would rather sit it out than sell. I'm thinking of opening a letting agency instead. That's what people are doing these days, leasing their property in the hope that things will pick up . . ."

Annika interrupted his tale of woe.

"The drug barons pay cash?" she said.

"If there's one thing they've got plenty of, it's cash. You said you were writing about money laundering? Building large, expensive houses is one way of cleaning up dirty money."

Annika looked at the man beside her. She really shouldn't be remotely surprised.

"So you know how money laundering works?"

Rickard Marmén smiled a very sad smile.

"Sadly I've never been blessed with any dirty money that needed laundering," he said, "but knowing how the washing machine works is no great secret."

"Would you mind telling me?"

"What do you want to know?"

She pulled her pen and notepad from her bag. Rickard Marmén poured another glass of wine.

"So they buy property?" she said.

The estate agent nodded.

"The laws are constantly being tightened up," he said. "Nowadays you can't just waltz into a bank with a sack full of dollars, the police will be there before you can say 'deposit account.' The banks and financial institutions have a duty to report anything suspicious. You have to be able to explain that you acquired the money legally."

"So you buy a house?"

"Or you buy a plot and build a house. As much as possible gets paid in cash. It's no problem for the builder to roll up at his bank with a bundle of notes, because he can explain that it came from building a house. He'll have receipts for pipes and cement and bricks. And then the house is there, all finished, and can be sold for x million euros. The drug baron can prove that he got the money from selling a house, perfectly legally. And then the money is back in the system."

"They must build a lot of houses," Annika said.

"And they must have a lot of luxury yachts that they sail about in," Rickard Marmén said. "That's why Gibraltar is so useful."

Annika put down her pen.

"I read about something called Operation White Whale," she said. "Some huge crackdown where loads of crooks were arrested, and more than two hundred and fifty villas seized. Apparently they used solicitors and companies in Gibraltar."

Rickard Marmén nodded enthusiastically and drained his second glass.

"That's it exactly!" he said.

Annika was taking notes.

"So how does it work? The money launderer sets up a company in Gibraltar," she said, drawing a circle in the middle of her page. "Then what?"

"Several companies," Rickard Marmén said patiently, reaching over and moving her notepad to his own lap. He drew several smaller circles around the first one.

"The barons feed money into a few of the companies, and then they start sending invoices to each other. For rent, perhaps, or consultancy services, import and export of goods, everything between heaven and earth."

"But none of that is actually real?" Annika asked. "All the invoices are false?"

The estate agent poured some more wine.

"Are you sure you don't want any?"

Annika pointed at the circles.

"So when all the invoices are there, then it's perfectly all right that the money is there as well?" she asked.

"Hey presto," Rickard Marmén said. "Dirty drug money has become lovely clean company profits, all of it audited and signed off by solicitors and bankers and accountants. And Gibraltar is completely tax-free, which of course is wonderfully practical!"

"But doesn't anyone check to make sure that it's all above board?"

"Of course. All the solicitors and bankers and accountants."

"Solicitors and accountants in Gibraltar?"

"Exactly."

She was starting to realize why Patrik had been so keen for her to interview someone practicing there.

"You don't happen to know a Swedish solicitor I could interview?"

"In Gibraltar?"

He rolled the wine around his mouth as he thought. Then he swallowed loudly.

"Not a Swede," he said, "but a Dane."

"Does he launder money?"

Rickard Marmén smiled again.

"Like I said, sadly not for me. Would you like me to call him?"

"If you wouldn't mind."

She went through to the toilet while Rickard Marmén, swaying slightly, made his way round his desk and dialed a number with the prefix 350. There was no toilet paper, and the washbasin had dark gray tidemarks.

Rickard Marmén had evidently cut back on cleaning costs.

She stood and looked at her reflection as she heard the estate agent's voice rising and falling out in the shop. It was obvious that Annika had been crying. Her eyes were red and her lashes looked like spiders' legs from the clumped mascara.

She realized how incredibly tired she felt.

Then she heard the telephone being hung up out in the office. She dutifully flushed some water in the basin and went back out to Rickard Marmén again.

"Stig Seidenfaden will see you in his office first thing tomorrow," the estate agent said. "Do you feel like heading down to the harbor for a bite to eat?"

She smiled, but felt ready to collapse.

"Thanks," she said, "but I've already eaten. Now I need to go and write an article."

Rickard Marmén tutted unhappily.

"All work and no play makes Jack a dull boy," he said.

"Oh," Annika said, "I think you're pretty good fun."

"I was thinking more of you," the estate agent said seriously as he switched off his computer.

They headed out through the door together.

Rickard Marmén pulled down the obligatory metal shutter and secured it with a padlock to a hook in the pavement.

"Let me know if there's anything else you need help with," he said, then waved and disappeared into the alleyways leading to the harbor.

The lobby was completely empty. There wasn't even any sign of the woman in reception.

Annika hurried in and up to her room without meeting anyone. Best of all, there was no sign of Lotta. Relieved, she slumped onto the edge of the bed and stared down at the marble floor.

That's how I see things, she thought. If I can avoid confrontation, if I don't have to talk and explain myself, then I've won. If I can talk about work, and make use of other people's expertise in my work, then I feel good. As long as someone answers my questions and does what I say, all my anxiety fades away.

She straightened her back.

And that's not very healthy, she thought. It might even be worthy of its own diagnosis. What if I am actually mentally ill?

Maybe she ought to go to see a shrink after all, like Anne Snapphane had been trying to persuade her to do for so long.

Or else she could try to change her behavior. Make an effort to be more accommodating, even with people who didn't do as she said. How hard could that be?

She stood up and walked around the room restlessly. People with far worse problems than hers managed to fit in. They had the capacity to appreciate love; it happened all over the place, all the time. It happened in damp prison cells, where men were locked away because they were scared of their closest relatives. It happened in half-empty hamburger joints, where people with a disabled child managed to stick together and love both each other and life.

She sat back down on the bed and pulled her bag onto her lap. She took out her mobile and sat there with it in her hand. She had to let Lotta know they would be going to Gibraltar early the next morning. The question was whether she should call her or send a text. She hesitated for half a second, then decided to text her. Then she clicked to check the list of missed calls.

Thomas's number was second on the list, after the government office.

She looked at the time, quarter past eight, then she gulped and pressed *Call*.

The phone rang, once, twice, three times, four . . .

"Hello, Thomas here . . ."

She had to clear her throat.

"Er, hello," she said. "It's me."

"Hi, hello!" he said. "How are you?"

A double greeting. So he was surprised to hear from her.

"I saw you called me," she said. "Sometime this morning?"

"Yes, I did! Can you hold on?"

He disappeared from the phone for a few seconds, and she heard him say something in English in the background.

"That's better," he said. "I'm outside now."

"Where are you?"

"At the hotel, the Parador. A golf resort right by the sea, and right under the flight path to the airport. If you hear something that sounds like the Third World War, it'll be the easyJet flight from London bringing a load of British tourists on a package holiday to Torremolinos . . ."

The rest of his words were drowned out by the terrible roar of a plane coming in to land.

"That was it," he said, and she couldn't help laughing. He must have had some wine, he wasn't usually this lighthearted.

"Did you want anything particular when you called?" she asked feebly, transferring responsibility for the call onto him.

"Er, yes," he said. "I got a call from the insurance company this morning. Do you remember that damage assessor, Zachrisson?"

She shut her eyes and remembered a small man with a wide, dishonest smile, in a glass-walled, high-rise office with chrome furniture.

"How could I forget?" she said.

"He called me and said we're going to get the insurance money. Do you know if anything's happened?"

She laughed with relief, so it really was true.

"They've identified the person who did it," she said. "It's a woman who's in prison in the US. She's not going to be extradited, so there won't be a trial, but any suspicions against us have been dropped."

She said "us" rather than "me," but he didn't protest.

"That's brilliant," he said simply.

She gulped, then said:

"Do you want to celebrate?"

"Celebrate?"

"What are you doing tomorrow evening?"

"The negotiations are due to finish at four or so. We were going to have dinner."

She bit her lip, making it bleed.

"Okay," she said, feeling a wave of embarrassment spread across her face. "Of course. You've got dinner planned . . ."

There were a few long moments of silence down the line. She shut her eyes and put her hand over them.

"Mind you, it's just the Scandinavian delegation," he said. "The Norwegians have come along for the ride as usual, taking part in all the things they like about the EU, but refusing to pay for any of it . . ."

He fell silent.

"I could interview you about how the negotiations have gone," Annika said.

"It might be a bit hard to summarize without . . ."

"You can just say that the discussions have been very reward-ing, that you're making good progress, and that everything's going as well as could be expected."

He thought for a moment, then made up his mind.

"They can manage without me. Where shall we meet?"

She felt a flutter of happiness in her stomach, and had to stifle a squeal of joy.

"I'm staying in Puerto Banús," she said, trying to sound fo-cused. "Have you ever been here?"

"Once, with my parents when I was fourteen. Where are you staying?"

She gave him the name of the hotel and some basic directions, the first section of the toll motorway, but not the second, because then you end up in Estepona and you don't want that.

They arranged to meet in the lobby at eight o'clock.

Then they hung up, and she remembered that she was sup-posed to be writing something, but she was feeling so tired that she pulled off her skirt and top and crept under the covers, her mind full of confused but hopeful thoughts, and fell asleep just as the lights came on along the motorway.

Dawn came later to the west of Spain than any other part of Europe.

That wasn't the result of any discrimination on the part of the sun or the weather gods, but a political decision by the Spanish authorities. They decided that the whole of the Spanish mainland should share the same time zone as the rest of Europe, one hour ahead of Greenwich Mean Time, which made no geographic sense. Annika was standing on the beach in shorts, a hooded jacket, and trainers, watching the sun rise over Puerto Banús at half past seven in the morning. The same sun was shining on the other side of the sea, hitting the red mountains of Morocco, but there it was only half past five.

She looked out across the water for a while, thinking about time and what we do with it.

Her last day at work on the Costa del Sol. She would be flying home early the following morning. She hadn't written up a single word of any of the interviews she had conducted. All the material existed only as fragmentary notes in her pad or as digital information on her mobile. It would take days to go through it and structure it into anything that was publishable. And none of the articles felt particularly interesting. She hadn't had any time to do what she'd really been hoping to do: Check out the members of the Söderström family.

There has to be a motive for this crime that we haven't identified. Executing an entire family is an expression of serious fucking brutality. The killer was making a point. We don't know which one of the victims was the real target. Sebastian Söderström was a charming slacker, Veronica Söderström was a well-regarded solicitor. If you don't ask any questions, you don't get any answers. Suzette vanished without trace on December 30 last year. The worst of it may not be that she's dead.

She put the thoughts out of her mind.

The wind had got up during the night. It had changed direction, and the air was cooler now. She was freezing in her skimpy shorts.

Gibraltar was going to be a nightmare. They needed pictures from there, and they'd have to get some good shots of the Swedish girl who was going to spill the beans about her jet-set lifestyle. The fact was that the girl might end up being the only person they could print a picture of in any of the articles; that all depended on whether the solicitor was willing to be photographed.

This wasn't going to win any prizes for journalism, she knew that already.

Mind you, her articles never did. She covered the wrong subject areas, in the wrong medium. Heavy politics with a shaky hand-held television camera was a cast-iron way of getting nominated, along with sensitive articles in one of the pompous morning papers about children or old people threatened by council cuts, and war of course. War was actually easiest. You just needed an old man holding a white flag on some road in Iraq, and you could get Picture of the Year.

She raised her face toward the bloodred sun for a minute or so, then turned back toward the hotel. If she was in luck, she'd have time to eat breakfast before Lotta came down.

They bumped into each other outside the lifts. Lotta got out of one just as Annika was about to get in the other.

"Britain hasn't signed up to the Schengen Agreement," Annika said. "You'll need your passport. We'll set off in half an hour."

Then the doors closed and Annika was carried up toward the third floor.

She showered, got dressed, gathered her things together, and wondered how she was going to persuade Lotta to pick up her camera.

It was ridiculous, she thought, that the most troublesome part of an already difficult assignment was working out how to get the photographer to do her job.

She knew Patrik was expecting an utterly corrupt solicitor, and Swedish, obviously, who was prepared to have his name and photograph printed alongside an article in which he explained how many billions he had laundered for the drugs mafia.

She doubted whether Rickard Marmén's acquaintance was planning to volunteer that sort of information.

This had every chance of being a really excruciating interview.

How nice of you to see me, tell me, have you been bought off by the mafia? Oh, really? And what do you think about the fact that your colleagues have been?

She would just have to let him explain how the setup with companies hidden from official oversight worked, and ask him if he saw any dangers or shortcomings with it, and then bulk out the article with Rickard Marmén's description of how money laundering worked. And she would have to sew it all together so that the Dane was the personification of an activity that he didn't actually represent, ideally in such a way that the paper wouldn't get sued.

She could hear Anders Schyman's voice in her head: *It's just a question of how you frame the article.*

She left her room, closed the door, and headed toward the lifts.

*   *   *

Lotta had even more equipment with her than the previous day: the rucksack with her camera and lenses, a large flash, a tripod for the camera and another for the flash, a circular screen to direct the light, and another bag whose contents Annika had no idea about.

"Do you really think you need to take all that?" she asked.

Lotta didn't answer, just carried it all purposefully out to the car, first the rucksack, then the two tripods, and finally the screen and bag.

"We only need fairly straightforward pictures," Annika said. "Really just four: a general view of Gibraltar, a shot of Main Street, a portrait of the solicitor, and one of the girl in Estepona."

Lotta got in the car and started the engine. Annika got in the passenger seat with her bag on her lap. She pulled out a bundle of papers, notes, and printouts, and set to work reading and making notes on them. She knew she would end up feeling carsick, but it would be worth it to avoid having to talk.

The photographer drove up onto the N340, then turned right toward the toll motorway. She didn't say a word until they were halfway to Estepona.

"Your outburst yesterday was completely unacceptable," she said, glaring straight ahead through the windscreen.

"Not now," Annika said, without looking up from her papers. "Not on the motorway."

Lotta was gripping the steering wheel so hard that her knuckles were white.

The drive was shorter than Annika had dared to hope. They arrived at La Línea, the Spanish border town that had practically merged with Gibraltar, after just half an hour. They drove along a four-lane highway that followed the coast, with the vast rock of Gibraltar rising up in front of them, 430 meters straight up from the sea according to Annika's printouts from Wikipedia.

"Try to find somewhere to park," Annika said. "It's supposed to be really difficult to drive across the border in a car, and there's no guarantee that they'll let us through at all seeing as we're in a hire car."

Lotta jerked her head.

"I'm going to take good pictures, and for that I need good equipment. I can't drag everything with me, so I'll have to take the car across."

"To get the pictures we need, you don't need all that studio equipment," Annika said.

Then Lotta had to brake sharply. The cars in front of them formed an enormous queue that they couldn't even see the front of.

Annika sighed. They waited for a minute. Two minutes. Five minutes.

Then she opened the door and got out.

"I'll go and see what's happened."

It was considerably cooler here than in Marbella. The sea on her right was the Atlantic, and the water she could make out beyond the rock in front of her was the Mediterranean, and the wind was coming from the Atlantic. She was glad she'd decided to wear her jeans and a sweater.

She walked past car after car, some hundred meters, until she could see where the queue started. Then she turned and went back. Lotta had moved about four meters. She got back in the car.

"This is the queue for the border crossing into Gibraltar," she said. "We can probably expect to sit here for a couple of hours if we're going to drive across. At least."

"You don't respect my integrity as a photographer," Lotta said. "I have to be able to feel that I'm happy to put my name to everything I produce. You tell me to take a nondescript picture of an ugly prison, when it would actually be possible to take a really dramatic photograph of the same thing."

Annika swallowed hard.

"Maybe," she said, "but it's the ugly prison that's important for the article. It doesn't matter that there are loads of women with goats and furrowed faces around us, because right now we're here to write about drugs and money laundering."

"I'm not talking about women with furrowed faces, I only took those pictures so I had something to do while I was waiting. Of course it's possible to take good pictures of a prison, but you have to follow the light, you have to work with the picture. Be there at dawn and dusk, see how the colors change . . ."

"So why weren't you there then?" Annika asked.

"You're the one who takes all the decisions! You're the one who says when we're going somewhere and where we're going. You treat me like I'm your secretary."

"Have I stopped you from taking the initiative? Have I said no on any occasion that you've suggested something? You've got exactly what you wanted every time you've opened your mouth!"

Lotta looked down at her hands and tried to stifle a sob.

"This isn't easy," she said. "I'm completely new to this, and you're Annika Bengtzon. Do you really think I dare suggest to you what we should do?"

Annika heard herself gasp.

"What do you mean, 'you're Annika Bengtzon'? What the hell's that supposed to mean?"

"Everyone knows how you treat temps. Do you think I wanted to come on this job, and spend four days in your company?"

Annika stuffed all her papers in her bag, opened the car door, and got out.

"Where are you going?" Lotta shouted from inside the car.

"Take whatever fucking pictures you want to. I'm going to interview the solicitor. See you at the airport tomorrow morning."

She slammed the door behind her and marched off toward the border crossing with her bag over her shoulder.

*   *   *

There was no queue at all to cross the border on foot. She showed her passport and left the Spanish side, walked ten meters or so across no-man's-land, and entered the British border post.

The building looked like an underground station in some London suburb. The ceiling was low and arched like a tunnel, the floor gray-blue, the walls painted concrete. There were a few tired potted plants and a Coca-Cola machine, and a machine selling disgusting British chocolate. A sweaty, red-faced Brit was sitting at a desk and gave her passport a desultory glance as she walked past.

She stopped at the tourist information office at the end of the tunnel, and asked for a map of the city with City Mill Lane marked on it.

"Go over the runway," the tourist guide said, pointing through the door, "then up to the left, over the drawbridge and in through the city walls, and you'll be in Main Street. When you get to The Plaza turn left again, and City Mill Lane is a bit farther up the rock."

She said thank you and went out of the door, and found herself in Great Britain, on Winston Churchill Avenue. She hoisted her bag up onto her shoulder, and began to cross a landing strip that stretched from one sea to the other.

This was where Veronica Söderström had worked. She had crossed this border every day, crossing this landing strip to get to work. Or did she usually drive? Did she sit in that long queue, or had she found some way of avoiding it? Why on earth did she put up with it?

There had to be a very good reason why she had established her office in Gibraltar.

The number of people crossing the landing strip was fairly small. There was a cold side wind blowing from the Atlantic, and she hunched her shoulders and pulled her sleeves down over her fingers. Her pulse slowly calmed down. She forced Lotta's words from her mind, *"Do you think I wanted to spend four days in your company?"*

She was trembling as if she were actually freezing.

In front of her were some hideously ugly concrete apartment blocks, with washing hanging off them. The car park outside was old and rusty.

There might be a lot of money here, she thought, but it doesn't show in the look of the place.

The center of the city was older, better looked after, and seriously commercialized. The main street had ornate benches that no one was sitting on, and elaborate lampposts and rubbish bins, and hundreds of tax-free shops for tourists. It was a kaleidoscope of jewelers and off-licenses and fashion boutiques, department stores and mobile phone shops and toy shops, and, thank God, camera shops.

She went inside one of them and asked for a decent digital camera with a wide-angle lens and a simple zoom, a large memory, and a charged battery.

I can use it to take pictures of the children afterward, she thought. After all, I'll soon have the insurance money.

She sat down on one of the ornate benches outside the shop and skimmed through the English-language instructions for the camera. It was as simple as she had been hoping. Point and click. The camera automatically adjusted everything, from the aperture to shutter speed and focus. She dropped it into her bag with the rest of her clutter and carried on along Main Street.

Ten minutes later she found City Mill Lane, a narrow, winding street with no pavements clambered up the western side of the rock. She set off up the road, getting out of breath thanks to her heavy bag. The noise from Main Street below died away and soon there was total silence up among the buildings. There was a smell of dust and sausages.

Number 34 was a brown door between a travel agency and a barbershop.

The Danish solicitor Stig Seidenfaden had a very modest office on the second floor of the old building in City Mill Lane. He received her with a formal bow and showed her into a small conference room where tea and scones had been laid out.

"So you're a good friend of Rickard Marmén," he said, looking at her with interest. "How long have you known each other?"

Annika sat down on one side of the table, and Stig Seidenfaden sat down at one end.

"We meet up for dinner every now and then," she said vaguely. "Rickard often helps me with contacts . . ."

A secretary came in with a sugar bowl, which she put down on the table, then she glided out silently and closed the door behind her.

There was a short and slightly oppressive silence once the secretary had left. Annika looked around. Three windows filled almost the whole of the wall facing the street. You could see right into the building opposite, into another conference room that looked very similar to the one she was sitting in. It was very quiet. The sun creeping through the top few centimeters of the window was making the dust up near the ceiling dance.

Stig Seidenfaden cleared his throat and leaned forward across the table.

"Rickard told me that you were interested in interviewing a Scandinavian solicitor in Gibraltar," he said. "There aren't that many of us, and of course one of our number died last winter."

"You mean Veronica Söderström?" Annika said.

The man nodded.

"We tend to stick together, us Nordic types down here in the sun. Rickard's friends are my friends. How can I help you?"

"Did you know Veronica Söderström?"

Stig Seidenfaden poured some tea from the pot and sighed.

"We weren't close friends, but naturally we knew each other. Some tea?"

Annika moved her cup and the solicitor filled it. The china was delicate, decorated with roses and a gold rim. The saucer was chipped.

"What sort of law did Veronica Söderström specialize in?"

The solicitor looked rather surprised.

"Her practice was somewhat broader than mine. She dealt with business cases and crime. She was also authorized to work as a public notary, I seem to recall. I only provide corporate services."

"Businesses and taxes?" Annika said.

He nodded.

"Can you explain how the tax system in Gibraltar works?"

He nodded once more and stirred his tea.

"People have been able to register tax-free companies here since 1967," he said, "but it wasn't until Spain joined the EU in 1985 that things started to take off."

She had taken out her pen and notepad and was making notes.

"Is anyone allowed to register a company here?"

The solicitor leaned back in his chair, holding the small handle of the teacup tightly and sticking his little finger out.

"There are certain criteria that need to be fulfilled. The working capital of the company has to be over a hundred British pounds."

He paused to give her time to write it down.

"No resident of Gibraltar is allowed to be the ultimate owner of the company. The company is only allowed to conduct its business here if all its income is derived from sources outside Gibraltar."

She glanced at the man, at his serious expression and bulging stomach beneath his shirt.

Was this what Veronica Söderström had traveled to Gibraltar every day for, to do this? To uphold some sort of washed-out British business morality in a make-believe country on the edge of Africa?

"The company must have its official address here, and keep its register of shareholders here. And lastly, the proprietor must be able to attest to his good standing and financial status."

She made an effort to look interested.

"Who provides those references?"

"They have to be given by a bank, a solicitor, or an accountant."

Annika nodded; this was what Rickard Marmén had mentioned.

"And there's no official oversight of companies registered here?"

"No. All information is treated as confidential, and isn't entered on any public register."

"And there are no taxes?"

"There's no income tax here, no tax on company profits, no stamp duty on the transfer of shares, and no taxation at source. The only thing that's obligatory is a fixed tax of 225 British pounds each year."

Annika couldn't help shaking her head.

"It seems remarkable," she said, "that something can work like this in modern-day Europe."

"Not for much longer," the solicitor said. "The rules are changing, this system's coming to an end in 2010. The EU is putting a stop to it."

She looked up at him as he sipped his tea.

"But there'll be alternative solutions," he said. "There always are."

"Will there be any more transparency after 2010?"

"I can't imagine that there would be," the solicitor said. "Have you tried the scones? My wife made them."

"Your wife?"

"And secretary."

He spread some marmalade on one of them. It crunched as he bit into it.

"I've spoken to people who describe Gibraltar as the biggest money-laundering machine in Europe," Annika said. "What's your opinion about that?"

The solicitor carefully chewed his scone, picked up a napkin, and wiped the marmalade from the corners of his mouth.

"I'm a solicitor," he said, "not a prosecutor. I have to trust my clients. If they say that a source of income is legitimate, then it isn't my job to question that information. We have to remember that. But I only provide references when I can personally guarantee the good standing of my client."

"Do you see any dangers with this system?"

He leaned forward over the table.

"This system wasn't constructed by lawyers and solicitors," he said. "We just make sure that it's adhered to. Any solicitors who actively participate in money laundering, who set up fake companies and ski some sort of slalom around the legislation—well, I dissociate myself entirely from them."

"Do you know of any like that?"

He looked at her and smiled.

"Even if I did, do you think I'd tell you?"

She smiled back politely.

"No," she said, "I doubt it. Would it be all right if I took a picture of you?"

He raised his eyebrows in surprise.

"Yes," he said, "I suppose so. Where? Here?"

"In your office, perhaps? With some files and documents in the background?"

Usually it was best to avoid pictures of men sitting behind desks, but in this case it would serve a purpose. The reader would see the files and wonder what they contained, and would hear the washing machine rumbling in the background.

He shook his head.

"I don't let anyone in there," he said.

Smart man.

She took out the camera and switched it on, and held the viewfinder up to her right eye.

It looked a bit odd. There was a potted plant in the background, and the solicitor was sitting directly between her and the plant. As a result, it looked as though the man had a plant growing out of the top of his head.

"Perhaps we could move closer to the window?" she said. "For the light . . ."

She positioned the man beside one of the windowsills, with his profile facing the glass. Then she stood in front of him. The daylight was soft and indirect. Half the solicitor's face was clearly visible, and the other half was in shadow. The effect was rather striking.

She took several pictures of him sitting at the table as well, and then she was done. They stepped out into the little hallway again, and the secretary-wife materialized on silent feet and asked if everything had gone all right. She spoke English with a British accent.

"Very well," Annika said politely. "And thank you for the scones, they were delicious."

Then she realized she hadn't had one.

"Veronica Söderström," she said quickly. "Where was her office?"

"I suppose it's still there," Stig Seidenfaden said. "It's over in Tareq's Passage. Opposite the church."

Annika did up the zip on her bag, shook his hand and thanked him.

"Say hello to Rickard," Stig Seidenfaden called down the stairs after her.

The stream of people on Main Street had thickened into a dark mass. The street led vaguely uphill, and she took out the camera and stood on one of the benches. Using the telephoto lens she compressed the crowd still further, then took a few portrait shots and several in landscape.

There, enough establishing shots.

She stood there for a few minutes trying to identify a suitable subject for a photograph: a young man with broad shoulders and jeans that clung to his thighs.

He was walking up Main Street with his arm round his girlfriend. He was even wearing a sports shirt.

"Hello," Annika said, walking up to him with her hand out.

Taken by surprise, the couple stopped and shook her outstretched hand: an instinctive reaction in Westerners.

Annika explained that she was a photographer, and asked if she could take a picture of the young man from behind, because she needed an anonymous picture of a young man to illustrate a newspaper article.

The man lit up, but his girlfriend was unhappy.

"What's the point of that?" she said.

"What sort of article?" the young man asked.

"It's for a Swedish paper, the *Evening Post*," she said. "Have you ever seen it?"

He shook his head.

Annika positioned him so he was facing a dark-gray building, asked him to spread his legs and hook his fingers in the waist of his jeans, and put most of his weight on his right leg.

He was almost a carbon copy of Niklas Linde.

She took a series of portrait and landscape shots, then asked him to turn his head slightly to the left. The sun was hitting his hair and back, putting his profile in shadow.

That would do as an anonymous picture of the heroic Swedish police officer on the Costa del Sol.

She thanked him for his help.

"When can I see the picture?" the young man asked with interest.

"Keep an eye on the online edition, the Swedish *Evening Post*," Annika said.

She put the camera away and made her way to the church. It was white, and looked like all the churches in Pedro Almodóvar's films. In front of it was a small square. On the far side were two alleyways, each entered through an archway: Giro's Passage to the right, and Tareq's Passage on the left.

She headed off to the left. The archway led straight through the building at the end and into a narrow alley. She was met by the deafening roar of a huge air-conditioning unit and stood there, at something of a loss.

The old buildings lining the alleyway were poorly maintained. Electricity cables hung like lianas between the windows. Water and drainage pipes had been stuck to the outsides of the buildings, making them look misshapen. All the shutters on the windows of the lowest two floors were closed and locked with padlocks.

She walked farther down the alley and found a door with an entry phone but no identifying label. Round the corner was a small brass sign:

VS Counseling
Barrister—Solicitor—Commissioner for Oaths
International Legal Services
International Corporate Services

VS, for Veronica Söderström.

But where was the entrance?

She walked on another ten meters, passing an estate agent's that looked closed, and a chemist's that was just opening up, and stopped to think.

What had Veronica Söderström spent all her time doing in this run-down building?

Did she fight to defend those let down by society? People who had been wrongly convicted? Did she arrange contracts worth billions for the fishing industry?

Or did she launder money?

If you don't ask any questions, you don't get any answers.

She looked down at her clothes. Trainers, jeans, and a bobbly sweater from H&M: There was no way she was going to pass as a chief executive or international investor. She walked determinedly toward the unlabeled entry phone. She pressed the button hard, and held it down. Eventually it came to life with a great deal of crackling.

"Yes, what is it?" a voice said in an American accent, sounding young, male, and annoyed.

"Hello, my name's Annika Bengtzon, and I need some help with a legal problem," she said. "Can I come up?"

The phone was still making a noise. So the irritated young man hadn't hung up.

"A legal problem?" he said. "I can't help you with that. I'm very sorry."

Annika didn't believe that for a moment. He didn't sound the slightest bit sorry.

"I can go somewhere else," Annika said, "but Veronica would have wanted me to come here first."

Another silence, the same crackling from the phone.

"You knew Veronica?"

"I'm their stable manager. I look after My's pony."

After a few moments' hesitation the lock on the door clicked.

She hurried to push the door open and stepped into a pitch-black stairwell. The door closed behind her and she blinked a few times to get her eyes used to the dark. Then she saw a luminous red button just to the left of the door. She pressed it and the lights came on with an audible click.

A naked bulb was casting an uncertain light over a small entrance hall. A narrow staircase led up steeply in front of her. The walls and ceiling had seen better days. The floor must have been beautiful once upon a time; under a layer of dirt she could make out a blue, white, and brown mosaic.

There were two doors, one on the right, one on the left. They were both barred and padlocked. She headed for the stairs and started climbing up them, almost literally.

There didn't seem to be any other businesses in the building. The doors on the first floor were barred as well.

The office of VS Counseling was right at the top of the building, on the second floor. On the door to the left was a similar brass sign to the one down in the street. She couldn't see a doorbell and knocked so hard it hurt her knuckles.

The door opened so abruptly that she had to take a step back.

"Good morning," she said shyly, holding out her hand. "Thanks for seeing me."

The young man really was very young. He was dressed in a neatly ironed shirt and tie, suit trousers, and polished leather shoes. His expression softened as he looked her up and down. She evidently wasn't a threat.

"Henry Hollister," he said, sounding rather less irritated now.

"I've never needed legal advice before. This all feels rather strange for me."

"Come in," he said, stepping aside to let her into the office.

It looked like an old flat that hadn't been changed very much to adapt it to its new function. The doors were all open, three small rooms off to the right, a kitchen straight ahead and a larger room off to the left. It was completely quiet. The office seemed utterly deserted, apart from the young American. There was a smell of coffee and unaired fabrics.

"Can I offer you anything to drink?" Henry Hollister asked.

"No, thanks, I'm fine," Annika said.

The young man showed her into the large room on the left. It was a conference room, very similar to Stig Seidenfaden's. Solicitors in Gibraltar evidently never saw people inside their own offices.

They sat down opposite one another, and Henry Hollister frowned deeply and folded his hands on the table.

"Well," he said, "how can I help you?"

"I'm not actually the one who needs help," Annika said. "It's my brother. He's been arrested for possession of drugs, hash."

There was a surprised silence. The man looked at her and blinked several times.

"Possession of hash?" he said. "Where?"

"In Puerto Banús," Annika said.

"But possession isn't a punishable offense under Spanish law." Shit, shit, shit. She hadn't realized that.

"The police have accused him of intending to supply," she said.

"How much cannabis are we talking about?"

She gulped hard.

"Four kilos," she hazarded.

The young man blinked again and leaned back in his chair.

"Well," he said, "it would be hard to claim that amount was all for personal use. I'm sorry, but this isn't something that I . . ."

Annika leaned across the table and took hold of his hand.

"You've got to help me," she said. "He's in prison in Málaga, in a *polígono* right next to the airport . . ."

Henry pulled his hand away in horror.

"I know that prison," he said, "but I can't help you. I'm not a solicitor, just a legal assistant. I'm not qualified for active work, I'm just holding the fort for the time being."

Annika gave him a curious look.

"Holding the fort?"

"Yes, until the new owner arrives."

"Has the firm been sold?"

"It's been transferred within the holding company."

Really, *transferred within the holding company.*

She sniffed.

"Spanish legal procedures take forever, my brother's going to be shut away in there for years if I don't do something. How long will I have to wait?"

"The only thing outstanding is some sort of legal formality before the new owner can come down; it might take another month, six weeks . . ."

"Why can't he come down sooner?"

The young man looked uncomfortable.

"I don't actually know."

Annika let out a deep sigh.

"It was so tragic about Veronica," she said. "Imagine if that terrible break-in had never happened. She'd have sorted this out in no time."

The man gave her a curious look.

"Do you really think that?" he said. "I never heard of her doing any work on minor felonies in Spain."

Annika looked surprised.

"Really? I thought she did. She was always away so much, what did she spend her days doing?"

"Veronica was a business solicitor. She spent most of her time on contracts and negotiations for various international companies."

"Oh," Annika said, trying to sound disappointed. "I always thought she defended innocent people, like my brother. That's what it says on the sign downstairs, *Legal Services.*"

Henry's mouth curled into a slight grimace.

"You've no idea what criminal accusations get made against international companies," he said. "The authorities are so suspicious of successful businesses in this part of the world. It's quite different from the USA, where I come from. There free enterprise is actually encouraged."

Annika nodded cheerily.

"What sort of companies did she work with most?"

"Import export," Henry said, then looked like he was biting his tongue. He leaned toward her.

"How did you say you knew Veronica, again?"

She tried to smile and could feel her feet starting to itch.

"I look after My's pony. We haven't found a buyer for it yet, so I ride it every day so it doesn't lose its condition. It's a lovely horse, have you ever seen it?"

The American stood up.

"I'm sorry," he said, "but I can't help you."

She sighed unhappily and stood up as well.

"I suppose I'll have to try and get help somewhere else. Do you know of any good criminal law firms?"

"I'm sorry," the man repeated.

She smiled, and tried to put a bit of extra sparkle into her eyes, then held out her hand.

"Thanks for seeing me," she said.

He suddenly looked worried.

"Listen," he said, "don't tell anyone you were here talking to me. Call and book an appointment to see the new owner once he's settled in."

She pretended to be surprised.

"Okay," she said, "no problem."

They went out into the cramped hallway. On the wall outside the conference room was an ornate diploma, framed behind glass.

The Faculty of Law at the University of Oxford.

Veronica's diploma.

"If you know anyone who'd like to buy a really lovely pony, you can always call the stables," she said, closing the door behind her.

The sound of it shutting echoed between the walls. The light had gone out and the stairwell was as dark as before. She felt along the wall and found the switch.

Then she hurried quietly down the stairs.

Out in the street she stopped, out of breath, as if she'd been rushing upstairs, not down. Then she took a last look up at the building and hurried along the alleyway and round the corner. She stopped outside the closed estate agent's and fished her pen and notepad out of her bag. She sat down on the pavement and quickly jotted down what she had found out during her conversation with the young American.

Veronica had studied law at Oxford University in England. She was primarily a business solicitor, even if the sign on the wall mentioned *legal services* as well. She never worked on Spanish criminal cases. She handled contracts and negotiations for international businesses involved in import export. These international conglomerates were evidently the subject of "criminal accusations" every now and then. Perhaps that was when Veronica's *legal services* came into the picture.

After her death the firm was transferred "within the holding company." So there was clearly a company with a number of proprietors that now controlled Veronica Söderström's law firm, unless it had always done so.

The new owner, a man, was waiting for some sort of formality before he could "come down" and take over the running of the firm. Come down from where? Somewhere more senior, or from the north?

For the time being the office was manned by just an American legal assistant who was clearly so bored that he let people in off the street, something he had presumably been instructed not to do.

That much was clear from his parting remark, "don't tell anyone you were here." His smart appearance suggested sporadic contact with the outside world, otherwise he would have been wearing gray jogging trousers and a sweatshirt. Did the holding company pay unannounced visits to the office?

The building housing the office was a mystery in itself. Why was most of the building shut up and abandoned? Property prices here had gone through the roof; she'd read about that on Wikipedia. Ordinary people who worked in Gibraltar almost always lived on the Spanish side of the border, in La Línea, where housing costs were just a third of what they were in Gibraltar.

She glanced up at the window of the closed estate agency. It looked like it hadn't been open for a while. There was a little row of dead insects along the bottom of the window.

She got up and brushed the dust from her backside, and leaned forward to check out the cost of property in Gibraltar.

There wasn't much to choose from in the window, just faded pictures of a handful of villas and apartments, with little information about them and obviously no addresses. Carita had told her that Spanish houses might be on sale with ten different estate agents at the same time. No one ever had exclusive rights, so the agents always concealed the addresses in an effort to stop other agents from muscling in.

She glanced at the pictures and realized that none of the houses or flats were in Gibraltar, they looked just like all the others on the Costa del Sol.

Then she stiffened. Thought her eyes were deceiving her. She took a step closer to the window and wiped the dust from the glass.

Existing Freehold Villa.

Ideal Family Home. Ideal Investment.

The picture of the villa that was for sale, close to the top-right corner of the window, was faded and had slightly curled corners, as if it had been there for a while, exposed to sun and damp. There was no indication of where the villa was, how big it was, or what its price was, but Annika recognized it. A mixture of two and three floors, terraces and balconies, bay windows and pillars and arches, curved balcony rails and ornate iron railings. At the top was a tower with arched windows in all directions. The pool, the light, the mountainside in the background.

It was the Söderström family home in Nueva Andalucía.

The picture had to be several years old, because the trees were much smaller than she remembered, and there was a cement mixer in the bottom corner.

She moved toward the door to see if there was any indication of opening hours. Nothing, just a brass sign referring visitors to a website.

A Place in the Sun
Your Real Estate Agents on the Coast.
Visit us at www.aplaceinthesun.se

She stared at the sign and read the last line twice.

A place in the sun, dot, se.

Why dot, se?

Why would an estate agent in Gibraltar have a Swedish domain address?

She took out her notepad and wrote down the address. Then she moved back to the window to see if the villa had any sort of reference number.

It didn't.

It wasn't particularly surprising that it was for sale, she thought. Obviously the executors would have to sell it, like the pony. But why not use a new, better picture?

Unless the picture had been there ever since the Söderström family bought the villa. Veronica worked just round the corner, so obviously she must have walked past and looked in the window to see what was for sale, maybe that was how she first found it. Maybe she bought it through this particular estate agent, and they just never got round to removing the picture from the window.

She looked at her watch, it was time to head to Estepona.

Suddenly she realized that she didn't have a car.

The bus station in La Línea was in the Plaza de Europa, a round-about just a couple of blocks from the border. There were buses leaving for Estepona all the time, the next one due to set off in ten minutes. She bought a ticket at the counter, 3 euros and 64 cents, just as the bus rolled into the station. It was noisy, and belched diesel. She climbed on board and felt the floor rock. There was a smell of oil and disinfectant. The seats were stripy blue velour, and there were grubby curtains in the windows. She had a sudden flashback to the school bus that used to take her from Hälleforsnäs into Flen and on into Katrineholm.

Just like the school bus, the Spanish local service was slow, calling at every stop. A distance that would have taken fifteen minutes by car took an hour and a half. The bus drove into every tiny hamlet and stopped to let people on and off at every junction. Outside Marina de Casares she dozed off for a while. She woke up when a boy with a surfboard got on in Bahía Dorada.

The road wound along the coast. The surface of the water was white from the wind. The sky was bright blue and completely free of clouds. She could tell they were approaching Estepona.

It was hardly the city's fault that Julia had thought it was so awful there, she thought as the bus turned off toward the harbor.

The main street followed the beach. Palms and orange trees lined the road, and the wind was pulling at the treetops. The sun-beds on the beach were empty, but at the simple restaurants by the shore people had started to gather for lunch.

She suddenly realized how hungry she was.

The young jet-setting Swedish girl she was going to meet was called Wilma. Niklas had texted her the girl's mobile number.

She got off the bus at Avenida de España, pulled out her note-pad and mobile and called the number.

Wilma answered on the first ring. It sounded as if she had been holding her mobile all morning, waiting for the call. She sounded very excited about the chance to "tell her story in the paper," as she put it.

They arranged to meet in the beach restaurant below the bus station.

"Annika Bengtzon?"

Annika looked up from the menu and knew at once that the series of articles had been saved.

Wilma looked amazing. She fulfilled every single one of Patrik's criteria: young, blond, too much makeup, and a pair of seriously enlarged breasts.

Annika stood up and shook hands with her.

"It's great that you were able to see me at such short notice," she said.

"Well, you want to do your bit, don't you?" Wilma said, sitting down opposite her.

All the men in the restaurant had put their cutlery down and were staring at them.

"What would you like?" Annika said. "Have whatever you want."

"Have you tried the *almejas*? They're a sort of mussel they catch out on the reef. Or *mejillones*? They're a bit bigger. They've got shellfish here you've never seen before."

Wilma closed her menu authoritatively.

"Shall I order for you?" she asked, evidently not expecting to be contradicted. She leaned back and waved the waiter over. Her nipples were clearly visible through her tightly stretched T-shirt.

"*Camarero, queremos mariscos a la plancha, con mucho ajo y hierbas. Y una botella de vino blanco de la casa, por favor!*"

"Goodness," Annika said. "Where did you learn to speak so fluently?"

The girl looked at her in surprise.

"At school," she said. "Why?"

Annika took out her notepad and pen.

"How old are you?" she asked.

"I'll be twenty in July."

"You know I got your name from Niklas Linde?" Annika said. "He said you wouldn't mind telling me about life down here on the Costa del Sol . . ."

"I want to warn other people," Wilma said, smiling warmly at the waiter as he put a misted bottle of white wine and two glasses on their table. "*Gracias, señor, quiero probarlo.*"

She rolled the wine around her mouth for a moment with a practiced gesture, then nodded in approval. The waiter filled their glasses, then glided away.

"It might look like life down here is all bars and nightclubs and guys with flashy cars, but there's another completely different side of the Costa del Sol," Wilma said, sipping her wine.

"The drug dealers want to get rid of as much of their stash as possible down here," she went on. "That saves them the hassle of transport, and losing any of it on the way up through Europe. You don't drink wine?"

Annika looked up from her notepad in surprise. The girl was like a walking, talking headline generator. She just had to sit here taking dictation: This series of articles was starting to look pretty good.

"Er, yes, I'm just not thirsty."

She drank a symbolic sip; the wine was unpleasantly sharp.

"You *loca!*" Wilma said. "You don't just drink wine because you're thirsty! It's incredibly easy for young girls to be charmed by the good-looking guys down here. They're nice and suntanned, they've got big yachts and fast cars, and use girls as disposable goods. I see it time after time, Swedish girls turning up here thinking they're going to marry a millionaire and live the high life in some huge villa in Nueva Andalucía, but all that ever happens is that they get hooked on coke and end up nervous wrecks."

"What about you?" Annika said. "Have you tried cocaine?"

Wilma nodded, suddenly very serious.

"Yes," she said, "and I bitterly regret it. I got picked up in a raid back in February, but that probably saved me. Talk about a warning! As luck would have it, I was questioned by Niklas Linde, and he put me on the right track. I mean, he's just brilliant. Do you know him?"

Annika picked her glass up and took a large gulp.

"No," she said. "Not at all. I've just interviewed him a couple of times."

"It actually makes you feel a lot safer knowing the Swedish police has such competent officers."

"Can you tell me about the raid?"

"It was a private party down by the harbor, in Puerto Banús, I mean, in rooms above one of the clubs. The police came in at half past two at night with sniffer dogs and everything, and searched everyone. Of course it was really horrible, but actually really good at the same time."

"Are you going to be charged?"

She shook her head.

"No, I only had a few grams for personal use."

Ah yes, Annika thought. Possession alone wasn't a punishable offense.

"So what were you doing at the party? What was it that attracted you to that lifestyle?"

The waiter came over with their food, an enormous dish laden with grilled shellfish, swimming in oil, garlic, and herbs.

"*Ah, qué bueno!*" Wilma exclaimed in delight, clapping her hands and setting about the food.

Annika peered suspiciously at the prawns and mussels and lobsters and all the rest. She wasn't fond of shellfish, and would much rather have meatballs with lingonberry sauce if she was given the option. She prodded a prawn tentatively.

"I felt special, chosen," Wilma said. "Imagine, little me allowed to be here with all the beautiful and famous people. Princess Madeleine has been, she stayed at the Marbella Club. I never met her, obviously, but I got to know a lot of other celebrities."

"Did you know Sebastian Söderström?" Annika asked, trying not to sound too eager.

Wilma wolfed down half a small lobster and nodded enthusiastically.

"That was so awful, what happened to him. Who could have imagined that? Just think, we were at his daughter's birthday party just a week or so before they died."

Annika let the prawn drop.

"You went to a child's party?" she asked skeptically. She couldn't really see Wilma eating birthday cake in My's bedroom.

"No, you *loca*, it wasn't the little girl's birthday. The other one, Suzette."

Annika stared at her.

"You were at Suzette's party? When? Where?"

"Actually in the same place that got raided a few weeks later. Above one of the nightclubs by the harbor. If you buy four whole bottles of vodka you're automatically allowed to use it. It's very popular."

"And that's what Suzette did to celebrate her birthday?"

"No, *loca,* it was her dad. He wanted Suzette to make friends, so he invited the lot of us, all the younger ones. Sebbe was always so generous, free drinks and champagne, champagne, champagne all night long."

"Did you get to know Suzette?"

Wilma let out a deep sigh.

"Well," she said, "that young lady really didn't want to be there. She sat in a corner trying not to talk to anyone. I don't know when she left, but after a while she just disappeared."

"And when was this?"

"Just after Christmas. Boxing Day, I think. There were a few girls snorting lines in the toilet, and Sebastian was furious. He was really antidrugs and all that, and he threw them all out, just like that . . ."

"You know Suzette's missing?"

Wilma nodded, gathering together the last of the mussels.

"I read about it, it's just so awful."

"Have you got any idea where she could be?"

"No idea."

"Did she have any friends?"

"I really don't know. I only saw her that once."

"So she never used to hang around the harbor partying?"

Wilma shook her head firmly.

"Maybe once or twice, but she wasn't a party animal. If she was, I'd have known about it."

She drank the last of her wine and refilled her glass.

"So what do you do now?" Annika asked. "Do you work, or study?"

"Work," Wilma said. "I'm a consultant. I help Scandinavian companies to set up on the Costa del Sol."

Annika stared at the young woman.

"You?" she said. "Help Scandinavian companies . . . what with?"

"Finance, and getting established," she said.

Annika tried to focus her thoughts.

"And business is good?"

"Are you kidding? I know every rich old man on the whole Costa del Sol."

Wilma leaned forward, so that Annika was staring down into her massive cleavage.

"There's just one simple rule," she said in a low voice. "Never sleep with them. Because then they lose all respect for you."

Annika drank what was left in her wineglass and ordered a mineral water. Wilma finished off the rest of the bottle.

Annika asked some dutiful questions about Wilma's background and childhood (Vikingshill outside Stockholm, parents IT consultants, two younger brothers), then asked what advice she had for young women who wanted to try their luck abroad, what they should look out for, and what they should focus on, then the wine was finished and the plates cleared from the table.

"Shall we take some pictures?" Annika said. "Maybe down on the beach?"

Wilma lit up.

"That's a brilliant idea! How lucky that I've got my bikini with me!"

She pulled a tiny piece of cloth from her handbag and dangled it in Annika's face.

"Great," Annika said. "We'll try some with the bikini, and some with clothes, then the editors up in Stockholm can decide what works best."

She paid the bill. Even if the restaurant seemed basic, with its woven raffia roof and open sides, the bill wasn't remotely basic. It cost more than Annika's plane ticket.

They went down onto the beach. Wilma wanted to start with the bikini shots, and Annika didn't object. She pulled off her T-shirt, and Annika noted that the scars from her surgery were in her armpits. She slipped the bikini top on, then wiggled her hips until the G-string was in place.

Then Wilma posed cheerily on a sunbed with Estepona in the background. They wouldn't be able to use any of those pictures, but Annika snapped a whole sequence just to keep Patrik happy.

"We should probably take a few of you looking more serious as well," she said.

Wilma suddenly looked extremely serious and stern, as stern as anyone wearing a minuscule leopard-skin bikini possibly could.

"And then a few with clothes on too . . ."

She told Wilma to walk along the shore with her heels in her hand, looking out to sea with a thoughtful expression. It all worked very well. The sun looked hot and merciless, and Wilma was alone and vulnerable on the long white beach.

She looked in fascination at her new camera. This was actually great fun. And it wasn't exactly rocket science.

They split up outside the bus station and Annika sat down to wait for the next bus to Puerto Banús.

There was no sign of Lotta in the hotel lobby. Annika had no interest in any further confrontations on the subject of photography, so she greeted the woman behind the reception desk with a breezy *buenas tardes* and sneaked quickly up to her room.

It was quarter past six.

She dropped her bag on the floor and walked restlessly round the room.

An hour and forty-five minutes before she was due to meet Thomas.

The thought made her stomach knot.

She curled up on the bed and pulled the bedspread over her head. Everything became dark and silent. She lay there quite still, listening to her own heartbeat until the air ran out and she had to push the bedspread back.

She and Thomas hadn't actually sat down to talk to each other since the divorce, not once. On one occasion he had come up to the flat in Agnegatan, that Sunday evening after she got back from Spain the first time. It had been a rather strained meeting. Annika had been keen to make a good impression, and Thomas had been trying to act like he wasn't bothered. The children had rushed round like mad things, chasing each other through the rooms and yelling and laughing until Thomas told them to behave.

He thought the flat was "nice."

She said it was "nice of him to call in."

She had cried for ages that evening, and now she was going to meet him again.

She looked at the time, an hour and a half left.

She got up from the bed, sat down at her laptop, logged into the hotel network, and surfed randomly around the Swedish news sites. The *Evening Post* was leading with the earth-shattering news "Ten fine wines to make your May Day party go with a swing."

And there was me thinking it depended on the people you were with, she thought.

Below the wine story were two financial articles: The first expressed outrage at how mean Ingvar Kamprad, the founder of Ikea, was. The second was horrified that this year's Swedish Eurovision entry was using a private plane for a publicity tour. It wasn't entirely clear which of these was most deplorable.

The other evening paper was running with "Payday shopping in the sun!" then "How to escape the luxury gap." She gave up. She closed the news sites and went into her Facebook page. It had been a while since she had last logged in. She had eight new messages, all of them from Polly Sandman, Suzette's best friend back in Blackeberg.

Most of them were long, thoughtful musings about life and death and love, but occasionally Polly wrote short messages or just wanted the answer to a specific question.

Annika worked through the messages from the top, which meant she read the most recent one first. It contained a short, blunt question:

"Is it full moon at the same time all over the world?"

Annika blinked at the screen.

She didn't actually know. It couldn't be, could it? Maybe it could.

She made a mental note to find out.

The next message was a long story about a reality soap star who became an astronaut.

The third one consisted of three sentences:

"Suzette's mum has sold their flat. She's thrown out all Suzette's things. I don't know where she's moved to."

Annika read the message twice and felt her throat tighten.

Suzette meant nothing. She was in the process of being completely erased. Everything she had been, thought and liked was being wiped away, and nobody cared.

The message was dated April 16.

I really must keep a closer eye on this inbox, Annika thought.

The following three messages all contained gloomy poems about missing friends.

The penultimate one was short, just two sentences:

"I've had a really weird email. I think it's from Suzette."

Annika's heart started to beat so quickly that her pulse was pounding in her veins, and she started breathing faster.

I think it's from Suzette.

She glanced quickly at the bottom of the page: Polly Sandman was online. She clicked on Chat, which brought up Facebook's own instant message facility, and typed: "Hi Polly, Annika Bengtzon here! What was the weird email you got? Why do you think it's from Suzette?"

She sent the message, then stared at the screen. She saw that she had a *new request*.

Rolle in Mellösa wanted to add her as a friend.

It took a few seconds before she realized that Rolle in Mellösa was Roland Larsson, the boy she had gone to school with and who had a crush on her the whole way through, Jimmy Halenius's cousin.

She stared at the screen and wondered if he was actually serious. How many grown adults voluntarily spent their free time on this sort of thing?

But on the other hand there were people who spent their working lives helping fraudulent businessmen avoid tax by registering companies in places like Gibraltar.

She clicked to accept Roland as her friend. She looked at the time. Maybe Polly wasn't at her computer? Maybe it was just on in her room while she was out with her friends or something?

The next moment the chat box pinged.

"Do you believe in messages from the other side? In the olden days the dead used to speak through spirits, maybe they use email these days?"

Annika replied briefly and bluntly: "Not a chance. What did she say?"

There was a short pause.

"The message was from Gunnar Larsson. There was nothing in it."

Annika stared at the reply. Her pulse slowed down. What was this nonsense?

"Gunnar Larsson?" she wrote back. "Who's that?"

The reply came quick as a flash.

"That's a secret."

"Polly," Annika wrote, deciding to be dramatic. "If this has anything to do with Suzette, you have to tell me. It could be a matter of life and death."

It took several minutes before the reply arrived.

"Gunnar Larsson was our maths teacher in year 9. He was so stupid and old that Suzette and I wanted to play a trick on him. We set up an email account for him, mr-gunnar-larsson@hotmail.com, then we sent dirty emails to some of the girls in the class. We don't know exactly what happened, but Gunnar Larsson had to leave the school."

Annika read the message twice.

"He was fired because of the emails you sent?" she asked.

"Don't know. He was only a relief teacher, so maybe he had to leave anyway. But we got really scared. We swore we'd never ever tell anyone about Mr. Gunnar Larsson's emails."

Annika's heart started to speed up again.

"And now Mr. Gunnar Larsson has got in touch?"

It took eight minutes before the answer came. Annika had time to chew off most of her thumbnail.

"Only me and Suzette know the password to Mr. Gunnar Larsson's email. I have to go now, we're going out for dinner. Bye for now!"

Then she went offline.

Annika sat there staring at the screen with a faint buzz in her ears.

A blank email from a Hotmail address—what did that mean?

The fact that it came from Hotmail meant the sender had to know the password for that account.

The fact that it was empty suggested they were in a hurry.

It didn't necessarily mean anything, but it could be a sign of life.

She clicked to open Polly's last message, which turned out to be the start of the story about the reality soap star/astronaut.

Annika sat in front of her laptop for a minute or so. Then she wrote a short reply:

"Here's my mobile number. If Gunnar Larsson emails you again, I want you to call me."

She typed her mobile number, looked at the time, sent the message, and shut down her laptop.

She would have to hurry if she was going to have a shower.

He was standing in the lobby with his back to the lifts.

He was wearing the same suit as when she had bumped into him at the conference center, the slightly shiny Italian one that fitted so well across his hips.

She walked up behind him, breathing in the smell of his aftershave.

He had showered too, and shaved.

"Hello," she said quietly.

He turned round and ran his eyes over her. No direct sign of appreciation, but no attempt to distance himself either.

"Hello," he said. "Shall we go?"

She walked past him and out onto the street.

She was wearing her jeans and slightly pilled sweater, and had her bag with her, as usual. She had actually packed her best dress in her case before she flew down, a bright red sleeveless thing that she had bought on impulse in the Christmas sales. She hadn't had Thomas in mind when she packed it, but Niklas. She had put it on first, but felt overdressed and stupid. As if she were trying too hard.

He had his hire car parked outside the hotel. He unlocked it by remote, then opened the passenger door for her.

"Where are we going?" she asked.

"I've booked a table at a place just above here."

"Not in Istán?"

"What?" he said, looking confused.

"Nothing," she said, and got in the car.

He got in beside her, just as he had done hundreds of times before, fumbling with the key and checking the gears were in neutral, then pausing a moment before turning the key. Breathed out, tested the accelerator, looked in the rearview mirror, then forgot to release the hand brake before pulling away.

He headed up toward Nueva Andalucía. She was looking straight ahead through the windscreen, intensely aware of his presence: long arms and legs, narrow fingers, broad shoulders. She shivered and wrapped her arms round her.

"The porter at the hotel recommended this place, and gave me directions," he said. "Apparently they specialize in grilled meat. I assumed you wouldn't want fish or shellfish?"

She didn't answer.

They swept past the bullfighting arena.

"How are your articles going?" he asked.

She closed her eyes. This was what they always did. Skirting around the important things. Saying a load of words that never meant anything.

"Fine, thanks," she said. "Not enough time, a lazy photographer, too little preparation, but it'll probably work out okay. How about you?"

He sighed, but still sounded fairly cheerful.

"This whole business, trying to coordinate economic legislation throughout Europe, is a much bigger task than I realized to begin with. I'm going to be on secondment to the department for a while before this is done. It feels good to be entrusted with something of this significance by the heads of the department."

She looked out of the side window.

Why did he always have to tell her how fucking important and talented he was?

They sat in silence as the car climbed upward. They were on a different road from the one she had driven along with Niklas, so at least they weren't on their way toward La Campana. The sun was low, coloring the walls red. Bougainvillea tumbled over fences and rooftops, glowing like fire in the sunset.

"I've been thinking," she said. "We have to try to make sure we get on well, you and me, for the children's sake."

He glanced at her, but said nothing.

"I interviewed a guy yesterday," Annika said. "He's twenty-six years old, and he's locked up in a windowless concrete cell in Málaga. He'll be lucky to get out before he's thirty, and there was no need for him to end up there in the first place."

Thomas didn't respond, and turned into a large car park outside a place called El Picadero.

"The porter told me this place used to be a ranch once upon a time," he said. "There were horses here until just a few years ago, in fact. I thought you might like it."

The restaurant was a low, long building with flame-colored tiles and a large covered terrace stretching the entire length of the front. Lanterns with candles in them were hanging under the roof.

"Do you want to sit outside?"

She nodded.

They got a table for two some distance from the door.

"I've been doing some thinking as well," Thomas said once they had sat down and ordered water and wine. He played with his napkin and shuffled his feet restlessly under the table, just the way he used to when he was worried and nervous about something.

"It was wrong of me not to say anything about Sophia," he said. "You knew about it, and I wish you'd said something, but it wasn't your fault. That things turned out the way they did. Not exclusively, anyway."

Annika looked down at the tablecloth. She knew what he meant, and realized how hard it had been for him to say it. That was the closest she was going to get to an apology.

Evidently he wasn't finished, because his feet were still shuffling about.

"That's why I think we should be honest."

She nodded, yes, that's what she thought too . . .

"So you can also say . . ."

She blinked, not understanding.

"If you were ever with anyone else."

She looked down at her napkin.

"Never," she said. "Not with anyone, not once."

The waiter arrived with their drinks. Thomas tasted the wine. Annika took a thirsty gulp of her mineral water.

"How about afterward?" he said when the waiter had disappeared.

She looked off toward the car park. The only man she had been with was Niklas Linde.

"That policeman?" Thomas said. "Or Halenius?"

The old fury, hidden under a layer of scarcely frozen ice, poured out in all its fetid rancor. She got halfway up from the table, her chair jabbing into the diner behind her.

"You've got a nerve!" she said. "Cross-examining me about who I've slept with the moment you get a chance."

I can walk back to the hotel, she found herself thinking. I can ask for directions. It can't be more than five kilometers.

Then she looked round. The others diners were looking at her curiously. The man she had rammed her chair into moved forward unhappily.

She was about to do it again: run away from confrontation and hide her head in the sand.

She blushed and sat down.

"Sorry," she said.

Thomas looked extremely embarrassed.

"Those people over there are Swedish," he said, nodding toward a table by the entrance. "They would have heard you even if they're deaf."

"Sorry," she repeated.

The waiter appeared beside them and asked if they were ready to order. They hurriedly picked up their menus.

"Apparently the steak is what we should have," Thomas said. "It gets cooked at the table on a red-hot slab of stone. It's supposed to be really good."

Annika closed her menu without answering.

Thomas ordered a few starters and *carne a la piedra*.

The waiter disappeared.

"The children," Annika said. "We have to put aside any disagreements between the pair of us, we have to be able to talk to each other without it always being so fucking volatile. For the children's sake."

He nodded.

"I've been thinking about that too," he said. "How different things are now. We used to share the children, but now I'm the only one taking responsibility."

She looked at him.

"No, Thomas," she said. "While we were married I looked after the children and you looked after your career. Not at the start, but once I was on leave after that business with the Bomber, you left me to it. Whereas *now* we're sharing responsibility, the two of us."

He looked at her in astonishment.

Annika didn't look away, but stared right back. He'd started to get some gray hairs by his temples. The wrinkles around his eyes were more clearly defined than before. He'd put on weight as well. Maybe Sophia Fucking Bitch Grenborg baked cakes. Thomas had a weakness for cake.

Silence descended. A cricket started to chirrup in the grass alongside them. Others answered it from some distance away. A dog barked.

The waiter arrived with their starters, one plate of finely sliced ham, and another with cheese and walnuts.

"I thought we could share them?" Thomas said. "Have you tried this? *Jamón Ibérico de Bellota,* it's the best in the world."

They ate without talking. Annika couldn't stop once she'd started. She wolfed down the ham and the cheese, *queso manchego,* and endive salad with walnuts in a gorgonzola cream until she was quite breathless. She drank water and actually a whole glass of wine.

The darkness was getting thicker, and soon formed a wall around them.

"Have I told you what Ellen said the other day when we were on our way to preschool?" she said. "*When I get old, you'll be dead, and then you'll come back.*"

Thomas laughed.

"We have a daughter who believes in reincarnation."

"Exactly," Annika said.

"I wonder if she's had a previous life, and who she could have been?"

"Mahatma Gandhi?" Annika suggested.

"Well, not Joseph Stalin, anyway," Thomas said. "She's far too scared of blood."

They laughed.

At that moment his mobile rang. He pulled it out of his inside pocket, peered slightly long-sightedly at the screen, hesitated, then stood up and turned his back on her.

"Hi, Kalle," he said, walking out to the car park.

She watched him, suddenly completely deflated.

Their son was calling him, but he didn't want the boy to know that he was having dinner with her, because it would be too complicated to explain to Sophia.

She got up and threw her napkin on her chair. There had to be some limit to the humiliation. She was expected to sit there and tell him whom she was sleeping with, but he couldn't even own up to the fact that they were having dinner together.

She'd made it a couple of meters into the car park when Thomas caught sight of her.

"I miss you too, Kalle," he said. "Do you know who's coming now? There's someone here who I think would like to talk to you."

She stopped midstride. He was standing four or five meters away, holding the phone out to her.

She practically ran toward it.

"Kalle?" she said.

"Mummy?"

Warmth welled up inside her, bringing tears to her eyes.

"Hi, Kalle, how are you?"

"Mummy, guess what, I've lost a tooth!"

She laughed and stopped a tear with her finger just below her eyelashes.

"Wow, another one, how many is that now?"

"Loads! Do you think the tooth fairy knows the way to Grev Turegatan?"

"Leave it in a glass of water and you'll see that it's turned into a gold coin by tomorrow morning."

"Mummy?"

"Yes?"

"When are you coming home?"

"Tomorrow. And I'll see you on Monday when I pick you up from afterschool club."

"I miss you, Mummy."

She closed her eyes and cleared her throat.

"And I miss you too. Is Ellen still up?"

"She's asleep, she's just a baby."

"Well, you should be asleep too. Sleep well now. I love you."

She smiled at the warmth inside her and waited for the lines that the boy usually said at the end of every phone call, "I love you, Mummy, you're the best mummy in the whole wooorld," but it didn't come.

"Mummy?"

"Yes?"

"Are you going to marry Daddy again?"

She opened her eyes and saw Thomas walking around the car park the way he did when he got nervous. He never could stand still.

"No, darling, I'm not. Here comes Daddy, so you can say nighty-night to him as well."

She passed the phone to Thomas and went back to her chair, and sat there staring out into the night. It was completely dark now. The warmth of the day was still lingering, and the wind had died down. Thomas ended the call and put his mobile away.

The waiter removed their starters and came back with a frame on which he placed a spitting-hot stone slab. Then he laid out thin slices of marbled T-bone steak and vegetables, and three different sauces, and showed them how to melt fat directly on the stone, then fry the meat in the fat. It hissed and crackled and smoked and steamed.

Annika stared enchanted at the flame burning beneath the frame, listening to the crackling sound from the stone.

"I miss you sometimes," Thomas said.

She thought he was going to say something else, but he didn't.

"Why?" she said eventually.

He put another slice of meat on the stone.

"You never went with the flow. You always said what you thought. I was never very happy when I was discussing anything with you, but I always ended up wiser."

She didn't answer.

Thomas fried and sliced the meat.

She was still full from their starters.

The flame under the frame flickered and went out.

The waiter came and took their empty plates away.

Neither of them wanted a dessert or coffee. Thomas picked up the bill and paid with a credit card she'd never seen before. He signed with his usual, looping signature, and left a ten-euro note as a tip.

"Is the state footing the bill for this?" she asked.

"Hardly," he said. "After all, I don't want to end up in the *Evening Post*."

She laughed.

"It's my private account," he said. "We have a joint one for food, travel, and other shared expenses . . ."

Annika turned her face away, toward the darkness. She really didn't give a shit about their shared fucking account.

He saw her reaction and looked at her, embarrassed.

"Sometimes I wonder if we tried hard enough," he said.

She shivered, it was getting cold now. She was pleased she'd put her ugly old sweater on.

"Shall we go?" she said.

"Maybe we could get a drink somewhere?" he said. "Somewhere down by the harbor?"

"I don't think so," she said. "I'm pretty tired."

They left the restaurant and walked out into the car park. There were hardly any cars left.

"Do you miss me?" he asked. "At all, ever?"

All the time, she thought. Every day. Whenever I'm alone. Or do I?

She took a deep breath.

"I don't know," she said. "Not as much now. At the start it was awful. The fact that you were gone was like a black hole inside me, it was like you'd died."

She stopped beside the car.

"It would probably have felt better if you had died, because then at least I'd have had the right to grieve."

"I never wanted that," he said. "I never meant to hurt you."

"You should have thought of that before," she said.

"I know," he said.

They got in the car and drove in silence through the streets of Nueva Andalucía. The sky was dark and starless, clouds had rolled in from the Atlantic during the evening.

"It was on a night like this that the Söderström family were gassed to death," Annika said. "A cloudy night, but colder. They had the heating on in all the bedrooms."

"Are you sure you don't want to come and have a drink? A beer, maybe, or just a coffee?"

"Maybe a beer," Annika said.

They parked at the Hotel Pyr and walked down to the harbor.

Great crowds of people were milling about in the street by the harbor. They shuffled slowly out of the way whenever a Lamborghini wanted to get through. The row of bars and nightclubs lining the quayside were pumping out light and music into the darkness outside.

Thomas was heading toward the Sinatra Bar.

"Can't we walk out onto the pier?" Annika asked.

She didn't want to run into Niklas and his girls.

They walked past the lighthouse and carried on out onto the breakwater. The wind was cold and Thomas did his jacket up and turned up the collar. Annika stuck her hands in the pockets of her jeans. They were walking close to one another without actually touching.

"There's a lot I wish I'd done differently," Thomas said into the wind. "I wasn't thinking about the consequences. I was just thinking that you were so cold and difficult and emotionless."

"She was the easy way out," Annika said. "You do have a tendency to just *end up* doing things."

He nodded and stopped, without looking at her. Off to the southwest there were scattered lights on the shore of Africa.

"I know I made mistakes," Annika said. "I was running away too. And I'm pretty sure we could have sorted things out, if we'd tried to get help."

Now he looked at her.

"Do you think it's too late?" he asked.

At first she thought she'd heard him wrong, that the wind was playing tricks on her.

"Too late?" she said.

He put his hand on her cheek and kissed her.

First she went completely rigid. His lips were soft and cold. She realized her nose was bunged up, because she found she couldn't breathe through it. She pulled away and wiped her nose with her hand. He kissed her again.

"Come on," he said in a low voice.

He took her hand and led her back toward the lights on the quayside.

She went with him, her fingers laced in his, and it struck her that he had always held her hand this way; imagine, forgetting something like that. She moved closer to him, because her injured forefinger was hurting.

They walked round the harbor and back toward the hotel, along streets that quickly became empty and cold when the music and lights no longer reached them.

The reception desk was unmanned, the sound of a television coming from the little office behind.

They walked quickly and silently through the lobby and got into the farthest lift. Annika pressed the button for the third floor and Thomas brushed her hair aside. She caught sight of her reflection in the mirror as he kissed her earlobe.

She closed her eyes.

Her room was completely dark. Thomas turned on the lamp in the ceiling and turned to face her.

"I want to look at you," he said. "See if I remember you right."

Does he fantasize about me? she thought.

She pulled off her sweater and T-shirt, and her bra caught in the bottom of the sweater. She was wearing the red one, the one she had bought to go with the smart dress she'd chosen not to wear.

He put his hand on her shoulder, stroked her arm, cupped his hands around her breasts.

The way he used to. The way he knew she liked.

She unbuttoned his shirt, following her fumbling fingers with her eyes, button by button. Then she looked up at him.

His eyes, oh, how she loved his eyes.

"You know," he said, "I've really missed you."

Me too, she thought. Every time things are silent around me, every time I'm alone, that's when I miss you.

He undid her bra and put it on the bedside table. Unbuttoned her jeans and stroked her backside.

"You've lost weight," he said.

He's remembering wrong, she thought. Sophia's just sturdier than me.

She pulled off his shirt and let it fall to the floor. He'd developed a bit of a belly. She put her hand under his navel and left it there for a moment. The way she used to. It felt like she'd never done anything different.

Afterward he fell asleep on his back with his arms stretched out, but Annika lay awake with her head on his shoulder, staring into the darkness.

SATURDAY, APRIL 30

Annika paid for both her own and the photographer's rooms. She signed the credit card bill, then headed straight out onto the street with her suitcase.

She stood waiting on the pavement for a few minutes. There was still a chill in the air, the sun hadn't yet risen above the Sierra Blanca.

Her plane left at ten o'clock, and Thomas's at quarter to four.

He was going to drive her to the airport, then he was going to get his things from the Parador.

It felt as though nothing odd or unpleasant had ever happened between them.

The divorce was just a bad dream, something she had imagined. Everything was the way it always had been, and now they were going home to get the children and then they would go back to the flat on Kungsholmen; there'd be loads of washing to do and they'd have to remember to get some milk. Her parents-in-law would be waiting for them out on the island and . . .

Suddenly she felt short of breath. Her chest felt tight and the sounds of traffic faded away. She fumbled for her suitcase and sat down on it gingerly, leaning forward so she could breathe better.

His car glided up alongside her.

"What's up?" he asked, hurrying up to her. "Aren't you feeling well?"

She waved her hand dismissively.

"No, no," she said. "I just had a bit of a turn . . . felt a bit dizzy. It's nothing."

She glanced up at him.

They hadn't made love that morning. He hadn't showered. He hadn't borrowed her toothbrush; he'd never dream of doing something as unhygienic as that.

He looked at her with genuine concern in those wonderful eyes, bright blue, and she took his hand and allowed herself to be pulled up and led over to the passenger seat. He brushed her hair from her face and put her seat belt on. Then he put her suitcase in the boot, closed it, and made sure it was properly shut. Then he went round to the driver's side and got in, looked at her, and smiled. His hair had fallen across his forehead and his shirt was open at the neck.

She made an effort to smile back.

"I don't regret it," he said.

Not yet, she thought.

"Me neither," she said.

Then he pulled away.

The motorway was almost deserted. Once they reached the toll road they didn't see any other vehicles. They sat in silence beside one another. Thomas was concentrating on the motorway and Annika was staring out to sea. She couldn't see Africa, it was too misty.

At this rate they'd be at the airport in half an hour.

She would get out of the car and kiss him rather tentatively, then she'd go inside the Pablo Ruiz Picasso terminal and the sliding doors would close behind her, and then the illusion would be over.

Their flights would take off, then there'd be the baggage belts and the taxis with their fixed rates. And then she'd be sitting up in her three-room flat on Agnegatan and he'd be taking the last boat out to Vaxholm to his parents' summerhouse in the archipelago, where Sophia and the children would be waiting for him, Kalle and Ellen clingy and expectant, Sophia warm and cooing.

And then this car journey would feel strange and incomprehensible.

She noticed a smell of old socks and looked up; they were passing the San Miguel brewery that was right next to the airport.

It was almost over.

Thomas headed up the ramp for *salidas*, departures. The airport was obviously utterly chaotic no matter what time of the day or week it was. An official in a fluorescent yellow jacket waved them toward an empty space a few meters from the terminal doors.

She took a deep breath.

"Are you feeling better?"

She nodded. Looked at him. His expression was open and bright. He meant her well, she was sure of that.

"I'm fine," she said, and brushed his hair from his forehead, the blond fringe that he hardly ever bothered to comb.

She leaned over and kissed him, so lightly that she almost couldn't feel it.

"Let me help you with your case," he said.

"There's no need," she said, but he'd already opened the door and got out, and was on his way round to the boot.

She got out, her legs heavy as lead, and took her case, and he kissed her on the forehead.

"I'll call you," he said, looking at her as though he really meant it, and she smiled back without replying, then turned round and headed toward the doors.

When they slid shut behind her she stopped and blinked.

It was all gone.

Annika drifted round, looking in the shops, until it was time for her flight. She bought sweets and toys for the children, wine and spirits for herself, even though she would never drink it, and a travel pack of various lipsticks from Dior that she would probably never use.

Lotta was waiting by the gate. She had her rucksack containing her camera, but she must have checked in the rest of her equipment.

Annika sat down beside her without saying anything.

Lotta started and moved a few centimeters away from her.

"Don't worry," Annika said. "I only bite when there's a full moon."

"I realize that I haven't done very well," Lotta said, sounding terrified.

Annika looked at the photographer; her face looked scared and defiant.

Lotta had spoken to someone. She'd probably called the paper and demanded to speak to Pelle, head of images, or Schyman himself, and the conversation couldn't have gone well. Now she felt even more unfairly treated, but would have to swallow a whole load of shit if she wanted to keep her job.

"The articles are all sorted," Annika said, picking up a copy of the previous day's *Daily Mail*.

She held the paper in front of her and stared at the pages without reading a single word until they boarded.

They were in seats next to each other. Annika took the window seat. Because she hadn't slept more than an hour that night, she fell asleep as soon as the plane had got into the air, and didn't wake up until they were on their descent into Arlanda.

The baggage carousel spat out Lotta's bags, all five of them, before Annika's little suitcase appeared.

"I'd be grateful if you didn't mention our collaboration to anyone at the paper," Lotta said once she'd piled all her things onto a trolley.

Annika looked at the photographer, trying to work out what she felt about the pale young woman.

She couldn't summon up anything but indifference.

"What collaboration?" she said.

The photographer made do with this and headed off through customs.

Annika stayed where she was and watched her disappear along the corridor with its vast portraits of famous Swedes wishing visitors welcome to their home town.

She bought the evening papers in the arrivals hall and read them as she ate a fairly unpleasant salad in a 7-Eleven. Then she took the express train into Stockholm and decided to walk from the station.

The sky was steel gray and there was rain in the air. The wind was damp and cold, and cut to her marrow and bones. She struggled across Kungsbron toward Fleminggatan. The small wheels on the suitcase kept catching in the grit on the pavements and in the end she gave up and carried it instead.

By the time she reached her flat her arm felt completely numb.

She put the case down on the hall floor and decided to put off unpacking it, just as she always did.

Instead she went into her bedroom and ended up staring at the framed drawing of the girl and the horse that was hanging over her bed. Little My, eight years old, who was left to mourn her? What trace had she left on the world?

Annika lay down on top of the bedspread. With her eyes opened she lay and listened to the sound of the building breathing.

First the big noises, the ones indicating people, activity. Water running through the pipes. Someone flushing a toilet. Voices from someone listening to a radio.

She closed her eyes and listened for the other sounds, the ones beyond human concerns, and after a while she heard them. The quiet hum of the central heating, the creaking of the hundred-year-old beams, the soft whistling of windows and air vents.

Thomas was probably in the plane now. It would just have taken off and Spain would be disappearing below him, the mountains speckled with olive trees, the villages standing out white against the red soil.

Maybe Suzette was still alive. Who else could have send that empty email from Mr. Gunnar Larsson?

Suddenly she was struck by a thought that made her sit bolt upright on the bed.

What if Mr. Larsson himself had hacked the account? What if it wasn't Suzette trying to send a message, but a teacher bitter at being sacked, wanting to get his revenge on the people responsible for his dismissal?

If he had suddenly been sacked because of the emails, his employers must have confronted him with them. So he would have seen the address, and he could have gone onto Hotmail and tried to crack the password. It wasn't brain surgery. She'd done it herself a year or so before, with the email account of the murdered chair of the Nobel Committee, Caroline von Behring.

She leaped out of bed and into the hall, pulled her laptop from her bag and went into the kitchen. That was the only place she had an Internet connection. She'd thought about getting wireless, but hadn't got round to it. Besides, she wasn't sure it was good to have the signals bouncing around the whole time. The newsroom was a Wi-Fi zone, and sometimes when she got home she felt like she'd had her head in a microwave oven all day. It was quite nice to escape that at home.

Her laptop booted up and she went straight to her Facebook page.

No new messages. And Polly Sandman wasn't online.

She went into Hotmail and typed in the account name Mr-Gunnar-Larsson. She started with the obvious passwords: polly.

Invalid ID or password. Please try again using your full Yahoo! ID. suzette

Invalid ID or password. Please try again using your full Yahoo! ID. blackeberg

Invalid ID or password. Please try again using your full Yahoo! ID.

She wondered how many attempts she could make before the site shut her out. Maybe there was no limit; she had no idea.

She gave up, left the Hotmail site, and went back to her Facebook page instead. She wrote and asked Polly if she thought Gunnar Larsson could have cracked their password.

She was left sitting there, staring at the screen.

She hadn't called Niklas before she left. He had asked her to; it was the last thing he said before she got out of his car the day before last.

Maybe he had something to say to her, something he couldn't say with Lotta listening.

She clenched her fists tight, feeling her fingernails dig into her palms.

Then she logged into the national ID register and searched for "niklas linde" without specifying any particular geographic area.

Too many results (ca. 170). Please refine the search terms.

She removed the phonetic search option, to remove anyone called Lind or Lindh, and searched again.

Ten hits, eight of them with the surname Linde. Four of them lived in Skåne, one had been deregistered and had moved to Switzerland, and three were registered in the Stockholm area.

She looked at their dates of birth, and immediately saw which one was her Niklas.

Linde, Bo NIKLAS Yngve.

Registered address: ÄNGSLYCKEVÄGEN 73, 245 62 HJÄRUP

Region: 12 SKÅNE

Council district: 30 STAFFANSTORP

Parish: 06 UPPÅKRA

He was thirty-six years old.

She tried a new search, looking for the surname, Linde, the postcode 245 62, and gender: female.

Bingo. Three results at the same address.

Linde, Anna MARIA, thirty-three years old.

Linde, Kajsa ELENA, ten years old.

Linde, Alva NATALIE, three years old.

His wife, and two daughters. So, did he have any sons as well?

She performed a third search, Linde, male, postcode.

Bingo again.

Linde, Bo OSCAR, eight years old.

She stared at the name in front of her. A boy, like Kalle. Oscar. Presumably he was busy losing his teeth and calling to tell his dad, who was away working on the Costa del Sol down in Spain.

Nice work, Niklas. A wife and three kids in Hjärup, wherever the hell that was. Somewhere outside Malmö, at a guess. A proper little idyll, presumably. Ängslyckevägen, "happy meadow way" indeed.

Her mobile started to ring out in her bag. She got up from the kitchen chair, stubbing her toe on the table, and limped out into the hall.

"Annika?"

It was Niklas.

She glanced quickly over at the computer—was there some way he could trace her searches?

Probably, but that could hardly be why he was calling.

"Hello," she said in surprise. "I'm back in Stockholm."

"Listen," he said, and now she realized how abrupt he sounded. "I've got some questions for you. Can you give me the answers now?"

She went back to the kitchen table and clicked to get rid of the national ID database and the details of Niklas's whole family.

"Sure," she said, putting all her weight on one foot with the other in the air. Her little toe hurt like hell.

"It's about Johan Zarco Martinez, the Swedish citizen you met in prison in Málaga on Thursday."

"Okay?" Annika said.

"Can I ask you what you talked about?"

"Of course you can, but I don't know if I'll answer. Not because it was anything particularly secret, but you know how it is, confidentiality of sources, integrity and . . ."

"He's dead," Niklas said. "He was found dead in his cell this morning."

Annika slid down onto the chair, suddenly feeling weak at the knees. The hum of the laptop faded away and she could hear her blood pulsing.

"Dead? How?"

"There's going to be a postmortem, but the doctor was able to identify a couple of things straightaway. His pupils were myotic, extremely small. That's characteristic of morphine overdoses."

Annika shook her head as if she were trying to clear her thoughts.

"Morphine? But how could he get hold of that, stuck in prison?"

"That's what I was going to ask you. You were one of the last people to visit him. Did he ask for drugs when you were there?"

Her heart speeded up, and the palms of hands were getting clammy with horror.

"No," she said nervously. "He did say he wasn't very fond of cocaine. He said he preferred beer."

She gulped and nodded to herself.

"Yes, that was it," she said. "He asked if we had any beer with us. He said it was pretty easy to smuggle it in."

"But you didn't have any beer with you?"

"Of course not."

"What did Carita say during the interview?"

"Nothing, pretty much. She interpreted and got us in, but obviously Johan could speak Swedish."

"What did she say afterward?"

Annika took a deep breath.

"Nothing. Well, actually, she asked me what Johan had whispered to me right at the end, just as we were leaving."

"Whispered? What did he whisper?"

"Nothing much, he hugged me and asked me to help him get out of there. I didn't answer, because there was nothing I could say."

"Why did Carita ask about that?"

"No idea."

"Were you working with Carita yesterday?"

"Yesterday . . . what, Friday? No, I was doing interviews in Gibraltar and Estepona, in Danish and Swedish. Why do you ask?"

Niklas fell silent. The line crackled and hissed.

"Carita visited Johan Zarco Martinez in prison yesterday afternoon. Because she was already registered as a visitor, they saw no reason to stop her going in."

"Are you absolutely certain it was morphine? It couldn't have been something else?"

She was feeling dizzy and slightly sick.

"Unless one of the guards supplied Jocke with the morphine, it must have been Carita. She's the only person who had the opportunity. Jocke had no contact with the other prisoners, and he didn't have any other visitors."

Annika had to lean back against the kitchen wall and close her eyes.

"That's impossible," she said. "I've been around her house. I *know* her. She's vain and racist about Brits and is seriously in love with her husband . . . But what does she say? Haven't you spoken to her?"

"We'll put out a warrant for her with Interpol as soon as the postmortem has been conducted."

"Why? Has she gone missing?"

"The house is shut up. Her husband didn't show up for work this morning."

Annika opened her eyes and stared at the kitchen cupboards.

"So the whole family has gone? The children as well?"

"Did Carita say anything to you about her background, about her family?"

"How do you mean?"

"The first place we look is with relatives and close friends."

Annika could hear her own voice from far away, as if someone else was using her vocal chords.

"She grew up in Beverly Hills, and met her husband, Nacho, there. He's a pediatric doctor, from Colombia. They lived in Bogotá in the early 1990s. Her father-in-law, Victor, I think his name was, was chief of police there and was murdered by the mafia, and they had to leave, because the mafia wipes out the whole family, so there's no one left to inherit . . ."

"Anything else?"

She screwed her eyes shut.

"Her parents ran a biotech company, Cell Impact. When they died she inherited the business and sold it straightaway, because she didn't know anything about that sort of thing. They used the money from the sale of the business to buy the house in Nueva Andalucía."

"You may be called in by my colleagues in Stockholm for a more formal interview at some point, but that's enough for me for now. Well, take care . . ."

Annika stood up from the table.

"Wait a moment," she said. "Has the death been made public? Can we write about it in the paper?"

"You'll have to check with the Foreign Ministry press office. Nothing I've told you is official, as I hope you appreciate."

"One more thing," Annika said before she changed her mind. "Why didn't you tell me you were married?"

There was complete silence on the line.

"Oh, Annika," he finally said. "Do you feel disappointed?"

She cleared her throat.

"No," she said. "Just dirty."

There were limits. She was never going to turn into a Sophia *Fucking Bitch* Grenborg.

"Maria knows," he said. "Not everything, and no names, but that doesn't matter. I'll never leave her. She knows that."

You're deceiving yourself, she thought. One day you'll meet someone you can't resist, and then she'll be left standing there, your wife, in Ängslyckevägen, all alone with her empathy and tolerance.

More silence on the line.

I ought to tell him about Suzette, she thought. About the email, and the fact that she might be alive.

"Was there anything else?" Niklas asked.

Annika didn't answer.

"Well, then, take care."

He hung up.

She stayed where she was, paralyzed.

She felt like throwing up, or crying, or maybe both at once.

Carita visited Johan Zarco Martinez in prison yesterday afternoon. . . . We'll put out a warrant for her with Interpol as soon as the postmortem has been conducted.

It just wasn't possible. The Colombian mafia didn't carry leopard-skin handbags and wear high heels.

Beer. Morphine. Dead men.

Size thirty-seven shoes. Few men have feet that small.

She got up and went over to the sink, turned on the cold water, and drank straight from the tap. She closed her eyes and let the water wash over her face, run down her neck and under her collar.

Who was she to decide whether or not someone was a criminal? The two Nordic police officers had recommended Carita, because they'd used her as an interpreter as well.

She turned off the tap, tore off some kitchen paper, and wiped her neck.

Criminals some way up the hierarchy probably looked just like anyone else. Lipstick and a page cut, leopard-skin handbag, and high-heels: Why not?

She sat down at the kitchen table again. Closed her eyes and saw the villa in Nueva Andalucía before her, tried to understand what had happened there that night. She tried to see Carita before her, pumping gas into the house and stepping over the dead bodies of the children . . .

She let the thought go, it was impossible.

Could there have been some misunderstanding?

Was Carita the victim of some sort of conspiracy?

Or was she mad?

She shook her head to herself, no, not mad, but obsessed. You don't kill seven people unless there's a very great deal at stake. Or do you? If you simultaneously love your family and get upset because your British neighbors won't contribute to the pool mainte-nance guy's wages?

She got up and drank some more water, this time from a glass.

Carita had been extremely clever. Carved out a quite brilliant position for herself.

By interpreting at police interrogations she knew exactly what anyone under arrest had said.

By allying herself to Annika she managed to get an insight into the work of the inquiry.

And she herself was responsible for Carita gaining access to the prison.

She jumped when her mobile started to ring. Number with-held, presumably the paper. Probably Patrik.

"Yes," she said, "I'm home."

"Er, hello, this is Jimmy Halenius."

Oh fuck, not him as well.

"Hello," she said flatly.

"Is this a bad time?"

"Someone I interviewed on Thursday has just been found dead in his prison cell and I've just found out that my interpreter is probably a killer for the Colombian mafia," she said.

"Oh shit," Jimmy Halenius said. "Which prison?"

"Málaga."

"Zarco Martinez? Bloody hell. We've just requested his extradition."

"Too late now," Annika said.

"And the mafia killer?"

"A woman who worked as an interpreter for the police in Málaga."

"Oh shit," the undersecretary of state said again. "Would you like to come round and have dinner with me this evening?"

"I've got some writing to do," Annika said. "If I can get acknowledgment from the Foreign Ministry, Zarco Martinez will probably be the lead story tomorrow."

"I understand," Jimmy Halenius said. "Good luck with the Foreign Ministry. You'll need it."

She put her mobile down and stared at her laptop.

She couldn't write about Carita that evening. It was too tenuous. Besides, there wasn't even a formal warrant out for her arrest yet. She could count herself lucky if she was able to find anyone who could confirm that the young man was dead. She wouldn't be able to get verification of the cause of death, the morphine, or his last visitor, Carita.

And she couldn't make any direct link to the murder of the Söderström family either.

Annika stretched her back and scratched her head.

Where could they have gone? They couldn't go back to Colombia, the whole family had been forced to flee, hadn't they? They'd had to abandon the good life in a cozy suburb there when

Nacho's father, the chief of police, was murdered by the mafia. And the mafia wiped out entire families, so that no one was left to inherit anything . . .

She could suddenly see Carita before her, outside the house, that rainy day when the policeman had let them in, when she first became aware that there was another daughter, a girl called Suzette.

Another child? Carita had said, eyes wide open, her face completely white.

She had noted Carita's reaction, but had thought she was just upset at the whole story.

You didn't kill them all, Annika thought. There was someone left, an heir. A serious miscalculation.

She had to take a walk round the flat, into the children's rooms, stroking the sheets on their beds.

Then she roused her laptop from standby mode and went onto Google.

Carita's father-in-law, the murdered chief of police, maybe he was on some Spanish-language page, held up as a hero of democracy? Victor? Victor Gonzales?

She got 965,000 results.

She tried *victor gonzales policia bogota.*

The number of hits shrank to 179,000.

She pushed the computer away and looked at the time. She ought to phone Patrik and tell him about Zarco Martinez. If nothing earth-shattering had happened in the world of television, if no one had tripped over during a live broadcast or something equally serious, his death would probably be the lead story, assuming she could get the story confirmed.

She did a quick calculation.

What were the chances of anyone else finding out about the death and getting confirmation of it before she did?

Zero, pretty much.

So there was no reason to call Patrik until she had something to offer him.

She reached for her bag and pulled out the notepad where she'd jotted down the main points of her interview inside the prison. She leafed through her scribbled notes as she reached for an apple that had seen better days. Then she picked up her mobile and dialed the press office at the Foreign Ministry. She took a big bite and slurped up the apple juice, leafing back through the interview with Wilma in Estepona, and her visit to Gibraltar. There was a click on the line and a woman answered.

"You've reached the press office of the Foreign Ministry, can you hold?"

She spoke with elaborately enunciated vowels.

"How long for?" Annika asked, but the woman had already put her on hold. There was a hiss on the line, like distant tinnitus.

She sighed loudly and hoped someone could hear her at the other end. Obviously she was going to use the prison interview in tomorrow's article, news had to come before any series of articles. She picked up the pad again and carried on leafing through it.

Was there anything else she could use now?

Her eyes fell on a web address she had jotted down, from the building round the corner from Veronica Söderström's office.

The closed estate agent's, with the Söderström family villa in the window.

There was a click on the line.

"Hello?" Annika said.

No answer, just more tinnitus.

She put the apple down, pulled her laptop toward her and typed www.aplaceinthesun.se into the address box of Internet Explorer.

She took another bite while the computer did its thing.

Welcome to A Place in the Sun, your Real Estate Agent on the Coast!

The website looked like all the other estate agents' she had looked at when she had checked house prices and properties around the world, albeit perhaps a little more basic. This was no big agency. The logo was in the top left corner, brash and ugly. Maybe there was some information about the family's villa on the site?

Another click on the line.

"Hello? Hello!"

On the left, beneath the logo, was a list of various subsections: *Home, Property Search, New Developments, About Us, Contact.* She clicked on *Property Search* to look for villas in Nueva Andalucía, but the link led nowhere.

"Foreign Ministry press office, can you hold?"

"Hello?" Annika said, letting go of the laptop. "I've already been on hold . . ."

There was another click and the buzzing returned.

She threw the apple core in the drainer of the sink.

Fucking stuck-up diplomats, she thought, and clicked on the *About Us* link.

She found herself looking at the usual opening drivel in English: "Buying a property in Spain is a dream for a lot of people, but it's also a serious investment. So you need the very best advice and guidance from an established company. Since we opened our first office on the Costa del Sol in 1968, we've helped thousands of people to find a new home on the Spanish coast . . ."

She clicked to get off the page, and found herself on the contact page instead. She was about to close the window when she spotted the agents' email addresses:

astrid.paulson@aplaceinthesun.se

ernesto.zarco.martinez@aplaceinthesun.se

She stared at the two names, as her skin broke out in goosebumps all over her body.

Astrid Paulson.

Ernesto Zarco Martinez.

Astrid Paulson was Veronica Söderström's mother's name. It could hardly be a coincidence, two women with the same name, spelled exactly the same, just round the corner from the office of the daughter of one of them.

Had Astrid Paulson been an estate agent? And who was this Zarco Martinez?

She hung up, leaving the woman at the Foreign Ministry to her fate.

She quickly googled "ernesto zarco martinez," and got 133,000 results. Hopeless.

She stared at the screen until her eyes started to water, searching hard in her memory.

She'd seen this very name somewhere before, but with something else added. Another name, perhaps, or an address?

She thought for a while, then opened the search box for the laptop's own hard drive. She clicked to search for documents ("word processing, spreadsheet, etc."), and used the advanced search to look for a word or phrase in a document. Then she searched the entire hard drive for Ernesto Zarco Martinez, with capital letters in the right places just to be on the safe side. It would take a while, but if she'd ever written that particular combination of names, the search function would find it.

A happy little dog appeared on the screen, waving its tail as the computer searched. She went out to the toilet, had a pee, washed her hands and face, and went back to the laptop. The dog was wagging its tail. No results so far. She went through to the landline in her bedroom.

"Foreign Ministry press office, can you hold?"

"No!" she said loudly. "Absolutely not! If you won't talk I'm going to write my article anyway!"

There was stunned silence at the other end, no tinnitus.

"Er, what's this concerning?"

"Are you aware that a Swedish citizen has died in prison in Málaga?"

The person at the Foreign Ministry drew a deep breath.

"We haven't received any information to that effect."

"That's as may be, but I happen to know that this death has occurred."

She gave the woman all the facts about the case, and said she would call back in an hour for confirmation. That ought to get them moving.

Then she went back to the kitchen.

One result.

She felt her pulse quicken as she clicked to open the document.

It was an old website that had been cluttering up the laptop's memory, in temporary Internet files, a page from a company search on the national database that she must have made ages ago.

It was about a company called Advice Investment Management AB, described as providing "financial advice and business development and associated activities, but nothing that could legally be deemed to be banking or credit-related."

She scanned down the page and came to the board members.

The company had two full board members, Lena Yvonne Nordin from Huddinge, and Niklas Ernesto Zarco Martinez from Skärholmen. One deputy director was listed: David Zeev Lindholm from Bondegatan in Stockholm.

She forced herself to breathe calmly and steadily.

She recognized the image in front of her. This was where she had seen the name Zarco Martinez before. She knew exactly where it was from: her research into the bizarre business activities of the murdered police officer David Lindholm.

Niklas Ernesto Zarco Martinez from Skärholmen was known as Nicke in Sweden and Ernesto in Spain. So he was Jocke Zarco

Martinez's older brother, and he had run a business together with Yvonne Nordin, the triple murderer from Sankt Paulsgatan.

She went back to her search: The dog with the wagging tail had found another two results containing the name in question, then stopped. He had evidently finished.

The first was a company record for a defunct cleaning business in Skärholmen. It had been run by Lena Yvonne Nordin and Niklas Ernesto Zarco Martinez.

The second was a record from the national ID database.

Niklas Ernest Zarco Martinez—deregistered. Person deceased.

He had died on Christmas Eve eighteen months ago.

She nodded to herself, that's right. She remembered the search now that she saw it again.

Suddenly she began to tremble.

She realized what she had in front of her.

There was a connection between the Zarco Martinez brothers, Yvonne Nordin, David Lindholm, and Astrid Paulson, Veronica Söderström's mother: They had run companies together, worked together, and now they were all dead, all in a violent or destructive way.

Then a thought popped into her head and she went back to the website again, www.aplaceinthesun.se.

She looked at the garish logo in the left-hand corner, the words set out vertically inside a beaming sun.

A
Place
In
The
Sun

Then she read the initials, from the top down, and felt the room start to spin.

Apits.

Niklas was wrong. The drug business on the Costa del Sol, Apits, didn't mean Airport Passenger Intelligent Transport Systems, or Analogue Proprietary Integrated Telephone System.

It meant A Place in the Sun.

PART 3

After Whitsun

THE ANGEL AT GUDAGÅRDEN

To start with, there was only sky and meadows. Air and space and wind.

There were Mother's strong arms and the scented starchiness of the bed linen. The pattern of the scrubbed floor tiles, the shimmering water of the lake, and the singing in the evenings.

> *He has opened the pearly gates*
> *So that I may come in*
> *Through his blood he has saved me*
> *To keep me with him.*

She had no early memories of Father. He was there at a distance, always on the edge of her vision, because he was so tied to the earth: land, farm, words. She herself was always slightly elevated, without any real contact with the ground, and that was because she was an Angel.

That's what Mother always said.

"You're my little angel," she said, or *Du bist mein Engel,* because with Mother she always spoke her own language, the Angels' Language.

And she would float and dance over Gudagården like the blessed little child she was, conceived without sin with the approbation of the Lord. Father didn't like her talking to the other children on the farm, but she did anyway, because God, He talks to everyone, and He sees and hears everything. And everyone was kind and friendly toward her, smiled, and said nice things, because of course she was the preacher's daughter. Everyone except the Troll Girl.

It was a mystery.

The Angel was a bit scared of the Troll Girl. Not much, because as an Angel she was of course the servant of the Lord, and no one could be more safe than God's host of children, but the Troll Girl hid her voice and had narrow black eyes that could see around corners.

The only person the Troll Girl was prepared to show her voice to was the Princess, the most beautiful of all princesses in the whole world; in fact she was almost an angel too, because she could actually speak the Angels' Language. She had heard the girls talking to each other up under the roof where they lived. They only spoke when they thought no one was listening, and the Princess told stories about the Castle Among the Clouds, and the Troll Girl talked about the Little Match Girl who froze to death and became a falling star in the sky.

But the Troll Girl's weasel eyes saw her down on the stairs and drove her away with hard fists.

Then came the day when Wall-Eye put his hand on the Princess for the first time. The Troll Girl hit him in the head with a stone, and he let go of the Princess and rushed after the Troll Girl, who hid right at the back of the tool shed.

And the Angel, she saw it all, and she knew that the task of angels is to protect and help, so she followed them into the shed and saw how Wall-Eye found a knife and circled around the Troll Girl with the knife blade sticking out.

"Thou shalt not kill," she said in her high, clear angel's voice, and Wall-Eye looked in her direction, angry.

"Get out of here," he said.

But angels help people in need, even troll girls, so she took another step into the tool shed.

"Honor thy father and thy mother: that thy days may be long upon the land," she said.

"Ma's dead and Dad's been locked up to dry out, that's why I'm in this hellhole," Wall-Eye said, his voice cracking.

"We should fear and love God that we may not harm our neighbor's life or cause him suffering, but help and defend him in every danger and need," the Angel said, going up to him and taking hold of the knife blade.

Wall-Eye sniffed, let go of the knife, and ran for the door.

It was completely quiet once the boy had disappeared. The dust danced in the rays of sunlight. The Troll Girl was staring at her open-mouthed, and then she let the Angel see her voice.

"Why did you do that?" she asked, and all of a sudden the Angel felt bashful.

"Thou shalt love the Lord thy God with all thy heart," she said, "and thy neighbor as thyself. So Jesus says."

The Troll Girl took a step toward her and her eyes narrowed.

"Are you a bit simple?"

The Angel shook her head.

And from that day on she was allowed to go with the Troll Girl and the Princess wherever they went around the farm. Father and Mother didn't want her to join in with the sowing and reaping, but she replied with the words of the Lord, "in the sweat of thy face shalt thou eat bread," and then they let her be. Together they whirled around, between the mist's frosty down, at rest and play, and the Angel learned of other worlds, where there was a great man who lost a mighty war, and cold nights in damp cellars where drunken men bought drink and love. Yes, they did everything together, through summers, autumns, winters, and springs, until that night in August when the terrible thing happened and the Troll Girl and the Princess vanished from Gudagården forever, and the Angel's long journey down toward the underworld began.

—Original Message—

TT NEWSFLASH: Filip Andersson cleared.

Press Conference: Lawyer Sven-Göran Olin's office
Skeppsbron 28, at 10.30 am.
   (nnnn)

TUESDAY, JUNE 14

It felt like summer was never going to arrive. There hadn't been a single day when the air had felt mild. The north winds had the whole country in a cast-iron grip, and the weather forecasters had nothing good to say.

Annika pulled her jacket tighter round her throat as she headed for the bus. Rain was lingering in the treetops. She passed the billboards for that day's papers outside a 7-Eleven: *HOW TO GET AWAY TO THE SUN* on one, and *RAIN FORECAST FOR MIDSUMMER* on the other. Sadly her paper had the negative message, and their competitors the optimistic one. So there was no doubt who was going to win the circulation war on this particular day.

She missed the bus and waited in the doorway of number 32, Hantverkargatan to escape the rain, which had now decided to fall. She looked up at the arched doorway above her head: This was where she and Thomas had lived together for several years. It all felt so unreal, like something she'd read about or seen in a film.

He hadn't been in touch since that night on the Costa del Sol.

He had said he would call. *I'll call you,* that was the last thing he said when he dropped her off at the airport, and he had looked like he meant it, but he hadn't.

She hadn't called either. In fact she had actually bought Kalle a mobile phone and taught him how to recharge it, so she wouldn't have to call the flat on Grev Turegatan when she wanted to say good night to the children.

She missed them already, even though she had had them for the Whitsun weekend and had only just dropped them off at school and preschool.

She hadn't heard anything from Niklas either, but she hadn't been expecting to.

Not even Jimmy Halenius had called, but that was probably down to a mass breakout from Österåker Prison, which was having serious political consequences. Obviously, all the opposition parties were calling for the justice minister's resignation, as if he had personally driven the bulldozer through the wall of the prison. It looked like he was going to survive, as usual, thanks to a few elegant appointments and a large dose of natural political talent.

The bus pulled up and she scrambled on board last. She had to stand all the way to Gjörwellsgatan.

Tore the caretaker made straight for her when she came through the door.

"You didn't fill up the car the last time you borrowed it," he said, standing squarely in front of her.

Her mobile rang, and she fished it up at the end of the hands-free cable and checked the screen: a number she didn't recognize.

"Do you think I'm some kind of errand boy with nothing better to do than clean up after you?" he said.

"Hello?" Annika said into the phone.

"Annika? Hi! This is Polly."

The voice was high-pitched and bright, like a little girl's. She closed her eyes to shut out the whining caretaker. Polly, Polly Sandman, Suzette's friend. She'd never heard her voice before, just exchanged emails with her.

"Hello," she said, turning away and walking toward the newsroom. "How are you?"

"Next time you want a car from here you can whistle for it!"
Tore shouted after her.

"You said I should call you," Polly said. "If Suzette got in touch."

Annika stopped in the middle of the newsroom floor. Patrik
caught sight of her from the news desk and leaped to his feet,
bouncing toward her with a bundle of notes in his hand.

"Has she?" Annika asked. "She's been in touch?"

"As Mr. Gunnar Larsson," Polly said. "This time she wrote a
message as well."

"Press conference at Skeppsbron, half an hour," Patrik said,
handing her a printout from the bundle. "You're going at once,
with Steven."

"What?" Annika said, taking the earpiece out. "And who's Steven?"

"Filip Andersson's been released. New temp photographer."

"Hello?" Polly said in the earpiece.

Annika put it back in.

"Can we meet up?" she asked. "Bring your laptop or a printout
of the message. Where will you be at lunchtime?"

Polly mentioned a café on Drottninggatan, right in the city
center. Annika had never heard of it, which probably meant it was
terribly trendy. She saw a tall man, very young, festooned with a
load of camera cases, rushing toward her.

"Hi, I'm Steven."

She dropped her mobile in her bag and shook hands with the
new photographer.

"I suppose we should set off at once," Annika said, glancing
at the printout of the news flash from the agency that Patrik had
given her: number 28, Skeppsbron. In Gamla Stan, then, with
parking spaces on the quayside opposite the building.

"I can't drive," Steven said.

Great, Annika thought, and headed off toward the caretaker's
desk.

"No chance," Tore said when he saw her coming toward him. "You need to learn to fill the tank before you try that again."

"It's your job to fill the tank, and it's my job to think," Annika said. "Get me a fucking car."

She got the shabby old Volvo he usually gave her.

"What do we want from this press conference?" the photographer asked as Annika drove out of the car park. "Dramatic or formal? Who's the victim, who's the hero? Is there a bad guy?"

She glanced at him to see if he was making fun of her, but he seemed deadly serious.

"I suppose Filip Andersson is the victim, and the lawyer's the hero," Annika said. "Mind you, neither of them looks particularly good in their respective roles. Filip Andersson looks like a gangster and Sven-Göran Olin is a cuddly old uncle."

"And the bad guy is a well-dressed man with a suntan and trustworthy blue eyes?"

"The bad guy is an ordinary-looking woman who was shot by the police in the forest outside Garphyttan in December last year. Called Yvonne."

The photographer didn't say anything else.

The rain had stopped.

She crept through the heavy traffic in the city center. It would have been quicker to walk.

She parked on the quayside at Skeppsbron, paying 260 kronor for two hours. It would have been cheaper to take a taxi.

She looked at the time and wondered how long the press conference would go on for. If it looked like it was going to drag on, she was planning to abandon it. Her meeting with Polly in the café was more important, no matter what Patrik might say.

It might be a false alarm, she thought. It doesn't necessarily have to be a sign of life from Suzette. Polly was prone to dramatizing things.

The legal firm's waiting room was already stuffed full of jour-

nalists, television cameras, and radio transmitters, which surprised Annika. The fact that Filip Andersson was going to be
released had been pretty much obvious since last winter.

I suppose they're here to get a look at him, she thought.

She forced her way through the room and found an empty
chair next to the toilets. On the arm were the various sections of
that day's illustrious broadsheet. She sat down with a sigh and
opened the culture section. She flicked through it without reading
anything until she got to page 4, where she was brought up short.

The double-page spread was dominated by a review of a photography exhibition at Kulturhuset, entitled "The Other Side of the
Costa del Sol." The photographer, Lotta Svensson Bartholomeus,
was praised for having "captured and sensitively documented the
underbelly of the overexploited Costa del Sol: the women on their
way to market, craftsmen's abandoned tools . . ." The article was
illustrated by a close-up of the plate shears from the drug warehouse in La Campana.

Who'd have thought it? Annika mused, and put the paper
down.

She looked straight ahead of her for a few minutes with a growing sense of unease in the pit of her stomach. Then she picked up
the culture section again and stared at the strange picture, remembering Lotta's assertion that art was more real than journalism.

There was something about this that she didn't understand,
that much was clear.

How, in principle, could a broken pair of plate shears on a
warehouse floor be interesting?

What was she missing, seeing as she lacked the capacity to see
anything exceptional in it, as the reviewer claimed.

She folded that section of the paper into a hard little bundle
and stuffed it under her chair, then got up and stood beside the
toilets. She remained there until the doors to the conference room
were opened.

There was an immediate crush in the doorway. She heard Sven-Göran Olin urging everyone to calm down.

She waited until most people had gone in, then went through the doors and stood just inside them.

Up at the front, by an ordinary table with three chairs on the other side, the photographers and television people and radio microphones were all jostling for position. She could see Steven in the crush; he was much taller than all the others.

She tried to catch a glimpse of the exonerated murderer. He wasn't there yet.

The unease in her stomach showed no sign of letting up.

Filip Andersson had been locked up for five years, for a grotesque crime that he hadn't committed. Was it possible to emerge from something like that in anything like a healthy mental state, or did you have to be Nelson Mandela to cope with that?

She realized that she was about to get an answer, because a door at the far end of the room opened and Filip came in. He was dressed in dark trousers and a white shirt, and looked like he'd just had a shower. The sporadic clicking of the photographers turned into a torrent of automatic fire, the television lamps came on, casting a blue sheen over the whole room, and overmade-up television reporters performed animated pieces to camera.

The released man didn't look at any of them. He sank onto one of the three chairs and stared ahead of him without blinking. Annika craned her neck to get a better view.

He'd lost weight since they met in the visitors' room in Kumla Prison last autumn. His hair had been cut, and he'd shaved.

Sven-Göran Olin sat down beside him, and finally a young woman came in and sat on the chair at the end.

"It is with great pleasure," the lawyer began, "that we have today received the decision of the Swedish Court of Appeal to exonerate Filip Andersson entirely of all three cases of murder on Sankt Paulsgatan."

The torrent of camera clicks subsided slightly. The radio-reporters sat down.

"Filip Andersson has been locked up for over five years," the lawyer went on. "As I pointed out when the verdict of the City Court was announced, he was found guilty on very weak evidence, on both occasions. Everyone involved in the case seemed to be mainly preoccupied with making things easy for themselves."

By now there was complete silence in the room.

Annika looked at the man's face, trying to find any sign of feeling or emotion: relief, sadness, joy, or bitterness, but she couldn't identify anything at all. His face was utterly blank, his eyes staring fixedly at a point slightly above the heads of the crowd of journalists. His shoulders seemed broader; maybe he'd started exercising in anticipation of his release.

"A judgment of this sort means that we have simultaneously both more and less faith in the legal system," Sven-Göran said. "The fact that it is possible to raise an appeal and put things right in retrospect is positive. But at the same time it is very troubling that miscarriages of justice like this can occur in the first place."

You could have heard a pin drop. Annika studied her colleagues. They were all staring at Filip, their faces showing disappointment and uncertainty. What could they make of this in their papers?

Filip Andersson was pretty terrible in the role of victim. He didn't have a cute family gathered around him with cake and children's drawings, no beautiful wife holding his hand and gazing in gratitude at the cameras with teary eyes. He looked exactly like what he was: a slightly overweight, unscrupulous financier who had been in the wrong place at the wrong time. There was no way they were going to be able to summon up much sympathy for him among their readers.

"Seeing as the chancellor of justice has rejected our application, today we will be submitting a claim for damages against the

Swedish state," Sven-Göran said. "Filip Andersson is claiming twelve million kronor, five million of which represent reparations for the suffering caused, and seven million his loss of income."

The woman beside him stood up and started handing out printed documents, presumably copies of the claim for damages.

There was more murmuring in the room.

A record-breaking claim for damages wasn't going to make the public feel particularly sympathetic. Sven-Göran wasn't going to win any points in the media from this victory.

"Filip Andersson, how does it feel to be free?" one of the radio reporters shouted.

Sven-Göran leaned toward the microphone again.

"My client would prefer not to comment at the present time," he said.

"So why's he here, then?" a reporter shouted angrily from somewhere off to Annika's left.

"Olin forced him," someone replied. "He's conducted the whole case pro bono, and this is the payoff."

Annika didn't think the lawyer was getting much return on his investment, although of course he hadn't had to do a great deal. It had been her articles about Yvonne Nordin that had set the ball rolling, and the attorney general herself had requested the judicial review.

The woman distributing the documents had reached the back of the room, and handed one to Annika. Annika leaned over toward her and whispered in her ear:

"Can I have an exclusive interview with Filip? My name's Annika Bengtzon, I was the one who wrote the articles about Yvonne Nordin, which . . ."

"Filip Andersson isn't making any comment," the woman said expressionlessly. "Not now, not to anyone."

The other reporters around her were looking at her in disapproval, as if she'd just tried to jump the queue in the Co-op.

She glanced anxiously at the time.

If she couldn't get any comment at all, then the whole morning would have been wasted. It was impossible to write an article for the evening tabloids about a man who had nothing to say.

She decided to wait until the end to see if he could manage to utter a single word.

The journalists began to drift away. She stood aside and pretended not to see her colleagues as they streamed out into the hall.

"If he wants that amount in damages, he could at least have the sense to speak out about those lost years," a woman in the crowd said as she passed.

Filip got up from his chair behind the table; he was still pretty large and heavy. Annika slid to one side and made her way toward him along the wall.

The young woman who had handed out the printouts opened the door at the end of the room. Sven-Göran slipped out first. Filip Andersson turned his back on the room and began to walk toward the door.

"Filip!" Annika said in a loud voice. "Filip Andersson!"

He stopped in the doorway and looked round. His gaze landed directly on her. She stopped beside the wall.

Did he recognize her? Surely he must? He couldn't have received that many visitors in prison?

"What are you going to do next?" she asked loudly. "What are your plans?"

Incredibly slowly, the released man raised his left forefinger, then bent it several times, as if he were waving at her.

His left forefinger, waving. Waving.

She felt a shiver of terror run down her spine.

And suddenly she was back in that alleyway again, in Yxsmedsgränd in Gamla Stan, that Wednesday night after she'd visited him in Kumla Prison. She had been on her way home when two masked men had dragged her into a doorway. One of them had leaned over her, and the eyes staring at her through the holes of the balaclava were pale as glass. The other had held the point of a knife a centimeter from her left eye. "*Leave David in peace. It's over. No more poking about.*" Then the feeling when they grabbed her left hand and pulled her glove off, followed by the terrible pain that ran from her hand, up her arm and into her chest. "*Next time we'll cut your children instead.*" The cold of the cobblestones against her cheek, her thundering heartbeat in her ears as she watched their heavy walking boots disappear down the alley.

She looked up and met Filip's gaze, took a step back, and unconsciously hid her left hand behind her back.

Filip saw the gesture and smiled, then he turned round and disappeared from the room the same way he had arrived.

Her hand was still burning as she headed back to the car. The scar on her index finger was throbbing and aching, which hadn't happened since the very coldest days of the previous winter.

She put her hand in her jacket pocket and hunched her shoulders against the wind.

"He doesn't seem particularly humble," Steven said. "Mind you, maybe you wouldn't be if you'd been locked up for five years when you were innocent."

"No one's saying he's innocent," Annika said. "The only thing the Court of Appeal has concluded is that there wasn't sufficient evidence to convict him. There's a fuck of a big difference."

Steven fell silent again.

I'm too hard on temps, she thought. It serves me right that they don't want to work with me.

"I'm not going back to the newsroom," she said, trying to sound a bit gentler. "You'll have to take a taxi, I'm afraid."

Steven didn't seem upset.

Probably glad to get shot of me, she thought as she paid out

260 kronor for another two hours. She may as well leave the car where it was as there were no parking spaces on Drottninggatan.

Polly wasn't there yet. Annika clambered up onto an extremely high bar stool next to a table with a rolled steel top and neon legs. She tried to order a caffè latte from a waitress with a silver stud in her nose, but the girl snapped that it was actually self-service. So they weren't fashionable enough to offer waitress service. She decided to skip the latte and looked around the room.

It reminded her of the inside of a factory in some futuristic horror film. There were rusty lumps of iron on the walls for decoration, many of them wrapped in loops of multicolored neon. The coffee machine hissed, and the noise of a dishwasher could be heard out in the kitchen, along with the clatter of crockery. The music throbbing from the speakers made the German industrial metal of Rammstein sound like sing-along Europop.

Her finger ached.

It could hardly be a coincidence. He had waved to her with the same finger she had been cut in on the night after she had met him in prison and not done as she was told.

She put her hand back in her jacket pocket again.

The café was filling up, it was getting toward lunchtime. A surprising number of the customers seemed to be civil servants from the government ministries and office blocks in the city center, to judge by their conservative appearance: white shirts and dark trousers, exactly like Filip Andersson at the press conference just now.

She shivered with unease.

If Filip had ordered the knife attack that evening, he had been very quick off the mark. It hadn't been more than a few hours after her visit to Kumla. He must have been extremely keen to stop her snooping about in David Lindholm's past. Why?

It could hardly just be childhood nostalgia. They had run a

business together. David had had an affair with his sister, and got her pregnant. He had been Filip's trustee at Kumla, a position that involved providing support and acting as a contact person for people serving life sentences.

There was obviously something she wasn't supposed to find out about, something she didn't already know. David had a lot of dark sides.

Annika remembered Nina Hoffman's description of how he had treated Julia.

David Lindholm had kept his wife locked in their apartment, sometimes up to a week at a time. On other occasions he threw her out into the stairwell naked, until she got so ill that she had to go to A&E. He was notoriously unfaithful, disappeared for weeks without saying where he had been, shouted at her, calling her a whore and a slut . . .

Annika looked at the time.

What if Polly didn't show up?

She drummed the fingers of her right hand on the metal tabletop.

David had been an extremely contradictory character. While he had been a pig of a husband, he had somehow got away with becoming one of Sweden's most famous and respected police officers.

She knew he used to be violent from the investigations into complaints made against him at the start of his career in the police. She remembered Timmo Koivisto, the former drug addict she had met at the Vårtuna rehab center, and what he had told her about how David had smashed his head into a toilet wall, leaving him with permanent injuries.

Timmo Koivisto had been a dealer right at the bottom of the food chain. He supported his own habit by ripping off his employers and cutting the gear with icing sugar, then charging extra and pocketing the difference.

"Why did he do it? Why did David beat you up like that?" Annika had asked.

"They wanted to show me that I could never get away," Timmo Koivisto had said. "Wherever I went, they would find me."

And who were "they"? Annika had asked. Was he talking about some sort of drugs mafia?

"That's one way of describing them." Timmo Koivisto had replied.

She looked around the futuristic, nightmarish décor. She was in the right place, wasn't she?

To make sure, she took out her notepad and checked. Yes, this was the place.

She left her notepad on the tabletop and stared at the concrete wall.

David Lindholm, drugs mafia, the murders in Sankt Paulsgatan, Filip Andersson arranging for her finger to be cut . . .

"Annika?"

She looked up and saw a blond girl with a rucksack and padded jacket standing next to the table.

"Polly?"

The girl shook her hand politely, introduced herself, and sat down opposite her while she shrugged off her rucksack.

"I know," she said, leaning across the table so Annika could hear her. "I don't look like my picture on Facebook anymore. I've thought about changing it, but for some reason I don't want to. We took our pictures together, Suzette and me, and if I change it, it'll be like another bit of her vanishing . . ."

Annika looked at the girl; she seemed so grown up.

"And now you think she's got in touch?" Annika said.

Polly nodded.

"Do you want anything? I can go and get it."

Annika took out her purse and handed Polly a 100-kronor note.

"Just a glass of water for me, please."

The girl went off to the counter, which was actually a rusty metal table. Annika watched her. She must be sixteen, maybe seventeen. She seemed older.

She returned with a glass of water with ice and lemon, and a cup of green tea for herself. She looked rather apologetic.

"I know it was a bit silly of me," she said. "What I said last time."

Annika blinked several times.

"When I asked if you thought there was email in heaven. Of course there isn't, I know that. I suppose I was just hoping . . ."

She struggled onto a stool. She wasn't particularly tall, about the same as Annika.

"This time I know it's for real. Suz is alive," she said.

Annika tried to look at the girl without staring. Her face was calm and focused. She didn't seem either distraught or overjoyed.

"Have you got your computer with you?" Annika asked.

Polly nodded and pulled a laptop out of her rucksack.

"I'm in a bit of a hurry," she said. "We've got a student council meeting."

She started the laptop up, logged in, did a bit of clicking, then turned the screen towards Annika. The screen was covered by a picture of a smiling, black-haired girl hugging a chestnut horse.

"There's free Wi-Fi here," Polly said. "Hang on, I'll log in."

"That's a lovely picture of Suzette," Annika said.

"The horse's name is Sultan. He was Suzette's favorite. The riding school's sold him now."

The screen flickered, and a Hotmail page appeared below Windows Live. There was a banner at the top advertising some science magazine. Immediately below that, on the right-hand side, she saw the email address "mr-gunnar-larsson." The darker blue marker on the left was highlighting *sent*. There were two messages, both of them with nothing in the subject box. They had been sent to Polly's Yahoo address, the first one at the end of March and the second at 1437 the previous day, June 13.

"So this is Gunnar Larsson's email account?" Annika said. "The one you and Suzette set up to send dirty messages to girls in your class?"

Polly nodded.

"We deleted all the messages after Gunnar left," Polly said, shamefaced.

"But you kept the account?"

"We didn't know how to close it down."

Annika clicked on the first message, the one from March. Empty.

Then she clicked on the other one, from the day before.

> Hi Polly, you cant tell anyone about this email. You cant say anything to mum and DEFINITELY NOT the police. Theres no internet at the farm so i havent been able to email. Im at an internet cafe now. They dont know where i am, and Fatima would be furious if she knew I was writing.
>
> Im with Amira. Ive been here since new year. Ive got my own horse called Larache. Hes lovely, a mix of English and Arabian thoroughbred. Is Adde with anyone else? Dont tell Adde ive been in touch. You can answer this but I dont know when ill read it. We only go places like Asilah, but not very often.
>
> Big hug from suz

Annika read the message twice. Evidently it had been written on a fairly basic keyboard, without any Swedish characters. Asilah sounded like a place, it seemed vaguely familiar—where had she heard it before?

"Do you think it's genuine?" she asked in a low voice. "Is this how Suzette usually expresses herself?"

Polly took a sip of her green tea and nodded.

"She always writes '*big hug*,' and Suz with a small s."

"Who are these people she mentions? Fatima, Amira, and Adde?"

A shadow passed quickly over Polly's face, unless Annika was just imagining it.

"Amira's Suz's best friend. That's what she used to say, as if those of us here at home didn't count. I think Fatima's her mother. Adde is Suz's boyfriend. Well, maybe not boyfriend, they weren't really together; it was mostly that Suz had a crush on him. Adde's always got loads of girls . . ."

"What about Amira?" Annika asked. "How come she's Suz's best friend?"

"Her summer friend. Suz spent a lot of time on their farm when she was little. They're the same age."

"Where? In Spain?"

Polly shook her head.

"In Morocco."

"Morocco? In Africa?"

"They've got a farm there."

"Do you know where it is? This place she mentions, Asilah?"

Polly shrugged and pushed her teacup aside.

"But how do they talk to each other?" Annika asked. "They speak French and Arabic in Morocco, and Suzette couldn't really speak English, could she?"

Polly looked indignant.

"Of course Suz can speak English."

"Does she speak English with Amira?"

Polly shook her head and turned the laptop round to face her.

"Swedish, obviously."

"Hang on," Annika said. "Can I forward this to my own email?"

Polly hesitated, then looked at her watch.

"No," she finally said. "I promised to tell you if she got in touch. I have to go now."

"They speak Swedish to each other? How come?"

"Amira's half Swedish, isn't she? Her dad's from Sweden. Her surname's Lindholm."

All the noise around Annika vanished, the music and coffee-machine and crockery.

"Lindholm?" she said. "Her dad's surname is Lindholm? Do you know what his first name is?"

Polly put her laptop back in her rucksack and shrugged again.

"No idea. I don't think he lives on the farm."

"Could his name be David? Do you know if he was a policeman?"

The girl was pulling her rucksack back on now.

"Can I ask you something?" she said.

"Of course you can," Annika said.

"Don't say anything about this to anyone. Promise."

Annika looked at the serious young woman with the blond hair, so different to the heavily made-up, black-haired girl on Facebook.

"I won't say anything," she said. "And I won't write anything either. I promise."

Polly held out her right arm, shook hands with Annika, then disappeared out the door.

Annika gave her two minutes, then followed her out.

With a sigh of relief she left the noise of the hellish café behind her.

Suzette was alive. She was on a farm somewhere in the Moroccan countryside, where there was a girl the same age whose surname was Lindholm.

She stopped on the street, fished out her mobile, called international directory inquiries and asked to be put through to the Swedish Embassy in Rabat in Morocco.

After a good deal of ringing, an automated answer-phone message clicked in. A long harangue in French mostly just explained the opening hours for the visa section, and telephone times for other business. Annika had trouble keeping up; her French was almost as bad as her Spanish, but she realized it was already too late to get any information that day. She'd have to try again tomorrow.

She looked over toward Kungsholmen. She ought to go back to the paper and tell them that Filip Andersson wasn't talking.

People were sweeping past her, bumping into her, catching her bag, standing on her toes, hurrying, hurrying, hurrying off to lunch or the dry cleaners or meetings somewhere. Buses squealed and cars splashed through muddy porridge.

She looked down toward Hamngatan. Writing up that worthless press conference would take thirty seconds. Annika raised her mobile and dialed Julia Lindholm's home number on Bondegatan.

She and Alexander were at home, and Annika was more than welcome to pay them a visit.

Their flat was on the third floor of a rather dull block from the 1960s. The stairwell was dark and smelled musty. The only thing that looked new in the whole landing was the sign saying *LIND-HOLM* on the letterbox.

The police must have broken the old one when they broke into the flat after David was murdered, Annika thought.

She rang the bell and heard a distant *ding-dong* echo on the other side of the wall.

"Welcome," Julia said, throwing the door open wide. "How lovely of you to come and see us! Isn't it, Alexander?"

The boy, who had grown at a phenomenal rate during the

spring, was standing in the doorway to his room and staring steadily as Annika. He didn't answer.

Annika dropped her bag in the hall and hung her jacket up on a hook. Then she went over to Alexander and crouched down beside him.

"Hello, Alexander," she said. "Is it nice being able to play in your own room again?"

The boy turned round, went into his room, and closed the door.

"He's going to start back at his old preschool next week," Julia said. "The therapists have decided he's ready for that now. Have you been here before?"

Annika shook her head.

"There's not much to see, but my parents have redecorated and made it nice while Alexander and I were at Lejongården. This is the kitchen!"

She gestured toward a very ordinary 1960s-style kitchen with painted cupboards and a scratched stainless worktop.

"It suits the building well," Annika said.

"Yes, doesn't it? I really like it. And here's the living room . . ."

They went into a room with a television with oak parquet flooring and windows facing in two directions.

"We haven't got a balcony," Julia said, "which is a bit of a shame. It's really the only thing I wish was different. My bedroom . . ."

She opened the door to the room where her husband had been murdered. The bed was neatly made. The curtains were open.

Annika stopped in the doorway.

If David had done errands for the mafia in return for money, he hadn't spent it on his home.

"I know what you're thinking," Julia said. "How can I sleep in here?"

Annika took a deep breath and was about to protest, but just breathed out instead.

"He's gone, but we're still here. There's no way round that," Julia said. "Have you had lunch?"

Annika shook her head.

"I was thinking of doing meatballs and mashed potato. Frozen meatballs and instant mash, but it does the job. Would you like some?"

"Thanks, yes."

They went back out into the hall. Annika could hear banging from inside Alexander's room.

"He's decided to build a flying saucer," Julia said. "The therapists say I should let him do what he wants."

Annika sat down at the kitchen table while Julia got out a packet of powdered mash and a bag of ready-cooked meatballs.

"How's he getting on?" Annika asked.

Julia took a while to answer.

"He isn't the same boy as before, although I don't really know what else I was expecting. After all, he was a whole year younger then."

She stopped, holding a spatula in front of her face.

"You know what?" she said, turning toward Annika. "It doesn't really matter. I'm just so grateful that I've got him back."

Annika nodded. Julia went back to the meatballs. They were soon sizzling in a frying pan with some melted margarine. The sound was soothing and homely, the kitchen freshly painted and tidy, and Julia was humming bits of an unidentifiable song.

This ought to feel nice, Annika thought, but there's something about it that jars. The irregular banging sounds coming from the boy's room, perhaps, or possibly something about the spartan furnishings. Maybe it was just the echo of all David's lies. He had never been undercover on the Costa del Sol.

But there was no such thing as ghosts.

"How are you managing financially?" she asked, trying not to sound too intrusive.

"The flat's a freehold, and we inherited that, but there was nothing else. But David had life insurance, payable to those he left behind, and that's me and Alexander and Hannelore, of course. It was actually quite a lot of money, so that's what we're living off at the moment."

"What do you think you might do? Go back to the police?"

Julia shook her head.

"I want to study architecture. If I'm careful, the insurance money will last until I graduate."

She measured five deciliters of water into a saucepan and put in on the stove.

"Can I ask you something else?" Annika said. "Do you know if David had any connection to Morocco?"

Julia looked up at her in surprise.

"Morocco? No, none at all. Why would he have?"

"He never mentioned Morocco? Or if he knew anyone there?"

"Why do you ask?"

Annika took her time answering.

"He might have relatives there . . ."

Julia got the butter out of the fridge and a whisk from the cutlery drawer, poured some milk into a mug, added a large knob of butter and put it in the microwave, set it to two minutes, and pressed *Start*.

"The only time he ever mentioned Morocco was when he talked about his stepfather, Torsten. He disappeared in Morocco when David was in his late teens."

Annika sat still, searching her memory. Julia had said something about the missing stepfather on some earlier occasion.

"Did he ever find out about what happened to him?"

Julia got out three plates, glasses, and cutlery.

"I don't think David ever really got over it. They were very close. After all, he never knew his real father, so Torsten meant a great deal to him."

She stopped.

"It was the winter before David applied to Police Academy," she said.

Annika took the plates and laid the table.

"When you lived in Estepona, could David have gone to Morocco to look for Torsten?"

Julia looked at her, extremely surprised.

"No," she said, "it was all such a long time ago. I can't imagine that he did."

The microwave bleeped three times, the milk was hot, and the butter melted. The water was boiling on the stove and Julia poured a packet of powdered mash into the buttery milk and stirred it energetically with the whisk.

"Alexander! Lunch is ready!"

The boy emerged from his room at once and stopped in front of Annika.

"You're in my place," he said.

His voice was surprisingly dark, not at all the way Annika remembered it from that night out in the forest.

"You can sit here, Alexander," Julia said, pointing to the place that had been set at the end of the table.

The child's face contorted into a grimace, and a howl from the depths emerged from his mouth. He collapsed on the floor, his upper body jerking, his hands and feet banging the floor, as he screamed as loud as he could. Annika backed away in horror. Julia seemed neither surprised nor concerned, just got up and picked the boy off the floor, and rocked him in her arms until the tantrum had passed.

"Today you can sit in this seat," she said, putting the boy on the chair at the end of the table.

He fired a hostile glare at Annika, then grabbed his knife and fork, and set about the meatballs with gusto.

"Ketchup?" he asked between mouthfuls.

"Not today," Julia said.

Annika ate the powdered mash and heated-up meatballs in astonished silence. Sure, her children were angry sometimes, but she'd never seen anything like this outburst in such a small child.

"Can I get down now?" he said when he'd finished.

"Say thank you for the food and clear your plate away," Julia said.

"Thanks for the food," the boy said, then leaped off the chair and picked up his glass, cutlery, and plate in a somewhat unsteady grasp, and took them over to the draining board.

Then he left the kitchen without a backward glance, went into his room, and shut the door.

"The fact that I spent seven years as a beat officer makes it easier," Julia said with a sad smile. "Coffee?"

Annika looked at the time.

"I should probably get going," she said. "By the way, do you have any contact with your mother-in-law?"

Julia filled a kettle with water and got a jar of coffee out.

"No more than usual," she said. "We brought her round here last weekend, but she just wandered about looking for David. It was all a bit weird, so I don't think we'll be doing that again in a hurry."

"Which care home is she in?"

"Ramsmora."

"Where's that?"

"In Nacka. I know it's not far, but we haven't got a car and it's a bit tricky getting there on public transport. So we don't visit her terribly often."

"Would you mind if I went to see her?" Annika said.

Julia looked up.

"Why would you want to do that?"

Annika decided to be honest.

"Do you remember me asking if you'd ever heard the name Veronica Söderström, or Astrid Paulson?"

Julia paused, then nodded.

"She was that ice hockey player's wife."

Julia measured some coffee into a filter and pressed the *Start* button.

"I have reason to believe that David met her when they were children," Annika said. "You've never talked to Nina about that?"

Julia shook her head in bewilderment.

"Why would I have done that?"

"Nina once told me that they grew up together, David and Filip Andersson, Yvonne Nordin, and Veronica Paulson."

Julia started at the mention of Yvonne's name.

"We've talked about this before," Annika said, "about the fact they were like siblings. That means their parents must have known each other, or at least their mothers. Have you ever heard of a woman called Astrid Paulson?"

Julia adjusted the coffee filter.

"Wasn't she one of the people murdered in Spain last winter?"

"That's right," Annika said, "she was Veronica Söderström's mother. Have you ever heard her name in any other context?"

Julia shook her head.

"Astrid Paulson, and Nina's mother, and your mother-in-law, Hannelore, all knew each other."

"Did they?"

"Nina, Yvonne, and Filip's mother was called Siv. You knew her, didn't you?"

Julia put two mugs on the table.

"She died soon after we got married. I always felt rather sorry for Siv. She was a fairly severe alcoholic. You take it black, don't you?"

"Yes, thanks. David's real father, Klas Lindholm, what happened to him?"

"They divorced before David was a year old," she said, sitting down at the table. "He moved away, I don't know where. They didn't have any contact after that. He died a few years ago. David didn't go to the funeral."

"Do you know if he went on to have another family?"

"David inherited an old Saab and a summer cottage outside Kramfors when he died. He was the only heir."

"Do you know if he used to go to Morocco?"

Julia raised her eyebrows.

"You're really banging on about Morocco. What's this all about?"

Annika felt her face going red.

"I've heard about someone called Lindholm who's supposed to be living in Morocco, and I was wondering if it could be a relative . . ."

"Hardly," Julia said. "Lindholm's a very common name. There's one in the next building; we're always getting each other's post."

"Mummy?"

Alexander was standing in the kitchen doorway.

"Yes, darling, what is it?"

"My flying saucer's finished."

Julia lit up.

"How lovely! I must have a look. Would you like to see it too, Annika?"

"If I'm allowed to?" Annika said.

Alexander nodded.

They went into the boy's room, next to Julia's.

Half the floor was covered with a huge pile of pieces of board, plywood, and chipboard, all nailed on top of each other. A few sticks, probably broom handles originally, poked up toward the ceiling.

Julia clapped her hands in delight.

"That's wonderful!" she said. "I'm sure you could fly all the way to the moon in that."

The boy looked at her solemnly.

"I need to get higher than that," he said. "All the way to the stars."

"What do you want to go there for?" Annika asked.

He gave a look of utter surprise.

"To visit Daddy, of course," the child said.

Annika picked the car up from Skeppsbron. The parking ticket had expired and she had been given a 500-kronor fine. She tossed the penalty notice in her bag and called directory inquiries, and asked for a text containing the phone number and directions to the care home in Nacka.

The boy's dark stare was still burning inside her.

She shivered and started the car.

Slowly she steered toward Slussen and turned off onto Stadsgårdsleden. The traffic was heavy, sluggish as frozen syrup. It had stopped raining, but the sludge on the road splattered the windows and she still had to keep the windscreen wipers on.

There was a sixteen-year-old girl called Amira Lindholm in Morocco, on a farm outside Asilah.

Torsten Ernsten, David Lindholm's stepfather, had disappeared in Morocco.

As she was passing Skurusundet she thought the sky looked a bit brighter over to the east, where she was heading.

She carried on along the motorway toward Gustavsberg.

Where had she heard the word Asilah?

Who could have mentioned it to her?

Suddenly she heard Niklas's voice in her head.

It was saying something, and she was taking notes, something she hadn't used in her article because it hadn't seemed relevant, but what was it?

It gets shipped out of two small coastal towns, Nador and Asilah, in February and March.

They had been talking about the cannabis produced by the

hash farmers in Morocco. They had been sitting in the tapas bar in the conference center in Málaga, and Niklas had been pressing his leg against hers under the table.

She realized a moment too late that she'd missed the turning.

She had to take the next exit instead, then turned round and drove straight to Ramsmora care home.

The building was long and low, and looked like it had been renovated sometime in the 1990s, painted a glossy pink color that didn't suit the rest of the building or the windows and doors. Rustling birch trees framed the ugly building.

She pulled up in the visitors' car park and breathed out. She really didn't drive anywhere near enough, regardless of what Tore the caretaker might think, and it always felt uncomfortable when she was forced to.

She had closed the car door and was on her way to the entrance when her mobile rang.

It was Berit Hamrin.

"I'm sorry," she said. "I didn't mean you to have to go to that press conference."

"What press conference?" Annika asked, before she remembered Filip Andersson.

"I had to go to the dentist this morning, otherwise I'd have gone. Did he say anything?"

"Not a thing," Annika said, remembering his little wave.

"You know I don't think he's innocent."

Annika didn't answer, and carried on toward the entrance.

"Where are you?" Berit asked.

"I'm going to visit a confused old lady. She's a German Jew, and came here on the white buses after the war."

"She's German?" Berit said. "And came to Sweden on the white buses? You must have misunderstood."

Annika stopped.

"What do you mean?"

"The white buses picked up Scandinavians who were held in German concentration camps, Danes and Norwegians. There weren't any Germans."

"Are you sure?" Annika said.

"It was claimed that the buses were going to rescue other nationalities as well, but that turned out to be a lie. The only Germans that got anywhere near those white buses were dying prisoners who were moved between various camps. Pretty much all of them died."

Annika looked up at the tops of the birch trees. She really shouldn't be surprised. Nothing about these families seemed to be either true or normal.

"Why do you ask?" Berit wondered.

"I'll tell you later," Annika said. "I'll be back in a couple of hours."

She reached the door, scraped the mud from her shoes, and stepped inside the care home.

There was strip lighting in the ceiling of the lobby, reflecting off the polished linoleum floor. A few pictures of indeterminate subject matter hung on the plastered walls, and there was a sharp smell of antiseptic disinfectant.

She stopped inside the door and listened.

Two corridors led off from the entrance hall, one straight ahead and the other off to the right. She couldn't see anyone, but somewhere she could make out the murmur of voices. To the left she could just make out a dining room through a half-open door. She walked over and pushed it open. Two women in their fifties turned toward her as if on command. Their voices fell silent at once.

"Hello," Annika said. "I'd like to visit Hannelore Lindholm. Which room does she live in?"

The women looked at each other and whispered something.

Then one went off toward the kitchen while the other came toward her.

"My name's Annika Bengtzon," Annika said, holding out her hand and smiling. "I know Julia and Alexander. She told me that Hannelore visited them at home in Bondegatan last weekend and . . ."

"I know who you are," the woman said. "I'm Barbro, I'm the manager here. We do read the papers at Ramsmora. I know you were the one who found Alexander."

The woman fell silent, came a step closer, and looked at Annika curiously. She was very red under her nose, as if she had a cold and had been blowing her nose too much.

"Are you going to send something to the paper?"

People generally couldn't tell the difference between the various types of articles in the daily papers: long, explanatory reports, incisive interviews, sharply focused news stories, diaries, notes, op-ed pieces, or adverts. For a lot of people, including the manager, Barbro, everything was just "something" you sent in.

"No," Annika said. "I'm not going to write anything. I'd just like to see Hannelore and talk to her."

"About what?"

Annika adjusted her bag on her shoulder.

"Do I have to tell you?"

The woman blushed.

"This way," she said, turning on her heel.

She led the way through the lobby and carried on straight ahead, along one of the corridors. Annika followed behind her. Her frame bounced energetically with each step. Annika could sense that Barbro felt hurt.

"Ramsmora Residential Home is a very particular place. We focus on a number of particular areas," she said over her shoulder. "We have forty-eight apartments in total. We strive to make the atmosphere as homely as possible. We have a care-home section, some sheltered housing, and a section for people suffering from dementia. That's where we are now."

The walls were pink. A painted row of darker pink flowers divided the wall along the middle. After a few meters the corridor opened out and became wider, with a carpet in the middle of the floor. There were groups of armchairs and small tables placed at regular intervals along one wall. The other wall contained a series of doors, some open, others shut.

"So Hannelore Lindholm has been diagnosed with dementia?"

"I can't discuss the medical details of our residents," Barbro said, stopping at one of the closed doors and knocking on it. She pulled it open and went in without waiting for an answer.

"Hannelore," she said, far too loudly, as if the old lady was hard of hearing. "You've got a visitor."

Then she let Annika into the room. She remained standing in the doorway with her hand on the door handle.

"Thanks," Annika said. "I'll be able to find my own way out."

Barbro hesitated, then turned and walked out, closing the door behind her.

Annika was left standing there with her back to the closed door. On her right was a bathroom, on her left a rudimentary kitchen. The rest of the flat consisted of a single room that was seriously overfurnished. A heavy, cracked leather sofa, an ornate writing desk, bookcases made of yew, and a narrow bed in the corner closest to the kitchen. The furniture looked exposed and out of place on the yellow linoleum floor. There was a smell of dust and furniture polish.

A woman with long white hair was standing over by the window, fiddling with a potted plant. She didn't seem to have noticed that Annika was in the room.

Annika cleared her throat loudly.

No reaction.

"Mrs. Lindholm?" Annika said. "Hannelore? My name's Annika Bengtzon. I've come to talk to you."

The woman at the window cast a surprisingly alert glance over her shoulder.

"What do you want, then?" she asked in a completely normal tone of voice, as she turned her attention back to the geranium again.

"I'd like to talk to you about Astrid and Siv," Annika said.

The woman's hands stopped in the middle of what they were doing. She turned round. Annika noticed that she had her hands full of brown leaves. She was strikingly attractive.

"Is Astrid here?" she asked.

She had no trace of a German accent. On the contrary, she had the same Södermanland accent as Annika.

"No," Annika said. "She's not here at the moment. Shall we sit down?"

Hannelore Lindholm hesitated.

"I just have to get rid of this rubbish first," she said, heading over to the little kitchen in the corner of the room.

Annika pulled off her jacket and dropped it and her bag on the floor by the door, then went over to the sofa and armchairs.

"When is Astrid coming?" the old woman asked, looking expectantly at Annika.

"Astrid won't be coming again," Annika said, sitting down in one of the armchairs. "Perhaps you could tell me a bit about her?"

"Where is she?"

Annika looked at the woman before her. She was tall and slender; her back was bent but her shoulders straight. Her hair had been carefully washed and brushed. Her eyes were large and bright blue, and the look on her face reminded Annika of a surprised doll. She had rouge on her cheeks.

She had walked round the flat on Bondegatan looking for David, even though she had been told countless times that he was dead. So there was no point in Annika telling her Astrid was dead, when she might already have been told and forgotten.

"She's on the Costa del Sol," Annika said, because she didn't actually know if the bodies had been moved, or, if so, where to.

Hannelore sat herself down on the sofa.

"She's so happy there," she said. "Does she still have the estate agency?"

"Oh yes," Annika said.

Hannelore laughed.

"Astrid's so courageous," she said. "She's always the one who dares to do all the dangerous things."

She smiled and nodded for emphasis.

"What sort of thing does Astrid dare to do?" Annika asked.

The answer came promptly and easily.

"Jump off the biggest haystack. Ride the wild bull."

Hannelore laughed at her memories.

"She's crazy!"

The laughter died away. Annika waited. Nothing else followed.

"Where did Astrid jump off the haystacks?" Annika asked.

The surprised expression returned to Hannelore's face.

"At Gudagården, of course! She's already there when I arrive. She's the only one who's kind to me."

She leaned over an antique table and lowered her voice.

"Astrid's a very good person," she said quietly. "She always looks after anyone who's weak or scared. She's not a little troll girl at all."

Annika couldn't help blinking. The old woman really was completely confused. Maybe it would be better if she asked some easier questions.

"Could you tell me a bit about yourself?" she asked.

Hannelore looked up, then glanced around the cramped room.

"I live in a castle," she said. "In a castle high above the clouds. I dance in *die Halle* for all the animals."

She raised her arms and made graceful gestures in the air, her hands floating as she closed her eyes. There was something enchanting about the expression on the woman's face, as if there really was another reality concealed within Swedish geriatric care, another room besides this one in Ramsmora care home. Annika looked at her for a long time, until she started to feel a bit uncomfortable.

"Where are your parents?" she asked.

The woman's movements froze and she opened her eyes.

"I'm not allowed to talk about Mother and Father," she said.

She looked frightened.

"Why not?"

"Onkel Gunnar and Tante Helga have forbidden me."

She tucked her hands under her armpits.

"But you can tell me," Annika said.

The woman pulled her feet up beneath her and huddled up, shaking her head vigorously.

"He'll hit me even more if I ever say anything about Mother and Father," she said.

"Who will?"

"Onkel Gunnar."

Her voice was a monotone now, and she stared in front of her as she spoke.

"I came to Sweden on the white buses that Count Folke Bernadotte and the Swedish Red Cross so generously put at the disposal of those in need," she recited.

"But that isn't true, is it?" Annika said.

Hannelore glanced at her but said nothing.

"They forced you to lie, didn't they? Why?"

The woman blinked as though she were about to start crying.

"Because Father was an officer," she said in a very thin voice.

"An officer? A German officer during the war?"

She nodded.

"That castle you used to dance in, what sort of place was that? Was it a real castle?"

She nodded again.

"Berghof," she said in the same little voice.

Annika started. She wasn't great at history, but she'd seen almost every episode of the miniseries *Band of Brothers*.

"But that was Hitler's home in Bavaria," she said. "The one they used to call the Eagle's Nest."

Hannelore wrapped her arms round her knees and hid her face against her legs.

Annika looked at the woman, her soft white hair flowing over her legs. Her hands were clenched around her lower arms, white hands with blue veins and pale pink nails.

Hannelore wasn't Jewish, Annika realized. She had never been in a German concentration camp. On the contrary, she was the daughter of a Nazi officer, so high up that the family had visited Berghof at least once. Her Jewish background was a retrospective fabrication put together by the people she called Onkel and Tante. Who were they? Annika had never studied German, but those sounded like family titles. Were Gunnar and Helga distant relatives who had taken her in after the war? And who thought it sounded better and more noble to look after a poor Jewish girl who had survived a concentration camp than the daughter of a senior Nazi officer?

But why had she given her son Jewish names, David Zeev Samuel? Was that a way of repaying some kind of psychological debt?

Unless the boy's father, the elusive Mr. Lindholm, had chosen the boy's names? And he could have been Jewish, of course . . .

The woman was slowly rocking on the sofa in a slightly odd way.

"Can you tell me about Siv?" Annika asked.

Hannelore stopped rocking. She straightened her back, her shoulders relaxed, and her arms let go. Her vision cleared and she looked at Annika.

"Is Siv here?" she asked.

"No," Annika said, "she's in Södermanland."

The woman seemed content with the answer. She nodded in agreement, looking slightly concerned.

"Poor Siv," she said.

"Why's that?" Annika asked.

Hannelore leaned toward Annika.

"She's so easily taken in. She really believes in God and heaven and all the other things that Onkel Gunnar preaches. When I first arrived at Gudagården she actually thought she was an angel, because that's what Tante Helga had told her. How stupid!"

She shook her head to emphasize what she had just said.

Annika was looking at her thoughtfully.

Hannelore didn't seem to have any difficulty remembering her childhood. In fact it seemed as if she was still there. What she was saying was probably true.

The girls had grown up together on a farm somewhere, presumably in Södermanland seeing as Hannelore had the same accent as her. They had shared the same childhood experiences. Something that happened back then bound them together so tightly that they stayed in touch when they were grown up.

"What happened at Gudagården?" Annika asked, studying the woman's reaction carefully.

Hannelore Lindholm blinked.

"Happened?"

"When did you move away from there?"

Hannelore got up from the sofa so quickly that she knocked the antique table over. She went over to the window and began picking at the plant again, hard and spasmodically.

The question had upset her. Annika went after her and put her hands on the old woman's.

"Come and sit on the sofa," she said. "Let's talk about Siv and Astrid."

The doll's eyes turned to look at Annika.

"Is Astrid here?" Hannelore asked.

Annika led the woman back to the leather sofa.

"I'd like to talk about Torsten," Annika said.

"Torsten isn't here," Hannelore said, and her eyes looked suddenly heavy.

"No, I know," Annika said. "He's in Morocco. What's he doing there?"

Hannelore was fiddling with her skirt. Her lips moved, but no sound came out.

"Does Torsten often go to Morocco? What does he do there? Do you know?"

Hannelore started singing, something monotonous and incomprehensible, maybe in German.

"Don't you want to talk about Torsten? Has he upset you?"

She stopped singing.

"Torsten never came home," she said. "He went to the farm, and he never came back."

Annika felt the hair on the back of her neck stand up.

Theres no internet at the farm so i havent been able to email

"Where is the farm?" she asked. "Who's at the farm?"

Hannelore was staring straight ahead without moving.

Annika waited.

She sat there for a long time, trying to understand the limits of Hannelore Lindholm's memory.

Julia had said she had been taken into care after Torsten disappeared. She seemed to remember that he hadn't come back after his last trip. How long ago could that have been? David had been a teenager, and he would have been forty-three now. Twenty-five years ago, in other words, when Hannelore herself would have been about forty-five. Maybe she still had memories from that time.

He went to the farm and he never came back.

"Is David in Morocco as well?" she asked.

Hannelore Lindholm lit up.

"No, no," she said. "He's coming to get me soon. We're going to go home."

She got up and went over to one of the bookcases, opened one of the doors, and started to pile the books on the floor in front of it.

"Hannelore," Annika said, going over to the woman. "Come and sit on the sofa. David's not here yet, we'll have to wait a bit longer."

The woman hesitated, then nodded and left the books where they were on the linoleum floor.

"David doesn't have an easy life," she said. "All the other children have a father."

Annika got the woman to sit down again, and sat down beside her on the leather sofa.

"Why doesn't David have a father?" she asked.

The woman started picking angrily at her cardigan.

"They got cross with each other. He shouted at Astrid. Is David coming soon? He should be here by now, shouldn't he?"

Annika could hear footsteps and voices in the corridor, the clatter of crockery on a trolley. She took a deep breath and looked directly at Hannelore Lindholm.

"Can you tell me about Fatima?"

The woman looked at her uncomprehendingly.

"Who's that?"

Annika waited a few seconds before she replied.

"Fatima's at the farm," she finally said. "With Amira."

Hannelore's eye fluttered round the room.

Annika waited, then asked:

"Can you tell me about Julia?"

The woman's hands fumbled over her skirt.

"Alexander, do you remember him? David's son?"

There was a knock on the door, and Barbro the manager stuck her head into the room.

"How's it going?" she asked, looking inquisitively at Annika.

"We're just having a chat," Annika said, rather sharply. "We'd appreciate it if we could be left in peace."

Barbro came into the room and closed the door behind her.

"It's time for your medicine," she said, unlocking a cabinet in Hannelore's bathroom.

"I don't want my medicine," Hannelore Lindholm said. "It makes my head feel so fuzzy."

The manager took something from the cabinet and locked it again, then came out into the room again and went over to the sink.

"Don't throw dead leaves in the drainer," she said clearly and slowly. "Just remember that we have to come and clean up after you."

The manager filled a glass with water, then went over to the old lady.

Hannelore sighed, took the pill, and swallowed it with a sip of water.

"That's it, well done," Barbro said in her loud voice for people who were hard of hearing.

She turned to Annika.

"I'll have to ask you to leave now," she said. "Hannelore needs to rest."

Annika looked at the time. It really was time for her to be getting back anyway.

Hannelore went and sat on the bed with a look of resignation in her doll's eyes. Annika followed her and took her hand.

"Thanks very much for the chat," she said.

Hannelore blinked in surprise and looked at her.

"Who are you?" she asked.

Annika patted the old woman's hand, then went over to her bag, slung it over her shoulder, and put her jacket over her arm.

"Julia and Alexander send their love," she said. "They'll come and see you again soon."

Hannelore was gazing over at the window and didn't seem to hear her.

It had started to rain again. Annika ran out to the car, discovered that she had forgotten to lock it, and threw herself into the driving seat, tossing her bag on the seat beside her.

She pulled out her mobile and checked the screen: one missed call, from Patrik's mobile.

The head of news would have to wait.

She closed her eyes and thought. The rain was drumming on the roof of the car, and streaming down the windscreen.

Hannelore, Astrid, and Siv grew up together on a farm in Södermanland called Gudagården. The patriarch of the house was called Gunnar, and he wasn't above beating children. Hannelore was the daughter of a Nazi, and related to the farmers, who were hypocrites of the highest order seeing as they beat the little girl into lying about her past.

The three girls grew up and stayed in touch with each other. Their children in turn came to be like brothers and sister: David and Filip, Yvonne and Veronica, and little Nina.

She started the car and made her way onto the motorway as she dialed the number.

Nina Hoffman answered at once, the way she usually did, and gave her full name.

There was no noise in the background, so Annika assumed she was at home or in her office. At least she wasn't in a patrol car or in some noisy custody-unit corridor.

"I was at the press conference when your brother was released," Annika said. "Do you know what he's going to do now?"

"I'm grateful for what you've done, but I don't owe you anything," Nina Hoffman said. "You'll have to ask Filip what he's planning to do next."

Annika slowed down and pulled into the inside lane.

"Okay," she said. "On a completely different subject: Do you know anything about a farm in Morocco?"

The windscreen wipers were going at top speed. Nina didn't answer.

"Hello?" Annika said. "Hello? Nina?"

"Yes, I'm here."

"I've just been to see Hannelore Lindholm," she said. "I talked to her about your mum, and Veronica Söderström's mother, Astrid . . ."

"What on earth for? What do you want to go poking about in our family for? Why can't you just leave us alone?"

She didn't sound upset, just determined.

"Hannelore is a sick, confused old woman. You've got nothing to . . ."

"Nina," Annika interrupted, slowing down even more. "Did your mother ever mention a farm in Morocco?"

There was a hissing sound on the line.

Nina was silent for a few seconds.

"Why do you want to know?"

"I know there's a farm somewhere outside Asilah in northern Morocco, and it's got something to do with Astrid Paulson and David Lindholm and all the rest of you . . ."

"What do you mean by that? 'All the rest of you . . '?"

"A woman called Fatima, with a daughter called Amira? Ever heard of them?"

There was a click, then complete silence on the line. Nina Hoffman had hung up.

Annika bit the inside of her cheek. Damn.

Nina knew something and she didn't want to talk about it.

A lorry pulled up alongside her, splattering the windscreen with sludge.

Annika put her mobile away and tried to concentrate on driving.

*   *   *

Tore had left for the day, thank goodness. She handed the car keys back to the evening-shift caretaker and told him the car needed filling up and could do with a wash as well. Then she went and got a claim form for the day's expenses, and wrote down the cost of the car park, as well as the parking fine. They were supposed to pay any fines themselves, but there was no harm in trying . . .

"How much do you want about Filip Andersson?" Annika asked as she passed the news desk.

"Did you get an exclusive?" Patrik asked.

"Nope."

The head of news pushed his chair away from the desk and looked at her with a resigned expression.

"Where have you been all day?"

Annika stopped beside him, taken aback.

"Checking a few things," she said. "Why?"

"Not the things you should have been checking," he said, putting his hand on a bundle of notes beside his computer. "How are we supposed to publish a paper if the reporters don't show up for work?"

She closed her eyes and made up her mind not to get angry.

"Give me the notes," she said, opening her eyes. "What is it, some television celebrity burping during a live broadcast? Or has the man with the world's longest nose got hay fever?"

Patrik grabbed the edge of the desk and wheeled himself toward it without answering.

"Oh well," Annika said. "It can't have been that important, then."

She went over to the day reporters' table and got out her laptop. She opened an ordinary Word document, gathered her thoughts, then started to type up what she had learned during the day.

She started at the end, with Nina not wanting to talk to her anymore. Then Hannelore and her confused childhood memories,

Julia and Alexander and their brittle existence, and then she reached Suzette. She stopped, and could see the desktop of Polly's computer in front of her, the black-haired girl with her arms around the large horse, the radiant look in her eyes, and the smile on her face.

"Annika? Can you come into my office for a moment?"

The editor in chief, Anders Schyman, was standing in the doorway to his glass box.

"What?" Annika said. "Right now?"

"Preferably."

"Sure," she said, logging out of the network to avoid having her password changed, a nightmare that seemed to be the new game among night editors with too little to do.

Schyman stood there patiently waiting for her. She left her jacket on top of her bag on a spare table, and followed him inside the glass box.

"Close the door."

She slid the door shut.

"Has something happened?" she asked.

"Sit down," he said, pointing at a chair.

Annika remained standing, and didn't say anything. Schyman sat down behind his desk.

"How do you think it's working, you being a reporter?"

She looked at her boss intently, trying to work out what he really wanted.

"Okay," she said. "It's quite fun. It's not exactly rocket science, not with Patrik at the news desk."

"I've received a number of worrying reports about the way you treat your colleagues," the editor in chief said.

Annika stiffened.

"Patrik says you come and go just as you please. You can't behave like that. He has a responsibility to me and the management team, and he has to be able to rely on you being at work during the hours you're paid for . . ."

She folded her arms.

"He's been in here telling tales," she said. "He's annoyed because I didn't rush back to his little notes quickly enough."

"Patrik's not the only one who's fed up with your attitude. One of the temp photographers called me in tears when you were in Spain on that job about the Costa Cocaine. She said you'd abandoned her outside a conference center and gone off with some bloke, and not come back to the hotel all night. Then you went around by yourself, taking your own pictures, instead of working with her."

Annika took a deep breath.

"Nothing I did was 'photogenic' enough, so the photographer refused point-blank to get her camera out. And I had my hands full. I couldn't sit there holding Lotta's hand, listening to her telling me how clever she'd been in Tehran . . ."

The editor in chief raised one hand to stop her.

"She's been getting great reviews for her exhibition at Kulturhuset," he said, "so she can't be completely without talent."

"Those were the pictures she was running round taking instead of doing her job," Annika said.

Schyman leaned forward, his elbows landing heavily on the desk.

"You have to think about the way you act," he said. "Your behavior toward Patrik has been terrible ever since his first day as head of news. Almost as bad as some of the others were toward you when you were head of crime. Patrik doesn't want you on his shift anymore, and I can't say I blame him. So I've agreed to transfer you."

Annika wanted to sit down, but stood where she was, paralyzed.

"What do you mean?" she asked. "Transfer me?"

"Have you got any ideas of where I can put you?"

"Are you serious?"

Schyman sighed.

"Are you interested in a freelance contract?"

She gasped for air.

"What the fuck is this? Are you *firing* me?"

The editor in chief got up, squeezed round his desk, pulled out one of the visitors' chairs, and said: "Sit down."

Annika sat down. The chair was lower than she expected and she jarred the base of her spine as she landed.

"Can you see how Patrik might have had trouble handling you?"

Her instinct was to argue, pointing out Patrik's overhasty decisions and journalistic incompetence, his superficial judgments about news, and his poor instincts, but instead she just stared in front of her and refused to answer.

"Do you want to work nights again?" the editor in chief asked. "Or be copy editor? In charge of the letters page? Or something online? A news anchor on the web, how about that?"

She looked up at him. How could she possibly be a problem? She managed to bring home all the news editors' odd stories, she found missing children in the forest and uncovered terrorists and Nobel killers and Yugoslavian mafia gangs . . .

"I think you're being bloody ungrateful," she said. "You make it sound like I spend all day sitting around drinking coffee, but I bring in more stories than anyone else . . ."

"I'm not questioning your competence, just your attitude."

"My *attitude*? Is that more important than the fact I come up with the goods? Haven't you got enough yes-men around you?"

The editor in chief's face darkened.

"This isn't a question of me wanting people who don't contradict me . . ."

"Of course it is. You're just like every other male boss. You want well-behaved girl reporters who are cute and friendly and who always do whatever anyone tells them. And I'm never going to be like that."

Silence descended on the room.

"What's going to happen to me?" Annika asked. "Honestly?"

Schyman bit his lower lip.

"I've always defended you," he said. "Hell, I've gone further than that, I've gone into battle for you. The chairman of the board wanted to get rid of you, but I put my own job on the line to keep you . . ."

"Oh, my heart bleeds," Annika said. "If the board ever gets to overrule you and starts hiring and firing staff, you're finished as a boss, and you know it. You don't have to pretend with me."

Silence descended again.

"Are you interested in what I've spent the day doing?" Annika asked. "Instead of following up Patrik's little notes?"

Schyman didn't answer.

"You remember the fatal gassing in Nueva Andalucía? The missing sixteen-year-old girl, Suzette Söderström?"

He nodded.

"I think she's alive. I think she's being held prisoner on a farm in Morocco. I've been going round talking to people who might have information about that farm and where it might be, how she came to be there, and who might be there, and . . ."

The editor in chief put his hands over his face and groaned.

"Annika, Annika, Annika," he said. "There was a sabotage alarm out at the nuclear power station in Oskarshamn this afternoon, and we didn't have a reporter we could send."

"I heard about that on the car radio," Annika said. "It turned out to be nothing. A welder who had a trace of explosives on a plastic bag with an IFK Norrköping logo on it."

"But we didn't know that to start with. The fact remains that we didn't have a reporter to keep an eye on the story."

Annika stared at her boss.

"Well, that's hardly *my* fucking fault! I'm not the one who's just got rid of half the staff!"

Schyman stood up.

"We aren't going to get any further," he said. "I'll give you the rest of the week to think about where you want to be transferred."

Annika remained seated, with a dizzying sense of free fall. Then she forced herself to get up, left the glass box, and closed the door without looking back.

Patrik stared at her as she walked across the floor of the newsroom, obviously he knew what they had been discussing. He must be feeling on top of the world.

She couldn't bring herself to look at him, just went back to her laptop, and tried to hold back the tears burning inside her.

There were other places she could work. There had to be some other media company in Sweden that was willing to employ her. And she could manage without a job for a while, with the insurance money she was about to get.

At the end of June she would finally be getting compensation for her burned-out house, six million kronor plus a quarter of a million for contents. Admittedly, Thomas would get half of that, but the plot would also be put up for sale and ought to bring in another couple of million. She'd checked online, there was only one vacant building plot in the whole of Danderyd, and that was on the market for 4.4 million.

Maybe getting fired wasn't such a tragedy after all.

Maybe it could be the start of something new, something good.

Maybe it would be a good idea to go freelance, then she could do exactly what she wanted without anyone else interfering . . .

But she wanted to feel she belonged somewhere. She wanted her own chair, her own pigeonhole in the post room.

She sat down at her computer, shut her eyes, and took several deep breaths, then logged in and opened up the document she had been writing. She had reached Suzette's email, and tried to recreate it from memory.

"You can't tell anyone about this email. Not Mum, and not the police. There's no internet at the farm so I haven't been able to email. Fatima would be furious if she knew I was writing.

"I'm with Amira. I've been here since New Year. I've got my own horse, called Larache. He's a mix of English and Arabian thoroughbred. Don't tell Adde I've been in touch. You can answer this but I don't know when I'll read it. We only go places like Asilah, not very often.

"Big hug from Suz."

She read the email through twice, then sat there staring as the screen.

It was completely ridiculous that the paper wasn't interested in Suzette's story. Why were girls with horses so completely uninteresting?

Besides, there was something bigger going on underneath, something shady and out of reach about the whole thing, about Astrid and Siv and Hannelore and their families, something she was only just starting to appreciate the extent of.

"What did Schyman want?"

Patrik was standing beside her, unable to conceal his triumph.

"To wish me a happy birthday," Annika said. "You know perfectly well what he wanted. He told me you want to get rid of me."

The head of news sat down on the desk, on top of her notes.

"You're a good reporter, Annika," he said. "If only you could learn to . . ."

"Spare us both," Annika said, grabbing her notepad. "If you're quite done, I'd like to get on with what I was doing."

Patrik got up reluctantly.

"Shouldn't you go home? Tomorrow's another day."

She looked up at him and made a decision.

"I'm not feeling well," she said, "so I won't be coming in at all tomorrow. I need to go to the doctor's; it's probably streptococcus."

He looked at her skeptically, but said nothing and went back to his desk.

Annika clicked to close the Word document and went onto the Net instead.

There were flights from Stockholm to Málaga every morning.

There were boats between Algeciras and Tangier all the time. She'd realized that from the adverts along the Costa del Sol motorways.

There was bound to be some way of getting from Tangier to Asilah. Morocco couldn't be that big.

She went onto Google Maps and typed in *asilah morocco*. A couple of seconds later she was staring at a satellite image of a town on the Atlantic coast of north Africa.

It looked like it was fifty or sixty kilometers from Tangier.

She took a couple of quick breaths and glanced over at the editor in chief's glass box. It was dark, Schyman must have gone home without her noticing.

She hesitated for a second or two, then went onto the booking page for the early morning flight to Málaga.

There were a few seats left on the plane, departing at 0645.

FALLING THROUGH THE SKY

The Angel hit the ground with a thud once the Troll Girl and the Princess had disappeared. She was confined to bed with a fever and strange blisters on her hands, and was prescribed liniment for her chest and the prayers of the congregation.

Father and the farms people searched the surrounding area for three days and three nights. Then the runaways were reported to the Child Welfare Commission. The girls were officially declared missing, but not Wall-Eye. He was no longer a ward, since he had come of age the previous month.

The silence at Gudagården was large and mute. Father took on the task of retribution, and mortified his own flesh in penance, as well as that of the farms people. This wasn't received well. People had tolerated the fact that he beat the foster children, but adult farmhands who earned their own daily bread didn't take kindly to being whipped by their master.

Soon Father and the Angel were left to deal with the sowing and reaping on their own. Despite Father's prayers for the Lord's assistance, they didn't manage to lift the potatoes before the first frost.

Not a word was heard from the runaways, so Father took in more foster children. He didn't want any more girls who could run away, just boys of working age. And he got the worst ones, the ones no one else wanted, and he whipped the exhortations of the Lord God into them until their backs bled. Then he worked them until they couldn't even think of dissent. He no longer searched for any that ran away, merely left them to the Lord's Mercy and the Flames of Hell.

The Angel was fourteen when Gregorius came to the farm.

He was very different from all the other boys, because he was dark and thin and quietly spoken, he never started fights, and he wasn't boastful or noisy. He smiled his strange smile and inspired respect among the gang of boys, possibly even fear. Those who chose to pick on him woke up with strange injuries or had peculiar accidents.

The Angel was drawn to him like a moth to a flame, and like a careless insect she got her wings burned so badly that she was never able to fly again.

She was fifteen years and eight months old when Mother realized that she was pregnant, and by that time Gregorius had been gone from the farm many weeks. Father beat her legs and back and crotch to shreds, intending to whip the sin out of her wicked body, but all he succeeded in doing was to give her scars that stayed with her for the rest of her life. Then she was locked away in the loft where the Troll Girl and Princess had been made to sleep, beneath the frost-engraved glass of the attic window. And, just like her predecessors, she climbed over the roof tiles and down the fire ladder as soon as her wounds had healed enough for her to be able to run.

And she ran.

She made her way to the road under cover of the night's darkness, through the village and out onto the main highway, and early that morning she got a lift with a lorry driver who was going all the way to Gnesta. He asked what a little girl like her was doing out on the road so early in the morning, and she said she didn't want to talk about it, and he said he wouldn't say anything if he could be a bit friendly with her. And of course the damage was already done so she saw no real harm in letting him have his way.

Her wounds stung when he took her, and she felt the earth close above her head, never to open again.

Here you have your life, here you have your underworld.

He drove her to Mölnbo. From there she got a lift on a milk truck that was on its way to Södertälje.

By that time it was already evening, and she was very hungry.

She spent the night in a hollow next to the railway track, shivering like a dog, but she knew that there wasn't far left, because the Troll Girl had told her about her mother. She had been out on release for a long time, and she wanted to take care of her daughter, but the Child Welfare Commission said no, because they thought it was better for the Troll Girl to be raised in the Righteousness and Discipline of the Lord at Gudagården.

What no one knew was that sometimes the Troll Mother would come and visit her little girl, always at night when the roof was clear of snow and the girl could use the fire ladder, and the Angel knew her address.

How she was going to find it in the big city of Stockholm was something she had given no thought to, but it wasn't too difficult. A cab driver took her to number 28, Tyska brinken, in return for the same payment as the lorry driver from Mölnbo, and then she rang on the door.

The Princess opened it.

It took her several seconds before she recognized the Fallen Angel.

They looked after her on the truckle bed in the kitchen for several weeks. Her wounds were infected, she fell into a fever, and the child in her belly wasn't well. But in the autumn, just before the child was due, the Troll Girl took them all, her mother and the Princess and the Fallen Angel, to the cinema to see an almost new film from America.

The Troll Girl had already seen the film several times, and knew all the dialogue by heart. It was called *A Place in the Sun*, and it was about a poor young man who went to work for his rich relatives, and fell in love with a beautiful girl, and he was prepared to do anything for her sake, even murder someone. The film was terribly sad and the Angel wept, for the pregnant girl, Alice, for the handsome, weak George, and his love for the divine Angela, and because he was so unjustly executed in the electric chair.

Afterward they went to a café and drank coffee and ate buns.

They didn't say much, but they were all thinking how unfair life was.

The Troll Girl paid the bill and gave the waitress a generous tip.

Before they got up from the table she leaned forward and took the others' hands in hers. Her voice was low and dark, and her troll eyes were black as she prophesied their futures.

"We deserve a place in the sun," she said. "Each and every one of us, and all of our nearest and dearest. And that's what's going to happen, I promise you that."

The words burned their way into the Angel's body, and then the first contraction came.

The little boy was born at dawn the following morning.

———

She didn't bother going to bed.

She stayed at the paper, printing out everything she knew about Hannelore, Astrid, and Siv and their children, about Carita Halling Gonzales, and all she had done; she read up about Algeciras and Morocco and Asilah; she thought through what she needed to do, and when it was half past two she went home to pack. She took just her bag containing her laptop, the camera from Gibraltar, her toothbrush, and a change of underwear. At four o'clock she got a taxi to the airport, boarded the plane as soon as she could, and slept like a log.

She woke up as they were landing and tried at once to call the Swedish Embassy in Rabat. Another long harangue in French, which she thought meant they weren't answering the phone yet.

She went straight from the plane to the car-rental desks on the floor below.

There were more people there than ever before; she presumed the tourist season had started. She moved quickly and easily through the crowd because she didn't have any luggage this time.

She hired a Ford Escort from Helle Hollis, managed to find her way out of the increasingly chaotic airport, and noticed they had built a vast Ikea warehouse next to the motorway since she was last there, unless she just hadn't noticed it before.

It wasn't as hot as she had been expecting; the thermometer on the dashboard said twenty-six degrees. The sunlight was hazy and dull, strong enough to make her eyes itch even though it wasn't casting any shadows.

She drove west, past Torremolinos and Fuengirola, then turned up onto the toll road and speeded up. The landscape had changed since she was last there. The verdant vegetation was gone. Everything looked yellow-brown and burned, with just a few hints of dark olive-green.

Soon the signs for *Tickets Ceuta Tanger* began to appear along the side of the road. She passed the Hotel Pyr in Puerto Banús on her left. The roadworks were still going on, and she had to slow down just in front of the hotel. She peered up at the third floor and tried to work out which room had been hers, but couldn't tell.

To her right the huge walls surrounding the villas of Nueva Andalucía rose up. She turned off the motorway and headed upward, past the bullfighting arena.

You need to get the right exit from a total of seven roundabouts, Carita had said the time she invited her to that party.

She made one mistake and had to make her way back to Plaza Miragolf, but after that she got it right.

The gateway was less ostentatious than she remembered it, unless she was just starting to get used to them. What a terrible thought. She pressed various buttons until house number 20 opened the gate without asking any questions. She drove in.

The development Carita had lived in had looked like a model village that evening, and it made the same impression in daylight. The houses clambered up the mountainside, a pastel-colored pastiche of a southern Spanish mountain village. The waterfall by the pool burbled, the bushes were in bloom, and the glass of the lampposts sparkled.

She parked outside *casa número seis,* wound the window down, and looked at the house.

There were white aluminium shutters over all the windows.

Blue-and-white police tape hung from the terraces and balconies of all three floors.

Annika switched the engine off, got the camera out of her bag, and stepped out into the sunshine. She stood beside the car for several minutes, just studying the house. There was no movement anywhere around her. No sound apart from the waterfall. It was as if all the houses had been abandoned, not just Carita's.

She adjusted the focus and took a few pictures, some general shots of the area, and some of Carita's cordoned-off house. She hesitated, then clambered up onto a raised flower bed, and took some pictures of the terrace behind the cordon. As long as she was standing on the flower bed she wasn't guilty of trespass, or at least she hoped not.

The terrace looked the way she remembered it. That was where she had stood talking to Rickard Marmén that evening. The potted plants were still there. A hose on a timer led along the edge of the terrace from the tap. The plants would survive long after their owners had vanished.

She jumped down from the flower bed and went and rang on the bells of the houses in the neighborhood: She didn't want to waste the opportunity to use the well-worn headline A TOWN IN FEAR. She got no answer. She found the pool-maintenance man and asked him if he knew where the Halling Gonzales family had gone.

He looked at her suspiciously; no, he didn't keep tabs on the residents, they came and went all the time, or they rented out their houses. It was pretty much impossible to know who was where. She asked when the police had been there and was told that it was a while ago now, some time after Easter. He didn't know anything about any of that, he added.

She thanked him and walked back to the car, looking up at the houses and trying to work out which one was number 20. Someone was definitely home there, because they had let her in through the gates.

The house was apricot-colored, and was one of a row on the far side of the pool.

The woman who opened the door had the same quintessential Scandinavian look as Carita. She had bleached hair, a dark tan, a bit of a face-lift, and was wearing gold sandals. Annika didn't recognize her from the party last winter.

Her name was Tuula, and she was Finnish, and she had nothing but good to say about Carita. Carita had been on the committee that looked after things for the residents, and she kept everyone informed about the meetings and increases in ground rent and shared activities in plenty of time. Her children had never thrown the sunbeds in the pool, which wasn't something you could say of the British brats and their parents; imagine, having people like that here! Carita was always the person who called the water company when there was no water, or the electricity company when there was a power cut, because, of course, she spoke fluent Spanish.

"And garbage collections," Tuula said. "Who's going to call the council about the rubbish now?"

"Apparently Carita is under suspicion for a serious crime," Annika said, trying to look concerned.

Tuula merely snorted.

"The Spanish police," she said, "everyone knows what they're like. Lazy and corrupt, down to the very core. Everything is all *mañana, mañana* in this country. They're probably only blaming her because she's foreign."

Annika thanked her and went back toward the pool. The Finnish woman's reaction was hardly surprising. Even the worst criminals had their supporters. There were still people who thought Pol Pot was a really great guy.

She stopped and looked out over the golf course that spread out across the valley below, then took out her mobile, found the number, and called Knut Garen.

He answered on the fifth ring.

"I'm just calling to say that I'm on the Costa del Sol, and I'm planning to write about Carita Halling Gonzales," Annika said. "Does anyone know where she's gone yet?"

"No idea," Knut said. "The Spanish police have been checking the passenger lists of all planes and ferries, but she must have got out another way."

"Could she still be in Spain?"

"If she is, the whole family must have access to a completely different identity, with different schools and homes and bank accounts. We don't consider that very likely. What are you planning to say?"

"Anything I can get confirmed, by you for instance. Has her arrest warrant with Interpol been made public?"

"Not yet," Knut said.

She bit her lip; that was a mistake.

"Bu it might well be made public this afternoon. The Spanish police got the results of some DNA tests back from England yesterday, and they link her to the gassing in Nueva Andalucía just after New Year."

Annika's pulse quickened.

"Link her how?"

"The safe and the other vehicle used in the break-in have been found."

"Where?"

"The long-stay car park at Málaga Airport."

Annika was walking back to her car.

Very smart of Carita. If she'd abandoned the car by the side of the road or in the middle of nowhere, someone would have noticed it sooner or later. A car could be left in the unmanned, long-stay car park of a large airport without anyone thinking it odd.

"Was there anything in the safe?"

"It had been blown open. It was empty, apart from a few traces of the explosives. But inside the car they found strands of hair and pieces of skin, and yesterday it was confirmed that they match Carita's DNA."

"You had something to compare it to?"

"From the search of her house," Knut said. "I think they got the DNA from her toothbrush."

Annika looked up at the house.

Poor Jocke Zarco Martinez must have been party to a great deal of information. Carita sacrificed her whole existence to kill him. She didn't even take her toothbrush with her when she took off.

Then she remembered a thought that had occurred to her during the night.

"I didn't see any broken walls in the Söderström family home," she said. "Where was the safe?"

"There were safes in all the bedrooms. This one was in one of the rooms on the ground floor."

She frowned. She wasn't aware that there were more bedrooms there, other than Suzette's.

"Whose room was it in?"

"Astrid Paulson's."

She blinked.

Of course.

"What could she have had in there that was so valuable?"

"Cash, deeds, documents, diamonds, codes, sensitive information, take your pick."

Annika rubbed her forehead.

Of course Astrid's safe would be the most interesting in the house. Not Veronica the money launderer's nor Sebastian the financial disaster's, but Astrid's. She was the one who was here first, she started her own business, she'd been running an estate agency on the Costa del Sol since 1968.

"How much of this can I write?"

"The head of the preliminary investigation will make the formal decision to arrest Carita in her absence this afternoon. At the moment there's a warrant out for her for the manslaughter of Zarco Martinez. We know she gave him the morphine, but it's not clear that she intended to murder him. But as of this afternoon those suspicions will be expanded to cover eight cases of murder. And when that happens, any restrictions on publication will be lifted. I wouldn't expect anything else."

Annika took her notepad and pen from her bag and scribbled down the information.

"Eight cases?"

"The family in the house plus the thieves and Zarco Martinez. Now that we know how it all fits together, the prosecutor can assume she meant to kill him."

"Can I call and get this confirmed later on this afternoon?"

"Of course you can."

They were silent for a moment.

"Why?" Annika finally asked. "Why did she do it?"

Knut didn't answer.

"But you knew her," Annika said. "You worked with her. What was her motive?"

The police officer sounded weary.

"Money, I assume," he said. "Status and recognition, maybe, a life of luxury . . ."

Annika looked up at the terrace, with its blossoming hibiscus bushes.

"But why choose to become a criminal? I mean, she didn't have anything like that in her background. Quite the contrary, with a father-in-law who was chief of police in Bogotá . . ."

Knut coughed.

"Yes," he said, "we checked out what you said about Carita's background. It wasn't entirely correct."

Annika couldn't think of anything to say.

"Her father-in-law, Victor Gonzales, was one of Colombia's

biggest cocaine barons. He and his wife and daughters were executed by another cartel fifteen years ago. They blew up his cocaine lab and burned his house down."

Annika could feel her cheeks burning, and not just because of the sun.

"But Nacho and Carita survived," she said, "because they were in Sweden visiting her parents."

Knut Garen sighed.

"Fifteen years ago both of Carita Halling's parents were in prison in the USA. They used to run a company called Cell Impact, then it went bankrupt, but to avoid scandal they started falsifying invoices and cooking the books."

Bloody hell, she really had been gullible.

"But now they're dead?" Annika said.

"Our colleagues in Sweden have spoken to them," Knut said. "They live in a small village outside Borlänge. They haven't had any contact with Carita since they were released from prison, and that was ten years ago now."

Annika closed her eyes. Had the interpreter spoken a single true word during all the days they spent together?

Yes, some of it was true: her father-in-law's name and the fact that he had been murdered, and her parents' company. She probably did grow up in Beverly Hills, and maybe she did meet her husband the way she described. And her love for him and the children wasn't necessarily a lie.

Annika looked up at the police tape round the terrace and recalled Carita's twittering presentation of her guests, how pleased and proud she had sounded when she spoke about them. *His wife was an international model, their daughter's a Spanish horse-jumping champion. She's a partner in a law firm in Frankfurt, he used to run a bank in Kenya . . .*

"Do you think you're going to find her?"

"People who are used to daylight usually pop up sooner or

later. Terrorists and freedom fighters are different: They can spend forever hiding away in caves. But Carita wants to go out for meals in restaurants, send her children to good schools."

"Did she carry out the murders of her own volition? Or was she contracted, or forced to do it?"

"The murders link Zarco Martinez, the Apits organization, and the Söderström family," Knut said. "But we don't know what Carita's motive was. We're hoping to find out when we catch her."

Annika thanked him for his help and ended the call.

Then she realized that she had forgotten to ask about Niklas Linde.

There was a traffic jam through San Pedro de Alcántara, but after that the traffic flowed fairly freely. She passed through the unjustly maligned town of Estepona with no problem and carried on farther west.

As she reached the top of the hill by the junction for Torreguadiaro, the rock of Gibraltar rose from the sea in front of her like a huge iceberg. Immediately behind it she could make out the Rif Mountains of Africa through the mist.

Then all the road signs began to appear in two languages, Spanish and Arabic.

Algeciras was a messy city, quite different from the neat, picturesque places she had visited so far in Andalucía. The ornate letters of the Arabic alphabet rushing past her only heightened the sense of unfamiliarity.

She wondered how she was going to find the harbor, then realized that the word *PUERTO*, harbor, was painted on the tarmac of the motorway.

Low palm trees lined the six-lane autostrada. She followed the arrows, which led her onto an island covered by a forest of huge cranes. Cargo ships crowded the quays as far as she could see. Thousands of containers were stacked up, being loaded or unloaded in a sort of chaos that reminded her of an anthill. On Wikipedia she had read that Algeciras was the sixteenth busiest port in the world. She looked around in astonishment and wondered what the fifteen that were busier than this looked like.

She parked the car by the Estación Marítima and headed toward the Terminal de Pasajeros.

The building reminded her of the Silja Line Terminal in Stockholm's Freeport, just a bit less organized. There seemed to be a number of different companies that sailed to Tangier. Large boards up in the ceiling announced departures and arrivals, just like in an airport. She saw that she had missed one boat to Tangier by just a couple of minutes. The next one wasn't for another fifty-eight minutes. She bit her lip and looked at the time; it was already after two o'clock in the afternoon. The crossing to Morocco would take a couple of hours, then she had to get through customs and find some way of getting further south. She had read online that there were trains and some sort of bus taxi, a *grand taxi*, between the cities.

She bought a ticket for 33 euros and took the escalator up to the departure hall. The Sala de Embarque was built entirely of speckled gray granite, and was the size of a football pitch. She checked in, no, she didn't have any luggage, and was told that passport control would be open in quarter of an hour and that she could go aboard then. The cafeteria was open in the meantime, the man said, pointing to a door on the far side of the football pitch.

The cafeteria was almost as big, and just as deserted. She ordered a *cafe cortado* and a *bocadillo con jamón serrano y manchego* from a waitress with a gold stud in her nose who was wearing pink underwear. She couldn't help noticing this because her jeans were slung so low that her belt was at the same level as her backside.

She was seriously hungry. Seeing as she had been asleep on the plane she had missed the chance to buy one of their gluey sandwiches. She devoured the large baguette in three minutes flat.

Then she tried calling the embassy in Rabat again.

This time the French voice told her that telephone hours were over for today.

So she dialed Rickard Marmén instead.

He picked up at once.

"Annika!" he said cheerfully. "Have you managed to find a new life that suits you?"

"I decided to keep the old one," she said. "I'm in the middle of doing it up, actually. Listen, have you ever done any property deals in Morocco?"

"Can you hold on a moment?"

He took the phone from his mouth and said something in Spanish to someone next to him.

"Morocco?" he said when he came back. "Sure, Morocco's an up-and-coming country. What did you have in mind? I've got two villas overlooking the sea outside Tangier, and several nice projects off plan . . ."

She clenched her left fist in triumph.

"Are there any property registers in Morocco? Public ones?"

If he was surprised by the question, he didn't show it.

"Yes," he said, "there are, but only in printed form. You can look at them all you like, but you have to do it in person. They haven't been computerized. And they're in three different languages, French, Spanish, and Arabic."

She bit her lip.

"If I have a name," Annika said, "and a city, is there any way of finding out where that person lives?"

"Hmm," Rickard Marmén said. "You want to find an address in Morocco?"

"If possible."

"And you've got the name of the person, and you know which city they live in?"

"Exactly."

"Well, you could try going through a *muqaddam*."

"A what?"

"The local civil servant, there's one in charge of each district. They distribute voting cards, keep a record of who lives where, sign applications for ID cards, and so on . . ."

She closed her eyes and breathed out. She would have bought a house off Rickard Marmén just to make him happy.

"On a completely different subject," she said, "what do you know about Asilah in Morocco?"

"A sleepy little dump, although they restored the medina fairly recently, it's supposed to be quite smart . . ."

"Would there be a muqaddam there?"

"In Asilah? Bound to be."

"And how do I find him?"

"It's probably no harder than finding the police station. Just ask someone. And if you go to Asilah, be sure to try the food at Casa García. You do like Spanish food, don't you? It's on the main road into the city, looking out over the harbor. Well, I need to get going, love. Was there anything else?"

"I'll be in touch if I make a mess of the renovations."

"You'll be more than welcome."

The waitress with the gold stud in her nose took her plate and coffee cup away.

When passport control opened she was at the front of the nonexistent queue.

She got a stamp and was ushered into a glass corridor that hung high above the harbor. Beneath her were hundreds of lorries, all of them either heading onto or off one of the ferries.

She had to show her passport one more time before she was allowed onboard the boat itself, then she was plunged back into a feeling of déjà vu from a school trip to Finland in the mid-1980s. She seemed to recognize everything, from the tired blue carpet to the duty-free shop and the bar at the front with its maritime theme.

She walked about the various decks, and concluded that she and the lorry drivers, who all seemed to know each other, were the only passengers.

Outside the women's toilet on deck six she discovered the explanation for her memories of bitter winds and the bleak archipelago: The instructions for the fire alarm were in Finnish. The boat had had a previous existence on the Stockholm–Helsinki route.

With a dull clanking sound the ferry pulled out and began to head toward Africa with long, lurching rolls. Annika settled down in the maritime-themed bar.

They passed dozens of ships in the seaway as they followed the Spanish coastline westward. She saw towns and villages float past, sandy beaches and olive plantations and wind turbines.

It occurred to her that she was traveling along the new iron curtain, between the first world and the third, then suddenly she started to feel ill.

She had forgotten that she always got seasick, no matter how small and insignificant the swell was.

Quickly she took out her laptop, to have something else to think about. She moved to a table with a plug socket in the wall alongside, then opened a new document and wrote a news article about the fact that the gassings in Nueva Andalucía were on their way to being cleared up.

Interpol had issued a warrant for the arrest of a Swedish woman living on the Costa del Sol in Spain, on suspicion of eight counts of murder. Five of the victims were Sebastian Söderström and his family.

She referred to Knut Garen as her source, in his capacity as Nordic police representative on the Costa del Sol. She wrote that the suspect and her family had disappeared from their home without trace, and that the police believed that they had fled the country. She mentioned the fact the car had been found at Málaga Airport, and the DNA evidence, the expanded arrest warrant, and Interpol. She also mentioned the link to Jocke Zarco Martinez's death, and the fact that the suspect had been the last person to visit him in prison before he died. The article was short and concise. She saved it, then looked at the time.

One and a half hours left.

She opened another new document and wrote an article about what sort of person Carita Halling Gonzales was. Obviously any decision to publish the name and picture of a suspected criminal wasn't hers to make; that was down to the person legally accountable for the paper's publication. She thought for a moment, then decided to call Carita "the Swedish jet-setter."

Annika wrote that "the Swedish jet-setter" had lived in the well-to-do district of Nueva Andalucía (anywhere that wasn't a suburb full of concrete high-rises was a "well-to-do district" in the evening tabloid jargon), and that she had worked as a translator and interpreter, occasionally for the media and the Spanish police. She described the woman's social life with her friends, how she had been active in the local residents' association, and had stood up for her neighbors.

She quoted Tuula, the Finnish neighbor, anonymously.

Then she saved the file to the hard drive, clicked to close the document, and looked out across the sea.

The strait had got narrower. The mountains were so close to the ship that she felt she could touch both continents at the same time if she stretched out her arms. She was still feeling sick.

She opened up the article she had already started about how Carita had set about carrying out the mass murder in Nueva Andalucía. This was a completely different sort of article, a long, detailed description of what had happened that night in early January.

She described how the woman had planned the murders of the

Söderström family and the two Romanian crooks. How she had got hold of gas, beer, and morphine, how she had stolen or bought the codes for the alarm, and recruited the unfortunate criminals. How they drove up to the villa along roads wet with rain, injected themselves with the naloxone derivative, then headed carefully round the pool on the terrace to the ventilation unit at the back of the house, laden with a gas canister, a lump hammer, and a large crowbar . . .

She went on to describe how the thieves loosened a pipe from the fresh-air intake and attached it to the gas canister, then turned the valve and listened to the hiss as the gas poured into the house, into the bedrooms, the children's rooms . . . Then they had waited in the darkness. The gas alarm had gone off. Lights had come on in the bedrooms. Could the cries of the dying children be heard all the way out to the ventilation unit at the back of the house, or hadn't they even had time to cry out?

She went back to her old articles and reread them.

One effect of fentanyl poisoning was lethargy. Those affected became incapable of action. The mother and two children had been found lying on either side of the closed door, unable to cry out to each other or open it, yet still fully conscious. Their muscle control had diminished until it finally ceased altogether. They were dead within a matter of minutes.

No, there probably hadn't been any cries.

Annika looked up at the horizon to try to suppress her nausea. She could sense a change in the water around her; it had a different tone, a different resonance. The ferry had left the Mediterranean and entered the Atlantic.

She went and bought a bottle of mineral water, then carried on with her article.

They broke in through the terrace door. The gas alarm was shrieking. Everything else was completely silent. First they made their way up to the parents' bedroom where the alarm was located, stepping over the dead children and pushing the double doors open. Maybe that was difficult, because the mother was lying on the other side. Maybe they had to shove the doors open, kicking the dead woman's body aside. Then they switched off the alarm, and with that the hardest part of the job was over. Now they had plenty of time.

They began by stealing the safe. The two men smashed down the wall surrounding it, a time-consuming and noisy job. Then, when they were done, they carried it out together to the woman's car.

And then she had driven off, with the safe in the boot, and probably the gas canister as well, seeing as that hadn't been found.

The car, and the remains of the safe, were dumped in the airport car park.

The thieves stripped the villa of art and rugs and jewelry, just like it was Christmas.

They didn't know they had just four hours left to live.

Annika saved and then closed the document.

The ferry was swinging south, leaving Spain and Europe behind. It was rapidly approaching the Moroccan coast. Small fishing boats began to appear around them, more and more of them the closer they got to the shore. In the end there were about a dozen bobbing about like colorful floats.

The sun had passed behind some clouds and the sea was gray. Rain was hanging heavily above the Rif Mountains. She could make out buildings along the shore, tall and white, as well as a number of cranes.

She closed her laptop.

She got a message on her mobile from Méditel, a mobile operator welcoming her to Morocco.

She put everything away in her bag and went out on deck. The wind pulled and tugged at her hair. She felt less sick immediately.

The construction boom from the Costa del Sol seemed to have

spread across the strait. She could see people on the beaches, cars on the roads, shops with big plate-glass windows.

She had never been to Africa before, but this was nothing like she'd been expecting.

The ferry slowed down, the deck and walls shaking as it approached the quayside to dock. She looked at the time: They'd been late leaving Algeciras and the crossing had taken almost half an hour longer than the promised two hours. It was now quarter to five. She paced about restlessly, hoping that the muqaddam observed the Spanish custom and stayed open for part of the evening.

The lorry drivers and workmen gathered on deck five, chatting to each other in a mixture of French and Spanish and Arabic. None of them seemed to be in any great hurry. She positioned herself strategically beside the door she had entered the ship through, hoping to get off as soon as she could, but nothing happened. There was a lot of banging and crashing somewhere below her, and she presumed that gangways and ramps were being fixed in place.

Then the door opened. Not the one she was standing next to, but the corresponding one on the other side. She ground her teeth in frustration at the misjudgment but meekly took up position at the back of the queue.

It took an eternity.

First she had to fill in a form, listing all her personal details, her profession and her address in Morocco, the purpose of her visit, and how long she was planning to stay. She knew better than to say that she was a journalist, and put "writer" as her profession.

Two customs officials and two border guards were checking all passports and travel documents with irritating thoroughness.

"What do you write?" one of the customs officials asked suspiciously in English, fingering the laptop in her bag.

"Textbooks for schoolchildren," Annika said.

They let her through without any further questions. She had

to go down two decks, across the car deck and through a narrow metal corridor to reach the gangway.

She stepped ashore in Morocco and took a deep breath. The air smelled of sea and burned rubber.

She was channeled into a glass corridor like the one she had walked through to reach the ship in Algeciras, surrounded by a similar view of articulated trucks and containers and cranes.

She stopped inside the terminal building, sat down on a bench in the arrivals hall, and called Knut Garen. Méditel seemed to work fine, the police officer sounded like he was next door.

"The arrest warrant has been made public," he confirmed. That was all Annika needed.

She took out her laptop and connected to the Internet using the WAP on her mobile. It would probably cost a fortune, but she opened her usual Outlook Explorer page and composed a new message to Anders Schyman. Using Bluetooth, she sent off all three articles about Carita: the arrest warrant, her as a person, and the actual crime, plus one of the pictures she had taken outside the prison in Málaga on her mobile when they visited Jocke Zarco Martinez. Carita had managed to end up in one of the pictures, albeit only in the corner, but you could see that she was blond and was carrying a leopard-skin handbag and wearing high heels.

The "Swedish jet-setter" in person.

Finally she attached two pictures of the area where Carita had lived, one general shot with the pool and waterfall in the foreground, and then one of Carita's row house with the police cordon fluttering in the wind.

In the email itself she wrote some captions for the pictures, gave a brief explanation of what had happened, gave Carita's full name, and told Schyman that her parents lived outside Borlänge, then said he could do what he liked with the articles.

It took forever to send the email. She was worried the connection would fail and she'd have to start all over again, but it didn't, and eventually the pictures and articles had been whisked away. She breathed out and packed everything away.

That's for all those damn notes, she thought as she walked out of the terminal building.

The sky was overcast but the light was sharp. She squinted up toward the city as it clambered up the mountainside, and realized that she was now facing her next problem: how to get to Asilah.

"Taxi?" an older man in blue jeans and a grayish-blue jacket asked, as he leaned against the outside wall.

"Asilah?" she said quizzically.

"Twenty-five euros," the man said.

Twenty-five euros? All the way to Asilah? That was less than half what she paid to get to Arlanda Airport that morning.

"Okay," she said.

"My car is over here," he said in heavily accented but reasonable English.

She followed the man toward a car park alongside the terminal. His neat haircut and relaxed gait reminded her of someone she knew—Thomas's dad, maybe?

He walked over to a yellow Mercedes with a taxi sign on the roof, opened the door to the backseat for her, and closed it after she got in.

"So you're going to Asilah?" the man said, glancing quickly at her in the rearview mirror. "It's a very nice little city."

She put her bag down beside her on the vinyl seat.

"Will it take long to get there? I'm in a bit of a hurry . . ."

"Not long at all. This is a very good car. It's been to Rabat, Casablanca, the Sahara, all over the world!"

He started the engine and steered the car through the harbor with a practiced hand, then out into the streets of Tangier. Annika was looking out through the side window.

It looked just like Marbella. The streets were lined with palm trees. Modern white buildings rose up toward the sky, and there were bars and cafés and car-rental companies along the pavements.

"A million people live in Tangier now," the taxi driver said. "Everything's new. Europeans come over here and buy up the land. They build hotels and golf courses and shopping centers. It's very good *bizniz* for people here, legal *bizniz*. Very good."

She watched the buildings sweep past and decided not to ask about the illegal bizniz. She presumed part of it consisted of what Knut Garen had told her about: the hash plantations up in the mountains, and the distribution chain leading to Europe.

She went on looking out of the window.

How on earth had Suzette managed to get into this country without a passport? Within the Schengen area you could travel anywhere without having to show any ID, but the check on the ferry had been rigorous. She had very rarely had to answer questions about her occupation and the purpose of her visit before. How had Suzette, with no money and just sixteen years old, managed to get through without customs and the border guards sounding the alarm?

"This is a very good place to live," the taxi driver said. "The atmosphere is relaxed, good food, good weather."

They were driving through a residential district with a forest of television aerials and satellite dishes on the roofs. She saw women on their way to shops and markets, some with their hair covered, others without. They passed petrol stations and mobile phone shops and a large football stadium that was still under construction. The residential housing thinned out, and industrial buildings took its place. They passed a Hotel Ibis, a large Volvo showroom, and a Scania dealer.

Suzette had been here for several summers, driving along this road, looking out at the fields and car showrooms and petrol stations, sitting in her grandmother's arms and playing with her friend Amira, and for her Africa had been perfectly nor-mal.

"The factories produce goods for the European market," the driver said, pointing. "Moroccan workers are much cheaper than Europeans."

He gestured toward the other side of the road, to a thin line of trees along the shore.

"Families come out here at weekends," he said. "They cook on open fires, read books, play with their children."

"How come you speak such good English?" she asked. "Have you lived in England?"

He cast a quick glance at her in the rearview mirror.

"Never," he said.

"Did you learn English at school?"

"No."

"So you've got English friends?"

He didn't answer, and she didn't ask any more questions.

They were heading south along the coastal road. It clung to the Atlantic coast: To her right Annika could see vast sandy beaches, completely deserted. To her left there were rolling fields and hills, soft and friendly, nowhere near as harsh and dramatic as the Med-iterranean coast of the Costa del Sol. There seemed to be flowers everywhere, an overwhelming display of blossom.

The man carried on talking, telling her how people from Qatar had discovered the Moroccan coast and had started buying up land and building huge villas with big pools, and other things that were probably perfectly true but not terribly interesting. She shut off his voice and looked out at the landscape.

How was she going to find a muqaddam in Asilah? Where was she going to start? Who should she ask?

Then she looked at the man behind the wheel and slapped her forehead: God, she was stupid! She had the best guide in the world sitting right in front of her.

"Excuse me," she said, "but do you know if there's a muqaddam in Asilah?"

He looked at her in surprise in the mirror.

"A what?"

She tried to make the word sound right.

"A muqaddam?"

"Ah, a muqaddam!"

He swallowed all the vowels, pronouncing the word as *mqdm*.

"Of course there's a muqaddam in Asilah."

She looked at the time. Half past six.

"Does he have an office, do you think?"

"Sure, he has an office."

"How long is it open?"

"Until five o'clock."

She leaned back in the seat and felt her mood sink. Oh well, if the taxi driver could help her find the office; she could book into a hotel and go back there first thing in the morning . . .

"We'll probably make it in time," the driver said. "We're only a few kilometers from Asilah now."

She looked at him in astonishment, then looked at the time again. It had just gone half past six.

"But," she said, "didn't you say the office closed at five o'clock?"

The man's eyes twinkled in the rearview mirror.

"You didn't put your watch back when you got off the boat, did you? It's half past four here."

She took a deep breath; of course, she'd completely forgotten that! There was a two-hour time difference between Spain and Morocco, even though they were on the same longitude. She quickly turned her watch back two full hours. As she looked out of the window again she saw the sign for Casa García rush past on the other side of the glass. That was the restaurant that Rickard Marmén had recommended. They must have reached Asilah.

A moment later the driver slowed down.

"Can you help me?" she asked. "I need to ask the muqaddam something, and my French is really bad."

The taxi driver pulled into a car park, stopped the car, and turned round to face her.

"You want to ask about someone?"

"A woman called Fatima, she lives on a farm somewhere near here."

He nodded, and looked as though he were thinking.

"Whereabouts?"

"That's the problem. I don't really know. Do you think the muqaddam would know?"

He nodded, more firmly this time.

"Her name is Fatima? If Fatima lives on a farm near Asilah, then the muqaddam will know."

He switched off the engine.

"We'll park here, and walk to the muqaddam."

They followed a sign showing the way to the *Quartier Administratif*. Annika stayed half a meter behind the man, letting him set the pace. He wasn't walking very quickly.

They reached a pedestrianized street with low residential buildings on both sides. There were pots of flowers and herbs along the pavement. The taxi driver stopped a man dressed in white and asked something in Arabic. The man answered and pointed, the taxi driver nodded, the man bowed, then they talked and talked and talked, and then finally they carried on.

"That green door up ahead," the taxi driver said, raising his hand. "Fatima? On a farm near Asilah? Does she have a husband?"

"I don't know, I think he might be dead," Annika said.

The driver nodded again.

He walked up to the green door and knocked. Without waiting for an answer he pushed it open and stepped into the darkness. Annika waited in the doorway, unsure of whether she should go in. She decided it would be best to wait.

The taxi driver went through a dark hallway, then into a room on the left at the far end. A triangle of light fell onto the hall floor when the door opened. Then it shrank and disappeared as the door was slowly closed. She heard the taxi driver greet someone, then there was a stream of Arabic, and after a while it sounded like tea was being drunk. She blinked in at the shadows in the hallway and shifted her weight from one foot to the other.

Some young boys were playing on a bicycle a bit farther down the street. They turned shy when they saw her watching them, so she turned her head away. A girl with plaits wearing a school uniform walked with a pink schoolbag on her back. A woman with her hair covered, wearing a long dress, passed by on the other side, talking animatedly into a mobile phone.

Then the door behind her opened and she turned round to see the triangle of light reappear. The taxi driver came out, leading a man in traditional Arabic dress behind him.

"Muhammed, the muqaddam in Asilah," the taxi driver said, taking up position beside Annika as though he were about to introduce her. Annika's mouth felt completely dry. How on earth did you say hello in Arabic?

But the muqaddam held out his hand and said softly:

"*Bonjour, madame.*"

Annika took his hand.

"*Bonjour,*" she muttered, embarrassed.

"Muhammed knows Fatima's farm," the taxi driver said. "It's up in the mountains."

"*C'est une ferme très grande,*" the Arab man said in his gentle voice. "*Les routes sont très mauvaises. Vous avez besoin d'une grosse voiture pour y aller.*"

"What?" Annika said, bewildered.

"The roads are bad," the driver said. "You need a big car. He's explained to me where it is. Do you want me to drive you?"

"One more question. Fatima's husband, does he live on the farm too?" she asked, looking straight at the muqaddam.

The taxi driver translated. The civil servant shook his head in reply, then raised and lowered his hands.

"He's dead," the taxi driver said.

"What was his name?"

More gestures, more shakes of the head.

"He was European."

Annika looked at the taxi driver.

"Yes," she said. "I'd be very grateful if you could drive me to the farm."

"Another twenty-five euros."

"You drive a hard bargain."

"But first I need to eat," he said.

The thought of food make her feel weak at the knees. The only thing she'd eaten all day was the baguette in the café at the ferry terminal in Algeciras.

"Okay," she said flatly.

They thanked the civil servant for his help, and he went back inside the building and locked the door. It was five o'clock.

The taxi driver, whose name also turned out to be Muhammed, thanked her for her offer of dinner but politely declined. Annika watched him sit down in a local bar, where he immediately struck up a conversation with some other men in gray-blue jackets.

She walked round the corner and got a table in the Spanish restaurant, Casa García. They would take an hour for dinner, Muhammed had decreed, so she ordered a starter (*jamón ibérico*), main course (*pollo a la plancha*) and dessert (*flan*). Afterward she was so full she could hardly move. She paid by card and then strolled off toward the medina, the old center of the city. She wasn't worried that Muhammed was going to disappear, seeing as he hadn't yet been paid.

The sun was sinking quickly into the sea. She stopped at the north gate of the city and looked out over the small harbor. Colorful little fishing boats were bobbing up and down in the shelter of the jetty.

This was supposed to be one of Morocco's main shipping ports for cannabis?

She had trouble believing that.

But of course she couldn't see the go-fast boats that Knut Garen and Niklas Linde had told her about. And it wasn't certain that they'd use the main harbor in the center of the city to load their cargo of hash.

She took a walk among the thousand-year-old buildings within the city walls. They had been tarted up and freshly painted, and looked like they had been built the day before.

The taxi driver was sitting waiting for her in the car when she got back. She slid into the backseat. Muhammed started the engine, and drove out of the city.

"You got some good food?" he asked.

"Very good," she said.

"Morocco has very good food, good couscous."

She didn't tell him she'd eaten at a Spanish restaurant.

Asilah disappeared behind them, drowning in the setting sun. The car headed east, across a railway line and under a motorway. Then the tarmac came to an end, replaced by a gravel track. Muhammed braked, turned the headlights on, and steered the big Mercedes over the rough road surface. The track was visible in front of the car as a slightly paler strip through the night, and she could make out bushes and crops and rocks along the side of the road.

When the last light of the motorway disappeared behind a ridge, darkness closed in around them like a sooty black sack. Muhammed wound his window all the way up, as if he wanted to shut it out.

"Is it far?" Annika asked, beginning to wonder if it would have been better to wait until morning before setting out for the farm.

"Not far," the taxi driver said, "but the road is bad. You have to be careful with the car."

She leaned back in the seat and stared into the darkness outside the window. The Spanish food was lodged in her stomach like a rock. She couldn't see anything at all outside, just the vague outline of her own face reflected in the window.

What had made David come here, to this godforsaken part of the world? Had he been shaken about in bad cars on even worse roads to get out to some little farm in the Moroccan outback? Had Suzette come this way as well, recently? Just a few days before?

Suddenly a scene from a film popped into her head, from the film *La Vie en Rose,* which she'd seen at the cinema with Julia a few months ago.

The boxer, Marcel, is sitting with Edith Piaf in a restaurant in New York, telling her about the pig farm he owns in Morocco, a modern farm with big, healthy pigs. His wife looks after it while he travels the world, boxing and sleeping with French singers.

She shut her eyes and let herself be shaken and jolted by the potholes and stones.

Men go out into the world while their wives stay at home to feed the pigs.

She leaned her head back and fell asleep.

"Madame? Madame! We're here!"

She sat up with a jerk. The taxi driver had turned round to face her in the backseat. He looked tired. She looked at her watch: half past eight. They had been driving for two hours.

She rubbed her eyes, getting mascara on her knuckles.

The night outside the car windows was just as impenetrably pitch-black as before, but above a hill to her right something was lighting up the sky.

She blinked a few times to help her focus on the object out there.

It was a bright yellow spaceship hovering like a glowing dish against the sky.

"What?" she said, staring up at the hill. "What's that?"

"That's the farm."

"That thing?"

She wound down her window. The wind blew into the car, bringing with it sand and pollen, and blowing her hair about.

"Can you drive closer?"

"Right up to it?"

"Yes, please."

Muhammed put the car in gear and slowly began to climb the last stretch toward the farm.

Annika stared in fascination at the bizarre sight in front of her.

Of course it wasn't a spaceship. It was a wall, a yellow, plastered wall that was several meters high, enclosing a very large area. Both the wall itself and the ground around it were brightly illuminated by powerful halogen floodlights.

"Are you sure?" she asked dubiously.

She'd been expecting a little farm with a few sheep and a couple of horses.

"This is the farm where Fatima lives, according to the muqaddam."

"Christ," Annika said.

The car stopped with a slight jolt in front of a large gray iron gate. The wall was crowned with a spiral of thick barbed wire. The floodlights were mounted along the top of the wall every ten meters, and two of them shone down directly upon the gate. She could see an entry phone and a surveillance camera.

She scratched her head; this was nothing like what she had been expecting. It looked more like Kumla prison than a farm.

"Where exactly are we?" she asked.

"Between Souk el Had el Rharbia and Souk Trine de Sidi el Yamani."

"Hmm," Annika said. "Are there any other houses nearby?"

"No other houses. An hour ago we passed a little village. There might be more houses in other directions."

"How far are we from Asilah?"

"Forty kilometers, maybe a bit more."

"Up in the mountains?"

"Up in the mountains, but not too high. Good farmland in Asilah."

She took a deep breath and opened the car door.

Seeing as she'd come all this way, the least she could do was call and see if anyone was home.

The taxi driver cleared his throat. She stopped and looked at him in surprise.

Payment, of course.

She sat down in the backseat again, and Muhammed switched on the little light in the roof so she could find her purse. She dug it out of her bag and pulled out three twenty euro notes.

"Don't have any change," the taxi driver said quickly.

She smiled at him.

"It's a tip," she said. "Can you wait until you see that I've been let in?"

He lit up and nodded enthusiastically.

"Of course. I'll wait."

She got out of the car, hung her bag on her shoulder, carefully closed the car door, and turned to face the wall.

Muhammed had stopped the car ten meters or so from the gate. She started walking. The track sloped upward, and the surface was poor. She blinked and squinted under the floodlights, then heard something buzzing and saw the surveillance camera zoom in on her.

She reached the gate. It was shiny and gray, as if it had just been smartened up with gloss paint. She touched the smooth surface carefully with her finger.

Then she went over to the entry phone and pressed the button next to it.

Ten seconds passed.

She was about to press it again when the speaker crackled.

"*Oui?*"

She cleared her throat quietly and flicked her tongue, trying to summon up the French she had learned at school.

"*Je m'appelle Annika Bengtzon. Je voudrais parler avec Fatima.*"

The speaker clicked, then fell silent.

She stood there by the wall, increasingly aware of the sound of her own breathing. The floodlights up on the wall hummed. In the bushes, just out of reach of the lights, she could hear animals and the sound of the wind.

She looked over her shoulder.

The taxi was still there.

Muhammed met her gaze.

"Problem?" he asked.

"I don't know," she said. "I think so."

"Do you want a lift back to Tangier? Fifty euros."

You've got to drive back anyway, Annika thought, pressing the button by the phone again.

The speaker crackled into life at once this time.

"*Oui?*"

More annoyed this time.

"*Je veux parler avec Suzette aussi.*"

I want to speak to Suzette as well.

The speaker hissed and crackled: They hadn't switched it off.

"*Je sais qu'elle est ici.*"

I know she's here.

"Maybe the farms people have gone to bed?" the taxi driver said.

Hardly, Annika thought, looking up at the surveillance camera. The farms people were still up, there was no doubt whatever about that.

The speaker clicked and went silent.

"I need to go now. Long way to Tangier."

Annika hesitated. Apart from the rustling from the bushes, there was nothing but silence.

Maybe it would be as well to drive back and try again in the morning, in daylight.

She turned to walk back to the taxi, but at that moment there was a clang from the wall and the gate started to open, one decimeter, two, three. Another floodlight became visible through the gap, shining right in her eyes and forcing her to put her hand in front of her face. She squinted and waited, then she held her breath and walked through the gap in the gate. At once the metal gate stopped opening and began to close again. She could hear it rumbling behind her and was seized by a moment of total panic, then there was a loud click as the lock snapped shut, and there was no longer any point thinking about retreating.

The floodlight shining in her face went out. She blinked against the darkness, still blind from the bright light. She heard Muhammed start his taxi, then turn round, and drive off.

There were two men standing in front of her. One was in his fifties, the other a boy in his late teens. They were both armed with some sort of automatic weapon. The guns were pointing straight at her.

She took a step back, her sight still affected by the floodlight. She could see various versions of it floating in front of her vision as pink balls of light. She tried to blink them away and see what was behind them. Some sort of yard, she thought. She was standing on gravel and stones.

"*Pardon,*" she said. "*Je ne veux pas causer des problèmes.*"

The older man said something to the younger one in Arabic. The boy came over to her and pointed at her bag with his gun.

"*Laissez le sac.*"

She put her bag down on the ground.

"*Donnez-le moi.*"

She pushed it toward him with her foot.

The older man took a step closer to her as the boy bent down and tipped the contents of her bag out onto the gravel. He poked through them with the barrel of his gun. Annika wondered if the lens of the camera would survive that sort of treatment.

"*Venez par ici,*" the older man said, pointing with his gun. She realized he wanted her to go with him. The boy gathered her things back in her bag and slung it over his own shoulder. So she wasn't getting it back, then.

She took a few cautious steps forward, now able to make out the shapes of buildings and vehicles.

As she had assumed, she was walking across a large, walled yard. There were buildings in two directions, in front of her and off to the left. She looked up at the building in front of her and gasped.

It was a residential house, and it was huge. Thirty meters long, three stories high, with balustrades and balconies on both the top floors. There were lights on in several of the windows on the top floor, but the light was faint, as though filtered through heavy curtains. A small lantern glowed above the doorway on the ground floor.

The older man was walking in front of her, and the young lad behind. It looked as if they were heading for the illuminated doorway.

The man knocked lightly on the door, and it opened up like a black hole.

"*Entrez,*" the man said, gesturing with his gun again.

She could hear her heartbeat pounding in her ears and gulped hard.

Then she stepped through the door. The darkness was solid but the air light. She was in a large hall, a big, open space.

"*À droite.*"

She had to think for a moment, then turned to her right.

A door opened in front of her. She got a light shove in the back and stumbled into a room containing a desk and an old chair.

"*Attendez ici.*"

The door closed behind her. She heard a key turn in the lock.

She looked around and breathed out. At least it wasn't pitch-black in here. A small table lamp was shining on the desk.

There had to be someone here called Fatima, otherwise they wouldn't have let her in. And as soon as she mentioned Suzette's name the gate had opened.

She took a few steps over to a window hidden behind closed curtains. She pushed one of the curtains aside to look out, but couldn't see anything. It took her a few seconds to realize that there were closed shutters on the outside.

Then she heard a rattle from the lock. She let go of the curtain as if she'd burned her hand and quickly went back to the spot in the middle of the room where the armed man had left her.

A woman in her fifties wearing traditional black clothing came into the room. She said something out in the hall, then closed the door behind her.

Then she turned toward Annika. She was tall, almost one meter eighty, and had neatly made-up black eyes and large rings on her fingers.

"You wanted to talk to me?" she said in perfect Oxford English.

"Are you Fatima?" Annika asked.

"I'm Fatima."

"My name is Annika Bengtzon," Annika said. "I'm from Sweden. I work for a newspaper there, called . . ."

"I know who you are."

Annika took a deep breath but couldn't manage to say anything.

Fatima walked around the desk and sat down on the old chair.

"Why have you come?"

She looked at Annika with eyes that were used to giving orders.

Annika had to make a real effort to stand her ground and not back away.

At least I'm in the right place. She knows who I am. So she also knows what I do.

"I'm a journalist," Annika said. "I want answers to some questions."

Fatima's face didn't move a muscle.

"Why would I answer your questions?"

"Why not? If you haven't got anything to hide?"

Fatima looked at her intently for a whole minute.

"Maybe you can give *me* some answers," she eventually said.

"Me?" Annika said. "What about?"

"Where's Filip?"

Annika stared at the woman.

"Filip?" she said. "Filip Andersson?"

Fatima gave a curt nod.

Annika cleared her throat. It was no secret that she'd attended the press conference after his release. She had nothing to lose by answering.

"He was released from Kumla Prison yesterday morning. I saw him at his lawyer's office on Skeppsbron in Stockholm yesterday, just before lunchtime. I haven't seen him since then."

She paused.

"I have no idea where he is now."

"What time did you see him in Stockholm?"

Annika thought for a moment.

"Approximately quarter to twelve," she said.

"Does he have a passport?"

"A passport?"

She thought.

Were prisoners serving life allowed to have passports?

She'd once written an article about a prisoner who hadn't been allowed to attend his mother's funeral in Scotland. The young man had been desperate, but the rules were completely inflexible. His passport had been seized when he went inside, and that applied to anyone who was sentenced to serve twelve months or more. She could still remember which paragraph of the law dealt with the issue, paragraph twelve of the Passport Act.

It was out of the question that anyone sentenced to life would have a passport.

And getting a new passport issued took five working days; she knew that, because she had tried to get the process speeded up herself a few years ago, and had failed miserably.

He might be able to get hold of some sort of provisional travel document out at Arlanda. Anne Snapphane had managed to do that once when she was going on a charter holiday to Turkey.

She shook her head.

"Not an ordinary passport," she said. "Possible a provisional one."

"Is Sweden part of the Schengen Agreement?"

Annika nodded.

"So he can travel within Europe on a national ID card?"

She nodded again.

Fatima got up from the chair, went over to the door, opened it, and said something in Arabic in a low voice. Then she closed the door again.

"Do you know him?" she asked. "You know what sort of man he is?"

Annika hid her finger behind her back.

"I interviewed him once, but I don't know him."

Fatima went and sat down behind the desk again.

"I've answered several questions now," Annika said. "Can I ask one in return?"

Fatima didn't move. Annika took that as a yes.

"Is Suzette here?"

The woman still didn't move. She didn't even blink.

"What makes you think she'd be here?"

The woman didn't question the premise for Annika's inquiry. She didn't want to know who Suzette was. Which meant that she had to know.

Annika thought hard about her answer. She couldn't let on that Suzette had managed to write an email, because that would get the girl in trouble.

"Suzette has a very good friend called Amira. She's told her friends about her; it's no great secret. Amira lives on a farm with horses outside Asilah. If you know who I am, then you know that I write articles. I've written about Suzette; I was very affected by what's happened to her. I wanted to find her."

There was a knock on the door, and Fatima went and opened it. Annika heard voices muttering in Arabic. Fatima stepped out into the hall and closed the door.

Annika waited five minutes, then the woman came back.

"We'll talk more tomorrow. From now on you'll be staying here as our guest. Ahmed will show you to your room."

Then she disappeared, and the young man appeared in the doorway. He handed Annika her bag, empty except for her toothbrush, notepad, pens, and the change of underwear. They had taken her laptop, mobile phone, and camera.

"*Suivez-moi*," he said. Annika took her almost empty bag and followed him.

They walked through the dark hall, over to a stone staircase on the left-hand side. It led up steeply through the floors and ended in a heavy wooden door. The young man pushed it open, and they emerged into a poorly lit corridor.

"*Allez*," he said, then followed her almost the entire length of the corridor. He stopped beside a narrow door on the left-hand side.

"*Ici*," he said.

Annika stepped inside the room and felt the door close behind her.

She turned round to ask how long she was going to be kept there, only to hear a key being turned in the lock.

DEATH ON THE BEACH

Wall-Eye was a bit simple in the head. People said his father once hit him so hard across the face when he was little that his eye got dislodged and he ended up deaf in one ear, but that might just be talk. He was among the first foster children to arrive at Gudagården, and he never made much of a fuss.

He had just one weakness.

He couldn't stay away from the girls, and especially not the Princess. He would hide among the reeds when they bathed, he crept up on them from behind and squeezed their breasts and backsides, he pressed up against them and rubbed his genitals against them.

The Troll Girl always had to keep an eye on him so he couldn't get at the Princess.

The girls were thirteen and fourteen on the evening when the Princess didn't manage to get away. He got hold of her down on the beach where the reeds were at their thickest; he ripped off her bathing suit and put his hand over her mouth. He took her with such a frenzy that the violence and sand tore at her innards and left her drenched in blood.

The Troll Girl and the Angel had been running errands to the local shop, to buy sugar and salt, and when they got back to the beach he was busy pulling his trousers back on, facing away from them, toward the water. The Princess was lying lifeless and soaked in blood at his feet. The Troll Girl moved silently and quick as lightning, quick as the weasel she was, she picked up a stone and ran up on light feet and hit him in the head, and this time she didn't stop hitting him. The Angel stood there, mouth open in a silent scream as the Troll Girl hit him and hit him and hit him, until the blood stopped running and the gray sludge from his shattered skull lay strewn over the sand.

"Go and get spades and bandages," she told the Angel as she carried the Princess to the water to wash her.

And the Angel ran in to Mother in the kitchen with the sugar and salt, and asked if they could sleep in the hayloft that night, and they could, and then she dragged the spades and the little crowbar all the way down to the lake, and she and the Troll Girl spent all that night digging a suitably narrow but deep grave behind the big oak tree on the shore. First they cleared the dead leaves and twigs away, and the sand was soft and easy to dig, but the tree's roots were hard as steel, and the Angel had to fetch an ax. It was almost light by the time they were finished. The Princess had recovered slightly, and they all joined in to drag the limp body into the grave. One of his shirtsleeves got caught on a tree root, so the Troll Girl had to clamber down into the grave and pull it loose. The corpse fell on top of her, and the others had to help her climb out.

They shoveled the blood and brains in first, then they filled the hole up with tree roots and soil and sand, and then they scattered the leaves and twigs over the top again.

Then they sat and wept together, out of fear and exhaustion, standing in a tight huddle on the sand by the lake below Gudagården, and promised each other that they would never tell.

The Princess was fourteen, and the Troll Girl was thirteen, and the Angel, she was only ten.

And for the three of us I have had this book printed, just the three copies, one for each of us.

And all this, every single word of this, is true. Because the Angel—that's me.

Annika woke up with the sun shining in her face. It was oppressively hot in the little room. She had eventually managed to get to sleep with all her clothes on, lying on top of the narrow bed that filled up half the floor space.

She sat up wearily on the edge of the bed and squinted out at the sunlight. It was pouring in through a pair of small-paned French doors that weren't shuttered. She got up to open them, but they were locked. There was a pair of thin yellow curtains hanging on either side of the glass, and she pulled them closed in a vain attempt to shut out the heat.

She was desperate for a pee. She went over to the narrow door and tried the handle.

Locked.

She sat down on the bed again, brushed some locks of sweaty hair from her forehead, and looked at the time. Half past six in the morning. After hours of worry and torment she had fallen into a troubled and exhausted sleep. She took off her jacket and the T-shirt under it was soaked with sweat.

She looked round the room. Last night she hadn't been able to find a light switch and had had to feel her way to the bed, where she curled up in the darkness. Now she could see why. There was no electric light in the room.

One wall of the room was taken up by the bed she was sitting on, and the other by a large, solid wooden desk with a rickety chair in front of it. On top of the desk was a lantern and a box of matches.

What sort of room was this? A guest room? A nursery? Servants' quarters? Or was it a cell?

Right now it was definitely the latter.

She got quickly to her feet, went over to the door, and banged on it as hard as she could with her right fist.

"Let me out!" she shouted in Swedish. "For fuck's sake, I need to go to the toilet! Hello! Can you hear me?"

She stopped banging and put her ear to the door to hear if anyone was coming.

All she could hear was her own heartbeat.

She waited five minutes, then sat down on the bed again.

She had to pee, that was simply a fact. She'd just have to do it on the floor if that was the only option.

Then it suddenly occurred to her to look under the bed.

Sure enough, there was an enamel bedpan under there. Almost exactly the same as the one her grandmother had kept under the bed out at Lyckebo, in her cottage in the woods near Hosjön, where there were no drains.

She pulled the pot out, shrugged her jeans off, and closed her eyes in relief.

Afterward she pushed it back under the bed, as close to the wall as she could reach.

She sat down on the chair by the desk.

The house was completely silent.

Her grandmother never got to meet Ellen and Kalle.

Her children had never peed in an enamel bedpan in a drafty cottage beside the waters of Hosjön.

When she got the money from the insurance company she was going to buy a place out in the forest in Södermanland.

She got up to go and bang on the door again but stopped herself.

They weren't going to let her out just because she kept banging. And beating her hands to shreds wasn't a particularly constructive thing to do.

Her bag had fallen to the floor beside the desk. She picked it up and took out her notepad and a pen.

She chewed the pen and thought through what she knew.

The woman called Fatima knew Filip Andersson, and she knew he'd been released from Kumla. Her questions about his passport meant she thought he was going somewhere. The fact that she hadn't shown any surprise when Annika mentioned Suzette meant that the girl was actually here, or else she knew where she was being hidden.

The farm she was in was large and wealthy. The little she had seen of the buildings and walls was very well maintained.

Annika got up and went over to the French doors, drew the curtains, and looked out.

She couldn't see much, just the yard she had crossed the previous evening, the inside of the wall, and rolling fields on the hillsides beyond. She was at the very top of the large farmhouse. To the right was the smaller building that presumably contained stables and outhouses.

Then she saw a young woman in a headscarf emerge from the outhouse, in the company of two young boys. Could that be Amira?

She pressed her nose against the glass.

No, this woman was much older; she must be more like twenty-five. She was holding one child in each hand and was walking toward the gate through which she herself had come the night before.

Outside the walls, as far as she could see, stretched vast fields of verdant vegetation. She couldn't make out the shape of the leaves from up in her window, but she was sure they weren't potatoes. On Wikipedia she had read that *Cannabis sativa* was a very hardy, fast-growing plant that could survive in most climates and at altitudes of up to three thousand meters above sea level. As far as the European market was concerned, most of it was grown among the Rif Mountains of northern Morocco.

Annika recalled Knut Garen's telling description of the rhythmic drumming that echoed through the Moroccan mountains in the autumn months, *da-dunk, da-dunk,* as the pollen from the cannabis plants was beaten out between layers of fine cloth.

There was a rattle from the lock and the young man from the previous day appeared in the doorway.

"Suivez-moi."

She put her notepad and pen back in her bag and followed him.

"Laissez-le ici."

He wanted her to leave her bag. So she wasn't going anywhere, and would be coming back here. Unless . . .?

"Où allons-nous?" she asked.

Where are we going?

Her French really was pretty awful.

He didn't answer.

"Qu'est-ce que vous faites maintenant?"

What are you doing now?

"Ne vous inquiétez pas," the boy said.

No need for her to worry.

They went down a different staircase, first Annika, then the boy with the gun behind her. It was a much broader flight of stairs than the one they had come up the previous evening. It was covered in thick carpet, and led down to the first floor of the house. They found themselves in a large stone hall with doors in three directions, all of them closed and barred. The doors and walls were all dark and richly ornamented, with even some gilding. There were heavy stone and bronze statues in various alcoves. In place of the fourth wall was a well of light reaching from the ground floor all the way up to the eaves. The staircase carried on downward; she could see all the way to the front door she had come in through the night before.

The young man stopped outside a large pair of double doors on the left-hand side, opened one of them, and ushered her in. She noted that there was a large key in the lock.

She did as she was told and heard the door close behind her, then the click of the lock.

She was in a library. The walls were covered with built-in bookcases with masses of books, some of them leather-bound, as well as other more modern books. There was both Arabic and Latin lettering on the spines.

There was no other way out.

She went over to the three windows and tried opening them, one after the other. They were all locked.

She stopped in the middle of the floor, between two uphol-stered sofas in bloodred leather. Beside her was an ornate marble-topped table with a solid bronze ashtray on it. She kicked out at the table, but only ended up with a sore toe.

In one corner stood an old table with four chairs, and on the table was a tray laid with breakfast for one person.

So they weren't going to let her starve.

She walked over to the table and looked suspiciously at the food. She recognized the pita bread and the vegetables alongside it, but the bean paste in the middle looked dodgy.

She sat down, picked up the fork, and tasted the beans. She didn't usually eat beans, even though the GI diet was so popular, but this bean paste was actually pretty good. It tasted of garlic and parsley.

She ate up everything, washing it down with sweetened tea.

She had just finished the last of the tea when the lock rattled.

Her stomach lurched, she didn't want to go back to that stifling cell upstairs.

But it wasn't the young man with the gun coming back.

It was a slender girl with big eyes and jet-black hair.

Annika gasped.

"Ha!" the girl said. "I'm starting to understand what they say. I thought they said they were going to give you breakfast in the library, and I was right."

She closed the door carefully behind her and leaned back against it with her eyes shining with curiosity.

"Is it true that you work for a newspaper?"

Annika nodded.

"And you're Suzette?"

The girl smiled broadly. She was wearing jeans, a T-shirt, and trainers.

"What are you doing here?" she asked.

Annika studied the sixteen-year-old: She seemed happy and healthy. It didn't look like she'd been suffering.

"I wanted to see if you were here. There are a lot of people looking for you."

Her face darkened.

"No one cares," she said. "Not really."

"Your mum's worried about you, she's really concerned."

The girl walked away from the door and threw herself onto one of the leather sofas.

"Oh," she said, "she only cares about her pathetic job. I just got in the way, and I cost too much money."

She half-lay on the sofa with one leg dangling over the armrest. Annika sat in silence and waited for the girl's curiosity to build up again.

"No one knows I'm here. How did you know?"

Suzette was evidently aware that she was being kept hidden. She probably wasn't supposed to be here in the library at all.

"The most important question is probably *why* you're here," Annika said. "And how you got here."

Suzette shrugged her shoulders and smiled.

"Do you want to interview me?"

"If you want to be interviewed."

"Ha!"

She threw her head back.

"Fatima would never agree to that. I'm not allowed to tell anyone where I am."

"Why not?" Annika asked quickly. "Are you a prisoner here?"

Suzette picked at her fingernails, but she was still smiling.

"Fatima came to get me," she said. "She told me to tell everyone I was going somewhere else, and then we came here."

Whatever the reason why the girl was being kept out of the way, it didn't seem to be anything that bothered her at all, that much was abundantly clear. What she was saying was probably true. Francis, the tennis coach, had said that Suzette was too disorganized to plan any sort of advanced disappearing act.

"But you didn't have your passport with you," Annika said.

Suzette sat up on the sofa, annoyed, dropping her trainers to the floor.

"Fatima's got her own boats, hasn't she; she doesn't have to go through customs. She uses her own private harbor."

Is that so? Annika thought.

"And you've been here ever since?"

The girl nodded.

"Do you want to be here?"

She stopped nodding and sat completely still.

"You know what happened?" she asked, her eyes filling with tears. "With the gas?"

Annika got up from the breakfast table and went and sat on the sofa opposite Suzette.

"Yes," she said, "I know what happened. I wrote about it in the paper."

The tears overflowed.

"They were, like, so little, and so cute. Leo could be really annoying, but he was so little. My was lovely, really lovely. She loved horses, just like me . . ."

The girl put her hands to her face and wept for several minutes. Annika sat quietly and waited for her to stop. In the end she wiped her eyes and nose with the back of her hands and looked up at Annika. Her makeup was smeared all over her face.

"Hang on, I'll get you something to wipe your face with," Annika said, then went and got her unused linen napkin from the breakfast tray.

Suzette blew her nose loudly and wiped the mascara from her cheeks.

"And Grandma as well," she said. "She was my best friend."

Annika sat down again.

"Astrid, you mean?"

The girl nodded.

"She always said I was her little princess, even though she wasn't my real grandma."

She blew her nose again.

"She was the one who brought me here the first time. The farm was our special place."

Annika tried to sound calm and neutral when she replied.

"So you and Astrid used to come here together?"

The girl nodded.

"What for?"

"Grandma knows Fatima well, they do *bizniz* together. And Amira's the same age as me, and she's had her own horse since she was four. We used to come and stay here every summer."

"Isn't it difficult talking to Amira?" Annika asked, even though she knew the answer.

"She speaks Swedish, doesn't she, because her dad's Swedish. She had Swedish nannies all the time when she was little, and Grandma used to send her all sorts of Swedish children's videos."

Suzette laughed.

"Imagine, sending *Seacrow Island* to Africa!"

Annika leaned forward.

"What's Amira's father's name?"

Suzette fell silent and frowned.

"He's dead. He didn't live here, I never met him. But her mum's name is Fatima and her sisters are Maryam and Sabrina, and Maryam is married to Abbas, and they've got the cutest little children in the world, two little boys. But Sabrina's not here at the moment, because she's studying at Harvard, and Amira's going there as well, as soon as she's finished her International Baccalaureate exams . . ."

Annika tried to look as if it was perfectly normal to study at Harvard.

"Did Maryam go there as well?"

"No, she did two years in Cambridge, like Fatima, but she wanted to come home and get married to Abbas, so obviously that's what she did. Fatima doesn't make anyone do anything. She doesn't force me either, because I don't like studying. I've got a horse of my own, Larache. He's a mix of English and Arabian thoroughbred, and he's the sweetest horse in the world. I want to work with animals and horses, and Fatima thinks that's a good idea."

She nodded to emphasize the point.

"You don't have to be top of the class," she said. "I help Zine and Ahmed—the foreman and his son."

"Did Grandma Astrid think it was okay, you working with horses?"

The nodding got even more intense.

"Of course she did. I mean, Grandma grew up on a farm, even if they weren't very nice to her there."

Annika leaned back in the chair and tried to calm down.

"Did Grandma use to tell you what it was like when she was little?"

Suzette lay down on the sofa and threw her legs over the armrest.

"Sometimes. Her stories were all pretty sad . . ."

Then she jumped and leaped to her feet.

"You know what?" she said. "There's a book about Grandma and her friends."

She spun round and ran over to one of the bookcases in the corner behind the breakfast table.

"A book?" Annika said, turning round on the sofa to see what she was doing.

"Er," Suzette said, running her hands over the spines of the books. "It was here somewhere . . . here it is!"

She held up a thin, stitched pamphlet with a white cover with no picture or other decoration, just the title and name of the author.

"They've got all the Emil and Pippi and Goldie books and all that stuff," Suzette said, "but this is pretty much the only adult book."

She handed it to Annika.

"I've read it. It's a bit weird."

Annika stared at the book.

A Place in the Sun
by
Siv Hoffman

"And you found this here? In the bookcase?"

She opened the imprint page. Printed by a vanity press twenty years ago. Nina's mother had evidently had ambitions to be a writer.

"It was where I just found it. There's no proper system, not like the school library. Everything's all mixed up . . ."

There was a noise from the lock in the door and Annika and Suzette both stiffened. Annika sucked in her stomach and slid the book inside her jeans, then pulled her top down over it and hoped that the book didn't show.

The young man called Ahmed came into the library, holding his gun in front of him. His eyes opened wide and he shouted something at Suzette in Arabic, who got up quick as a flash and slipped past him onto the stone landing.

"*Allez!*" he shouted angrily at Annika. "*Dépêchez-vous!*"

"Yeah, yeah," she muttered.

He wanted her to hurry.

It was considerably cooler in the room now. Someone must have aired it. Which meant that it must be possible to open the window somehow. Someone had also left a jug of water and a glass on the desk.

The footsteps disappeared down the corridor and she pulled the book from her jeans and put in on the blanket. Then she crouched down and looked under the bed.

Someone had emptied and rinsed out the bedpan.

She sat down at the desk and took out her notepad and pen.

Quickly she wrote down what Suzette had told her, filling in the gaps with her own thoughts and conclusions.

Fatima had secretly collected Suzette. She must have known that something was likely to happen, and for some reason she wanted to get Suzette away from the Costa del Sol without anyone knowing.

Because she liked the girl, maybe. Because Suzette was her daughter's best friend. Or did she have some other, less noble reason? Was Suzette a hostage? In exchange for what? And from whom?

Her next thought made her stop writing.

If Fatima knew that Suzette needed to be saved, then she must also have known that the Söderström family were in danger.

She could be mixed up in the murders herself.

Maybe she was the person who ordered them to be carried out?

Suddenly the walls felt even more restrictive.

Annika put her pen down and got up to try the door. Still locked, of course.

What if they didn't let her out again?

What if they kept her here forever?

Who knew where she was?

No one, except Muhammed the taxi driver from Tangier.

She felt her throat tighten and the classic symptoms of an approaching panic attack, tunnel vision, tingling in her fingers, the feeling of utter terror inside.

She stumbled to the bed and lay down on her stomach, facing away to the side.

There's no danger, she tried to persuade herself. If they really did want me dead, then they'd already have done it. They wouldn't have let me in in the first place. Fatima may grow dope, but she's not a murderer. That's why she picked up Suzette; Fatima cares about people . . .

She lay there without moving for a long time, concentrating on breathing normally.

She really ought to have grown out of these panic attacks by now.

She got up cautiously and went over to the window. It was still locked.

She couldn't see anyone outside. The skies had darkened, black clouds had rolled in from the Atlantic. It looked like they were going to get some rain.

She looked down toward the building below her.

The top floor, where she was now, was more sparsely decorated than the rest of the house. That suggested it was meant for servants, or had been added later.

The middle floor seemed to be the main social part of the house. She didn't have much sense of what was on the ground floor. It had been dark when she arrived, but from the outside it had looked much more basic than the floor above. On the way to Asilah she had seen similar farms. Maybe this was the way houses were built in Morocco: You started with a fairly basic ground floor, then added to it as your finances allowed.

The building was huge, it must be at least a thousand square meters. And parts of it were extremely lavishly appointed. This was a wealthy farm. It was quite clear that Fatima belonged to the premier league of hash farmers.

She turned round. It was starting to get darker inside the room as well.

She sat down at the desk, picked up the pen from where it had fallen to the floor, and started to make a list of the farm's inhabitants.

How many people lived here?

To start with, Fatima and her three daughters: Maryam, Sabrina, and Amira. Maryam was married to Abbas, and had two little boys. They were probably who she had seen from the window that morning. Sabrina was at college in Boston, so she wasn't here at the moment. Zine, the foreman, and Ahmed, his son, must be the men with the guns.

Then there had to be servants, people who emptied bedpans and worked in the fields. Zine the foreman had to have someone to be foreman over, after all.

She put her pen down and went and sat on the bed. She leaned over the foot of the bed and pulled out the book that Suzette had given her down in the library, Siv Hoffman's labor of love, *A Place in the Sun*. She pulled the pillow out from under the blanket and put it against the wall to cushion her back.

She opened the first chapter and started to read.

As she read about "The Princess in the Castle Among the Clouds," "The Little Troll Girl with the Matches," "The Angel at

Gudagården, Falling Through the Sky," and "Death on the Beach," and other strange tales, the Atlantic rain began lashing the window panes, and the wind tore at the plants in the fields around the farm.

In the afternoon came the lightning.

It had got so dark in the room that she had had to light the little lamp so she could finish the book.

She read the last page, closed the book, and didn't know what to think.

Could that really be what had happened, or was it just a piece of fiction with literary pretensions?

A flash of lightning followed by a clap of thunder made her get up and look out at the mountains. They were completely black. Lightning chased across the sky, to the sound of rumbles and cracks of thunder.

What would she do if a bolt of lightning hit the house and set it on fire?

She recalled the smoke and flames on the other side of her bedroom door in the house in Djursholm, and how she had opened the window and lowered the children down in the bedclothes. Here she was trapped like a rat in a shoebox.

A thousand-watt bolt of lightning followed by a terrifying crack of thunder shook the whole house, almost making her lose her balance. She screamed, and her breathing became short and shallow, and she took the three steps over to the door and yanked at the handle. It was as unresponsive and solid as the door of a bank vault.

She ran over to the window and looked intently at the lock on the French doors. They opened outward. The lock was part of the handle, in the middle of the window, at waist height. She pushed at it, hard. The doors didn't move.

She looked down at the farm. The lights had gone out. The electricity had been cut.

She gulped and tried to calm down; she'd never been scared of lightning before.

The house was made of stone and the roof was tiled, so it couldn't be particularly flammable.

It wasn't the weather that was her main problem, it was her own foolhardiness.

Who had any idea of where she was?

She sat on the bed and tried to think carefully.

Schyman knew she was on the Costa del Sol, as long as he had actually received the email with her articles. It wasn't absolutely certain that they'd got through.

If there was any kind of search for her, then passenger lists and passport control would show that she had entered Morocco. So at least they'd know which country she was in.

Her service provider's list of calls made on her mobile would show that she had called Rickard Marmén, and he could lead them to the muqaddam in Asilah. And he, in turn, could tell them that she had been asking about Fatima's farm.

So she hadn't just disappeared without a trace, even if it had been incredibly stupid not to tell anyone where she was going.

There was a crack of thunder above her head, and she ducked instinctively.

How long would it be before anyone started looking?

Monday at the earliest, when she was supposed to pick the children up.

There was another crash, not thunder this time but something else, a shorter, sharper noise from down below.

She went over to the window, leaned forward, and peered down at the yard. The little lantern was reflecting off the glass, and she moved it aside and blew it out.

Then she huddled up and peered out through the bars of the window.

The gate in the wall was half open. The metal at the bottom was warped and smoking.

She frowned and tried to focus properly.

Yes, the metal gate was actually smoking.

The bang had been an explosion: Someone had blown the lock off the gate.

She leaned forward and saw movement down in the yard, black figures sliding through gray sheets of rain. Two, no, three of them moving toward the house, then something flared and she heard a different sort of noise.

She gasped.

They had guns, and they were using them.

She fought an intense impulse to crawl away and hide under the bed. Instead she pulled her dark jacket on over her pale T-shirt so as not to be seen. She pulled the hood over her hair and cupped her hands against the glass.

There was more noise, several shots this time, and fire was returned from somewhere inside the house. She heard a scream and one of the shadows fell. It was one of the intruders. Zine the foreman and his son must have hit him.

The two other shadows zigzagged across the yard, now firing constantly. The flashes from the barrels lit them up so she could see their faces.

They were white men, pale Europeans.

Then another of the men fell, the one closest to the house. She saw him land on his back immediately below her window.

The remaining man stopped, stood up to his full height, and seemed to be thinking.

Then he walked calmly toward the house and disappeared from Annika's field of vision. She sat and waited, and after a short while he reappeared.

He had someone else with him, a man, or a child; he was dragging him by the hair, into the middle of the yard, where he let go of him. The youth lay there squirming on the ground. It looked like he had been hit by one of the shots.

Annika caught a glimpse of his face, contorted by pain and fear. It was Ahmed, the foreman's son. The black-clad man leaned forward, aimed the barrel of his gun at the boy's head, and fired. The gun jerked in his hand. Ahmed twitched, then lay still on the ground, and Annika thought she was going to throw up.

The gunfire ceased. That must mean that the foreman had been disarmed as well, and was possibly dead.

The man stayed where he was in the yard. She saw him lift his head and study the building in front of him, and quickly pulled back into the room so he wouldn't see her in the window.

She waited a whole minute before daring to look out again.

The man was gone.

Then she heard a shout from somewhere on one of the floors below her, then more screaming.

Suzette, she thought, the little boys, Amira, oh God, he's going from room to room, shooting everyone!

Her pulse started to race and she assumed she was about to die.

Soon he would have worked his way through the lower floors and then he would come up to where she was.

She looked round, forcing her panic back down.

Shouting and screaming, which she had been on the verge of doing, would obviously be bloody stupid.

She had to get out of there.

Breaking the window was out of the question. There were forty little leaded panes of glass in each door, she'd never be able to squeeze out.

She had to find a way to open the windows and get down to the ground.

She had used bedclothes before and survived. And at least there wasn't a fire this time.

She tried throwing herself at the window frame, but she didn't have enough space to take a proper run-up and couldn't get enough force in her shove.

Then she glanced at the desk and knew what to do.

She pushed the desk over toward the window, got up on top of it, shuffled forward so that her feet reached the lock, pulled her knees back as far as possible, then kicked as hard as she could. The thunder rumbled. The doors creaked and the desk moved back a bit, but not far. She took aim again and kicked four more times, then she had to get down and push the desk back in place again.

After the seventh kick the door flew open with a crash. The thunder answered up in the clouds. The rain swept into the room and she was drenched in an instant.

In two swift movements she tore down the pale yellow curtains. She pulled the sheets off the bed, noting to her relief that they were made of decent linen. With her fingers trembling she tied the curtains and sheets together with reef knots—thank God she'd been in the scouts. She tied one end to the balcony railing, and tossed the other end over the edge.

It stretched almost all the way to the ground, swaying in the gusts of rain.

Would the rain make the fabric slippery?

Probably.

She hesitated.

Maybe it was better to stay in the room? Maybe the man wouldn't come up this far?

At that moment she heard another shot from below.

She took three deep breaths, then stepped out onto the little balcony and climbed over the edge.

It was a very long way down to the ground.

She crouched down on the other side of the railing, grabbed

the curtain, and tested to see if it would hold. It did, but the weight would get heavier the farther down she got. The rain lashed at her face, making it hard to see.

Oh well, she didn't need to look, at least not downward, she just needed to lower herself down along the wall until she reached the ground. As long as she could get over her fear of heights, it ought to work.

She let go of the balcony railing and came close to falling straightaway. She was breathing so hard that it drowned out the claps of thunder. She clung on for dear life and realized that she had to let go with one hand. She eased her grip. The fabric burned at her hands. Then her feet touched the wall and she steadied herself and began to lower herself down, one step, two steps, another step, far too big, the skin of her palms scorching, and she made it past the first knot, past the next floor, as her arms started to ache. She passed the second knot, she ought to be halfway now, her arms were getting numb, she loosened her grip slightly, her palms burning, then the third knot, and then she lost her grip. She tumbled to the ground and landed awkwardly on one foot. The gravel cut into her lower arms. She lay there quite still, just listening. The rain was still pouring down, she was soaked to the skin. Her ankle hurt badly.

She could hear voices.

From inside the house.

She sat herself up. It seemed lighter down on the ground than up in her window. She could see the stable block as a dark shape maybe thirty or forty meters away. The mangled gate was creaking in the wind far behind her, and off to one side in front of her the door to the house was hanging open.

With a twisted ankle she wasn't going to be able to run away from anyone. Getting out through the gate and hiding among the hemp plants was one option, if she could make it that far. The stable was much closer, but then she'd have to go right across the open yard, and she didn't know if the stables were going to be unlocked.

She heard a child's heartrending scream from inside the house. She looked toward the open door.

There was a faint light from the floor above.

Swaying slightly, she got to her feet. Just a couple of meters away from her lay one of the men who had been shot, staring up at the sky. The rain was falling on his open eyes.

She limped slowly over to him. The crunch of the gravel was drowned out by the torrents of water. She recognized those eyes. Pale, almost white. They had laughed at her as they cut into her left forefinger.

The man's gun was by his side, some sort of automatic rifle that she'd only ever seen before in American action films. She picked it up; it was astonishingly heavy.

Ahmed lay ten meters away. Half of his head had been blown off. She looked away.

In a flash of lightning she saw something moving down by the gate. She stiffened, staring intently through the veils of rain toward the opening in the wall.

Then she saw it again. She was quite sure. It was the shape of a person running past the shattered gate.

Her legs crumpled and she dropped the gun. Oh God, oh God, just don't let them shoot me.

On all fours she crawled toward the wall of the house, got to her feet, then ran at a crouch toward the doorway with adrenaline pounding in her ears.

By the entrance she stopped and peered inside the hall. She couldn't see anything, and threw herself into the darkness of the house and pressed her back up against the wall. She slumped down, breathing so hard that it echoed throughout the house, and put her hand over her mouth to muffle the sound. The thunder rumbled on. The child was crying. She glanced out through the doorway but couldn't see anyone outside.

She couldn't stay where she was.

She got up and tried to lean on her foot. It hurt badly, but it was just about bearable.

As quietly as she could she moved away from the front door. She grabbed the banister of the stairs to rest, and peered upward.

The voices were coming from one of the rooms up there. She could hear a man's voice, then a woman's. She couldn't make out what they were saying, but it sounded like English.

She went up a few steps.

"You emptied the accounts in Gibraltar. Where's the money?" The man's voice, almost shouting.

"Yes, I emptied them," Fatima replied, her voice thick with fear. "I warned her about the raids in Algeciras, but Astrid wouldn't listen. I knew what was coming, and I saved what I could."

Annika took several more steps.

"You sold us out," the man said. "You wanted to force us to use your supply chain, with your grotesquely overpriced rates, and when Astrid refused you tried to get rid of us."

She recognized the voice.

It belonged to Filip Andersson.

Annika used the banister to heave herself up the last few steps. The stone landing of the smartest floor of the building was in darkness. The voices were coming from the room next to the library where she had eaten breakfast. She looked down at the thick carpet under her feet, it seemed to run the whole length of the hallway.

"The police had you all under surveillance," Fatima said. "I warned Astrid, but she refused to listen. She said she had no choice."

The double doors were ajar, letting a thin strip of light out into the hallway. Annika moved along the wall and peered in through the gap between the door and the frame.

The room was a large sitting room. Filip was standing with his back to the door. A white shirt collar stuck out from inside his black waterproof jacket. A pool of water had formed by his feet.

"Of course she felt under pressure," Andersson said. "She'd withdrawn the money to finance that fucking tennis club."

Annika moved so she could see more of the room. It was dimly lit: She could see a candelabra with two candles, and two oil lamps. At the far end of the room she could see Fatima, sitting on a flowery chintz sofa with a little boy in her arms. One of her grandchildren, of course. Suzette and another young girl, presumably Amira, were sitting together in an armchair, holding each other's hands. They looked utterly terrified. Two other women were standing in front of them, presumably servants. They were both crying. Beside them stood a man and the woman she had seen in the yard that morning. The woman was holding the other little boy in her arms: Maryam and her husband, Abbas, and one of their sons.

It looked as if Filip had gathered together everyone he could find and ordered them into the sitting room. None of them seemed to have been shot or injured.

"You shouldn't have brought in such big shipments," Fatima said. "You should have let me handle it."

"And you should have kept your hands off the Gibraltar accounts. Where's the money?"

Fatima didn't answer.

"I'll count to ten," Andersson said. "Then I'll start with the kid in your lap. One."

Annika pulled back. There was a rushing sound in her ears and her hands were trembling. What should she do? Call someone? There must be a phone somewhere? She hadn't seen one, nor any phone lines leading to the house.

She looked down the stairs: nothing but darkness.

"Two."

Annika realized what Filip was about to do. He was going to

kill all of them, regardless of whether or not he got the money. The little boys, Suzette, Amira, the weeping servants, he was going to shoot them all the same way he had executed Ahmed.

What should she do?

"Three."

He wasn't standing far from the door, two, two and half meters. She looked round the hallway.

It was dark, she could hardly make out anything.

Then she limped quickly off toward the library and blinked in at the shadows inside.

She heard his voice from within the sitting room.

"Four."

She focused her eyes as hard as she could, and looked round the room, at the leather sofas and books and table. The tray was gone.

Then she caught sight of the bronze ashtray on the marble table between the sofas.

She limped over and picked it up; it was just as solid and heavy as it looked. Her foot hurt even more as she limped back toward with the door with the heavy metal ashtray in her hands.

"Five. Where's the money?"

"It's not your money, Filip. We can come to an agreement, you and me. Put the gun down and let the children and servants go, then we can sit down and work out a solution."

"Six. I negotiate my way. Try asking Astrid. Ask her who owns all her cherished fucking codes and records and company deeds these days. Seven."

Annika hopped back toward the sitting room on one leg.

"Filip, there's been more than enough death and misery now . . ."

"Eight."

"Okay, Filip, I'll tell you where the money is."

Annika peered into the room again. Filip was heading across

the floor, toward Fatima and the child, with light, almost playful steps.

He's enjoying this, she thought. He's going to do it.

"Nine."

She'd only get one chance.

Annika raised the ashtray above her head, took a deep breath, then rushed into the room. Filip was three meters away. The muscles in her arms ached, and pain shot up her leg every time her foot hit the floor.

One of the weeping women saw her and screamed.

With all the strength she could muster she smashed the ashtray into Filip's head.

The man had noticed her in the corner of his eye. He turned round just as the bronze ashtray hit him.

Annika saw at once that she had failed.

The ashtray didn't hit him on the back of the head, but on his ear and shoulder. He staggered and dropped his gun but remained standing.

"What the . . . ?"

Annika threw herself forward and grabbed the gun, the same as the one lying beside the dead man outside. She tried to shove it away, toward the others, but Filip was faster than her. He grabbed the gun from her hands and kicked her, and she ended up on her back beneath him. He aimed the gun at her forehead. She saw his face twitch as he recognized her.

"What the fuck are you doing here?" he said, sounding genuinely surprised.

Annika couldn't bring herself to answer. She was close to peeing herself in terror.

Filip put a hand to his ear and found blood on his fingers. She saw the surprise fade from his face as fury took over.

"I warned you," he said. "You really shouldn't stick your nose into things that are none of your fucking business!"

He took off the safety catch and aimed the barrel at her fore-head, just as she'd seen him do with Ahmed, and she thought about the fact that she had two children, that he mustn't do it.

Then his head exploded.

The women screamed as the sound of the shot rolled round the room.

Annika stared at the body swaying above her for a moment, the joints loose, as if it had no skeleton. In a panic she scrambled backward with her hands so that it wouldn't land on her when it fell. The body hit the Persian carpet with a soft thud. His shoes ended up right next to her face.

The two servants' screams rose to a falsetto. Suzette and Amira were clutching each other in the armchair, and Fatima put her hand over the child's eyes. They were all staring at the door and Annika turned her head to see what they were looking at, and saw a shadow in the darkness out in the hallway.

She shuffled away from the body, away from the door, and bumped into a statue, knocking it over.

A figure walked into the room with an automatic rifle in its hands. It was the same gun Annika had picked up but then dropped outside in the yard. The barrel was smoking.

Suzette and Amira screamed.

Annika looked up at the person holding the gun, at her sharp profile and shoulders, the wet ponytail, and pointed chin.

"They're going to kill us," Suzette screamed. "They're going to gas us all."

The woman didn't seem to hear her. She put the gun down and went over to the dead man. She knelt down beside him and stroked his hand, which was still clasped around the trigger.

"Sorry," she whispered. "Sorry, Filip, but this has to stop."

Then she slumped to the floor and wept.

Abbas rushed over and grabbed the gun, took the safety catch off, and aimed it at the intruder.

Annika got to her feet and stood in front of the woman with her hands stretched out.

"Don't shoot her!" she cried. "Leave her alone. She's a police officer. Her name's Nina Hoffman."

The storm passed.

A warm wind began to blow. It swept in through the open front door, up the stairs, through the stone hallway, and into the sitting room and library and all the other open rooms in the house.

Fatima stood up and handed the child she had been holding in her lap to Suzette and Amira.

She went over to the dead man on the rug and looked at him for a long minute. He was lying on his front, with his arms close to his sides, and the gun by his right side. The back of his head was gone. The women had stopped screaming. No one said anything. Not even the children were whimpering.

Then she looked up at Annika and Nina.

"Are there any more men here?"

Annika cleared her throat and tried to catch Nina's eye, but the police officer was staring down at the floor and didn't seem to have heard the question.

"There are two more out in the yard," Annika said.

"Zine and Ahmed?"

"Ahmed's out there," Annika said. "I haven't seen Zine."

Fatima nodded toward her and Nina.

"You two," she said. "Take the body downstairs and put it by the stable wall. Then you're to come back up here, roll this carpet up, and leave it on the floor of the washroom behind the kitchen. Then check which other carpets up here need washing, roll them up, and leave them against the back wall of the washroom."

Annika looked at the woman in astonishment. Fatima returned her gaze without moving a muscle. Then she turned to her son-in-law. Abbas was still standing there with Nina's gun raised and ready to fire.

"Abbas," she said, "get the electricity running again. Then you're to gather all the guns together and lock them up where they should be. Then get the digger out and the small trailer. Girls!"

She looked over at Suzette and Amira.

"Take the boys down into the kitchen. Get them something to eat. Then take them up to my bedroom and read them a story. Try to get them to sleep."

Amira was the first to move. She put her nephew down on the floor, heaved herself out of the armchair, took Suzette's hand, and helped her up, then went over to her sister and took the youngest boy from her arms. Abbas put the safety catch back on the gun, hung it over his shoulder, leaned over and pulled Filip's gun from his dead hand and left the room.

Then Nina moved.

She went up to the top end of the corpse and crouched down.

"We won't be able to carry him," she said in English without looking up. "We're going to need some help, otherwise we'll have to clean all the other carpets in the house as well."

"Amira," Fatima said to the girl, who went out quickly with the child in her arms and disappeared down the stairs.

Then Fatima said something to the servants in Arabic, and they left the room together with Suzette.

Annika couldn't bear to look at the corpse and turned away.

Amira came back with a bin liner and handed it to Nina, who quickly pulled it over the dead man's head and tied the handles firmly round his neck.

"Okay, let's turn him over first," she said to Annika, who did as she said.

"Grab his legs."

Annika did as she was told, simultaneously empty and full to bursting. In spite of the gloom the contours of the furniture were crystal clear, the colors incredibly sharp. He would have shot her, wouldn't he?

His body really was incredibly heavy. They couldn't manage to lift the whole thing at once, so they pulled it with its back dragging on the thick carpets until they reached the staircase.

At that moment the power came back on and the stone hallway was lit up by ornate chandeliers and lamps.

Nina swung the legs over the edge of the top step.

"You go first and pull. I'll keep hold of the head and try to stop the bag coming off."

Annika pulled the feet and trousers. The body slid down fairly easily; a couple of times she had to grab its stomach to slow it down.

The yard was illuminated by huge floodlights. They lowered the head to the ground and each pulled one of the legs. The bag split open and blood seeped out.

The two black-clad men who had run in through the gates with Filip were lying where they had fallen, hit by several shots to the chest. Ahmed had been moved; Annika could see the dark patch where his head had been lying clearly visible in the brightly lit yard.

"You can put him straight on the trailer," Abbas said.

He pointed to a tractor with a scoop at the front and a digger at the back. Behind the digger a small trailer had been hooked up to it.

"We'll need help," Nina said.

Together they managed to get the heavy body onto the trailer.

Without saying anything they went back toward the black-clad bodies. Abbas took the arms and Nina and Annika a leg each.

"Where's Zine?" Annika asked once they'd put the two men on top of Filip.

"He's alive, but he's lost a lot of blood. The only person here with the same blood type is Ahmed, and he's dead."

Fatima came out into the yard in a black garment.

Abbas climbed up into the tractor, started the engine, and drove off toward the fields. Fatima stopped beside them and watched the vehicle disappear over the brow of the hill.

"They'll never be found," Annika said. "Just like Torsten. That's right, isn't it?"

Fatima closed her eyes but didn't say anything.

"What did Torsten do?" Annika asked.

"What didn't he do? He deserved to die."

"Who killed him?"

"David."

Fatima turned round and walked back toward the house.

Annika heard the sound of the tractor fade and disappear.

At that moment the lights in the yard went out.

She went back inside the house and up the stairs, to bring down the bloodstained rugs.

The crops were rustling in the fields outside the walls. Annika sat down on the steps leading up to the house. She blinked to get her eyes used to the gentle darkness. Her eyes settled on the dark patch of gravel where the life had run out of the man with the pale eyes.

Nina came and sat down beside her.

"I recognized him," Annika said, pointing to the dark patch. "He was the one who cut my finger open."

Nina looked up at the sky.

The stars was sparkling and twinkling, clearer than Annika had ever seen them before. She felt shaky and oddly exhilarated.

They sat in silence for a long time.

"How are you feeling?" Annika asked eventually, looking at the woman next to her.

Nina picked up some stones, weighed them in her hand, then let them fall again.

"Numb," she said. "I've never shot anyone before. It was much easier than I expected."

She raised her arms and aimed an imaginary gun, closed one eye, and squeezed the trigger.

"It's hard to aim an AK-47," she said, letting her arms fall. "This one had a long barrel, otherwise I don't think I would have dared. I went down on one knee and shot him from below, because a bullet of that caliber could easily pass through the body, and I didn't want to hit anyone behind him . . ."

"You got it just right," Annika said.

Nina glanced at her.

"I was aiming for his body," she said. "The barrel must have moved. It was pure luck I didn't hit anyone else by mistake."

Annika looked away. Possibly relieved that the woman was a trained police officer, used to handling violent situations, and trained to use firearms.

"Why did you come?" Annika asked.

Nina replied in a quiet, focused voice.

"Filip came to see me on Tuesday, at lunchtime, and he wanted a passport. I asked him where he was going. 'The Costa del Sol,' he said, 'to sort out some business that's gone wrong.' I told him he could fly using just his national ID card, and then he got angry. I told him he'd have to go to the passport office, and that I'd try to speed up his application . . ."

She looked out into the darkness and wrapped her arms around her.

"That evening he called and asked if I knew where the farm was. 'Astrid was always so secretive about that farm,' he said. I said I didn't know what he was talking about. 'Stop being so sanctimonious,' he said. 'It's time you did something useful; there's only us left now. Apart from the kid.' I didn't know what he meant."

She fell silent and looked down at the gravel.

"Then he said, 'I bet you anything she's at the farm,' and then he hung up. That was the last time I spoke to him . . ."

Annika waited in silence.

"I wanted to talk to him," Nina went on. "I got the plane to Málaga this morning. That's why I came, to talk some sense into him."

"But how did you find your way here?"

Nina took a deep breath and glanced at Annika.

"Through you," she said. "You called that afternoon and asked the same thing as Filip, about what I knew about the farm, but you told me where it was. In Morocco, outside Asilah. I went to the muqaddam, and he said I was the second white woman in two days who'd come to see him with the same question, so I assumed you were already here . . . When did you get here?"

"Yesterday evening. They locked me up straightaway."

Nina rubbed her forehead and suddenly looked very tired.

"They knew Filip was on his way. They probably just wanted you out of the way until it was all over."

Annika looked at her. Nina sat for a long while without saying anything.

"I'll never be able to talk to anyone about this," she said.

Annika couldn't think of a response. She tried to imagine what Nina was thinking and feeling.

Was she remembering all the times she visited her brother in Kumla Prison? Was she thinking about the big brother who used to lift her up to the ceiling at Christmas and birthdays? Or could she no longer see beyond the criminal who was on the point of killing even more people?

"He was going to shoot me," Annika said. "You saved everyone."

Nina didn't move.

"I'm the last one left. It was up to me to put everything right."

* * *

Amira came out and asked if they wanted anything to eat.

Her Swedish was clear and fluent, with hardly any trace of an accent.

Annika didn't think she'd be able to keep anything down, but she got up and followed the girl inside the house, across the open hall and down a long corridor.

The kitchen was huge. It filled the whole of the eastern end of the ground floor, low-ceilinged but over a hundred square meters in area. There were twenty-four chairs round a rustic wooden table in the middle of the floor, with space for more if need be. There was cheese and fruit, lamb, vegetables, and a dish of cold couscous.

Annika and Nina sat down at the table and helped themselves to a bit of food. Annika chewed and chewed, and managed to swallow some vegetables and drank several glasses of water. She felt dizzy and shaky; the palms of her hands were full of blisters, and her ankle hurt badly.

When they had finished Fatima came into the kitchen.

"You two," she said, nodding to Annika and Nina. "Come with me."

She went out of the kitchen and into the hall, up the stairs and into the library. She sat down on one of the leather sofas, and indicated that Annika and Nina should sit down opposite her.

"I understand that you're Filip's sister," she said, looking at Nina.

Nina raised her chin.

"Yes," she said.

"I've heard a lot about you," Fatima said.

Nina didn't reply.

Fatima waited. No one said anything. Annika realized she was holding her breath.

"You're a police officer," Fatima said eventually. "Like David."

"Yes, but not like David. I've never been mixed up in the business, not like David and Filip and the others."

Fatima nodded.

"That's what David said. You were the only one who got away."

Nina cleared her throat.

"Why are you talking about my job? This doesn't have anything to do with my job."

"You're a police officer, and you killed your brother. I've got ten witnesses."

Nina didn't answer.

"Are you going to go to your superiors and confess what you've done?"

Nina looked away.

"Are you going to report him missing?"

"No."

"Never?"

"No."

Fatima looked at her intently. Nina didn't move.

"The other men, do they have families?"

"I don't know," Nina said. "Someone will probably notice they're missing."

"Can they be traced here?"

"I presume they flew to Málaga and got their guns there. Filip didn't have a passport, so my guess is that they chartered a boat and paid cash. I saw a car outside, an old SEAT. The passenger door had been broken open."

Fatima nodded.

"They must have stolen it. Abbas has already taken care of it."

Annika looked down at her blistered hands.

Filip Andersson and his thugs would never be traced to Morocco. They had already been buried alongside Torsten in some distant corner of the farm. They'd never be heard of again.

She shuddered.

Were there more bodies buried out there?

"Where's Carita Halling Gonzales?" she suddenly asked, looking straight at Fatima. "Do you know?"

Fatima raised her eyebrows.

"She's taken off, I don't know where."

"Why did she kill the entire Söderström family?" Annika asked.

The woman's eyes narrowed.

"You're a journalist," she said. "Your job is to poke about in other people's affairs. Are you going to write about my farm?"

Annika straightened her back.

"I'm going to do my job," she said. "I'm going to write that Suzette is alive. I want to interview her and let her decide how much she wants to say about her new life. I'd like to quote you as well, if you'll agree to that . . ."

"What about what happened here today?"

Annika blinked.

"You could have run away," Fatima said, "but you chose to come back. No one forced you to intervene."

Annika looked down at her hands. Fatima looked at her for a long time.

"Carita Halling Gonzales was Filip's eyes and ears on the Costa del Sol while he was in prison in Sweden," she said. "As the years went by she started to get sloppy. Astrid was able to embezzle large amounts of money, and shipments were delayed and seized. When Filip realized the extent of it, he gave Carita an ultimatum: her family, or Astrid's."

"That's terrible," Annika muttered.

Fatima pulled a face.

"It's not the first time Carita has tidied up. Do you know why you were let into this farm?"

Annika shook her head, unable to say anything.

"Do you believe in God, Annika Bengtzon?"

She gulped.

"Not exactly."

Fatima put her hands together on her lap.

"Well," she said, "you're fairly secular in Sweden. Do you respect people who do believe?"

Annika nodded.

"Then you understand that my God is the most important thing in my life? More important than my children and my family, my property, and my work?"

Annika didn't answer.

"According to my faith a man can have four wives. I was his first, and he took one other. That's how I see my marriage. I'm well aware of Western practices and traditions, and I expect you to accept mine."

Annika waited silently for her to go on.

"My husband and I, we only had daughters. But with his second wife he had a son, Alexander. You saved him, my husband's child, his only son. So I am in your debt, and that's why you were let in."

"I didn't think Muslim women were allowed to marry Christian men?" Nina said.

Fatima looked at her in surprise.

"David converted to Islam. Didn't you know?"

She stood up. Nina and Annika followed suit.

"You can stay here tonight," she said. "Abbas will drive you to Tangier tomorrow morning."

She looked at Annika.

"My duty as far as Suzette is concerned is finished," she said. "She can decide for herself if she wants to be interviewed. I believe in free will. God isn't an obligation, but a gift."

Then she sighed, and it looked like she slumped slightly.

"You're free to talk about what you've done here at the farm this evening," she said. "I don't make threats and I would never use force. I leave it up to your judgment to take responsibility for your own actions."

Some women started to sing in another part of the house.

"The window in your room is broken," Fatima said to Annika. "Amira will show you both to another bedroom. You'll find her down in the kitchen."

She waved them away with her hand, and from the corner of her eye Annika saw her turn toward the darkness outside the window.

Annika got her laptop, camera and mobile phone back. To her surprise she saw that she had a full signal on her mobile.

"Mum installed a mast," Amira said. "We've got our own power plant as well, with solar cells and wind turbines. It's enough for the house and the stable, but not when we have to light up the walls with the floodlights. Then it gets all weird and dark, like it was last night . . ."

"How's Zine?" Annika asked.

Amira's beautiful face twitched.

"He died," she said. "The funeral's tomorrow. This way. There are some backstairs."

She led them up the same narrow stone staircase that Annika and Ahmed had gone up the previous night. The lamps in the walls were shining much brighter now that the floodlights on the wall weren't on.

"The window in your room's broken," she said to Annika.

"I know. My bag's in there. Can I go and get it?"

She nodded.

"The door's open. Suzette and I have prepared the big room for you. It's much nicer, and it's got lights. Here's the bathroom."

She gestured to a door beside her.

Annika and Nina glanced at each other, then stepped into the bedroom they would be sharing. Annika made sure the door was left ajar. No one locked it behind her.

The room was certainly a lot bigger than her previous cell. It had two large beds, a big desk, two armchairs, and lights in the ceiling and beside the beds.

"I'm going to have a shower," Nina said.

She disappeared into the bathroom. Annika put her things down on one of the beds and went out into the corridor, back to her former cell, and opened the door.

The floor was soaked. The French doors were swinging slowly in the wind. The mattress was hanging off the bed from when she had pulled the sheets off, but her bag was still on the end of it. She splashed through the water and picked it up. Beneath it was the white book with the black lettering on the cover.

A Place in the Sun, by Siv Hoffman.

She picked up the book and put it in her bag, then went back to the bedroom.

She left the door ajar, sat down on the bed, and checked her mobile. It must have been on the whole time, because the battery was low and she had three missed calls. Thomas, then Anders Schyman, then Thomas again.

She had two new voicemails. The first was from her editor in chief, and it was short and to the point.

"I assume you didn't send those articles from your sickbed. Call me."

The second was from Thomas, and was slow and hesitant.

"Hello Annika, it's me . . . Well, I know I said I'd call you . . . well, you know . . . but I've been doing a lot of thinking, Annika, I really have, and I was wondering . . . can you call me? Soon? When you get this. Call my mobile, that would be best. Okay. Bye . . ."

She clicked to end the message and held the phone to her chest.

How strange he sounded. Surely nothing had happened to the children? He would have said if it had, wouldn't he?

She sat still for a moment, listening, as the water ran in the shower. Quickly she closed the door, then sat back down on the bed again, took a few quick breaths, and pressed *call*.

"I got your message," she said quietly when he answered.

"Good, hi, thanks for getting back to me," he said, sounding very official. "Can you hold on a moment?"

"Sure," Annika said.

The sound of water stopped in the bathroom. There was a clatter at the other end of the line, then the sound of a door closing, and now there was an echo, as if Thomas had gone out into the stairwell.

"Hello? Annika?"

"Yes, I'm here."

"Listen, this isn't a good time, but I've been doing a lot of thinking, and I really want to talk to you. Can we meet up?"

She cleared her throat and heard the toilet flush on the other side of the wall.

"I'm not in Stockholm," she said. "What do you want to talk about?"

"I think this is a big mistake," he said.

Annika closed her eyes.

"What? What's a mistake?"

"The divorce," he said quietly.

She opened her eyes, then her mouth, but no words came out.

"Annika?"

Nina came into the room with a towel round her hair and another wrapped round her body.

"There's not much hot water left," she said.

"Where are you?" he asked.

"Away on a job," she said. "Your message sounded so urgent that I wanted to call straightaway. Can I call you when I get back to Stockholm?"

"Sure."

The line went silent. Nina unrolled her turban and shook her hair loose. She put the wet towel over the armchair and stood in the middle of the room.

"One last thing," Annika said. "Are you standing out in the stairwell on Grev Turegatan?"

"Er, yes. Why?"

She rubbed her eyes with her fingertips.

So he was sitting at home, all cozy with his new partner, then, when his ex-wife called, he crept out into the stairwell to tell her he regretted getting divorced.

"Nothing," she said. "I'll be in touch."

They hung up.

"It didn't help," Nina said. "I still feel just as filthy as before."

She seemed as together as she always was, just as stable and focused.

Annika switched off her mobile: She didn't have her charger with her and needed to save the battery. Then she reached for her bag and pulled out the white book.

"Suzette found this in the library," she said.

She went over to Nina's bed and put the book down in front of her.

"Have you seen this before?"

"'*A Place in the Sun*, by Siv Hoffman,'" Nina read as she picked the book up. "What's this?"

"Read it, especially the chapter titled 'Death on the Beach.' See if you think what it says could be true. I'm going to have a shower."

Nina leafed through the book.

Annika went out into the corridor. The women were singing somewhere below her.

There was no hot water left. She had a lukewarm shower, washing her hair and body with some Wella shampoo she found on the shelf. Nina was right, the water and the synthetic perfume of the shampoo weren't having any effect on the strong odors coming from her skin, a mixture of terror and fish guts. She dried herself, put her clean underwear on, then went back into the bedroom.

She went over to the French doors and looked out. This room faced the other direction, away from the farmyard. The moon had risen over the hilly landscape, shimmering in the wetness of the leaves in the fields.

Cannabis sativa. Since prehistoric times mankind had grown the plant, using it for rope, textiles, birdseed, a high-energy grain, a medicine, and as a means of getting high.

Nina closed the book. Annika turned round. Nina bowed her head and closed her eyes, but it didn't look like she was crying.

"What do you think?" Annika asked carefully. "Could it be true?"

Nina tossed the book to the end of the bed, as if it had scorched her.

"No idea."

"And you've never seen this book before?"

"Mum didn't have a copy, I'm absolutely sure of that."

"Even though she wrote it?"

"I went through all her possessions when she died. There was no book like this among them."

Annika walked across the floor and picked the book up.

"If this is true, I can't imagine Astrid just left her copy sitting about on a bookshelf. Which means this must be Hannelore's."

She nodded to herself.

"That would explain how it got here. David found the book and brought it with him."

She leafed through it, and her eyes caught on the sentence: "And she would float and dance over Gudagården like the blessed little child she was, conceived without sin with the approbation of the Lord."

"How much do you really know about your mother's child-hood?"

Nina stood up and walked restlessly around the room a few times.

"What does anyone ever really know about their parents?"

"How about when they were grown up? Astrid and Hannelore and your mother?"

Nina sat down on the bed again.

"Before I was born, Mum worked with Astrid on the Costa del Sol. I don't know what she did there."

Annika went back to her bed. She put the book down on the floor.

"I was three years old when Mum and I moved. I have no memories of the Costa del Sol. We ended up in Tenerife, in an artists' collective where people made pots and painted sunsets and smoked grass. Mum called herself a poet . . ."

Nina stopped, it sounded almost as if she let out a little laugh.

"A poet, bloody hell . . ."

"Your brother and sister, they didn't go with you to Tenerife?" Annika asked.

"They stayed with Astrid in Marbella. They were both almost grown up by then, Filip was twenty-two, Yvonne sixteen. Astrid paid for their education; they both became economists. I missed them the whole time."

Nina pulled her hair into a ponytail, tying it with a band she had in her hand.

"I don't know why we moved. I don't know if Mum wanted to get away from Astrid, or if Astrid kicked her out."

"Why would Astrid have kicked her out?"

Nina slumped slightly.

"Mum had problems with various dependencies," she said. "She never got over them. Once we moved to Södermanland she stuck to drink, and meths toward the end, but she drugged her way through the whole of her adult life."

"Did you ever meet Astrid?"

Nina thought for a moment.

"She came to visit us in Tenerife a few times. But Mum talked about her quite a bit, and about Hannelore, always when she was drunk. All I know about Veronica, Astrid, David, Torsten, and Hannelore comes from Mum's drunken ramblings. She missed Astrid a lot."

"Did you see much of Hannelore?"

Nina shook her head.

"Never."

"How involved was Hannelore in Astrid's business dealings?"

"Not much, I shouldn't think. She's been mentally unstable her whole life. But Torsten, her bloke, acted as a kind of traveling salesman for the organization."

"For their drugs racket," Annika said. "That's what it was, after all."

They sat in silence for a while. The women's voices stopped singing.

"I read your article in the paper today," Nina said. "About the jet-set Swedish woman who murdered Astrid and her family."

Annika straightened her back.

"It was in the paper?"

"There was hardly anything else in it, it was on loads of pages. Who is she?"

So the email hadn't only arrived, it had fallen on fertile ground.

"Carita Halling Gonzales, a very good actress. She fooled everyone around her, possibly even herself. No one's that good at pretending. I've done a lot of thinking about her."

Annika shuddered. She crept under the blanket.

Silence descended for a few minutes.

"I knew David had another family," Nina said quietly.

Annika started.

"What? You've known about this for all these years?"

"Yvonne told me, but I didn't believe her."

Nina was looking straight ahead, but without seeing anything.

"It was more than five years ago now. I knew Yvonne was completely infatuated with David; it had been a kind of obsession since they were little. I went to see her to ask her to leave Julia alone."

She fingered her hair.

"That's when she told me that David had another family, a wife and three daughters. He could have several wives, four, according to the Koran, but Yvonne considered that she was his first wife, even though they weren't married. She was the one who got to him first. I thought she'd gone mad."

Nina pushed her hair from her face.

"So I broke off all contact. That was the last time I ever spoke to Yvonne."

"And then," Annika said, "some small-time crooks tried to get their hands on the drug money. Was it Filip who murdered those people on Sankt Paulsgatan? Or was it Yvonne?"

Nina stood up and went over to the window.

"Does it matter? They're both dead."

Annika looked at her stiff back, her straight shoulders, the ponytail that had dried to a perfectly straight whip.

"It wasn't your fault," she said.

Nina raised both her arms and pressed her palms to her forehead hard.

"Fucking bitch," she said in a low voice. "She vanished into her hash clouds or the bottom of a bottle, and dumped it all on me."

Annika waited, but Nina didn't go on.

"What?" she said. "What did she dump on you?"

Nina's stiff back seemed to slouch slightly.

"I grew up without my brother and sister, without any sense

of belonging, but it was still up to me to make sure we all stuck together. She just grabbed me and left."

"Maybe she wanted to spare you from a place in the sun?'

Nina didn't answer.

Annika picked the book up from the floor.

"Do you know where this Gudagården is?"

Nina let out a deep sigh. She swayed and grabbed hold of the window frame for support.

"I grew up there. Mum inherited it. We moved there when Gunnar and Helga died, that's why we left Tenerife. Mum was the only heir. They'd written a will saying they wanted everything to go to the church, but it hadn't been witnessed properly and was declared invalid."

Annika waited in silence for her to go on.

"Mum hated the farm," Nina said in a weak voice. "I could never understand why she didn't sell it. It was always eating away at her from the inside."

"Is there a lake nearby?"

"Spetebysjön is just below Gudagården. Or Solgården, as Mum renamed the farm. It's between Ekeby and Solvik, not far from Valla."

"I know Valla," Annika said. "One of my school friends lived there, on Häringevägen."

"The farm's on the same side of the railway line, on the road down toward Björkvik."

"Now I know where it is," Annika said.

Nina looked out into the darkness.

"Just below the farm there's a lake with a little sandy beach next to a big oak tree," she said in a toneless voice. "It's huge. But Mum used to say it was dangerous there, that there were strange currents and quicksand."

She turned around, went over to the bed, and picked up the book.

"What do you think?" she said. "Could this be true? Was that why I was never allowed to swim there?"

Annika put her hand on Nina's arm.

"There's one way to find out," she said.

A knock on the door made them both jump. They looked quickly at each other.

"Come in," Nina said in a low voice.

The door opened and Suzette and Amira came into the bedroom.

"Hello," Suzette said. "Can we come in?"

"Sure," Annika said.

The girls stopped just inside the door.

"Don't you want to sit down?" Annika said, gesturing toward the two armchairs.

They went over and sat down, one on each chair. Nina adjusted her position on the bed.

"Did you want anything in particular?" Annika asked, and Amira nudged Suzette in the side.

"Fatima says I can go home now," Suzette says. "I don't have to stay at the farm, because there's no danger anymore."

Annika nodded.

"But I don't want to leave," Suzette said. "I want to stay here, and Fatima says I can if I want."

Annika looked at her seriously.

"You mum back in Sweden has a right to know where you are."

Suzette nodded.

"I know. That's why I want to tell them that they don't have to look for me anymore now. I don't want to tell them exactly where I am, but I'd like to be able to send emails to Polly, and call Mum . . ."

She took a deep breath and her eyes filled with tears.

"I miss my mum," she said, "and I'd like to visit her, maybe next summer, when I'm grown up. But I don't want to live with her in that flat. I just want her to know that I'm okay, and that I'll go back and visit . . ."

Annika remembered Polly's message on Facebook, about Lenita selling the flat and throwing all of Suzette's things away.

"Would you like me to say all this in the paper?" she asked.

The girl nodded.

Annika looked at her.

"Have you really thought through what it would mean, staying here? Will you be able to go to school?"

Suzette shuffled in the chair, annoyed.

"Abbas is going to be the new foreman, taking over from Zine. I can go round with him and learn how to run the farm. It'll be like being an apprentice."

Annika moved to the edge of the bed.

"Suzette," she said, "do you know what they grow on this farm?"

The girl's eyes opened wide.

"Of course I do."

"And you think it's okay to train to become a hash farmer?"

Amira flew up from her chair.

"My family's grown hemp on this land for two hundred years," she said. "Why should we stop, just because the European Commission says we should? They can't make decisions about our lives."

The girl had clenched her fists in anger.

"So you think it's a good life, growing dope?"

"I'm going to be an economist," Amira said. "My sister's going to be a lawyer, and we're going to help run the farm and Mum's business."

"Do you think your dad would have wanted that? You and Sabrina and Maryam working with this sort of thing?"

Amira's eyes filled with tears.

"Maryam has a different dad," she said, "a bad man from Sweden who violated Mum. But my dad killed him and married Mum, and saved our family's honor."

Annika stared at the girl, thoughts racing through her head.

"A different dad? Was his name Torsten?"

"Dad did what was right for the family. He'd be really proud of me."

Annika lowered her eyes. When she raised them again she turned to Suzette.

"We'll have to sit down together first thing in the morning, and work out exactly what we're going to say in the article. And then I want to take a picture of you with your horse, so we can show that you're fit and well."

Suzette was smiling broadly.

Together the girls walked out of the room and closed the door behind them.

"So you got your article," Nina said, and Annika couldn't tell if there was resignation or sarcasm in her voice.

"And everything goes on," Annika said.

EPILOGUE

After Midsummer

The sky was gray as lead. The light that did find its way through the banks of cloud was dull and filtered to the point where only a dubious sort of daylight remained.

Annika parked the newspaper's Volvo up by the road. She switched off the engine, got out of the car, and stretched her back. She looked both ways along the deserted country road. This ought to be the right place.

Between Ekeby and Solvik, not far from Valla. On the same side of the railway line, on the road down toward Björkvik.

She gazed out at the traditional, red-painted houses that lay scattered across the landscape, wondering which one had once been known as Gudagården. She squinted in the thin light and tried to find the lake.

There it was. It was actually visible from the road. Spetebysjön, between Stensjön and Långhalsen, one of the thousands of lakes and waterways in Södermanland, her low-lying home province with its oak trees and fences and meadows.

She locked the car with a click of the remote, hung her bag on her shoulder, and started to walk along a ditch down toward the water.

The ground was soft and smelled of grass and cow shit. The wet soaked into her trainers. Obviously, she should have remembered to bring Wellington boots.

She caught sight of the police forensics team and the cordon in the distance. The blue-and-white tape and the bright yellow tarpaulins were the only flashes of color among all the gray green. There were four officers there, two digging, and two checking the soil that was being dug out.

Nina was standing some way from the cordon, wearing army-green rubber boots from Tretorn. A few other curious onlookers from nearby farms had defied the gray weather to come and see what was going on.

"Have they found anything?" Annika asked.

Nina shook her head. She didn't look at Annika, and was just staring implacably at the police officers who were carefully digging soil and sand from the beach behind the oak tree.

"How did you manage to get them out here?" she asked.

"I said I'd received a tip-off," Annika said, "and that the caller wanted to stay anonymous. They can't do anything about that. They're not even allowed to ask me who the caller was, because that would be a breach of the constitution."

Nina gave Annika a quick glance.

"I read your articles about Suzette."

"The constitution's come in handy there as well. Her mother called me, in a complete state, demanding to know where she is."

They stood in silence for a moment.

"Is everything okay otherwise?" Annika asked.

"I'm on temporary secondment as a duty officer for the summer."

"Do you know if anyone's heard anything from Carita Halling Gonzales?"

"Not a sound."

Annika took a step closer to her and lowered her voice.

"Has anyone reported Filip Andersson missing?"

Nina's shoulders stiffened.

"A young man called from Gibraltar. Apparently Filip was supposed to be taking over some sort of law firm."

That must have been Henry Hollister, Annika thought.

"And his lawyer's called twice, something about his claim for damages. I told him exactly what had happened, that Filip had contacted me to ask if I could speed up his passport application, but that I wasn't able to help him. There's been no official report that he's disappeared."

"And the others?"

"I don't actually know."

Annika looked out across the lake.

"And Julia? How are she and Alexander getting on?"

"Alexander's started back at his old preschool again. Apparently it's going very well. He plays with his old friends as though nothing ever happened."

"What about his tantrums?"

"They don't happen as often now."

They fell silent again.

In the end Annika cleared her throat.

"Have you said anything to Julia? About Fatima?"

Nina let out a deep, concentrated breath.

"No," she said. "Moroccan marriages aren't registered automatically by the Swedish authorities. It's up to individuals to tell the tax office that they're married, and David never did that. But of course he was married, which invalidates his marriage to Julia. Which in turn means that she wouldn't be counted as his next of kin."

Annika tried to follow her train of thought.

"And that would mean that she isn't entitled to his life insurance, which is all she's got to live on."

"Precisely."

Nina looked at her.

"Didn't the paper want to know where you'd been? When you met Suzette?"

Annika chuckled.

"They don't care where I've been; the only thing that interests them is where they can send me. Their latest offer is if I'd like to be the paper's Washington correspondent."

Nina raised her eyebrows.

"Wow," she said. "Impressive."

"Not really," Annika said. "It's mainly about getting me as far away from the newsroom as possible."

"How's that going to work with the children?" Nina asked. "Are you going to leave them in Sweden?"

Annika hunched her shoulders against the wind coming off the lake.

"Thomas might be coming as well," she said. "It's possible that the department will have a new policy proposal for him to . . ."

She was interrupted by the sound of cries and voices from the beach. There was frenetic activity in the excavated pit. The officers were making calls on their mobiles and their police radios were crackling.

The onlookers around them moved as one toward the cordon. Nina and Annika followed them.

The two officers with the shovels had dug so deep that their heads were scarcely visible over the edge of the hole.

"Could three young girls really have dug down that far in one single night?" Annika whispered.

"They were used to hard physical labor," Nina said quietly. "Sowing and harvesting and gathering hay . . ."

"Is it true, then?" one of the men beside them called. "Have you found a body down there?"

One of the police officers who had been checking the excavated soil came over to the onlookers.

"It looks like we've found the remains of a person."

"Who is it?" an old woman asked from a distance.

"We don't yet know what gender the body is, or how long it's been here. It'll be up to the forensics team and the pathologist to work that out."

"Could it be my brother?" the woman cried. "Could it be Sigfrid Englund?"

The police officer went over to her.

"Was he reported missing?"

"He's been missing since 1953, when he was twenty-one years old. He was raised as a foster child on a neighboring farm."

Annika turned and began to head back toward the car.

Nina hurried after her.

"Aren't you going to write about this?"

Annika looked up at the sky.

"I'll leave that to the local paper," she replied.

ACKNOWLEDGMENTS

This is fiction. All events and characters depicted are entirely the creation of my possibly somewhat morbid imagination.

But, as in all my novels, the events, physical locations, and laws and regulations are often, but not always, grounded in reality. As a result, I have, as usual, conducted some research.

I would therefore like to thank the people I bothered with numerous hypothetical questions. Their titles below refer to the positions they held at the time of my investigation.

For information about the European drug trade, and how narcotics are smuggled and distributed, I would like to thank Rolf M. Øyen, police attaché at the Norwegian embassy in Madrid and also Nordic liaison officer for Malaga, as well as Detective Inspector Göran Karlsson and Detective Superintendent Jan Magnusson of the regional narcotics unit in Stockholm. I would also like to thank the drug-squad officers working undercover whose names I can't reveal here: I've thanked them in person.

Kent Madstedt, chief district prosecutor at the Financial Crime Authority in Stockholm, for explaining how money-laundering and financial crimes are carried out in Europe.

Joakim Caryll of the information department of Stockholm Police, for help with contacts.

Hampus Lilja, judge referee to the Supreme Court, for information about how decisions are reached regarding applications for a retrial.

Fredrik Berg from the Office of the Prosecutor General, and public relations officer for the Public Prosecution Authority, for help with the procedures and formulations used in decisions of the Prosecutor General.

Anders Sjöberg, detective inspector for Interpol in Stockholm, for information about the criteria for international alerts via Interpol, both for missing people and suspects.

Anna Block Mazoyer, counselor at the Swedish embassy in Rabat, Morocco, for information about public registers covering people and property in Morocco.

I would like to thank Peter Rönnerfalk, chief medical officer at Stockholm County Council, for ongoing help with a whole range of things, but in this instance particularly for information about narcotic gases, naloxone, and fatal doses of morphine.

Thomas Bodström, chair of the Parliamentary Standing Committee on Justice, for proofreading and discussions on judicial and political matters.

Anna Rönnerfalk, psychiatric nurse, for help with the diagnosis and symptoms of patients suffering severe mental stress.

Niclas Salomonsson, my agent, and his staff at Salomonsson Agency in Stockholm.

Emily Bestler, my publisher, and all the dedicated staff at Emily Bestler Books (an imprint of Atria Books, at Simon & Schuster in New York).

Neil Smith, who translated it all into English.

Tove Alsterdal, my editor, obviously, who has been involved the whole way through, from start to finish, as always. Thank you for being there.

And, always, Micke Aspeborg, my love throughout all these years, for everything else.

Any mistakes or errors in the text are entirely intentional.